Halfway down she heard bowed cello. The groan came right through her. She sat on a step and held her breath. Boon, wherever he was, kept silent too. Not even the dust moved. Maybe it had been something in the fly loft, the open space above the stage where backdrops, cycs and drapes were dead-hung with ropes and counterweights. She knew rigging reacted to moisture. When no other note followed, she scooted down the steps.

"Boon?" she whispered. "Let's go."

The dog whined an eerie warning, but Mary Alice couldn't fathom the danger. Had Boon sensed a ghost?

She had no desire to return through the theatre where the image of a dead Jamie O'Malley might leap from the shadows, so she headed for the door to the outside. She smelled the dog's damp fur before she felt him bump against her. She tried to button the raincoat to protect the plays, but the latex gloves slowed her. She ripped them off and tossed them into the overflowing trash bin beside the door.

Buttoned up, she opened the door. She screamed and stumbled back, trying to slam the door closed. A bulky figure blocked her way...

NOW PLAYING IN CANA
A MARY ALICE TATE SOUTHERN MYSTERY
DINAH SWAN

"A wonderful, utterly charming mystery as southern as sweet tea and in the great tradition of Sue Grafton. Impossible to put down."

BLAKE CROUCH
author of the bestselling thriller PINES
and the new series from Fox, WAYWARD PINES

Books by Dinah Swan

Mary Alice Tate Southern Mysteries
Cana Rising
Now Playing in Cana

Women's Fiction
Hacienda Blues
Romantic Fever

NOW PLAYING
IN CANA

A MARY ALICE TATE SOUTHERN MYSTERY

by

Dinah Swan

Cover Design: Jeroen ten Berge
Book formatting and layout: TERyvisions
Photograph of the Author by Judith Reynolds

ISBN-13: 978-1482525052
ISBN-10: 1482525054

Now Playing in Cana is dedicated to the author's husband, Terry Swan.

CHAPTER 1

February 26, Monday

THE LIGHTS OF THE TOWN appeared. The foggy sleet had kept most of Cana, Mississippi's 15,000 residents at home, and the yellow Labrador named Boon seemed puzzled by this midnight run.

"We're almost there," Mary Alice told the dog, who eyed the wipers fighting a losing battle.

She'd explained to him about leaving her cell phone at the theatre, but now questioned the urgency.

When the car slipped into a fog bank thick as dough, she hit the brake. The old BMW fishtailed and spun a one-eighty sending the car into the opposite lane. The centrifugal force slammed her head against the window and sent Boon to the floor. Pelting ice was the only sound. Frantically, Mary Alice tried to crank the dead motor. There was no traffic, but any minute someone headed home from Mickey's or another local watering hole could barrel around the curve. Her fingers fumbled the key.

She heard her father's voice telling her exactly how to start the temperamental car he'd loved so much. The engine sputtered then caught. She turned it around and petted the dog that had crawled back into the front seat. He seemed fine, but she was shaking.

"A few more miles. Might as well go on, huh?"

The dog didn't look convinced.

She switched on a Memphis radio station, Roy Orbison cry-i-i-i-ing over somebody.

Going twenty, the car crept through the empty town square and eased to a stop in front of the theatre's door. With the engine quiet, the sleet ticked like nervous fingernails on the car.

Housed in a converted cotton gin, the Cana Little Theatre stood as a testament to what wealthy patrons could do for the arts. Wrapped in rosy hues, the jewel box boasted 200 seats, a fly loft, a trapped stage floor and a state-of-the-art lighting system.

"Come on Boon. Run for it."

The lab followed Mary Alice out of the car and after a quick detour through the largest puddle in the parking lot, skittered under the theatre's front overhang. He pressed his soggy fur against the glass while she found her key and unlocked the door.

A desk lamp glowed in the box office. Theatres didn't have light switches by the doors because sooner or later someone would accidentally flip on the lights during a performance and engulf Shakespeare's dark witches in hot white watts.

By the gleam from the office, Mary Alice made her way past photos of long-ago productions: Annie Oakley astride her horse, Blanche Dubois repeating that she had always depended on the kindness of strangers, and a photo from ten years ago of Mary Alice playing a woman who had shot her husband.

She pulled aside the heavy velour drapes that covered one of the auditorium entrance doors and stepped into the dark. A stark ghost lamp, one bright incandescent bulb in a shadeless floor lamp, stood center stage. Without the amber stage lights, the auditorium felt foreign, making her a trespasser. Still shaken by the icy spin-out, images from *Phantom of the Opera* crowded in. A dank subterranean grotto inhabited by a scarred madman.

If her mother hadn't bitched incessantly about her inability to reach her daughter, Mary Alice would have been home watching Claudette Colbert and Joel McCrea in *The Palm Beach Story*. She felt a "Do-Mama-In" fantasy setting up. A cherished childhood ritual, the mental movies had finished off her mother, Elizabeth Tate, in dozens of satisfying ways: an avalanche of Austrian cut glass, a fall from one of the balconies of the ancestral home, a choke on cheese grits.

This time she borrowed from the 1940's film. Joel McCrea was kissing Claudette Colbert. Then Claudette turned into Mother and Joel was suffocating her. His mouth clamped over hers like a Tupperware lid. Elizabeth struggled, flopped about and then lay still. Wind on the theatre glass rattled the fantasy loose.

She heard her dead father. *Honey, don't let your mama get to you.*

Only five months ago Mary Alice had almost been murdered, drowned in the lake. Since then Elizabeth Tate called constantly. She heard her daddy, *the past, which can't be changed, loves to be relived in endless repetitions. If you let yourself become a victim, and your mama will be happy for you to do that, you'll be as dead as if you'd been drowned.*

She straightened her back and marched forward into the gothic cavern.

Beside the aisle seat where she'd sat during rehearsal, she patted the floor for the missing phone. Her fingers grazed an unidentifiable gummy substance but no phone. Boon headed down the aisle toward the stage as Mary Alice returned to the box office telephone. She dialed her cell number and heard the tinny notes of Beethoven's *Ode to Joy*. Back in the auditorium she easily found the phone wedged between two seats.

"Hello?" she answered her own call. "Hello? Look if you're a prank caller you better start panting, or I'm hanging up." She closed the phone. Levity hadn't made the theatre any friendlier.

"Boon?" She heard him but couldn't see him.

The *ciaroscuro* shapes created by the scenery made her pause at the back of the theatre. Flats defined the walls, but they hadn't been painted yet, and the furniture pieces were mostly temporary. A heavy desk anchored stage left, and in a nook down right sat a daybed. Even unfinished, the set was already doing its job: forming an apparition where every night the characters' problems were analyzed and then, in some manner, solved. In the theatre King Lear and Willy Loman died, but balance was restored to the community. Here, life worked out. Always.

She saw Boon in the shadows, nudging the bed.

"No, Boon. Come on, let's get out of here."

Boon whined.

"No, no, no," she called, her voice echoing in the empty space.

In a dozen strides she was down front and up on the stage. The ankles at the foot of the bed stopped her. As she drew closer and her vision overcame the deeper darkness, she saw legs, torso, arms and head. The playwright, Jamie O'Malley, slept soundly on the rumpled bed.

Mary Alice laughed. Her friend, Kate, hadn't managed to entice the sexy guest artist after all.

"Jamie," she whispered. "Jamie?" she said louder.

He didn't move.

Before she saw it, she felt a sensation like a wash of low voltage electricity—sickeningly painful, but not incapacitating. And there was a smell, compelling because she couldn't identify it. She moved in, touched his shoulder and then saw that the blue bedspread was soaked black. Dull eyes looked at her without seeing.

Her brain rejected what she saw, but a primordial response unlocked her frozen legs and forced her to back away from the bed. She barely missed stepping on the gun that rested center stage.

"Boon, come," she croaked.

The dog whined, but followed, making damp tracks across the stage.

If she left immediately, someone else could find the body. She had to get out. Her breath came fast. But what if someone has seen her car parked out front? Jamie had been shot. The police would ask why she hadn't called. What could she say?

She edged to the front of the stage and sat down on the apron. Her arm stayed tight around her dog. Roy Orbison sang on in her head: "I was all right for a while; I could smile for a while." She felt the cell phone in her hand and pressed a programmed number. Like the freezing rain that coated the roads and power lines, fear stole over her, immobilizing her.

"Dear God in heaven, please answer." Her breath now came in sips.

Boon cranked his head around to look at the body.

"Hello." Police Detective Tom Jaworski didn't sound as if he'd been asleep. The cell phone screen said it was just after midnight.

"Tom, I need help," she whispered.

CHAPTER 2

February 27, Tuesday

P ERCHED ON THE STAGE'S LIP, Mary Alice dangled her legs in space as though sitting on a dock. She kept her arm firmly around Boon, his furry body a barrier between her and death. As though it were the dog that needed soothing, she stroked his head.

"Tom will be here. It'll be okay."

The dog let out a slow whine.

"He's going to call the police for us. We just have to sit tight." She rambled on aloud, whistling in the dark, about how Tom Jaworski was a police officer even if he was on part-time status now due to his injuries. He had been the one who listened to her when everyone else was ready to convict her friend, Sheree Delio. She massaged the dog's shoulders and chanted, "Sit tight, sit tight, sit tight."

When Boon turned his head toward the dead body, her eyes followed. Even in the dimness she could see Jamie's eyes looking right at her. A choking pressure rose as the terror overtook her senses. She looked away, bugging her eyes wildly into the void of the theatre whose black turned to the night waters of the lake. Like embers given a shot of gasoline, the memory roared to life taking her back to five months ago.

Her lungs hurt as she recalled swimming past endurance, swimming for her life. She gasped, screamed once and then everything stopped.

Far away, an unfamiliar voice repeated something. It was only when thirty thousand watts flooded the stage that she realized two police officers were holding guns on her. Blinking like a newborn, she raised her hands as high as her ears and then let herself sink below the shouting and hysteria back into the dark.

MARY ALICE WOKE WITH TOM Jaworski kneeling beside her. She wanted to tell him not to bend over. His back hadn't healed from the roll-over. But her mouth was too dry; her tongue wouldn't flex. Then she remembered Boon. She struggled up on her elbows and croaked the dog's name.

"He's okay," Jaworski said. "In my car. You must have fainted."

From her position on the stage floor, Mary Alice saw a uniformed cop with a hand on his holster standing behind Jaworski. The blinding bank of Fresnels behind him made him shimmer like a mirage. Two other policemen stood over Jamie O'Malley's body while a third shouted into a cell phone. A large woman wearing a shiny gray pants suit was scribbling in a small notebook. Mary Alice heard her bark, "Do not touch the body. Wait for the team." Mary Alice didn't recognize her.

"Tom?" Mary Alice said. The side of her head hurt.

"It's going to be okay." He lowered his voice. "I called Martin Sumner after you called me, but he called it in. Burke and his partner were half a block away. They thought you were—"

The thought of explaining her flashback amped up her headache. She didn't know what had happened, but was glad to call it fainting. Southern girls fainted all the time.

"They think I killed Jamie?" Her voice shook; she struggled to control her tears.

"Maybe." He shrugged.

A thumping, like bellows, started in her chest. She grabbed Jaworski's hand.

"But you didn't, and they'll find that out too," he said. "One thing at a time."

Mary Alice felt the eyes of the bulky, gray-suited woman on her. "Who's that?"

"Grendel."

Before Jaworski could explain, the woman, who Mary Alice thought looked a lot like Cathy Bates in *Misery*, approached.

"Ms. Tate? I'm Detective Claire Potts with the Mississippi Bureau of Investigation. May I ask you a few questions?"

Whoever she was, Claire Potts wasn't from the south.

Mary Alice looked at Jaworski and then nodded yes.

"Let's move to the auditorium seats. I don't want to contaminate the crime scene anymore than we already have." Her face said things were a mess, and it was all Mary Alice's fault. Jaworski helped Mary Alice to the front row of seats and sat beside her. Claire Potts stood over them, the notebook open on the stage apron behind her.

The detective asked Mary Alice how she happened to be in the theatre at midnight. Her tone from the start was accusing and sarcastic. As Mary Alice explained about her missing cell phone, and Jaworski corroborated her call to him asking for help, Potts took notes.

Mary Alice could tell that the more she talked, the less Potts liked her. Mary Alice imagined Potts thought she was a privileged local accustomed to getting away with everything from parking tickets to murder.

"You were speaking to your mother?" Potts asked.

"She called to make sure I'd be at the pilgrimage meeting," Mary Alice rushed on. "To plan the wrap party. Our home, Linnley, is on the pilgrimage—we do it every spring—the garden club raises money—tours of the antebellum houses—I was watching an old movie when—"

Jaworski touched her arm.

Mary Alice realized she was babbling and about to tell the detective how neither she nor her father could understand how people in 1942 thought Rudy Vallee had a good singing voice.

"I didn't kill Jamie," Mary Alice said.

"No one said you did," Potts said, her voice resonant and intimidating.

Mary Alice's unsolicited denial felt like a confession. She saw the coroner, Lofton Buress examining the body. The newly arrived forensic team taped both of Jamie's hands into bags. She recognized the new Chief of Police back stage. The old one was in jail. But it was clear that the MBI outsider who stank of tobacco was in charge.

"Ms. Tate, what was your relation to the deceased?" She cut her eyes to the body.

"To Jamie?" She couldn't believe he was really dead.

Potts looked at her without moving, without expression, letting her 175 plus pounds amplify the intimidation.

Mary Alice tried to slow and rank her thoughts. She pretended she was swimming. Although she was a befuddled suspect, she was a champion swimmer. First, she told the detective how she was acting in Jamie's play. *Easy strokes, no rush.* He was a visiting-guest playwright for the Cana Little Theatre. Did Potts want to know about the play, or why it was being performed? Probably not. *Breathe. Set a rhythm.* Second, she'd known Jamie forever. He was from Cana, but had left. She'd married and moved to Dallas. Would the detective want to know that Jamie had been popular in high school?

"We didn't have a relationship," Mary Alice said.

"I'll rephrase. You knew the victim?" Sarcasm saturated her question like bacon grease on cheap paper towels.

"He grew up in Cana. Everybody knows, knew Jamie."

Potts inched through questions about Mary Alice, Jamie, the gun, the other actors. "When did you last see the victim alive?"

"Last night at rehearsal."

"What happened at last night's rehearsal?" Potts asked.

"Chase Minor, he's the director, reworked the scene where the general taunts his family because he's been cut out of his father-in-law's will." She spoke cautiously and thought of how Detective Barbara Havers trapped naive witnesses. The fictional Detective Havers, who went for the jugular, had a lot in common with Potts.

"Taunts?" Potts repeated.

17

"Tease. Mock. Goad?" Mary Alice said. "I wasn't in the scene. Kate and I sat over there and watched." She pointed, regretting she'd offered the synonyms. Belittling her accuser wasn't smart.

Potts' face didn't change; she wrote a word on the notepad. "And?"

"One of the actors had trouble with his motivation." She hesitated, wondering if she might go into an explanation of the Stanislavski Method. She wished she had a few M & M's to suck on.

"Which actor?"

"Garth Buchanan." Mary Alice thought of every mystery she'd ever read. There was always an interrogation of a reluctant witness. She fought to say as little as possible but to give the impression of full cooperation.

"What was the problem?" Potts asked, irritated by being forced to probe each detail.

"Garth was confused and asked Jamie about his motivation. I don't remember the particulars." Mary Alice noticed the tiny pulse of Potts' eyebrows.

"Is that usual? To ask the playwright instead of the director?"

"Well, usually the director—but usually the playwright isn't here." Mary Alice worried she wasn't putting Chase in a very good light. "It wasn't clear who had authority."

Potts scribbled. "Then what happened?"

"They argued." There was no point lying. Everybody had witnessed the fight and seen Chase flounce out of the theater in high dudgeon. But perspective was everything. Maybe the others would say it was no big deal. And the others didn't know what Mary Alice knew about Chase and Jamie.

"Chase Minor and Jamie O'Malley?" Potts sucked her teeth.

"Yes. They disagreed about the character's motivation."

"As well as who should be deciding it?" Potts asked.

Mary Alice could see where Potts was leading. "Yes, but—"
She thought she should explain the joint responsibility of the
two men.

"How did it end?" Potts shifted her bulk and leaned on the
lip of the stage.

Mary Alice wished the detective would sit down. She felt
like a school child called in for hitting on the playground. But
then that was likely what Potts wanted.

"Chase left. He knew the assistant director would take over.
That would be Norton, Norton Pike. Everybody was gone by
nine-thirty."

"How do you know that?" The detective snapped the button
on her ball point pen. Mary Alice could read *Cash Advance-
Loans* on it. Snap, snap, snap. "Because I left then and saw the
parking lot empty. I didn't take roll but—"

"Tell me more about the argument between the director and
the writer."

Potts looked energized in spite of the late hour. Mary Alice
felt like road kill, but she knew she had to stand up to this bully.

"A disagreement." Mary Alice had already decided to lie or
at least not tell the full truth. Others could fill in details if they
wanted to, but it seemed clear that Potts would twist her words
into a scenario that would blame Chase Minor. Assuming Potts
couldn't blame Mary Alice.

"I don't remember the details." Mary Alice stood up. "Ms.
Potts, theatre people are emotional. They're artists." She stood
inches from the beefy detective.

"Was there yelling? Did they threaten each other?" Potts didn't give an inch in the tight aisle.

Mary Alice wasn't sure what she'd do if Potts leaned closer. "Of course not." But of course Chase had threatened Jamie. In the lobby, as he struggled into his coat, Chase had said, "I'll die or kill him before I take any more of his crap." Mary Alice was pretty sure that she and Kate were the only ones who had heard him. However, this fact coupled with the mounting circumstantial evidence made Mary Alice feel queasy.

The detective's expression said she suspected Mary Alice wasn't giving her the whole story. "Had they argued other times at rehearsal?" Potts asked. She made *argued* sound like fought.

Mary Alice wished she hadn't stood; Potts' cigarette breath was killing her. But sitting down again seemed like an admission of guilt.

Two men put Jamie into a black body bag.

This is how they wear you down.

Jaworski put his hand on her shoulder. She became aware of how important his support was to her. The chemistry between them had been pretty hot, and his standing by her now, implicitly against another cop, heightened the initial attraction. Even as she answered Potts' question she was aware of another part of her brain evaluating whether or not she could fall in love with Tom Jaworski.

"Sometimes they disagreed," she said. Others would testify to that fact that Chase and Jamie argued. But just because you hated someone or were jealous of him didn't mean you killed him. She heard the bag zipper screech, catch and finish home. But someone had killed Jamie O'Malley.

When she pulled her eyes from the body being loaded onto a gurney, she saw Jaworski whispering to Claire Potts. Mary Alice heard him say her name, post-traumatic stress, police and case. Potts looked like a Nikon on motor-drive.

"Just one more question Ms. Tate. Would you say Chase Minor was jealous of Jamie O'Malley?"

Mayday. Land mines.

"I have no idea. Why don't you ask him?"

"I will," Potts said. "I plan to talk to everyone, and I'll want to talk to you again." She smirked and sounded confident, like she'd come for sardines and scored Ahi.

Mary Alice could see nicotine stains edging each sharp detective tooth.

"May I go home now?" Mary Alice asked. She worked to sound self-assured. She knew anyone who discovered a murder victim was automatically a suspect. However, her Minnie Mouse pitched voice betrayed her.

"After we do a gunpowder test." Potts smiled and seemed to enjoy Mary Alice's discomfort.

"I didn't touch the gun."

"Then there'll be no problem." Potts half-mocked Mary Alice's southern accent.

Mary Alice looked down at the detective's pudgy hands. The nails and cuticles were chewed; ink stained the left middle finger.

"If this man was your friend, I'm sure you want his killer found," Potts said, stuffing her notepad in her purse.

"I do." Mary Alice stepped back fighting an urge to wipe her hands on her thighs. She hadn't fired a gun since she'd learned to shoot her Daddy's forty-five over six months ago. Mary Alice felt sure Potts was out to make Mary Alice betray herself or someone else.

"One more thing," Potts said. "After you called Detective Jaworski and had this flashback when you thought you were being drowned, why didn't you pick up the gun?" Potts easily pulled out her notebook and flipped it open. "You said you were terrified you were going to be killed."

Mary Alice thought of Colombo, the TV detective who always turned around with one more question. *She thinks I wiped my fingerprints off the gun after I shot Jamie.*

"Well Ma'am, I guess flight won over fight." Mary Alice liked calling her ma'am; she could see it bothered the detective.

Detective Claire Potts' acid look said that she was through with Mary Alice for now, but not forever.

Mary Alice watched Potts walk away. Her careful steps gave her bulk an oddly sensual quality. Mary Alice pictured a grossly fat Middle Eastern belly dancer she'd seen in a film. Potts ran her stubby fingers through her hair. Mary Alice looked away just as Potts looked back, zeroing in on her.

After the powder test, Jaworski drove her and the dog home. The sleet had stopped, but roads were banana-slick.

They crept along filling the silence with speculation, agreeing that Potts' presence in Cana would have been interesting under different circumstances. Cana had no female detectives. Never had.

At her door Jaworski asked, "Are you still seeing that therapist?"

"No. Are you working for my mama?"

He took her hands in his. "Finding a dead body unnerves most people. Coming on the heels of what happened to you a few months back, I'd be surprised if you hadn't blacked out."

She rested her head on his chest. He exuded warmth, and she wished she had the energy to ask him in. She remembered that scorching day in the hunting cabin and how close they'd come to ripping off their clothes and falling together on the dusty mattress.

"Thanks for everything. I'm okay." She wished she meant the second part.

"Get some sleep," he said. "I'll get your car back to you in the morning."

She stood in the doorway and watched him limp to his car. It was a ten year old Honda Civic, all he could manage since his newer Ford Explorer had rolled with him in it. Boon raced through a quick survey of the deck and pushed past her inside. She bolted the door, but knew that the lock couldn't really protect her.

She sat in bed in the dark petting Boon and feeling like she'd aged another ten years. Why had Claire Potts been so abrasive? Maybe that was how policewomen were trained in Detroit. But Potts was scary—something in her eyes. Mary Alice was pretty sure the detective planned to nail the killer fast, earn the praise of her boss and get the hell out of the purgatory that certainly Mississippi was for her. She knew it would be wise to placate Potts or at least not piss her off. But since grade school Mary Alice had not been able to abide bullies.

You need to be careful. Didn't your experience with Sheree Delio's case teach you something about criminal investigations? She heard her father's voice. James Tate had been a lawyer. His

23

stories about the vagaries and injustices of the law should have taught her something.

Yes, her experience with Sheree had been instructive. But there was another aspect of the investigation her father would not have imagined. Detective work was rife with excitement, thrills, lots of them cheap thrills. Since at least high school, adrenaline had been Mary Alice's drug of choice. However, she was selective about the stimulation for it. She preferred sexy older men who offered adventure, or running away, or lying about who she was. The fantasy of being someone else was always part of it. But finding dead bodies and almost being killed also got the adrenaline pumping.

Boon rolled toward her, claiming a few more inches of the bed.

She sank under the down comforter and fell asleep thinking about Tom Jaworski. He could save her if necessary. Embracing the Cinderella myth wasn't selling out if you were thirty-six with a divorce under your belt and a noisy biological clock down there, too.

CHAPTER 3

February 27, Tuesday

B OON'S WHINING WOKE MARY ALICE. She'd dreamed she'd
been caught in a net and thrown in a flash freezer. As her
limbs slowly stiffened, she wondered if she'd be eaten with
cocktail sauce.

Like a saggy balloon, she slogged downstairs to let the dog
out. Unfazed by the gray chill, Boon frisked across the meadow
tracking up the frosty grass. Late February in Mississippi rarely
had felt so bitter. In three weeks spring was officially due to
arrive.

Mary Alice noticed her car in the driveway—the '98 BMW
that still smelled like her daddy. Jaworski had delivered it as
promised. She put two fingers to her lips and blew a piercing
whistle. Seconds later Boon cantered toward her, ears pinned
back by the wind, mouth agape in a goofy smile.

She punched Kate Bishop's number at World Oasis while
she filled Boon's bowl.

"World Oasis Health," an earnest female voice intoned.

Mary Alice knew it was Pebble, one of Kate's two employees. Pebble's boyfriend, Strider, his wiry hair stuffed into a bulbous knit cap that matched hers, did all the stocking and heavy work. Kate didn't bother to explain the Rastafarian pair, and Mary Alice had never spotted either outside the store.

"Pebble, is Kate in? It's Mary Alice."

"She's making infusions this morning. I'll see if she can come." Pebble made the work sound like Kate was formulating a cure for lymphoma.

Mary Alice wondered how, if Kate knew about Jamie, she could boil herbs. It was after ten, and everybody in Cana probably knew about Jamie.

Boon's crunching topped the hum of the refrigerator, filling the silence of the wait.

"Hey."

Kate sounded like she knew.

"You know about Jamie?"

"Yeah," Kate said.

"We've got to talk," Mary Alice said.

"Can you come by the store? I can't leave right now."

Boon banged his nose around in his food bowl.

"Soon as I get dressed." Mary Alice hung up, fired up Mr. Coffee and dragged herself up the stairs. Since Jamie's arrival back in Cana, Kate Bishop had made no secret of her attraction to him. Kate made no secret of any of her feelings. What was she feeling now that he was dead? The shower's cold blast made Mary Alice think of Claire Potts. She needed to warn Kate about the detective. Kate liked to be perceived as an authority on lots of things and that made her talkative.

Mary Alice blew her hair dry and pulled on a worn pair of Gucci jeans and a heavy gray cotton sweater. In the mirror her all-American-brown-eyed-girl good looks were on strike. She changed to a periwinkle pullover and practiced smiling.

"Stay here," she told Boon, who waited by the door. "I won't be gone too long."

The dog dropped his head and shuffled to his therma-pad bed by the window.

"I swear," she said.

He lay down and placed a paw over his nose, his eyes never leaving hers.

"Don't give me the bean-eye. I can't stand it."

He looked away.

The car started on the first try.

The bare fields of Cotashona County glinted in the mid-morning sun that came and went through the clouds sucked up from Mexico. Closer to town she slowed for a pack of bicyclists dressed in bright spandex. The fancy road bikes didn't move over. She cut around them. When had serious cyclists with snotty attitudes invaded north Mississippi?

"It's a good thing for y'all that I'm a southern lady raised with manners or—" They might not be so lucky when a late-to-work Bubba-good-ole-boy flew by.

She parked behind Kate's store and entered through the back. Kate worked at a long stainless steel table pouring a dark liquid into small glass jars. Steam laced the tall windows, and the air smelled like edible incense.

Kate met Mary Alice with an embrace. As Mary Alice hugged her, she realized they both were crying.

Kate pulled back and tried to wipe her eyes on her plastic coated apron. "You found him. His body?"

Mary Alice explained how she happened to find Jamie O'Malley's body.

"Who would do this?" Kate asked. She ran her fingers though her short hair. Silent tears continued to trace down her face.

Mary Alice shook her head.

"That Potts creature thinks I did it," Kate said.

"What?" Mary Alice felt Mr. Coffee etching the lining of her stomach. She didn't believe Detective Potts really suspected Kate. As generous as she was, Kate Bishop also liked drama and cast herself as the leading lady in any handy scenario.

"They think I was the last one to see Jamie alive and that puts me at the top of Detective Potts' list." Kate switched off the burner of the tiny stove.

"Were you the last?"

"Obviously not."

"I mean the last before the killer."

"Who knows?" Kate slipped the apron off. "We'd planned to get together after rehearsal. But Jamie wanted to stay at the theatre. He said he could rethink scenes better on the set; that he'd come over in a little while. I left. My car was parked over here behind the store." She slumped into a folding chair and mopped her tears with a pot holder.

"But he never showed up." Mary Alice tried to imagine how it would feel to know the man you had a date with had been murdered.

"No." Tears oozed. "Never did."

Mary Alice saw that Kate's distress was genuine. Maybe because Kate had overcome so much, Mary Alice had come to trust her. Kate was earnest the way most new age health nuts were, but she was no spacey earth muffin. A born nonconformist, Kate Bishop was from the south but wasn't bound by its rules.

"When did you talk to Claire Potts?" Mary Alice asked.

"She came by this morning. Who the fuck is she?" Kate said.

Kate's use of spicy language was another reason Mary Alice liked her. In Cana ladies didn't swear, and the few women who dared weren't invited back.

"Mississippi Bureau of Investigation. Tom says they usually get involved in murder cases. She's new. Just happened to be in Cana."

"Lucky us. Is she staying?" Kate twisted the pot holder.

Mary Alice nodded. "She just moved to Mississippi from Detroit."

"Michigan?"

"She had some trouble up there. At least that's what Tom heard. I guess Cana is in her region, district, you know," Mary Alice said. Last night in the car Tom had shared what he knew of the MBI agent. Mary Alice hoped it was okay to tell Kate.

Kate rose and returned to the work table where she loosely placed lids on the jars of the cooling liquids. "She gets off intimidating people, making the ends justify the means."

The odors of Kate's preparations were making Mary Alice dizzy, but she could hear customers out front, and there was no place else to go. "Did you tell her about your date with Jamie?"

"I had to. She said they need to put together a time line of what happened when."

"Be careful with her, Kate. If what Tom heard is true, she needs to score."

"Ah, Detective Lindsey."

"You mean Kinsey, Kinsey Millhone. Kate, I'm serious. This isn't a mystery novel. She's dangerous."

"She asked me about Chase and Jamie's fight," Kate said.

"Fight? You told her it was a fight?" All of Mary Alice's alarms went off. Chase was vulnerable and here was Kate aiding the enemy.

"Mary Alice, you were there." Kate set a dozen tiny jars of different dried herbs on the table.

Mary Alice couldn't tell if they were related to the cooling jars of liquid or were a new project. "I saw Jamie fail to observe the boundary between writer and director. Big egos bumping around."

"But you have to—"

Mary Alice moved in close. "If you tell the cops they fought, next they'll get you to say that Chase was jealous of Jamie and wanted to kill him." How could Kate not see what was so obvious?

Kate gripped the edge of the table. "But it's true," she whispered. She'd stopped crying but now looked even more miserable.

"Damn Kate. Potts is not your pal."

"I didn't say Chase wanted to kill Jamie, but Mary Alice, he did say that. We both heard him."

"It's an expression. Hyperbole. Exaggeration for effect. Chase is Mr. Theatre, for God's sake," Mary Alice said. Again she prayed no one else had heard the pissed off director mouthing off. "Haven't you ever said, I'm going to kill him or her?"

"Yeah," Kate said. "That's why I didn't tell her what Chase said. But I did tell her about the argument, and that Chase is, well, might be a little jealous. She's going to talk to everybody, and someone is going to tell her Chase and Jamie have been at war since Jamie got here." Locked into self-justification mode, she talked fast.

Kate was frightening Mary Alice. Things looked much worse for Chase than she'd thought. She tried to calm her voice. "It's all words right now, but Detective Potts is writing 'em all down," Mary Alice said. "They were two artists in a temporary ego battle who, after the show opened, would be friends again. Does that sound right to you?"

Kate nodded. "I just want them to find the real killer."

"Then stick to the facts." Mary Alice felt like screaming. How could Kate be so thick? They'd never find the real killer if they arrested Chase Minor.

Kate looked wounded.

"You sure you didn't tell anybody else what Chase said?" Mary Alice asked. "That he was going to die or kill Jamie before he took any more of his crap?"

"One hundred per cent positive."

Mary Alice hoped it was the truth. She wanted to tell Kate everything she knew about Chase and Jamie's history. However, saying it in the context of murder turned a past grudge into a present motive. "After everybody left, did Jamie say anything to you about Chase?" Mary Alice asked.

"He laughed. 'Fuck him if he doesn't want to direct my play.' You know how he talked," Kate said. "But suppose after I left, Jamie was fooling around, rewriting the scene, acting it out and maybe the gun went off." She lowered her voice. "Mary Alice, I know Chase took his gun, the one we use, home last weekend."

Mary Alice knew it too and that Chase kept the gun loaded at home. "You think he brought it back on Monday? Forgot it was loaded?"

"It's possible." Kate removed the lid and held her finger over one of the small jars to test the temperature.

"I saw the gun on the floor center stage, ten feet from the bed. No way Jamie shot himself either deliberately or accidentally." Mary Alice thought but didn't say that Chase could have returned and threatened Jamie with his gun that he thought wasn't loaded. She could imagine the scene. With hindsight, she thought Chase had made a poor decision, a fatal error, to use a real gun for a prop.

"Ouch. Shit." Kate pulled her hand back. Brackish liquid slopped onto the table. Mary Alice grabbed a wad of paper towels and mopped the spill. Kate sucked her scalded fingers.

"Was the gun you saw for sure the one we were using in the play?" Kate asked.

"Looked like it. Anyway a ballistics test will tell." Mary Alice tossed the wet paper towels, missing the trash can.

"Did they find any fingerprints?" Kate asked.

"The police didn't share that with me," Mary Alice said. "I say let Chase tell about his gun." Mary Alice had hoped to find a comrade with whom she could discuss the murder and decompress her own fears. But Kate wasn't thinking clearly, and she may have unwittingly implicated Chase Minor.

"But—"

Mary Alice went to her friend, held her shoulders and looked her in the eye. "We have an outsider, Potts, looking to make a name for herself, make up for past mistakes, and make a quick arrest. Things can go wrong fast. I say we give them the barest facts and zero speculation."

"I never knew a man like Jamie," Kate said. Her tears recharged.

Kate's sad-dreamy expression made Mary Alice suspect that Jamie and Kate had not wasted any time becoming intimate. Kate hadn't said anything about sex. She wouldn't. But intimacy made people vulnerable, and maybe Kate knew more about Jamie and his enemies than she let on.

Pebble stuck her Rasta-hatted head in the door. "Kate, Mr. Pearlman wants to ask you about *Coffea cruda*."

"Be right out," Kate said.

Pebble smiled and backed through the door.

"Didn't you give me that for insomnia?" Mary Alice asked. The murder discussion was over for now.

"That's it. That quack Dr. Fuller got him addicted to Ambien."

"I took a Xanax last night."

"Fine. But if you start taking that shit everyday, you better tell me." Chameleon-like, Kate became her healer-self.

"Then you'd give me something really strong? That would work?"

"Yes."

"What?"

"A potent bowel cleanse. I better go see Mr. P."

Mary Alice wanted to warn Kate again about talking too much. She didn't think Kate got it.

Kate hung her apron on a hook by the door. Mary Alice followed her into the store. In her wake, Mary Alice smelled the aroma Kate, who never wore perfume, exuded. It smelled like the air outside a Nabisco factory on cookie day. Kate, who said she couldn't smell herself, swore it was nothing except that maybe because she didn't eat meat, she smelled a little different.

World Oasis, two blocks off the Cana town square, occupied a remodeled Nineteenth century dry goods store that still possessed its original pressed tin plate ceiling and wide pine plank floor. Full of light and yellows, it shouted robust health. The business should have failed in the first year. Not even nearby

Oxford with its university clientele had a health food store. But customers stood four deep at the check-out, and the take-out lunch crowd that came for Pebble's organic Vegan soups and wraps hadn't even shown up yet.

But Mary Alice suspected the real draw was Kate, who with her knowledge of nutrition, herbs and naturopathic medicine listened to people's ailments and helped them. More than one Cana physician grumbled about her practicing medicine and dispensing drugs without credentials.

"Katie, honey, will the show go on do you think?"

Mary Alice heard a voice she recognized as belonging to Vallie Leonard.

Mr. Pearlman, flapping a *Coffea cruda* pamphlet, hovered impatiently.

"Mrs. Leonard, we haven't been told yet," Kate said. She sounded polite but curt.

Vallie Leonard, a close friend and pilgrimage buddy of Mary Alice's mother, sponsored the Cana theatre. She'd paid for the new seats in the auditorium and the light dimmer board.

"Y'all might could postpone," Vallie Leonard said. "It's too awful. Poor Jamie coming home to let us do his play. One of Cana's brightest stars. It wasn't suicide, was it?" She adjusted her oversized sunglasses.

"I don't know," Kate said. "Excuse me please, Mrs. Leonard. Mr. Pearlman's been waiting for me." Kate quickly shepherded Mr. Pearlman into the homeopathic remedy aisle. Vallie lifted her chin and pursed her lips, but Kate was gone.

Mary Alice watched from behind a cereal display. She didn't want to discuss decorations for the pilgrimage or Jamie's murder with Vallie Leonard. A handsome man on a granola box looked at her, but she saw Jamie O'Malley. She remembered his eyes, the position of his body and the blood. *Not suicide.* Thirty boxes of organic flax cereal toppled to the floor. Pebble came to the rescue, and Mary Alice escaped out the shop's front door.

She walked toward the town square, focusing on the courthouse at the center. The clock still hadn't been fixed. What was she going to say when Agent Potts of the MBI reappeared with new tricks to make her reveal that Chase had hated Jamie since college because Jamie had betrayed Chase?

She turned into an alley that led to the lot behind Kate's store. The car was warm even though the sun had reneged on its promise to shine. In ten minutes she was turning off onto the gravel road that led to her home on the lake, the house her father had left her. She put the car in the garage and entered the kitchen. Boon and a blinking red light on the answering machine greeted her. Maybe Tom Jaworski had called. No, it was better not to check. Not yet. It could be Claire Potts or worse, her mother, ready to add murder to the list of Mary Alice's faults.

Boon followed her upstairs and joined her in the unmade bed. She knew she didn't make good decisions when she was tired, and she'd had only five hours of sleep.

Her gaze landed on the photos on the dresser: Mary Alice and her father on horses, her being awarded her first swimming medal, her father in his fishing boat. She squinted at her father's image hoping she'd hear his voice. She longed to hear him tell her how it was all good and only her resistance to what *was* caused pain. He made such ideas acceptable.

She felt exhausted, but sleep didn't come.

Why was Kate confiding in Potts? Potts was a bully trying to pull her career out of the toilet. Couldn't Kate sense that?

Mary Alice remembered how no one would listen to her when she was trying to prove Sheree Delio didn't kill Scott Bridges. Murder investigations turned the truth into a moving target. Maybe the emotion of it all had engulfed Kate. After all, her lover had been murdered. And without Mary Alice's knowledge of the past, Kate couldn't imagine that Chase would be in serious trouble. Maybe.

She pulled her knees up and burrowed deeper under the down comforter. She wondered if Jamie's killer had gone home after the murder and slept peacefully.

She remembered reading about a Burmese tribe who believed the soul, like a butterfly, leaves the body as it sleeps. They don't wake the sleeping lest the soul, being too far away, not have time to return. Could some passing soul-butterfly have witnessed Jamie's murder? And what about Jamie's butterfly? She didn't know the rules for the butterflies of the murdered. As she listened to Boon snore, she searched inside for her butterfly's vibration, ready to wing into the universe. But if she had one, it was quiet.

CHAPTER 4

February 27, Tuesday

" HELLO, THIS IS NORTON PIKE. There will a meeting of cast and crew on Tuesday evening February 27 at seven at the Cana High Auditorium. Please be punctual." That was all the answering machine message had said. With the playwright dead, the theatre group had some decisions to make.

In a stall in the CHS Girls Restroom, Mary Alice struggled to zip her jeans. They were her fat jeans. It was probably the M&Ms. Those or the oatmeal raisin cookies from the front of the Kroger's. Probably baked with lard. She'd read in *Ladies Home Journal* that to work off a single M&M, she'd have to walk the distance of a football field. A hundred yards per M&M.

The bathroom door swung open, banging the wall.

"Daddy would knock the living snot out of me if he found out," a girl said.

Mary Alice recognized Brenda Lee Chinault's voice. She played the General's immoral but sweet teenage daughter, a big role, and Brenda Lee was good in it.

"He ain't gonna find out now. Mr. O'Malley's dead."

Mary Alice thought the companion was a girl who hung around the theatre but wasn't in the play. Annette somebody. Mary Alice could imagine lots of secrets Brenda Lee might have from her daddy, but that this one involved Jamie O'Malley made her freeze.

"Shit. Can you believe they arrested him?" Brenda Lee said. Mary Alice heard articles from a purse being dumped on the vanity table. Both girls worked hard to look like the current pop vixen.

Arrested him, who?

"It was Chase's gun," Brenda Lee said. A discharge of hairspray covered Annette's comment.

Mary Alice stopped breathing, straining to hear what she didn't want to. The bad news quickened her pulse but thickened her blood. At least that's what it felt like, and it didn't feel good.

"I'm not voting to cancel the show," Brenda Lee said. "This is the best role I ever had."

Mary Alice pressed an eye to the crack beside the stall door. Brenda Lee curled her eyelashes; Annette practiced her poutyslutty look. While Brenda Lee, in spite of her cosmetic choices, looked beautiful, Annette, with the same style, looked more tawdry than sexy. Both girls looked well beyond their real ages.

"Can I use that shadow?" Annette asked. She had an animal instinct for selecting the right products to heighten her *Girls Gone Wild* look.

"Sure." Brenda Lee licked her lips.

Mary Alice eased back from the door, closed her eyes and willed herself to be invisible. She inhaled the perfume of the hairspray—dime store floral with a bass note of Pine Sol.

"I guess that Atlanta reviewer won't come now on account of Mr. O'Malley being dead," Annette said.

"But Jamie already talked to him," Brenda Lee said. "He swore to me. God, I hope he told the guy my name. Jamie said he'd, like, specially point me out to him."

"He ain't here to point," Annette said.

Mary Alice heard items going back into the purse. She couldn't believe even a naive teen like Brenda Lee thought a theatre critic was going to review any play in Cana, Mississippi.

Something hard, like a hairbrush, smacked the vanity table top.

"It's so fucking un-fucking-fair," Brenda Lee said. She seemed to have concluded that the reviewer, under the circumstances, wasn't likely to show up.

"Then maybe it don't matter," Annette said. "Like, you know, if they cancel the play."

"Shit. Come on," Brenda Lee said.

The pair left. Mary Alice felt the whoosh of air from the swinging door. She leaned against the cold metal of the stall not quite able to leave its protection. Chase Minor arrested for Jamie's murder. When? Why hadn't she heard before now? She pressed her cheek to the cold next to graffiti that claimed, *Raylene Jeeter's a ho.*

Mary Alice had known Chase for twenty years and had majored in theatre in college because of his influence. His style was over-the-top-dramatic, but his sharp wit and tongue never overwhelmed his kind nature. Chase had taught her that honesty was best in acting and in life and that interesting was better than pretty. "Audition for the bitch. Sweet young things are boring," he'd told her.

She opened the stall door and saw herself in the mirror. The lack of sleep showed in dark circles beneath her eyes. Her Mama would have said she needed Estee Lauder cream concealer. That and a husband. On the vanity top strands of Brenda Lee Chinault's long bleached blond hair lay like spent Mardi Gras serpentine. Mary Alice shook her shoulder length brown hair. She knew she was still pretty, but looking in the same mirror recently vacated by teenagers made her feel dowdy.

Why had Jamie O'Malley told sweet, barely eighteen-thing, Brenda Lee Chinault that he was having a critic take a special look at her? Mary Alice didn't need a Yale Drama School degree to figure that one out.

She turned off the lights and headed to the meeting.

Mary Alice entered the cavernous high school auditorium from the back. It looked and smelled just as it had when she attended eighteen years ago. She felt like a freshman tiptoeing into assembly for the first time and absorbing the stares of the older boys. She sat on an aisle ten rows back.

Norton Pike had already started. Standing in front of the high school drama club's half-finished set of *Grease*, the tall black man ran a hand over his slick head.

"I'm not going to talk about Jamie O'Malley's death." He lifted his chin, stretching out of his creamy turtleneck. "Y'all know that Chase has been arrested. What I want to talk about is if you want to continue or not. I can take over direction, but—"

Several people interrupted.

Even under stress, Norton looked svelte. His chunky perfect teeth were like iced *petite fours.* "Please wait," Norton said. "I see three options. One, cancel, two, postpone and three, on with the show." He held up three fingers, but didn't telegraph his choice.

Garth Buchanan, the General, stood. "Jamie O'Malley would have wanted us to soldier on—"

Heads all around bobbed.

"Norton, have you spoken with Chase?" the costumer, Fran Zimmer, asked. Garth Buchanan looked irritated at being cut off, but he sat down. Over 70, Miss Fran had been hemming pants and making costumes in Cana for over half of her life. Everyone deferred to her.

"No. Bill Burgess is representing him. I talked to him," Norton said, his long fingers grazing the lapel of his camel hair jacket. His silence and posture made it clear that he wasn't going to repeat whatever Bill Burgess had said.

"I mean, Chase might want us to go on," Miss Fran said.

"Or not," somebody said.

Evelyn Alexander raised her hand, and Norton nodded at her. "We cannot go on," she said with authority. "How will it look? Well-known writer murdered by director in little theatre. It'll be in the national news. Once again Mississippi yokels—"

"Probably be sold out for every performance," somebody said. A few laughed and then suppressed their own laughter.

Mary Alice had anticipated that the tacky factor might guide the group. She was surprised when Minerva Weeds spoke.

"We're all in shock, but we need to consider that the tickets, programs, posters and advertising have been bought and paid for and another play is scheduled in May. We can't postpone, and if we cancel, the theatre will be close to bankrupt."

Brenda Lee Chinault seconded Minerva Weeds' opinion. Minerva, who played the General's wife, was married to a retired judge, and had a successful career as a romance writer. Minerva Weeds wielded considerable influence.

Mary Alice was about to state that the arrest was a mistake and Chase would be back soon when Norton called for a show of hands.

A majority voted to go on with the show. The nay-voters seemed content with the decision. They could tell their friends at church that they had been against continuing, but that they were overruled. The price of democracy. Norton, apparently ready for this decision, announced that the police had said that the Cana Little Theatre building would be available on Thursday and that he wanted the full cast there at seven. He adjourned the meeting.

But almost no one left. Mary Alice joined the group clustered around Minerva Weeds, who denied she knew any details about Chase.

Mary Alice didn't believe her. Minerva would know what her husband, the judge, knew, and retired or not, he'd be privy to everything. Mississippi politics hadn't changed in spite many reforms. You were in or you weren't, and the judge was certainly still in.

"Maybe he just got mad," one of the actresses said. "A crime of passion."

"I can't believe it."

"Chase has him a temper," another added.

"I remember when Curtis left him."

Eyes bugged or rolled. Who could forget how crazy Chase had acted back then.

"Maybe he went temporarily insane," a man said. "That's not first degree murder."

Mary Alice felt her face go hot and her guts go cold. "Wait a minute. We're talking about our friend. Chase didn't kill Jamie," she said.

People looked down; one moved to another group.

"Well, sure, innocent until proven—"

"Yes. That's right," a woman said, but her tone lacked faith.

"You think Chase committed murder?" Mary Alice asked. Her voice quavered.

"He's in jail, Mary Alice. They have evidence," the man playing the General's son said.

"It's wrong. It's that Detective Potts. Can't you see?" Mary Alice said trying not to sound hysterical. "She's desperate for a quick arrest." She wanted to tell them what Tom Jaworski had said about Potts leaving her last job.

"That Yankee detective's a piece of work, all right," a man said. "I'm just saying."

The General took over. "Mary Alice, you know Chase and Jamie didn't get along, and that's putting it mild," Garth Buchanan said. "Maybe Jamie provoked him."

"Or it could have been an accident," a voice behind her said.

"Mary Alice, you were here. You heard them," someone said.

"Wasn't so much what they said, it was the way they said it," Garth Buchanan said.

"It's like Chase taught us in the acting class," the General's son said. "Every line has a text and a sub-text. Chase's sub-text said, 'Back off. I can't stand you. How dare you?' Stuff like that."

"I really thought one of them might throw a punch. I really did."

"Chase never wanted Jamie O'Malley to come at all," a man who was on the board said. "The board of directors forced him."

Like Molotov cocktails comments lobbed in from all directions.

"The police have jumped to a conclusion, but we don't have to," Mary Alice said. "Chase needs us." She felt dizzy. Softening Chase's guilt to manslaughter shocked her nearly as much as the accusation.

"Bill's a good attorney," someone said. "He'll sort it out."

Affirmative murmurs all around.

When you were in deep shit, you got Bill "Dead-Eye" Burgess even if you couldn't afford him.

Mary Alice tried again. "A murderer is loose. Don't y'all want the real killer caught?"

Yeses all around.

"Mary Alice, it's not up to us. The police know what they're doing."

"We need to let the professionals do their jobs."

Mary Alice clearly remembered how the professional Cana police had not known their asses from their handcuffs when they arrested Sheree Delio. Yet, once arrested, guilt stuck like barnacles.

The group broke up. Mary Alice felt sick. She watched Brenda Lee and Annette leave together and wondered about what Brenda Lee's daddy was going to knock the snot out of her if he found out, which Annette now seemed to think he'd never discover. Casting couch seduction? What else could it be? Mary Alice wondered if Kate knew Jamie might have been fooling around with Brenda Lee. And if those two ladies, why not others? Maybe lots of others.

Minerva Weeds touched her arm. "Chase will be out of jail tonight. Early morning at the latest." Moving like one of her romance heroines, she melted into a throng and disappeared.

Kate caught up with Mary Alice outside the auditorium.

"Can I catch a ride with you?" Kate asked. Around her neck she wound a muffler that looked like something Pebble had crocheted.

They walked to the car in silence. Mary Alice ran an internal monologue that pretty much went, *I can't believe it.*

Shivering in the cold car, they headed toward Kate's cottage in the old part of Cana.

"They think Chase is guilty," Mary Alice said. The defroster roared, but failed to clear the windshield.

"Not everybody. Not me," Kate said.

"Lots of them. That little weasel that plays the General's son going on about the sub-text. He never thinks about sub-text when he's acting."

"Ignore him. He's hormonal jerk." Kate pulled on a baggy cap that matched her scarf.

"Prick."

"Nobody knows what to think," Kate said.

"What happened to loyalty? What does it cost to assume Chase didn't do it?" Mary Alice furiously scrubbed the windshield. "What am I missing here? Is it homophobia?" They waited at the single stop light between the school and Kate's house. A crescent opened on the fogged windshield.

"No, no," Kate said. "Chase is the gay man that lets the homophobes think they're cool with gayness as in 'I ain't prejudiced against no homos. One of my best friends is queer.' "

"I cannot believe how they—"

"He's only been arrested a few hours," Kate said. "Burgess will get to work on a defense. He's one of the best lawyers in Mississippi."

"Kate, once the cops arrest someone, they stop looking for anyone else. The corollary to that rule is that the longer the time between the murder and the capture, the better the chance that the killer will never be caught."

"I know," Kate said. "There's another corollary that says you throw as much shit as you can and see what sticks."

Mary Alice turned onto Kate's street. "Poor Chase. He must be a wreck." She imagined the impeccable Chase Minor in a Cana jail cell. Would they have taken his belt and shoe laces? "I've got to help him."

"Mary Alice, give Bill Burgess a chance. If you try to save Chase, you might make it worse."

Mary Alice remembered how her efforts to help Sheree Delio had nearly backfired. She'd found a coat button in Sheree's apartment that the police missed. It was the only hard piece of evidence, the sole clue, and she had rendered it inadmissible. Mary Alice pulled into Kate's driveway.

"You want to come in?" Kate asked. "I have some really good tree bark tea. From Brazil."

Mary Alice thought Russian vodka might go down easier. "Hard to resist, but I'm going home. Thanks."

"We're still doing props, right?" Kate asked.

"Yes. Why?"

"We'll need to find another gun." Kate got out of the car and dashed through the cold to her door.

And a new bedspread. No business like show business.

On the drive home Mary Alice made a list of who seemed to support Chase and who seemed to want to throw him to the jackals. Minerva Weeds seemed sympathetic as did Norton Pike and Miss Fran. Her head ached. She wanted to call the county jail and see how Chase was doing if he was still locked up. She pictured him sitting in a corner looking like the Earl of Essex waiting for the gibbet.

Chase isn't helpless like Sheree. It's none of my business, she told herself. But she knew she couldn't live with that. How had the police established a motive? Were an argument over a play and ownership of the murder weapon sufficient for an arrest or had someone given the cops more?

Away from the lights of town, the car glided through the dark past quivering oaks, gums and loblollies. She turned on the radio, WRVR in Memphis. Counting Crows' rendition of *Big Yellow Taxi* played; "they paved Paradise and put up a parking lot."

Who else knew what she knew about Chase and Jamie and would want to tell it to the police?

Chase and Jamie had gone to high school in Cana together and stayed in touch even though Jamie went to college out of state. Both had wanted to be writers. While in college Chase wrote a play and sent it to Jamie for an edit. By that time two of Jamie's plays had been professionally produced. But nothing ever came of Chase's play except that six years later, he found out that Jamie had plagiarized the work and gotten it produced. Even though productions hadn't won awards or made Jamie rich, Chase had felt profoundly betrayed. Of everything Jamie could have done to Chase, stealing and then rewriting his play was as bad as it could get. Chase had loathed Jamie ever since.

Of course, Chase hadn't wanted Jamie to come to Cana. However, the board of directors did, and Chase didn't choose to tell them the reason why Cana's most successful writer shouldn't come home and help the theatre produce his play. Perhaps Chase felt shamed just as victims often feel the abuse they suffer is mostly their own faults. The board had made Jamie a visiting guest artist and his play the centerpiece of the season.

Mary Alice turned into her drive, glad to be home. The windshield finally had cleared.

She couldn't imagine who else knew about the ancient grudge. Chase had told her. Who else? But all of that had happened nearly forty years ago, and anyway, Chase was not the kind who could kill. He might craft an exposé, but he'd never murder anyone. His tantrums contracted into snits. He'd throw a gun before he'd fire it.

Boon, twitching with delight at her appearance, greeted her at the door. She scratched his neck, sending a shower of yellow fur to the floor.

Later, in bed with Boon hogging the middle, she reviewed it all for the dog, ending with still more questions. Why was she sure Chase was innocent? Did she have some infallible inner radar that detected guilt and innocence?

"So I'm just going to be supportive, go see Chase tomorrow. You want to go?"

She eased her legs under the dog, nudging him to his side of the bed.

Boon blinked twice.

"But I'm not going to get involved."

He rolled his eyes then looked away.

"I mean it. Sheree didn't have anybody to help her. This is different."

Boon turned over, reclaiming the inches he'd lost.

"But it won't hurt to ask a few questions. You think the police know about Jamie stealing Chase's play?"

The dog yawned.

"And if they do, who told them, and why'd they tell?" She knew people seldom acted solely in the interest of revealing the truth. Some, like Kate, merely liked to be perceived as being in-the-know, but others might have darker motives.

"So who profits if Chase goes to jail for killing Jamie?" Only one person, the real killer.

Boon sighed, glad to be half buried in a down comforter in a heated room with the person he loved most. Completely in the Now.

Mary Alice snapped off the light and struggled to reclaim a little turf from the 75 pound animal. Her mind jerked between past and future or rather to an imagined future seen through the fearful eyes of her past.

As she lay there, she thought about Jamie O'Malley. The talented, handsome and charming Jamie. Then she remembered that it was Jamie who had offered to come to Cana with his play. The board of directors had never imagined he'd really come. Hadn't he refused once years ago? Mary Alice had been in marital hell in Dallas at the time, but somehow she'd heard. Why had he changed his mind?

Don't it always seem to go that you don't know what you've got 'til it's gone? They paved Paradise—

CHAPTER 5

March 2, Friday

WHEN MARY ALICE TELEPHONED CHASE'S lawyer, Bill Burgess, he told her Chase was in seclusion. It was Friday; he'd been released on $200,000 bond the day before and was holed up at a friend's. Bill wouldn't say where, but he seemed pleased Chase's bail was so low. Numb, Mary Alice tried to think of something positive. She remembered it was the second day of March. Spring couldn't hide out much longer.

She arrived fifteen minutes late at Thorpe House for the luncheon meeting to plan the pilgrimage final party. Her mother's car sat next to a new black Cadillac Escalade that she assumed belonged to Paige Leonard. Approaching the house, she felt dwarfed by the monstrous Greek revival white elephant. Whereas her family's home, Linnley resembled a delicate Dogwood blossom, the Leonard's Thorpe House looked like a fat cabbage rose. While both homes were antebellum treasures and had been on the pilgrimage tour since its inception, Mary

Alice always felt like something bad was going to happen at Thorpe House. A young black woman Mary Alice didn't recognize struggled to pull open the massive front door.

"They're in the dining room," she said, pointing.

Mary Alice knew the way. She padded down the marble hall, her footsteps swallowed in the thick Chinese runner. The place reminded her of a fancy Victorian TB sanitarium she'd seen in a movie.

"The Cana Little Theatre did fine before Chase, and it will do fine after," Mary Alice overheard Vallie Leonard announce.

The ladies were discussing the murder and the arrest. Mary Alice paused outside in front of a mirror that soared fifteen feet above an antique bombe chest.

"Most gay men have explosive natures," Paige Leonard, Vallie's daughter-in-law said. "I hate to say it, but I can just see him blowing up at Jamie and grabbing that gun. He probably didn't know it was loaded."

"Artistic men are mercurial," Vallie said. "Well, that's my experience."

"Makes me think about that preacher's wife who shot her husband up in Tennessee," Elizabeth said. "You know, anger and a ready loaded gun."

Mary Alice felt like she'd just swallowed an iced tea glass of bilge. *They've convicted him.*

"But please don't let's talk about this mess when Mary Alice gets here," Elizabeth said. "She's a breath away from rushing in like a fool thinking she can save him."

"Must have been horrible finding the body," Paige said.

Mary Alice looked at her reflection in the antique glass, forced the storm from her brown eyes and pulled out the Cana High beauty queen face.

"Where is she?" Vallie asked.

"Here I am," Mary Alice said, entering the huge dining room. "Y'all talking about me?" Her smile assured them she was teasing.

The three looked as startled as little girls caught trying on their Mamas' bras and high heels. Speaking at once, they denied gossiping about anyone. Elizabeth Tate's expression melted into relief that her daughter had shown up. The two had spoken once on the phone since Mary Alice discovered Jamie's body. Elizabeth had demanded Mary Alice come home to Linnley, but Mary Alice had held her ground.

Elizabeth, Vallie and Paige sat at one end of a dining table that could accommodate twenty. Although every piece in the room had a pedigree, the room felt oppressive. The claw feet on the massive table seemed to bite into the dark burgundies and golds of the Persian carpet. The floor to ceiling windows which could have framed the 200 year old oaks and catalpas outside, were swathed in layers of shades, sheers and swags. The walls, papered in deep blue with hand-painted *fleur de lis* patterns, led the eye up, up to the ominously heavy gilt crown molding.

It was as if the space existed to enhance the worth of Vallie and Spence Leonard and resented being used for practical purposes like lunch. Even the most valuable and beautiful objects wore sneers.

Mary Alice joined the trio at the table, masking her ire with repeated apologies for being late. She seated herself beside her mother and realized the three ladies were dressed in similar jewel tone dresses and heels. She wore a new Ralph Lauren nautically inspired slacks outfit in navy and white piped with red chosen because it was slimming. Next to the others, she looked like she ought to help serve.

"I hope y'all like chicken salad," Vallie said. She sounded confident they would.

Vallie shook a small silver bell. Immediately her cook's head popped through the swinging kitchen door. "Clotil, you may serve now."

The woman, clothed in a white get-up that looked to Mary Alice like the uniform of a woman who refused to wear uniforms, disappeared and reappeared with a loaded silver tray.

"We were just talking about the flowers for the party, Mary Alice," Vallie said.

"Yes, Mother Leonard is buying them from a wholesaler in Memphis," Paige said. "That way we can afford some really nice party favors and stay within our budget."

Vallie Leonard waggled her fingers and shook her head dismissively—her thrift and cleverness were nothing.

Three generations of Leonards had made fortunes off Mississippi timber, cotton and real estate. Spense Leonard owned the Cana First National Bank. How much more could it cost to buy locally and garner goodwill?

"We should give away goodie bags," Mary Alice said, picking the green grapes out of her chicken salad. But her tongue-in-cheek suggestion was taken seriously, and Paige assumed the responsibility for scrounging up silken draw string bags filled with baubles and extravagant *bric-a-brac* that would delight the major donors of the Cana Pilgrimage.

Elizabeth beamed approval at Mary Alice's suggestion and ignored the pile of grapes on her daughter's plate which declared, "not fond of the Leonard chicken salad."

Without comment or question, Clotil worked her way among them with a heavy cut glass pitcher, refilling glasses with sweet tea.

Conversation turned to the weather, challenges of shopping in Memphis and the failure of the Mississippi legislature to hike the cigarette tax or lower the highest food tax in the nation.

"Delicious lunch, Vallie," Elizabeth said and the others cooed in unison their agreement.

"Clotil's a treasure," Vallie said, smiling at the departing cook. When the door swung closed, Vallie whispered, "But Lord a-mighty, I miss Mrs. Dickens. Now that woman could cook."

"Where is she now?" Mary Alice asked.

"Assisted living near Pontotoc. Had a stroke sometime back," Vallie said. She petted her pink napkin.

"I heard she has Alzheimer's," Paige said.

Neither Paige nor her mother-in-law looked the least concerned over the obvious downturn in life quality experienced by the former cook.

"Bless her heart; I heard she can't recall what day it is." With a long, perfect, coral fingernail, Paige released the beads of condensation on her tea glass into rivulets.

Although Paige was perfectly turned out, Mary Alice sensed a melancholy energy. Mary Alice had been eighteen when Paige, just twenty, had married Bobby Leonard. Paige, born dirt poor, had learned the moves and nuances of small town high society, but Mary Alice believed Paige Thompson Leonard would be more at home with a long neck at Mickey's Bar wielding a pool cue and an attitude.

"Paige darlin', you have just given me an idea," Vallie said.

Paige turned a blank look on her mother-in-law.

"I'll hire Mrs. Dickens to help us at the party. She might not can remember yesterday, but she'll remember peach cobbler." Vallie clapped her hands with delight.

"No," Paige said. "She won't be reliable."

"How do you know that?" her mother-in-law asked. "You talked to her?"

"No, but she has dementia or something like it," Paige said. "You don't get over that."

"Don't be silly," Vallie said. "Clotil can keep an eye on her. Poor old woman must be bored stiff at that home. Be like riding a bike."

"If she falls off that bike at the most important party of the season, we'll look like idiots." Paige dropped her voice an octave. "These guests fund the pilgrimage, and more important, they sanction it. If they didn't love it, it'd die."

"Paige honey, I am well-versed about the inner working of the pilgrimage," Vallie said in a sugared put-down.

"Shall I call her?" Elizabeth asked. She uncapped her Parker fountain pen and held it poised over her crisp cream note pad.

"I'll do it," Paige said. "I'll call."

"No, I'll get her," Vallie said. "You won't make her say yes."

Clotil entered carrying petite portions of tiramisu in Gorham crystal balanced on delicate rose plates with filigree edges.

Mary Alice wondered why Vallie wanted to risk hiring a woman who might be crazy and suspected it had to do with not letting Paige tell her what to do. "How many are invited this year?"

"Over a hundred," Vallie said. She flicked her wrist as if twice that number would be no serious challenge at Thorpe House.

Last year's wrap party had been at the Walker mansion, and Snookie and Cliff Walker had set a high standard with hundreds of pounds of oysters and mud bugs washed down with gallons of bourbon.

Vallie went over her list of who was in charge of what. Mary Alice was assigned the music. "Don't let the band get too loud," Vallie instructed. Next she outlined the rainy weather plan. "Chase was going to help me with that summer theatre tent he has, but now—"

All but Mary Alice looked at the floor as though the sewer had just backed up under the dining table and sludge was racing for the Ferragamo pumps.

"Poor Chase," Elizabeth said.

"I still can't believe it," Vallie said.

"He has a good lawyer," Paige said.

"Bill gets them off, guilty or innocent," Vallie said.

"I remember once Judge Weeds asked Bill if he didn't think the guilty ought to be punished," Elizabeth said. She was far more animated in the telling than the tale warranted.

Mary Alice could see her mother striving to swing the conversation away from conflict over Chase.

"Bill Burgess said," Elizabeth continued, "Judge Weeds, my fee is punishment enough." Elizabeth led Vallie and Paige in whoops of laughter. Mary Alice caught her breath.

"Chase couldn't have murdered Jamie O'Malley." Mary Alice said. She couldn't catch a single eye.

"I heard that the gun that killed Jamie has Chase's fingerprints on it," Paige said. She sounded sad about the fact. "And there aren't any other suspects, are there?"

"Not yet." She wanted to scream, "it's only been a day you over-privileged idiot, but that isn't the point."

"It's still early," Paige said. "The police or Bill will figure it out. I just thank God I was home with Bobby and Jim," Paige said. "After the way that Yankee detective woman treated Mother Leonard—"

"Chase didn't kill Jamie," Mary Alice said. She felt as though she'd been Tasered.

"Not premeditated," Vallie said. "But anybody can get angry and lose it. A loaded gun presented itself."

"It's not like those two got along," Paige said.

Mary Alice was stupefied by their responses. It was déjà vu from the theatre crowd. Chase was guilty, but it might work out okay because tricky Bill could get him off.

"I remember Jamie O'Malley when he was a boy," Elizabeth said, again steering away from the dangerous shoals of who-done-it. "He was smart, handsome, charming. Lord, did the high school girls chase him."

"After high school too," Vallie said.

"Before my time," Paige said.

"Was sweet to his Mama," Vallie said.

Mary Alice poked the dessert. It jiggled like belly fat.

"Came back here all the time to see after her," Elizabeth said.

"I'm determined that this tragedy will not damage the pilgrimage," Vallie said.

"Don't worry, Vallie, once word gets out, they'll be flocking here," Mary Alice said. She didn't care if she sounded bitter. "'Director kills writer in fit of pique.' They'll be driving up from Biloxi, down from Charlotte and over from Birmingham." She hoped Vallie noticed that she'd used her first name. Most people of Mary Alice's generation called Vallie Leonard by her last name or at minimum Miss Vallie, a familiar southern title reserved for mature ladies. Vallie was sixty-seven.

"Mercy, you're right," Vallie said, missing or ignoring Mary Alice's sarcasm. "Any publicity is good publicity. I better give Maxine a heads up about advance sale tickets."

Mary Alice wanted to throw her *tira misu* at the *grand dame*. Vallie was a long-time supporter of the Cana Theatre. Vallie and Spence Leonard had been the ones to fund the permanent artistic director's salary, boosting the community theatre to semi-pro status. Vallie had backed Chase all the way.

58

"We ought to run Jamie's play all month," Mary Alice said. "It's a crime scene. Have tours. Ladies and gentlemen, down stage right is where the body was found. On this very bed."

Elizabeth Tate's eyes flared and then pulsed alternately pleading and warning.

"Mary Alice, I know Chase is your friend, and I don't mean to say he's guilty," Vallie said. "However, when a man, even if he is a friend, is arrested for murder, things change."

Mary Alice rose from the table sending her napkin to the floor. Her right foot had gone to sleep, and she stumbled. "Look at the time. Y'all excuse me, please. I have a hair appointment. Y'all know Arleen waits for no woman." She smiled; her mouth felt full of warm glue. "Don't worry about the band. I'll keep them in line."

Goodbyes echoed. As she walked to the door, one foot on pins and needles, she could tell they were relieved to have her go. By the time she reached the front door, she heard the tinkle of feminine laughter.

The morning that had hinted spring might be on the way had turned to a gray afternoon. The steely mica sky threatened to strafe the earth below. In her car with the motor running, Mary Alice wiped away tears and unbuttoned the waist of her slacks.

Judases, all of them.

They had loved Chase and roared at his over-the-top antics. They respected his skill as a director, a maestro. Without Chase, all of Vallie's and the others' generous donations would have amounted to nothing. Cana had a top-notch, award-winning theatre because of Chase Minor. How could they abandon him so quickly?

But she was angry with herself too. Her defense of Chase had been weak and then she'd bailed. Chase had put up with these spoiled, rich people in order to have a theatre and to practice the art he loved. He'd helped the town and more to the point, he'd helped Mary Alice. And she hadn't had the guts to tell them what she thought of their judgments and their disloyalty. She felt like stepping out of the car and vomiting the Leonard lunch in the middle of the driveway.

She pulled out onto the wide oak-lined street, glad to be away from Thorpe House. In the rear-view mirror she saw half a dozen Hispanic men working Vallie's flower beds. One combed the lariope; one collected sweet gum balls; the others lifted and toted. Twenty years ago they would have been black men. She wondered what those men did now.

Her head ached, and she rummaged with her right hand in her purse for the remaining chunk of Toblerone that she knew nested there. The gas gauge needle pointed down. She turned onto Main Street heading for the BP station.

Tom Jaworski had all but told her Chase's fingerprints were on the murder weapon. She'd called to pump him for information. He hadn't known much else except that Chase had no verifiable alibi. She'd argued that of course Chase's prints were on the gun. He owned it. It was being used in the production. But the police, especially Claire Potts, thought differently. Where was Chase hiding out? He'd been forbidden to leave the area. The chocolate bar was missing too.

She pulled into the gas station. On the other side of the gas pump island sat a white pickup, a Ford F110. She got out of the car and swiped her credit card at the pump.

"Want me to pump that for you?"

She turned. Stony Cole dressed in brown Carhartts reached for the nozzle.

"Why thanks Stony," she said.

"You look a little dressed up to pump gas," he said.

She hadn't seen Stony Cole for ages, but old high school classmates surfaced every week. She'd lived in Dallas almost ten years with her now ex-husband, Dr. Cham Mauldin, but much of the Cana High class of 1990 had stayed put.

"Gonna rain," he said, sliding the nozzle into the gas tank.

The weather was safe. She figured Stony knew all about what had happened to her last fall. Newspapers state-wide had carried the story.

Fat drops struck the rutted asphalt. "I believe it already is," she said.

"Want me to fill her up?"

She nodded and smiled. "Thanks." She was relieved he hadn't brought up Jamie's death. Maybe he hadn't heard yet.

"This was your Daddy's car, wasn't it?" he asked. In seconds the meter jumped to $12.34.

"Sure was."

"Beemers never die."

The gas pump made appropriate gulping noises.

"Where are you working, Stony?" she asked.

"Tupelo. Making furniture." He told her about his three years upholstering sofas. The benefits package had kept him loyal.

He topped off the tank, replaced the nozzle and screwed in the cap. "You gonna stay around Cana?" He pulled off his Bulldogs cap, smoothed his brushy hair and replaced the hat.

"I guess. For now anyway." She smiled.

"Good. That's good," he said as though he might call her.

"Thanks, Stony," she said pointing at the pump.

When he opened his truck's door, she noticed another man sitting inside. He had his head down reading something, but she recognized Randy Wells. He'd been a bad boy in high school and, therefore, had been very attractive to her. He still looked a little like James Dean in the movie poster for *Rebel without a Cause.* Four years older and three grades ahead, he'd never noticed Mary Alice, but she'd known that if he'd nodded, she'd have jumped in his car and taken her chances. She found herself smiling.

Randy Wells didn't look up.

"Well, you take care now, Mary Alice." Stony pronounced her name, Mae-Ralice.

He cranked the truck and pulled away.

She waved and watched the two men drive off into the mist. When the truck stopped before turning, she saw the right brake light was out. It was too late to warn him. She imagined a zealous Cana cop pulling him over. She'd failed to alter her opinion of Cana's finest.

She turned the key in the ignition and then turned it off.

Inside the BP quick mart she selected a bag of salted peanuts, a Snickers and fountain coke. Whoever designed gas station marts knew what they were doing. A special rack held a cascade of small cellophane bags of Sather's Candy: Coconut Stacks, Circus Peanuts, Orange Slices, Caramel Creams and twenty more. Junk food flowed in tiers, stacks and heaps in disorienting diagonal aisles. Lighted by tracks of warm incandescents, dazed customers circled, loading items into their arms.

"That do it?" the woman behind the counter asked. A tender portion of her 200 pounds crested like a muffin top out of her jeans and rested lightly on the counter.

"Yes, ma'am."

Mary Alice drove slowly to the White Oak Cemetery. She alternated bites of the Snickers with handfuls of nuts and sips of Coke. Sweet, then salty then acid. She thought of the fat woman at the store and wondered if she'd become so large from a similar routine of taste sensations. She let Randy Wells replace the uncomfortable thought. He'd been married but was divorced. She wished she'd gotten a better look at him. In high school he had positively oozed testosterone.

She parked inside the cemetery as close to the Tate plot as possible. The rain gently splattered the car, turning the windshield into a kaleidoscope of grays.

"Daddy, I have to try to help Chase. That Potts woman is going to railroad this thing, and Chase is going to end up doing thirty years for manslaughter. I know Chase hated Jamie because he stole his play, but I know he didn't kill him." She took another bite of the Snickers and felt the caramel hold then stretch between her teeth. Her father, if he was listening, wasn't replying.

"I'm just going to start asking questions. Maybe Bill Burgess will let me help. Somebody killed Jamie, and that means somebody is lying about something or they're going to. I got to look for where the lies are." She spoke aloud and remembered she would need to buy another pack of index cards. Sue Grafton's fictitious PI, Kinsey Millhone always wrote her clues on cards. So did Masie Dobbs, the British PI creation of Jacqueline Winspear. Masie also created a clue map.

Through the blurred window she could see a dark green canopy in the distance. No funeral sprays graced the plot yet. The trip from womb to tomb was brief.

"The first thing I'm going to do is read all of Jamie's plays. If he stole Chase's play, maybe he stole somebody else's play." She finished the last of the peanuts and rubbed the greasy salt between her fingers.

The rain let up. She got out of the car and made her way on tiptoe through the sopping grass to her father's grave.

Be careful, Mary Alice.

She heard his voice as if he were standing beside her.

Don't let familiarity blind you to danger.

She recalled her father's belief that the best place to hide something was to put it in plain view.

"I won't do anything stupid, Daddy." Sometimes it seemed that her daddy could share the insight he had from his side of the veil. So why couldn't James Tate's ghost just whisper the killer's name? Obviously the rules didn't permit that.

Be careful who you talk to.

The rain began again, moving from sprinkle to pelt in seconds. She ran for the cover of the car and drove out of the cemetery toward home.

"Be careful who I talk to? The only way to help Chase is to talk to everybody." She passed an armadillo scuttling along the shoulder. She couldn't remember armadillos from her childhood. When had they come to Mississippi?

She'd hoped for calm support but felt spooked by her father's warning. Familiarity. Was the killer right under her nose? She realized she was driving way too fast. She slowed and switched on the heater.

Instead of turning onto her road, Mary Alice headed back into town. It was Friday afternoon, and if she wanted to talk to Bill Burgess before Monday, she had to catch him within the hour. Talking to Bill Burgess couldn't be dangerous.

CHAPTER 6

March 2, Friday

"How about a drink?" Bill Burgess asked, posing beside his massive barrister's desk. He pointed to a framed *petite pointe* sign above the light switch which read, *It's 5 o'clock somewhere.*

"Isn't the sun supposed to be over the yardarm?" Mary Alice asked. She thought Bill Burgess must be about forty-five, but it was hard to tell. His hair was silver, but there was a lot of it, and he had an edgy energy and the body of a marathon runner.

"What sun?" he said. "We need a drink to warm up. What'll you have?" He opened a cabinet revealing liquor bottles three deep. They looked like soldiers ready to present arms and march into battle.

"Scotch and water with a lot of water, please."

"If this weather is indicative of global warming, it's not working," he said, pouring her a double. "Branch or soda?"

"Branch, please." She watched him splash in a thimbleful.

"It's March second, for God's sake," he said, handing her the drink. "Let's sit over here." He walked to the twin leather love seats that framed a fireplace. When he pressed a remote control, the gas logs sprang to life.

Bill Burgess, who practiced law alone, had renovated a "walking-distance-to-the-square" brick bungalow. Built in the 1920s, the house now possessed a comfortable elegance the first owners would not have imagined. Although he could have also lived in it, he chose to remain in a six bedroom Tudor country home two miles out of town that his second wife had put them into. She was history, and word was that neither of Burgess' wives got zip in their divorces. There were no children. Dead-eye Bill had tight pre-nups and friends on the bench. At least that's what people said.

Mary Alice felt the burn of the scotch and wondered again why people worked to acquire a taste for it.

Burgess sat opposite, cool and unhurried, as if she dropped by every Friday.

"You're looking good, Miss Mary Alice," he said in a way that only southern gentlemen can.

His gray fox eyes never left her, and if she'd been wearing a skirt, she would have had to resist the urge to tug at the hem. "Thanks Bill. Ditto." She knew the extra pounds she'd gained made her face fuller and maybe more attractive. Her stomach and hips, however, paid the price. "Bill, I've come about Chase."

"Ah yes, Chase." He glanced at the dancing flames.

"I've called and called and driven by his house. Can you tell me where he is?"

He set down his drink. "Why don't I call and ask Chase?" He rose and walked to the door that led to a hall. "Be right back."

She watched him leave. He sauntered like a cat. In his absence, she considered dumping half of her drink, but felt that somehow he would know. As though she were filming, her gaze inched around the room. Everything from an antique brass globe to a collection of art glass paperweights rested in perfect balance as though the items themselves understood their high class origins. The handsomely framed art was subdued and original.

Burgess returned. "Good news. Chase hopes you'll visit him this evening." He refilled his drink. "He's at Judge Weeds' old cabin on the lake. I'm sure you know it."

"Is he okay?" she asked, glad to know not only where he was but also that, if she cut through the woods, he was only ten minutes away from her house.

"He's a mess, but Chase dramatizes so much I can't tell what's real. You'll see." He sat again and took a big sip of his drink. "You're living out at the lake now?"

"Yes. Daddy left the house out there to me." Of course he knew that. Everyone did.

"I thought your mama told me you were living at Linnley," he said.

"I was for awhile after—" she stopped, not wanting to go into the story. He'd probably heard it from every angle. "I'm at the lake now."

She sucked in a breath. Hardly a day passed when Mary Alice didn't think it was possible that her attacker had eluded the cops, the APB and the PI her mother had hired and would come back to finish the job—killing Mary Alice. She shivered. Thinking you could kill in self-defense wasn't difficult, but actually doing it might be. She couldn't see herself or Chase having the mettle to pull a trigger and end a life.

Burgess relaxed and leaned back. "It's kind of you to help Chase."

"He's my friend."

"He surely does need friends right now," he said. He looked down at the cubes of ice in his glass.

"He's been so good to me."

"How so?" he asked. Burgess sounded warm and genuinely interested. Bill Burgess knew how to get people to talk.

"I've known him a long time. He got me interested in theatre in high school. Made it serious, not recreation. He taught me that work you love is more fun than anything that is merely fun." She held the scotch with both hands as if to warm it up. "I had some trouble after Daddy moved out. Their divorce. Teenage stuff. Chase helped."

"Sex, drugs and rock 'n roll?" he asked.

She looked up, startled.

"Merely rhetorical. I'm sorry."

"I'm worried sick about Chase."

"He's in some trouble. I won't sugar-coat." Burgess finished off his drink. "Refused to plead guilty or plea bargain. I convinced the D.A. not to go for simple murder. The charge will be manslaughter."

Mary Alice remembered from Sheree's case that Mississippi had capital murder, which carried a death sentence, simple murder with no death but long prison terms and manslaughter which carried a maximum sentence of twenty years.

"So the D.A. thinks manslaughter will be a slam dunk, and he'll push for the full twenty?" Mary Alice asked. The panicky feeling made her gulp her drink.

"That's my thinking," he said.

His expression told Mary Alice that he was impressed with her knowledge and maybe also with her loyalty. It also told her Burgess liked the way she looked.

"In my opinion Chase is more bothered by what people think than he is by the actual arrest," Burgess said.

"It's crazy. Chase couldn't—"

"You're looking at this emotionally, and that's rarely how murder cases work," he said.

"What do you mean?" She set the scotch on the glass-topped end table where it immediately went to work creating a pool under itself.

"For example, have you met Ms. Potts of the MBI?" He raised his eyebrows.

"Yes. One of the police called her Grendel."

"Actually Grendel was male, but no matter," he said. "Potts may turn out to be an asset."

Mary Alice looked at him and waited for the explanation.

"She's arrogant," he said. "A fish out of water. Wants a quick kill. She'll screw up and give us something."

"Technicalities?" she asked. "What about Chase being innocent not to even mention finding the real killer?"

"I'm hired to make the jury find Chase not guilty, not necessarily to find out who is guilty. If the case gets thrown out, Chase will be just as free."

Mary Alice wanted to press him about Chase's chances. What did "in some trouble" mean? She also wanted the lawyer to let her help. While true she'd bungled a few times helping Sheree Delio, in the end, even Sheree's lawyer had recognized Mary Alice's contributions. And Burgess didn't know about her bungles. She decided to shut up about dismissal versus acquittal for the time being.

"You went to Ole Miss, didn't you?" he asked.

"Hotty, Toddy," she said, echoing the famous cheer. Burgess was changing the topic. She wasn't going to get anything more.

"I have two tickets to the Ole Miss— Arkansas basketball game next Wednesday. You interested?"

In the time it took to inhale, she weighed her options. She wasn't ready to date anybody, and if she were it would be Tom Jaworski, who was well outside of Cana society, risky and therefore a doubly attractive choice. Bill Burgess, however, was the pinnacle of professional Cana. After a few dates with him, she'd be labeled his new girlfriend. She didn't want that. However, refusing to go to the game wasn't going to advance her bid to help Chase.

"Mama's got me busy with the pilgrimage, so I'll have to check," she said. "I'll call you." She smiled, but caught his expression. He didn't like being put off. Well, too bad, she thought. He'd manipulated things so that now if she wanted to help Chase, she'd have to go to a basketball game. Even a conversation with Burgess felt like high stakes poker. There was something about the exchange that made her uneasy.

"The Rebels are doing better than they have in five years. That new coach—"

She heard him without listening. He was in the grip of a sports attack, a mostly male malady common in north Mississippi. A smile and occasional nod was all it took to keep the static going.

"Players-three-pointer-post-in-the-paint-rebound-in-the-bonus-time-out."

Mary Alice knew about true listening. Her father had taught her how careful listening creates a field of conscious energy whose importance supersedes the conversation. However, when men went off on ball games, she glazed over. For her, talk of ball fields precluded conscious energy fields.

Burgess darted behind his desk, jerked open the top drawer and held up two tickets. He continued, "Arkansas-dumb-ass-refs-last-year-in-Fayetteville-turnovers."

Mary Alice broke in, "I hate it when they call the hogs. Soooooooeeeeeee."

"It's creepy," he said. "I understand dumping Colonel Rebel, but, well, I don't really understand."

Apparently the mascot problem sobered him, and he turned from sports junkie back to lawyer. "I hope you can go. Let me know."

"I better get out there to see Chase." She rose and headed to the front door. "Thanks Bill." She understood Bill Burgess wasn't going to tell her more about Chase's case or enlist her help. She'd have to trade a date with Burgess for a position on the defense team. Or at least it seemed like it to her.

He walked her to the door. She felt him watching her as she walked down the sidewalk to her car. She pulled back her shoulders then realized that wasn't the part he was watching.

In the dusk the mercury vapor street lamps sputtered to life as though her passing turned them on. Why hadn't she told Bill Burgess the specific reason why she felt compelled to help Chase Minor? Chase had been the single sane voice she'd heard when her world was collapsing as her parents tore one another and her apart. Even after her father moved out to the lake house, the hatred flowed back and forth like the tide, and it always threatened to suck her out to deep water. But Chase got her involved in the theatre, made her work and refused to take no. When she would have preferred to have anesthetized herself with pot, Chase was the one who noticed what was going on and then invented a crisis and persuaded her that she had to help him. Chase was much more than a rescue project.

On the way home she stopped by Latrice Latcherie's catering kitchen, Laissez le Bon Temps, and bought bags of individual servings of frozen stew, soup and veggies. The grocery bill was astronomical; she hoped her check wouldn't bounce.

Judge Weeds' old cabin looked picturesque, but no one had cooked in it since 1955 when Minerva burned to cinders a twenty-five pound turkey. Minerva Weeds often used the cabin as a fictitious setting for the panting lovers of her romance novels. Everybody in Cana knew just how the brass bed squeaked before the crackling fire as characters with names like Lance and Annadelle worked their way through the verbs of lust. Minerva had occasionally decorated the cabin to suit a particular setting, once stapling twinkle lights on the entire ceiling and another time installing a bear skin rug which had later mildewed.

She passed a swath of two dozen Bartlett pear trees about to bloom. Slowing, she rolled down the car window and inhaled, but the vaguely sour scent had yet to emerge.

It wasn't fair that Chase should have to hide out, but if he did, the Weeds' cabin was an appropriate setting for the bigger-than-life director. As she drove she fought the chilly demons that told her Chase was going to jail no matter what she did. Again, she thought of her daddy's idea about a conscious energy field developing between two people if they listened carefully to one another. The ethereal field that emerged was far more important than the spoken words. She had felt it with her daddy and with only one other person. Chase Minor.

CHAPTER 7

March 2, Friday

MARY ALICE PASSED THE TURN for Coon Tail Landing and took the next left on a winding, pine straw thatched private road that led to the Weeds' cabin. The car snaked through thick woods that hugged the narrow road. If Chase wanted isolated, he had it. When the road split, she turned right toward the cabin. The left fork led to the boat ramp. Boon rode shotgun, his nose out the window. She'd detoured by her house to pick him up. Chase loved dogs, especially Boon.

Near the clearing, she spotted dogwoods which any minute would unclench their small white buds and lace the forest with traceries of snowy blooms.

As she turned off the engine, she saw Chase standing in the open back doorway of the cabin. Instead of a suit custom tailored by James Davis in Memphis, he wore khakis and a flannel shirt topped by a black barbeque apron. He smiled through a tired face. When he saw the grocery bags, he came to help.

Mary Alice hugged him. "I brought provisions from Latrice's."

He thanked her and hugged her again.

Boon leading, she headed inside avoiding a melodramatic scene. Her mission was to reassure and support Chase, not to stoke his fear.

Inside, it was clear that a spring cleaning binge had been interrupted. Yellow rubber gloves dripped over the sink faucet, a bucket of soapy water topped a step ladder and two stuffed garbage bags waited by the door for a ride to town. Everything was pulled down, out and apart. She supposed that after a few nights in the county jail, scrubbing felt good.

"Looks like you're striking the set," she said.

"Something has been nesting in the ceiling fan," he said, setting down the grocery bags.

"I brought a really good cab. Want a glass?" she asked.

"*Certainment.* I'm on happy pills, but I haven't taken one in four hours."

She went to work on the bottle of wine. "Can I help you clean?"

"No, I need my distraction. If I finish too quickly, I'll have to paint, and I'm allergic to volatile organic chemicals," he said. "Let me just finish this cabinet." He slipped on the shark yellow gloves. "I don't believe cabinet hardware can become this severely encrusted without intent."

She set the wine to breathe. "Refrigerator work okay?" she asked.

"It does now," he said, working the cabinet pulls like a masseur.

She popped open the old Westinghouse's door. Neat rows of bottled water gave way to a single row of Heinekens and then to juices sorted by color. One shelf up lay yogurt, pickles, two kinds of olives and small sizes of condiments, and one shelf down, sat fruits and cheeses. Veggies gleamed through the fogged plastic of the Fresh 'N Serv drawer. She closed the fridge and stacked the frozen foods in the freezer.

"There's a trail to my house through the woods by the lake," she said. "I want to show it to you."

"Yes, Little Red Riding Hood, I know all about it." He rinsed the sponge.

She wondered if he'd raked the path and edged it with even-sized stones. "Is that why you're dressed like Paul Bunyan?"

"When in Rome," he said. "All clothes are ultimately costumes." He minced like a runway model across the kitchen to the sink.

The banter was starting to get to her. Chase might be looking at a long sentence, and a prison uniform would be the only costume he'd wear.

"Didn't I teach you anything?" he asked.

"More than you'll ever know," she said. She poured two glasses of wine.

"You weren't expecting my Noel Coward Chinese silk robe here in the forest primeval?" He returned to his cabinet and inspected the hinges.

"Quit that and come sit with me," she ordered.

His back to her, he froze for a moment and then threw the sponge and gloves in the sink. "Okay, let's have it. What are they saying about me?" He took his wine and bypassing his usual sniffing and swirling, took a gulp.

"Who are they?" she asked although she knew who he meant.

"The Judas-Brutus-vipers. Start with the thespians," he said. "Let's sit on Minerva's leopard sofa. I don't think it has many fleas."

"Meow." Mary Alice vaguely remembered the sofa had gone African, but she couldn't remember for which novel. The other pieces looked like Pendleton and L. L. Bean had decorated, making the sofa stand out all the more. They sat, turning in to face one another. Boon nestled at Chase's feet. Occasionally the dog looked up adoringly.

She started to tell him that in light of the present evidence, lots of people thought it was possible he had shot Jamie—not premeditated, but still. Then she realized she didn't really know the hearts of people. Based on what she'd heard at lunch, maybe Paige, Vallie and her mother thought he was guilty, but even that wasn't certain. People were confused and shocked by Jamie's death.

My job is to reassure and to support.

"What anybody thinks doesn't matter. I'm here for you and others are too."

"I didn't do it," he said quietly without a trace of bravado. "I swear, Mary Alice. I know you heard me say I was going to kill him, but I didn't." Tears filled his eyes but then receded without spilling like a timely pull of the plug in an overfull bathtub.

"I know you didn't, which means somebody else did. We can find that person if we ask enough questions."

"I went home, had a drink, several, and went to bed until the cops woke me up at four." He bent to scratch Boon's head and to cover his emotions.

"Did anybody see you?"

"Apparently not. Bill has someone asking everybody between Corinth and Batesville if they saw me come home, which wouldn't necessarily prove I couldn't have gone back and, you know."

She sipped the wine, hardly tasting it. "It's impossible to always have an alibi."

"One always has one, but I don't have one that can be corroborated. And that's not the worst of it." He sat forward and untied the barbeque apron. "Someone told that Potts woman about my play. The one Jamie stole." He folded the apron.

"Oh my God," she said. "You know I didn't tell."

He tossed the apron on a chair. "Yes."

"And I didn't repeat what I overheard," she said. "The dying and killing stuff. Kate either. You need to know that."

He nodded. "I just can't think who else knew," he said. "Shit, it happened twenty years ago. I was too hurt to make a big deal about it, too embarrassed ever to tell anyone."

"You told me."

"I had to tell you a secret," he said. "A big one. To earn your trust."

She remembered when he had taken her into his confidence all those years ago; she hadn't realized why.

"You were tough. I couldn't help you unless you opened up."

She resisted patting him and thanking him again. She'd been such a pissy teenager. Why had he hung in when others hadn't?

"Maybe Jamie told someone," she said.

"He stole copyrighted property. He wouldn't be in a hurry to bring attention to the fact."

"He might. Didn't you tell me he claimed he just used your ideas and wrote a completely different play?"

"Exactly, the lying bastard."

"So if someone compared the plays, they'd notice the theft?" she asked.

"Probably. But that isn't going to help me. That's just going to prove that low phylum invertebrate's contention that I hated him because of an ancient grudge made fresh with new jealousy at his theatrical success and my obvious failure."

"Potts' words?"

"Mine with apologies to Shakespeare."

"Still, he might have told," she said. "Don't you see if we can find out who Jamie told about stealing your play we have a suspect or at least a place to start? Someone wants the cops to think you did it, and they may have from the beginning. Look, if we take you out of the picture we have a killer who knew about the stage gun. She or he brought the right bullets to the theatre unless you left it loaded."

"No," he said. "I took it home for the weekend. I keep a loaded gun. But I knew I wanted to use it for Monday's rehearsal, and I brought it back. Unloaded. You know how fanatical I am about safety."

He sounded certain, but she knew people swore to things that never happened.

"Somebody who wanted to kill Jamie used the gun, so they had to know it would fire," she said. "Maybe they brought their own gun too or another weapon, but the killer must be an insider. Knows about our rehearsals, Jamie's play and your prop gun."

"You think someone in the cast murdered him?" He sounded almost hopeful.

"I don't know, but that supposition would make me ask a lot of questions that I don't think Miss Potts is going to ask." She held up her glass. "Drink your wine."

"Potts." He looked to the ceiling. "Could I have worse luck?" Boon rolled onto his back and looked up at Chase, who kicked off his shoe and massaged the dog's tummy.

She agreed the coincidence of the murder and of Claire Potts being in Mississippi was pretty bad, but then Bill Burgess was counting on her cockiness. And her daddy would have said it's all good. Resisting *what is* caused pain. But Mary Alice couldn't see how Claire Potts' presence was going to help Chase.

"What does Bill Burgess know about your and Jamie's history?" she asked. "The plagiarized play?" she asked.

"I told him about the play." Chase shifted, propping his feet on Boon. "Stealing my work and passing it off as his own wasn't the main thing. It was the betrayal. Of me. But he did it to others too. Jamie stole girlfriends, wives, favor, position—whatever he wanted. And he got away with it. He was the charming Irish swain, feted and loved. The hint of a brogue even though he never set foot on the Emerald Isle. His one true gift, writing, he compromised."

Mary Alice could feel the hurt radiating off Chase, and she knew that the betrayal was all that really mattered to him.

"But Burgess told me the police knew about the bad blood between y'all," she said. "Not just the play."

"Christ, Jamie was contentious."

"How'd the police find out you two argued?"

"I have no idea," he said, weariness now in his voice. "Maybe it doesn't matter anyway."

Mary Alice had the sense that it did matter. If nothing else the information had made it easy for someone to frame Chase.

"Chase, how can I get Jamie's plays?"

"Only a few are published—the professionally produced ones. They'd be easy to get."

"What about the others?" she asked.

Chase looked uncomfortable. "I don't think I should tell you, Mary Alice. You might be questioned. Better you don't have to lie."

"Too late. You have them?"

"If they find out I have Jamie's plays, they'll use that against me. Don't you see?" His voice rose. "It'll further substantiate my jealousy of him."

"How?" she asked. Chase wasn't making sense. She could imagine him on the witness stand getting hysterical, his guilt quotient surging with his vocal pitch.

"Hell, I'm not sure how they'll twist it," he said. "In the context of a murder everything takes on a new meaning. The scripts are originals. Jamie gave them to me, but I can't prove it. They'll say I nursed a grudge for years."

Chase looked more and more like the wrung-out wash rag hanging by the sink.

"Okay, okay. Maybe that's why I should have them."

Chase shook his head.

"If I have them, nobody else will," she said. "Where are they?"

She watched him weigh the alternatives. She knew he didn't want to do anything to involve her, to incriminate her.

"At the theatre," he said.

"Have they searched your house?"

"Bill says so."

"The theatre?"

"Ask Bill."

"Where in the theatre?"

"With the *Thoroughly Modern Millie* costumes. Green box."

"Why'd Jamie give them to you?"

"He said he wanted me to know he hadn't stolen any of my other work. I had accused him of that." Boon repositioned himself, and Chase tucked his feet beneath him.

"When?"

"Right after he got here he brought the plays to the theatre in a great show of openness. Said he wanted us to be friends as we were in high school. Bygones, patching up and other hackneyed expressions."

"Did you read them?"

"Hell, no. He wasn't going to hand me anything that would incriminate him."

Mary Alice wondered if it were possible that Jamie had been sincere. She wished she'd known him better. Still, she knew him better than the cops did.

"How many plays are there?" she asked.

"Maybe a dozen."

Mary Alice finished her wine and set down the glass. "I'm going to read them." It occurred to her that it wouldn't take investigator Potts long to realize she needed to search the theatre. As lawyers said, time was of the essence.

"Mary Alice, I'd never kill him." He moved closer to her. "You could see how he undermined me in rehearsals, couldn't you? Questioning my choices; pumping up the actors' egos so they'd agree with him. I admit it. I wasn't strong enough to stand up to him."

She took his hand and squeezed it. "It's getting dark. I left out a curried tofu salad to thaw. Eat some." She stood and stretched.

"Maybe later. Definitely maybe later."

Boon, sensing departure, rose from his spot on the rug and trotted to the door.

"Stiffen that upper lip or chin or whatever Noel Coward would stiffen, honey, 'cause it ain't over."

"If you start with mixed clichés, I'm going to be sick."

"I'll be back tomorrow. You have a phone?" she asked.

"Bill gave me a cell phone. Told me not to use mine."

Mary Alice could imagine the calls Chase might get from the press and the whackos. And of course there was the fact that Chase was openly gay. Homosexuality didn't appear to figure in the case, but she knew that for some, it couldn't help but be a factor. She hoped Claire Potts wasn't one of them.

"Give me the number."

He did, and she collected her purse and her dog and stood by the door hating to leave him alone to scrub Minerva's dirty cabinets.

"You have some good books?"

"Yes. Lots. Do you?"

"Tons," she said. "They get me through."

"Bully."

She hugged him. "Take care of yourself, Chase. You know, eat, sleep, exercise?"

"Got it. Now you go home, Little Red. I have some drawers to line and valances to press." He opened the door, and the cool woodsy air rushed in. Boon bounded off the narrow back porch for the car. Dinner was overdue.

From the car she called out the open window, "I want to show you the path to my house tomorrow."

"I told you I found it. Off the road to the ramp, through the woods, by the lake, to the shore, back into the woods and to your house."

"Yeah and don't forget, the lake is mine."

"You may have it and all the scaled creatures within it with my blessing," he said in his grand opera voice.

In the rear-view mirror she watched him watch her. He'd always reminded her of the British actor, Michael Caine. However, tonight he looked like he might have just enough energy to implode and disappear.

She drove away into the dark of the woods with the windows down. Both she and the dog separated out the different scents of pine, moss, earth, dung and skunk. Boon was doubtlessly pulling in dozens more smells. As she slowed for a hairpin turn, she imagined all the eyes watching her. And then she heard it—a car or truck or even an ATV starting. It was impossible to tell the direction. Somebody was on the Weeds' property, and they were leaving it. It felt like the Grimm Brothers' forest now.

Mary Alice rolled up the windows as fast as she could, checked the door locks and accelerated, hoping to spot the intruder. The road twisted like those on television ads for super-ply tires. She slowed. Smashing into a tree wouldn't help Chase.

Finally she pulled out onto the asphalt pavement. To the right she could make out one red left taillight. Then it was gone.

She drove home in a mental fog. Bolstering Chase had taken all her energy, and the adrenaline surge put her over the edge. Depressed and frustrated, she allowed herself to cry, making sloppy, weepy noises. Boon looked concerned.

No matter what she had said to Chase, it didn't look good. He had no alibi, and his prints were on his gun which was the murder weapon. A detective was out to nail him, and somebody had helped her with some well-placed info about Chase and Jamie's past bitterness. But who? That seemed the place to begin.

"We have to accept what is? Right?" she asked the dog. "No point in wishing Chase isn't accused of murder because he is. Daddy says make friends with what already is because resisting, which is pointless, makes it worse."

Boon nudged the window, and she pressed the button that rolled down the glass.

"Why am I telling you?" Dogs always lived in the Now.

She felt how resisting the facts for the last few days had sapped her. Saying "no, it can't be" only wasted more energy. Yes, yes *it is*. But admitting you had a headache didn't negate taking an Ibuprophen.

"Food first, then index cards and tomorrow get Jamie's plays. The cast and crew had scheduled a workday at the the-atre. She'd have all day to poke around. And call Bill Burgess and say yes. The drive to and from Oxford to see the Ole Miss Rebels might prove instructive.

She dragged into the house, discouraged about Chase, but sure of one thing. Tonight she'd sleep for the first time in awhile because she'd decided something. She was in. Seeing Chase on the porch as she drove away had coalesced it all for her. It was no longer about asking a few questions, using her connections and pointing Bill Burgess in the right direction. She was going to do for Chase Minor what she knew he'd do for her if she were in a jam.

She wished her daddy were still around. She could hear him explaining how everything that seemed true was also, in a way, untrue. He'd tell her to ask if her facts were absolutely true and then to turn them around, reverse them. Was it absolutely true that Chase hated Jamie? No, he had loved him and trusted him. Still loved him. Chase was wounded. And did Jamie care for Chase? Yes, but Jamie knew he was vulnerable which would make him uneasy with his old friend. You fear those you've hurt. And who else had Jamie betrayed? Chase said girlfriends, wives. Who else?

The pile up of unanswered questions reminded her of Sheree Delio. Helping her had taught Mary Alice that messing around in other people's business could get you killed. But it'd be awhile before the killer realized she was doing any messing.

CHAPTER 8

March 3, Saturday

MARY ALICE EASED OUT THE side door of Mickey's Bar into the mist visible only in the glare of the parking lot lights. Inside, the cast and crew were putting away countless pitchers of beer after a long Saturday of set building. She knew they were also decompressing from the stress of Jamie's murder and Chase's arrest. If their feverish work had been an attempt to purify the theatre, they were now in the final phase of the ritual. The Bacchanal.

All afternoon, she had helped Fran Zimmer pull costumes from stock for later fittings. She'd failed to come across Jaime's plays, and with so many people around, she hadn't wanted to be obvious in her search. She'd worried that someone had moved the plays, and they'd disappeared into the jumble of the costume loft. It also occurred to her that Claire Potts had found them.

Her car sat at the far edge of the parking lot. She walked quickly between the cars lined up like rows of dark, moist beetles. Inside, Boon lay on the back seat snoring softly.

"Come on, boy. Let's take a walk," she said. She patted the small flashlight in her raincoat pocket.

Boon, stiff with sleep, stumbled from the car to a phone pole where he sniffed and then left his own scent behind. Mary Alice quietly closed and locked the car. Cutting through a side street and an alley with Boon on her heels, she reached the theatre in ten minutes. Keeping to the shadows, she ran across the empty parking lot to the theatre's side shop door. She worked her hands into latex gloves. Kinsey Millhone and Barbara Havers had taught her about fingerprints. She jammed her key into the lock, jiggled and twisted it. Nothing. Someone must have changed the lock. The police? She had only one option. She dreaded entering the theatre auditorium and revisiting the bloody murder scene. It had been weird enough in daylight with the cast around. Her muscles felt gummy as her body told her to go back to Mickey's and try again later.

Anticipating, Boon trotted to the front of the theatre. When she rounded the side of the building, she saw the dog pressing his fur against the glass doors just as he had done a week ago. His mouth gaped in a smile. Running about in the night in search of plays probably seemed like great sport to the dog, a Labrador retriever.

She hesitated, scanning the façade, reluctant to expose herself to the real or imagined dangers of the murder scene. The misty darkness amped up the fear factor. Leaving seemed the best choice. But she knew that the police were likely to search the theatre. If Potts found Jamie's plays and linked them to Chase, the discovery might be enough to force Chase to accept a plea bargain that would send him away for many years. Besides, Jamie's plays held more potential clues than anything else she could think of. Her favorite fictional detectives followed opportunities as they came up, even when danger was present.

Barbara Havers wouldn't walk away; neither would Kinsey Millhone.

The theatre front door key nested on the ring with her car keys. She inserted it and turned. Boon pushed past her through the open door, and she followed him across the dim lobby into the theatre auditorium. Her heart thumped; her breath quickened.

The ghost lamp on stage revealed the newly finished set: painted and stippled walls topped with molding, doors on hinges and draped windows. A Black Watch plaid bedspread covered the bed where Jamie's lifeless body had greeted her a few nights ago. A quick glance revealed that there was no corpse, yet the theatre felt menacing as though the residual pain of the week's events had taken over and was growing like mold in a coastal basement. The day's hectic set building hadn't been quite enough to cleanse the space, at least for Mary Alice.

A favorite college professor had regaled Mary Alice's theatre history class with stories about haunted theatres. He claimed John Wilkes Booth's ghost, still looking twenty-six years old, roamed Ford's Theatre in Washington. Mary Alice looked straight ahead and slowed her breathing.

Her footsteps echoed on the hollow stage as she crossed through the proscenium arch, heading for the relative safety of the scene shop.

"Boon, heel," she whispered and then heard the raspy echo.

Off stage right a wide double door opened into the scene shop. Above it, a loft held the costumes of past productions and Fran Zimmer's ancient Bernina sewing machine. It was pitch. She snapped on the flashlight and went forward.

"Boon, stay," she said, pointing to the bottom step.

She started up toward the loft. The wood steps groaned in the empty quiet. She thought of characters in scary movies who were always entering dark, dangerous places just like this one, and how she'd always cried, "Don't go." But they always did, and so did she. At the top, she misjudged a step, collided with a rolling rack of tuxedoes and sent it skittering into another rack. She sneezed in the dust cloud and stifled a second. Then she heard Boon's nails click on the concrete floor beneath. Something had attracted his attention.

Go. Move. Get the damn box and get out.

The beam hit a sign that read, *1920s -1940s*. Among the stack of boxes, none was green. Had Chase given her the wrong location? Should she search these? Hurry.

High in the loft, directly beneath the roof, she could hear water drip off the corrugated metal. Tap. Tap. Tap.

Following the silver pool of light, she crept to the back of the loft to a shallow closet marked, *Dance: Tights, tap and ballet shoe, Swine Lake Revue. Thoroughly Modern Millie* had lots of tap dancing. Six of the boxes were one shade or another of green.

Holding the flashlight in her teeth, she opened the first box and found black and flesh tights. The second held feather boas, which true to their name wiggled out of the box and refused to return. She went on to the next box, which contained 1920's era dress patterns. As she was about to close it, her light caught a file folder under the patterns. She slid it out and opened it. The plays. There were a dozen, all by Jamie O'Malley. Some had been written on an old typewriter; most had hand-written marginal notes. One manuscript, entirely hand-written, seemed to be a scenario for an unfinished play.

She poked an errant boa beneath the patterns, shoved the box back in the gap in the stack, closed the closet and retraced her steps to the loft's stairs. She snapped off the flashlight and stowed it in a coat pocket. Needing both hands to negotiate the steep steps, she shoved the fat file of plays into the waistband of her slacks and closed her raincoat over it. Gripping the two handrails, she slowly descended in the dark.

Halfway down she heard what sounded like a badly bowed cello. The groan came from the theatre, and it went right through her. She sat on a step and held her breath. Boon, wherever he was, kept silent too. Not even the dust moved. Maybe it had been something in the fly loft, the open space above the stage where backdrops, cycs and drapes were dead-hung with ropes and counterweights. She knew rigging reacted to moisture. When no other note followed, she scooted down the steps.

"Boon?" she whispered. "Let's go."

The dog whined an eerie warning, but Mary Alice couldn't fathom the danger. Had Boon sensed a ghost?

She had no desire to return through the theatre where the image of a dead Jamie O'Malley might leap from the shadows, so she headed for the door to the outside. She smelled the dog's damp fur before she felt him bump against her. She tried to button the raincoat to protect the plays, but the latex gloves slowed her. She ripped them off and tossed them into the over-flowing trash bin beside the door.

Buttoned up, she opened the door. She screamed and stumbled back, trying to slam the door closed. A bulky figure blocked her way.

Boon barked.

"Police. Don't move."

Mary Alice recognized the abrasive northern accent of Claire Potts, who blasted her with a searing beam of light.

"Shit fire. You scared me to death," Mary Alice said. She resisted touching the papers stuffed under her coat. "Boon, quiet."

The dog ceased his growling but remained poised to attack.

"Ms. Tate. What are you doing here?"

Mary Alice presumed that Potts remembered that Mary Alice had a key to the theatre. She couldn't remember which fictional detective or PI had said it, but one had opined that if you had to lie, it should be done with boldness. Cops read wimpy lies for what they were.

"Please get that light out of my eyes," Mary Alice said. "I've been here all afternoon with the rest of the cast and crew." She petted Boon's head.

Potts aimed the light down a few inches. "Where's the switch?"

"Pull the string on the overhead fluorescent," Mary Alice said. She didn't want to move, afraid the papers beneath the coat might crackle or slip out. She imagined a single page with Jaime's name on it wafting to the floor.

"You alone?" Potts asked.

"Me and the dog." Keeping answers brief seemed best. She didn't introduce Boon.

Potts turned on the overhead light and rotated 360 degrees, shining her flashlight into the far corners. She wore a water-repellant jacket that hadn't done its job. Her damp hair clung to her head like a rubber bathing cap. "Why didn't you turn on the light?"

"We were just leaving," Mary Alice said. "Came back for my prop list. It was in the office." She wished she hadn't offered more information than requested. Guilty people did that.

Potts set her jowls and looked skeptical.

Mary Alice could feel the dozen scripts straining the waistband of her pants. If Potts found them, Chase would be in even more trouble.

"I'm leaving now," Mary Alice said. "Come on Boon. Turn off the lights and lock up when you go."

"Where's the list?" Potts asked.

Mary Alice felt the sting of adrenalin; her teeth sank into her bottom lip. Potts smiled sickly, and Mary Alice concluded that the Yankee detective took a sadistic pleasure in catching people. From her left coat pocket, Mary Alice pulled a three day old grocery list and held it up.

Potts took it. "Chicken, potatoes?" she read.

"Food for the dinner scene. The potatoes are for ice cream."

"What?"

"Ice cream would melt too fast." She knew she was walking a fine line, but she took Potts for a bully and bullies fed on fear and weakness. Mary Alice didn't plan to feed this troll. "Mashed potatoes look like vanilla from the stage."

Potts handed back the list.

"You're on foot?" Potts asked. Her eyes swept the shop again, lighting briefly on the latex gloves on top of the trash.

Mary Alice realized that Potts hadn't yet searched the theatre beyond the crime scene. That was about to change.

"The cast and crew are over at Mickey's. Want to come have a beer with us?" Mary Alice asked. "It's straight across the square on the other side."

"I know where it is," she said. "Maybe another time." Her jaw flexed as if she were chewing a minuscule piece of gum.

Mary Alice could tell Potts was trying to work out some puzzle.

Potts stepped close to Mary Alice and lifted something from the front of her coat. "What's this?" Potts held a fuchsia feather in her pudgy fingers.

Mary Alice had barely restrained herself from jerking away and likely revealing the scripts hiding beneath her coat. "Looks like a feather."

The detective didn't say anything, but Mary Alice could almost see her jotting in her little notebook: *Suspect in theatre digging in feathers.* Getting out fast became critical. She stepped into the outside darkness. "Let's go, Boon."

Boon made a guttural, not-quite-a-growl at the officer and slunk out.

Mary Alice felt Potts' gaze on her back until she rounded the corner.

"Jeez. Stupid, stupid. Be careful who I talk to," she muttered to the dog. She picked up the pace.

It had been sheer luck that she had worn her raincoat and that her grocery list was in the pocket. Thank God she hadn't taken the bulky green box. She strode across the square to her car, loaded the dog and drove straight home.

In the study, she laid out the scripts on the desk. There were seven full plays. She'd been right about the manuscript; it was a scenario for a play. Perhaps this play had never been completed. The complete scripts bore copyright dates and one word titles including *Penance*, *Redemption*, *Contrition* and *Ascension*.

After reading only a few pages of the first in the chronology, she recognized it from what Chase had told her as the play that Jamie had plagiarized over twenty years ago. It was too late to read all the plays. She was tired and might miss something important. Instead she made a root-beer float and drank it while she laid out the five clue-cards she'd prepared.

Alexander McCall-Smith's character, Precious Ramotswe, the only lady detective in Botswana, frequently consulted Clovis Andersen's *Principles of Private Detection*. Madame Ramotswe's loyalty to the book had made Mary Alice order a copy of *Private Investigating 101*. It hadn't come yet, but Mary Alice already understood the usefulness of good notes.

She read the cards aloud to Boon. "*1. Somebody told the police about Jamie stealing Chase's play which resulted in a motive for murder. Who? Why? Did Jamie tell someone? 2. Somebody knew about Chase's gun being used in the play and the kind of bullets it required. An insider? 3. Somebody killed Jamie with Chase's gun. Had s/he planned to use this gun? Also brought another weapon? 4. Brenda Lee Chinault may have had sex with Jamie. Would her father/uncle/brother care enough to kill over it? 5. List of people who didn't like Jamie/maybe others he betrayed.*" This card had no names other than Chase's, but it occurred to her that she knew who else knew about Jamie O'Malley.

Her mother.

Looking at the cards fanned around the root-beer float, she wondered if Chase was being framed or if his arrest was a fortunate coincidence for the killer. Could the killer have known that Chase wouldn't have an alibi? Dumb luck for the killer?

Boon whined.

"Wait. I have one more card to do." She scooped the ice cream from the bottom of the glass, swallowed it and wrote, "*6. Who else doesn't have an alibi for Monday night, February 26?*" She added in parentheses, "*ask Bill and Tom.*" The point of using the cards was to repeatedly juxtapose clues to gain a fresh perspective. However, it didn't take much to examine only six cards. As she stacked the cards, she looked at the map of Cana and Cotashona County taped to the wall beside the desk. The population of each, 13,365 and 29,062 respectively, was printed in bold. Someone had marked Pilgrimage homes with pink dots. Thorpe House sat directly west of Linnley. What had Vallie Leonard said at lunch about Jamie? How often had he come back to Cana to visit? Did Chase see him? Who else did Jamie see? Who else knew Jamie O'Malley? She filled in card number 7.

She stacked the cards and held them between her palms as though the clues they held could penetrate her pores. Then she set them carefully on the desk not because they held a truth yet but because they were evidence of her commitment to help her friend.

Mary Alice turned off the desk lamp, crossed through the living room and out onto the mammoth deck that spanned the distance between the house and the lake and then jutted fifteen feet over the water. Boon darted out and made his rounds ending up by the small dock.

Mary Alice remembered firing warning shots at her ex-husband that had obliterated the deck railing. He hadn't bothered her since. She also remembered where she had been standing when Georgia told her that Sheree Delio was in trouble. Georgia Horn, director of the Women's Center, was on leave now in Atlanta, finishing a Master's Degree. Mary Alice missed her friend.

She saw Boon nosing around her father's inverted fishing boat, stored on the lakeshore for the winter. In the dark she couldn't see the trees across the lake that marked the secret underwater caves, but they were there and perhaps held the decomposing body of her would-be killer.

It had taken a lot of energy not to feel victimized, not to fear her own home and lake, not to get rid of reminders like the fishing boat or the dining room chandelier to which the killer had wired a dead buzzard. Nobody was looking for a body anymore; it'd been over five months. But soon the lake would be warm enough for her to swim, and while her muscles longed for a pull of several miles, part of her resisted. She wondered when the tinge of fear would completely fade.

Dead bodies reminded her that Jamie's funeral was on Monday. The autopsy in Jackson had delayed the burial. She marveled at how Jamie could be at a rehearsal Monday, February 26, and be in a cold grave the following Monday.

"Come, Boon," she called.

The dog, his inspection complete, ran to her.

She went inside and locked the sliding glass door. Boon escorted her upstairs. Lying in bed in the darkness, she relaxed and breathed deeply, watching each breath, and stopping all thought. She felt she wasn't breathing, but, as her daddy had said, she was being involuntarily breathed by life. She had little control. No one did. In the state of calm, she could feel she'd turned a corner. Chase had become more important than her fears.

Boon rolled with enough force to claim the center of the bed. Dogs knew what was important. Why did humans get it wrong so often?

CHAPTER 9

March 7, Wednesday

Bill Burgess picked up Mary Alice at 5 pm in his spanking-new black BMW. He'd suggested supper in Oxford before the game. The car's quiet, effortless flow of power contrasted with that of her '98 BMW and with her mood. She felt tight as a boxer's fist.

Jamie's plays, now read and reread, had produced one solid clue that she wanted to share with Burgess, but she was uncertain about how to approach him. Not only did she want him to look for another killer, she wanted to parlay her information for a place inside the investigation. She'd learned with Sheree's case the importance of being privy to details. Of course, in Sheree's case, she'd failed to tell Sheree's lawyer about a vital clue. The lawyer had banished her. But Mary Alice was savvier now.

As they pulled out onto the paved road, Bill said, "There's a bunch of CD's in there. Put on something you like."

"This is fine," she said. It was early Sonny Terry and Brownie McGhee. She wouldn't have changed it even if it had been The Chipmunks rapping.

"I got us a reservation at 208, but if you like someplace different, let's go there," he said. He drove slightly over the 55 miles per hour limit into the countryside set on the brink of spring.

"City Grocery?" he asked. "John just got another award for something. I think Yocona River will be too crowded."

"208's perfect," she said trying for a genial but not solicitous tone. She settled into the leather and new-car smell and tried to relax.

It's just business, she told herself. I need something and he needs something. I'm being silly. Still, using a date to pitch her ideas about Chase felt uncomfortable.

A mammoth SUV filled with Ole Miss fans clothed in red attire similar to theirs passed. They honked and waved.

"That was Ferti DeAngelo," he said.

Mary Alice was about to mention Jamie's funeral two days ago and then segue to his plays, particularly the one titled *Redemption*, but Burgess continued.

"Ferti sent me a case last year that may be the most unusual one I ever had."

Mary Alice had heard a million lawyer stories from her father, and she knew Bill was a consummate storyteller. She enjoyed legal tales. However, she felt anxious to get her own story out. Burgess, along with most of Cana, had attended Jamie's funeral. Now was the time to talk about Jamie.

"A fella, call him Dan, inherited about two million dollars from his aunt, his daddy's big sister," he said. "But the aunt stipulated that Dan had to prove his family lineage in order to collect. Dan's mother had given birth to him seven months after her marriage to the aunt's brother, and the aunt suspected Dan might not be legit." He looked over at her.

"His parents were dead?" Mary Alice said giving up on corralling the discussion to Jamie O'Malley.

"Everybody's dead, but Dan. So we have to go looking for DNA."

"Exhuming corpses?" she asked. "Oh my God." She hoped he wouldn't describe casket contents.

"Exactly. The first problem was that the daddy had died in a plane crash, and his remains were not only burned, but we had some doubt that they really were his remains." Burgess turned down the radio. "After the crash, it was hard to tell who was who." Burgess had a lush southern accent. Syllables rumbled up, their edges polished smooth.

"And his grandfather?"

Burgess smiled. "Have I told you this before?"

"No, no," she said. "Just seems logical." Great. Instead of sounding preoccupied, she'd sounded like a know-it-all.

"The grandfather's remains were easy to find and to be certain of, but his DNA didn't match."

"So no dough for Dan?"

"Not necessarily. Sometimes the DNA doesn't match when it skips a generation. But there're some new tests now that may help us," he said.

"What a strange bequest."

"Well, after the father died the mama remarried, and so Dan wasn't really in the aunt's family any more, so to speak."

"What happens if he can't establish his line?"

"Others in the family get the money. But here's the ace. The old lady's will gives Dan fifty years to prove his lineage."

"They'll all be dead in fifty years," she said. "Why doesn't Dan just negotiate with the others for a share? That way they'd all at least get something."

Burgess looked over at her. "Where'd you go to law school?" He smiled his approval. "That's just what I think is gonna happen."

Mary Alice struggled to link Dan and the elusive DNA to Chase and Jamie's play via Jamie's funeral, but before she could open her mouth, Burgess had shifted to the basketball game. The Arkansas Razorbacks had beaten Ole Miss earlier in the season but not by much.

"And they played in Fayetteville," he said. He spouted statistics about turnovers and free throws as if they were investments that had made him rich.

"They just kept losing at the line," he said. "Well, that freshman point guard was hot but—"

She nodded. The line meant something about free throws. Probably. She'd wait until the drive home to broach the subject of Chase. If Ole Miss won, Burgess would be exhilarated and receptive. Her interest in an Ole Miss victory shot up.

Mary Alice, who loved Oxford, couldn't help but notice how quickly it was changing. The General Sherman Landscaping Company seemed to be on the job. Closer to the historic square, condominiums sprouted like fungi. They were even tearing down churches to build condos.

They parked in front of Square Books. Mary Alice read the sign which listed writers due to appear for readings. Inside she could see a photograph of the crusty William Faulkner, who had lived in Oxford and in his novels, renamed it Jefferson. Across the square, a bronze of Oxford's most famous citizen enhanced the front of city hall. Faulkner would have loathed it.

At the restaurant on South Lamar, they were greeted by hordes of Ole Miss Alumni on their way to the game. Mary Alice knew lots of people, but Bill Burgess knew everybody. Though he seldom gossiped, she imagined he had a story about each. She ordered the veggie pasta dish; he selected shrimp and grits. Through drinks and dinner, long time friends and casual acquaintances joined by ties to Ole Miss moseyed about the restaurant, laughing, catching up and stoking the pre-game buzz.

Ole Miss had always been an exclusive club, and activities of the flagship university provided countless staging grounds for meetings. The Grove tailgating ritual before each home foot-ball game ranked as the top event.

After dinner, on the way to the car, Burgess draped his arm over Mary Alice's shoulders. She worried she'd smiled and nodded at him too much.

Burgess parked in the special Tad Smith Coliseum VIP lot and joined the throng all in red that converged on the Tad Pad. Seated center court and five rows up, they were surrounded by wealthy alums and star athletes from days past. Mid-week games didn't draw like weekend ones, but the new Rebel coach had exceeded all expectations and won the last few SEC games. As the place filled up, the decibels rose in proportion.

Mary Alice observed the subtle pecking order among alums created by casual visits from the university chancellor or retired coaches. The athletic director stopped to say hello, and Mary Alice could tell Bill was thrilled.

After the teams' warm-ups, the Tad Pad went dark except for flashing lights and the introduction of the starting lineup on overhead jumbo screens. Everyone stood and screamed "Hotty toddy, gosh almighty, who in the hell are we? Hey! Flim flam, bim bam, Ole Miss by damn!" the hallowed, revered cheer that made no sense but still worked to whip up the crowd.

"Arkansas players look tall," Mary Alice said to Bill.

"They are. We're going to have some giants next year. You wait. We're still suffering from lousy recruiting, but this Coach—"

Mary Alice watched the student section, nearly full, and fronted by six boys with naked, painted torsos bearing the letters REBELS, one letter per pale chest.

She thought about Chase. She'd visited him again, and in spite of his paint allergy, he was coating the cabin in Sherwin Williams' Blond. They'd walked the path to her house, and whatever bravery Chase had exhibited earlier was waning as he had time to think about what a lengthy jail sentence might be like.

He'd been arraigned and refused a plea bargain. His pre-trial hearing would be set soon. The prosecution was going to skip sending the case to the grand jury. And while the trial could be delayed for months, more time wasn't necessarily useful. The longer the killer went free, the less chance there was to find him. Or her. Trails grew cold fast. She had to make Bill Burgess listen to her.

A buzzer brought her back to the game just in time for a timeout. The Rebels' dance team, clad in skintight stretch pants and sparkly bra tops, took the floor and executed a series of kicks, spins, bumps and grinds, smiling sweetly as if their pelvic gyrations were completely void of sexual connotation.

She heard a man behind her say to another, "How come they're wearing britches?"

His companion said, "You want 'em in shorts?"

"What do you think?" he replied.

At the half, the Rebels were down by three points. Burgess bought cokes and a box of hard, dry popcorn that must have been left over from football season. In the second half the Rebels changed their game plan.

Bill explained that the coach liked to run a physical man-to-man defense that taxed the opponents. However, Arkansas had scored easily and often from the low post in the first half, and the Rebels had substituted a 2-3 match-up zone and dared their opponents to shoot over them.

The cheerleaders, who looked wholesome next to the dancers, led the crowd in something that sounded to Mary Alice like "gee-up."

"What are they saying?" she shouted to Burgess.

"D-up," he said. "D for defense."

"D-up, D-up, D-up," she yelled.

It had been decided early on that the refs were blind, stupid or both. They called hand checks on Ole Miss while ignoring Arkansas elbows. Boos exploded from the crowd. The lead teetered back and forth. But the home team surged ahead in the final two minutes, and Arkansas was forced to foul the Rebels early on in every possession to lengthen the game, and for once, Ole Miss hit its free throws down the stretch to ice the game.

The crowd went nuts as the Rebels paraded past the student section, high-fiving on their way to the locker room. Burgess grabbed Mary Alice in a hug she regarded as a positive sign for her chances of discussing Chase's case.

When David Kellum's post-game talk show on the car radio finished, she cut in fast before Burgess could get started. "Bill, I have to tell you something about Chase. I need you to hear me out. I haven't even told him this yet 'cause I wanted to see what you thought."

"I'm all ears," he said turning down the radio that advertised the services of yet another Oxford bank.

"I read a bunch of plays that Jamie O'Malley wrote over the last twenty years including the one Chase told you Jamie plagiarized."

"Oh?" He sounded interested.

The Oxford to Cana traffic thinned.

She liked that he hadn't interrupted. "But the play I think you should read is called *Redemption*." She watched his reaction in the dashboard light. Inquisitive, but noncommittal.

"Is it good?" he asked.

"It's autobiographical."

"Did Jamie say it's about him?"

"No, but as you know, the one thing about being from Cana is that you know everything about everybody. Lots of details are clearly Jamie. You'll see. But the main thing is that the main character, named Jeb, has come home to a small Mississippi town to claim the illegitimate son he fathered fifteen years ago."

"Sounds Faulknerian."

Burgess wasn't jumping to conclusions as she'd hoped he would. But then he was a lawyer.

"Jeb's obsessed with the boy who turns out to be his only child. Jeb stalks him, and begs the boy's mama to tell the boy who his real father is."

"Let me guess. The mama says, no way."

"Precisely," Mary Alice said. Burgess had bitten the hook.

"If she reveals her son's identity, her husband will divorce her leaving her penniless and at the mercy of public shame," he said.

"You got it." Mary Alice said. "The boy's mama never loved her husband, but she's become accustomed to his money."

"So the main character, this Jeb, his objective is to what, persuade the mama?"

"To claim the son at any cost."

"By whatever means."

"Exactamento."

"Is he successful?" Burgess asked.

"He threatens to force a DNA test and prove paternity."

"But Mama's not about to let the cat out of the bag, so she shoots him?"

"Almost. You'll see. But that's not what matters," she said.

"No?"

"Jamie couldn't have anticipated that somebody was going to shoot him," she said. "He couldn't have written about his own death."

He slowed. A group of nervous raccoons crouched poised by the side of the road.

"In real life, I don't think the son knows he's Jamie's son," Mary Alice said.

"So the mama in real life killed Jamie to protect her secret, preserving her wealth and status, and to protect her son, who she figured didn't need a no-count father showing up to possibly dispossess the boy of everything the cuckolded father offered." He tapped the steering wheel.

Mary Alice had a clearer idea of why Bill Burgess was such a successful lawyer. "How'd you know he was no-count?"

"They usually are," he said.

They entered the outskirts of Cana, and he turned onto a county road that connected to another near the lake. Mary Alice knew she didn't have much time to make her point.

"I know it's circumstantial, but if you read the play, you'll see that another person had a motive to kill Jamie."

"I'll see that a fictitious mother had a motive, Mary Alice."

"Jeb is Jamie."

"And how do we prove that? Even if countless details point to the similarity between Jeb and Jamie, all it does is raise a speculation. Many authors pattern characters on themselves."

"Will you read it?" she asked.

"Of course. You got a copy?"

"Right here." She pulled the play from her handbag.

"Mary Alice, I know you want to see Chase out of this mess, and you believe he's innocent. But don't get your hopes up about this play." He pulled into her driveway and turned off the engine. "Think this through a minute. Let's say we find an illegitimate son and his mama, and let's say her alibi isn't airtight. Even if you proved the paternity, which would be very hard to accomplish, you still haven't shown she shot him. But what you will have done is shown a young man that's he's illegitimate. You've torn up a family and likely incurred the displeasure of the entire town. But not necessarily helped Chase."

Mary Alice shut up. Precious Ramotswe of the No. 1 Ladies Detective Agency emphasized the importance of knowing when to be quiet. Burgess had agreed to read the play, and it would have to speak for itself. They could talk about what it meant later. In the meantime, Mary Alice could make a list of suspects: women of position who had known Jamie O'Malley and who had teenaged sons.

Of course, the son's age wasn't certain, but Jeb, would likely be the same age as Jamie. Jeb's concern about his declining sexual power motivated him to seek out his son. This was his only son. Ditto for Jamie O'Malley as far as anybody knew. It seemed likely that the son would be a teenager. If the son were fifteen, then Jamie had sex with the boy's mother around 1991. Mary Alice had been a senior at Ole Miss then.

Bill Burgess walked her inside the house but refused a drink due to an early meeting with a client the next day. "We're flying to Houston on his jet. Gonna drop him off, and the pilot will fly me back," he said.

"Time is money."

"I intend to charge him for the round trip."

"Thanks for taking me to the game. It's been a long time since I was at the Tad Pad." She thought of the Ole Miss football game she attended last fall. Weeks later she'd nearly been murdered. She guessed Burgess had come in to make sure no intruders lurked, and she felt a certain relief that he had done so.

"Pleasure was all mine. I'm glad you're okay." He paused, perhaps evaluating if he should say more about her state of mind following the attempt on her life. "I'm gonna run, but I hope to see you again. Maybe when all the pilgrimage madness has calmed down." He gave her a quick hug and a kiss on the cheek, stepped outside and walked to his car. As he got in, he waved the copy of Jamie's play she'd given him.

"Thanks," she called.

Mary Alice watched him drive off and thought how cool he was. He gave away nothing. He had acted in several Cana theatre productions, favoring small roles that stole the show. People still remembered his rendition of the judge in *The Best Little Whorehouse in Texas*. Didn't everybody always say successful trial lawyers were actors?

And she knew he was smart. Surely he'd see the dozens of parallels between Jeb and Jamie and come to the conclusion she'd reached. Of course, if she could point to a suspect and corroborate her evidence, that'd go a long way toward convincing him. Her favorite mystery writers had taught her that just the suspicion of another killer could be enough to divert a jury's guilty verdict.

In the study, she turned on the desk lamp and looked at her 3 x 5 clue cards. With the information from Jamie's play, *Redemption*, their number had grown to a dozen. Had Jamie been trying to redeem himself by coming back to Cana? Looking at the cards, Mary Alice understood what her next job was. She had to talk to her mother.

CHAPTER 10

March 10, Saturday

E LIZABETH TATE'S PILGRIMAGE OBLIGATIONS PREVENTED Mary Alice from immediately connecting with her mother. Tom Jaworski, however, had been available.

Standing outside his door, she felt excited, like an egret fledgling about to jump. From the beginning, the chemistry between them had been potent, and time away had not dampened it. She dropped the bronze pine cone knocker against the massive front door and heard the echoes within.

Jaworski rented a not-quite-completed house eight miles out of town that had been built by a restaurateur who'd gone bankrupt. It looked like a cross between a Mediterranean whorehouse and an Aspen ski lodge.

Tom Jaworski, wearing sweats and a Mississippi State Bulldogs tee shirt, opened the door. "Hey," he said, as if he'd been expecting her.

"You said to come anytime." She knew she sounded school-girl-nervous. "Is this a bad time?"

"Come in," he said, waving her in. "I'm finishing PT."

She looked blank.

"Physical therapy."

"Oh."

"You can watch."

When he brushed the back of her arm and shoulder, she felt a sensation down to the soles of her feet and back up to her groin. The jolt felt equally delicious and disconcerting. She didn't usually like cops or cop mentality. Particularly she disliked Cana police; her experience with them taught her they were macho, myopic and mean. Well, most of them. She questioned if she knew Jaworski well enough. On the other hand, Jaworski had helped her save Sheree Delio. He'd more than just stood by her. He'd nearly died for his trouble. And, finally, there was the fact that he was overwhelmingly sexy.

She held out the bottle of cabernet and then remembered the painkillers he took. "Can you have some?"

"Glasses are in the kitchen," he pointed.

She followed him into a massive great room anchored by a two-story field stone fireplace around which was placed all the furniture Jaworski owned: daybed, sofa, chair, end table with lamp and a large trunk that served as a table. The rest the house was entirely empty.

Mary Alice tossed her coat on the chair and went in search of a corkscrew and wine glasses. Jaworski settled beside the trunk on a thick foam pad and pulled his knees up to his chest. From the kitchen she heard him groan through an exercise.

She'd been to this strange house in the woods once before. After he got out of the hospital, she'd brought out frozen casseroles and chocolate. He said he couldn't remember. She poured the dark wine and returned to the den, stopping just past the granite breakfast bar. Jaworski strained to execute a twisting maneuver. Mary Alice sucked in a breath. He looked like he was doing a TV ad for exercise equipment. His muscles bunched and buckled as he worked. She wanted to touch him, maybe put her cool cheek on his chest and let her hands play over the contours of his bi and triceps, deltoids, obliques and on and on. Shazam. The sensation fired again.

"Done," he said.

She nearly dropped both glasses and the bottle.

He eased onto the cordovan leather sofa, and she joined him. They toasted health which seemed appropriate. The same person who had tried to kill Mary Alice had run Jaworski's car off the road. The car had plunged down an embankment and rolled three times, cracking Jaworski's back, ribs and collarbone and doing other damage that accompanies such injuries. He was back on the police force but at a desk he was anxious to get away from.

"You look nice," he said.

"Thanks." She'd worked hard to achieve the right look. Her jeans, tight as Teflon on a skillet, were expensive and well-cut. The wrap knit top hugged her curves and said feminine-sexy not slutty-sexy.

"I could make a fire," he said more as an announcement than a suggestion.

Mary Alice considered firelight and wine. From three feet away she smelled a concoction of sweat, shaving cream, and some primordial man-smell. It was a heady brew. She was glad she'd shaved her legs.

As he assembled kindling and logs, she browsed the half-full bookcases that flanked the fireplace. Most volumes related to law enforcement. They looked dismally technical unlike her *Private Investigation 101* which had arrived in the mail on Thursday. She'd read it twice; the chapter on interviewing and interrogating she'd read three times.

"Find out anything from the lawyer?" he asked.

She watched the play of muscles through his tee shirt. "Bill Burgess?"

"You said you were going to talk to him."

She wondered if he knew about the trip to Oxford for the basketball game. "He's doing the neighborhood, checking alibis, all the stuff the police should be doing," she said. "I think he hopes to get Chase off on a technicality." She watched him deftly arrange the logs, making the process look sensual.

"Burgess said that?"

"He said his job was to get Chase off any way he could, not to find the real killer."

"How's the accused doing?" Jaworski lit the fire which leapt up orange and hot.

"Getting more freaked out by the day," she said.

He sat beside her on the sofa, not close, but closer than a mere friend would have done. She told him about finding and reading Jamie O'Malley's plays and how one play seemed autobiographical.

"If Jamie was living what he wrote in that play, then he has an illegitimate son in Cana," she said. "And the boy has a mother who probably doesn't want anybody to know." And he might be having trouble getting it up. She didn't say that part.

"And you think she'd kill to conceal her son's—what?," he asked.

"Birth history? I know some would."

"Would you, if you were the mother?" He rotated his glass, spinning the wine up the sides.

She shrugged. "Maybe she wants to protect her boy."

"Maybe she needs to save face or fortune or both."

Finally, a colleague, she thought. Here was a trained detective who was helping her and not making fun of her. Maybe he took her seriously because Mary Alice had discovered Scott Bridges' killer. Whatever the reason, she relished his attention and respect. She recognized it was a big part of her attraction to him.

"You have suspects?" he asked. He stretched his arms, placing them on the back of the sofa.

Mary Alice dug in her purse for her list but visualized sinking back on the sofa and resting her head in the crook of his arm. "Thought you'd never ask." She pulled out the single sheet.

"How'd you choose?" he asked. He set his glass on the table but didn't reach for the list.

"I read about free and pay databases," she said. "I'm essentially looking for a missing person, right? The mother of Jamie's son." She sipped her wine.

He looked at her. His gaze was direct and keen. "There are databases for women who fooled around with Jamie O'Malley?"

"Almost. I narrowed down the time of conception to three years."

"Still, that's a lot of women."

"I cut out women who had moved. And they had to be here the summer of 1991 when Jamie's mother died."

He seemed to understand the significance of the limitations without explanation.

"You did this on the computer?"

"Cana High School Alumni records," she said. "My second cousin through marriage, Mattie Catherine McBride, maintains the web site."

Jaworski reached for his wine, and in the move, touched her knee. She didn't think it was accidental.

"And?" he said when she didn't continue.

"Huh? Oh. They have reunions all the time. It's like they never graduated."

"Cana High's Face Book?"

"Besides the web site, they print booklets every year. People send details of their lives, especially news of their children."

He took the folded list. "How many names you got?"

"Of just over a hundred graduates each year, half of whom are female, only about half of them lived in Cana between 1990 and 1993 and only a few of them had sons during the time that would make the boy a teenager now. I got eight names." She could still feel where his fingers had grazed her knee.

He read the list.

"I couldn't have done it without Mattie Catherine," she said. "I'd still be looking for Susan Hopper who hemorrhaged to death in 1991 after having stillborn twins." She felt high and not from the wine which was having a separate but parallel effect.

"Now what?" he asked.

"If Bill Burgess sees what I saw in Jamie's play, then he'll follow up on these women. At least check alibis." She finished off the wine, and he refilled her glass.

"You know any of these women?" he asked. He set the list on the sofa between them.

She nodded. "And their husbands." She smiled. "Am I going to get the 'be careful' lecture now?"

"Will it do any good?"

"No, because I'm not doing anything dangerous."

"You poke around and make a killer nervous, it's dangerous," he said. He looked into the flames that flicked like searing tongues.

"Burgess or the police are going to do all the poking," she said. "I just made a list." She held up both hands in a gesture of protest.

"Hang on, Little Miss Innocent." He caught one of her hands and held it. "Didn't you tell me about how when you're acting in a play you try to be the character? The magic something?"

She couldn't believe he remembered a conversation about theatre they'd had months ago. "Stanislavski's Magic If." Jaworski's grasp felt as though it had dual intentions.

"And?" He released her hand.

"If I'm playing Maggie in *Cat on a Hot Tin Roof*, I ask myself what would I feel or do if my husband wouldn't go to bed with me."

The mention of going to bed focused her fantasy like an electromagnet on fresh rolled steel. Mary Alice realized she was massaging her neck and pulled her hand down.

"Is that a common problem for women in plays," he asked.

115

She knew he was teasing her. "Usually the husband is going to bed with another woman instead."

He faced her. "If you were a woman with an illegitimate son who wanted to keep her secret, what would you do if, one, the father wanted to claim paternity, two, you shot him dead, and three, someone started poking around in your business?"

"I'm not going to poke."

"I ought to make you sign that," he said.

"You haven't heard anything about Chase's case?" she asked. She didn't want to think about putting herself in danger. Last time had been completely different. Emotion had clouded her judgment.

"I'm not on the case." He sounded disappointed. Cops, like generals, despised desk jobs.

"Y'all got a locker room," she said.

"Yes, but the head of the investigation isn't allowed in it."

"Claire Potts," Mary Alice said. "She scared hell out of me the other night." She described the Saturday night events in the scene shop. "It's like she knew I was lying about why I was there."

"Were you?"

"Yes, but that's not the point. She's disturbing."

"But not stupid."

"She a pal?"

"As a matter of fact, she joined me at lunch at Mickey's yesterday," he said.

He looked mischievous. Mary Alice saw that at home, Jaworski was much less reserved. A playful quality had joined his alert animal intensity.

"Lunch with Grendel?"

"The very one," he said. "I think she was lonely."

Mary Alice had difficulty visualizing Claire Potts and Tom Jaworski in a booth at Mickey's Bar.

"She confirmed Chase Minor's gun was the murder weapon—ballistics and fingerprints. But it appeared to have been partially wiped. Fired once at close range. The bullet destroyed the victim's aorta. Jamie O'Malley bled to death. The autopsy report put the death between ten and midnight."

"So they think Chase shot him and then did a bad job of wiping off his fingerprints?"

"An incomplete job," he said. "There were other smudges and partials, but his were identifiable."

"Anything else?"

"Everyone connected to the theatre has been interviewed, and only three were without verifiable alibis," he said. "Apparently none of them very interesting to her. Most people corroborated the idea that Chase Minor and Jamie O'Malley argued frequently. Some put it more strongly."

"I doubt Detective Potts got anything useful in her interviews," she said.

"Why's that?"

"Most people don't like cops or lawyers and don't want to help them."

"PI Tate," he said.

"It's in the book." She paused to see if he'd laugh at her. He didn't. "Add to that her aggressive style and that she's an outsider in the Deep South where insider counts."

"And that Yankee accent?"

She shrugged.

"You bought a book on investigating?" he asked.

"PI 101. Want to borrow it?" She glanced at his bookshelves.

"Touché," he said.

"The book says to create a bond with people you're interviewing. Make them want to help you."

"Bonds are not likely Potts' strength," he said.

She didn't say it, but they both knew that creating bonds with people was what Mary Alice was good at. In fact she was doing it with Jaworski.

"Did she happen to say who told her about Jamie stealing Chase's play?" she asked.

"No."

"Who are the three people without alibis?"

"Not sure of that either, but I think I'll find out," he said. "She invited me to dinner."

"Potts cooks?"

"I assume so. She's rented a cabin at Wyatt's RV Park."

"You're going?"

"No."

"But she might tell you—"

"But then it'd get weird if she decided I was using her," he said. "Your book didn't tell you about that?"

She wrinkled her nose at him. "Then how come you think she's going to open up and give you details?" she asked.

"I've been polite. Nobody else has."

"She got the hots for you?"

"I told her I was married," he said.

Mary Alice remembered when Jaworski had told her that he was married. She'd felt like she had when she dropped a hibachi on her foot. He'd been separated two years from a wife in California who'd refused to leave the wealthy, extended family that was suffocating her marriage. Her name was Alicia, and while she had no aspirations to be a north Mississippi detective's wife, neither did she aspire to be a divorcée.

"Potts just needs a friend," he said. "Has to talk to somebody."

Mary Alice thought of her attempts to use Bill Burgess and to keep it friendly. She regretted her subterfuge because Burgess probably saw right through it.

"She did seem interested in the fact that only one bullet was fired," Jaworski continued.

"Because?"

"It says something about the killer," he said.

Mary Alice figured that one fatal shot indicated a person who knew how to use a gun and hadn't been panicked when he or she fired. What else would be important? "But you can ask her about the three people without alibis?" she asked.

"It's better if I don't ask directly." Jaworski leaned forward and winced. "I've got to lay down. My back is seizing up."

"Oh, of course," she said. She couldn't help but feel that his injuries were partly her fault. She'd gotten him involved in Sheree Delio's case.

He crept to the foam pad, nudged it in front of the fireplace and sat down. The fire had calmed to embers with occasional flares. He lay down on one side of the pad.

For a couple of minutes neither spoke. Then he looked up at her.

She slid off her shoes, walked over and touched the pad with a toe as if it were a pool.

He extended his arm creating a space for her to nestle.

Beside him, she took her time tucking in close. He seemed to take in the fire's warmth and transfer it through his body to her. But the heat, which should have relaxed her, ignited her. She had to fight to keep from sighing. She turned to him; their lips met and stayed together for a long time.

"I can't do much," he said. "You know. My back."

She closed her eyes and thought that if he did anything more, she'd probably vaporize and be sucked up the flue into the night sky. Surrendering to the twin sister agonies, Lust and Longing, she took in a breath, and he took one with her. Exhaling, she felt she'd turned into one of the soft green weeds that undulated at the bottom of the lake.

Maybe he'd turn out to be typical cop or a weak man who couldn't get divorced or a bully like her first husband, but at that moment, he was pure natural male energy, the yang her yin desired.

By the time she left the house, the gray sky had split, revealing streaks of mauve and salmon.

Red sky in morning, sailors take warning.

Chapter 11

March 11, Sunday

Vodka overflowed the ornate sterling jigger as Elizabeth Tate prepared two Zing Zang Bloody Marys.

"This will pick you up," she said, pushing the tall glass toward her daughter. Watermelon pink lipstick coated a front tooth.

Mary Alice doubted liquor on top of only five hours of sleep was a good idea, but disagreeing with her mother was a worse one. She didn't mention the lipstick.

"Spring cometh at last," Elizabeth stretched her arms wide toward the view outside. She was good at posing and now resembled Joan Crawford in *The Women*.

Mary Alice admitted the view from Linnley's south sunroom was gorgeous. Only the early bloomers—forsythia, spiraea and daffodils—were in flower, but the temperature had risen with the winds of a warm front, and the fecund earth looked ready to burst.

"All ready for March 31?" Mary Alice asked. Today was Sunday, March 11, only twenty more days.

"You'd think after twenty-two years of pilgrimages there'd be no surprises," Elizabeth said.

Mary Alice sipped her Bloody Mary hoping the vodka would loosen the knots in her neck.

"Maria has a sick, as in dying-sick, aunt in California," Elizabeth said. "She says she has to go see her. What if the aunt lingers and she doesn't get back? Maria, not the aunt." She tasted her Bloody Mary and made tiny smacking sounds.

Maria had managed to remain employed at Linnley for a record-breaking six months by making herself indispensable. She'd rearranged every cupboard and drawer until Elizabeth couldn't serve a crumpet or tweeze her eyebrows without her housekeeper.

"Let me know if I can help," Mary Alice said. "I'll do anything short of putting on a hoop skirt."

Maria entered with a tray stacked high.

"Just put everything on the buffet," Elizabeth said. "We'll serve ourselves." She waggled her fingers at the buffet as though Maria might be unsure of its location. Clearly the housekeeper was in disgrace for anticipated abandonment.

The odor of grease—bacon, hollandaise and butter—snaked across the room like armed terrorists and kidnapped Mary Alice. Without a sound, Maria slipped from the room.

"Speaking of hoop skirts, Marjory Ann Battla swore to me the docent dresses were in fine condition. But when we opened the boxes, we were greeted with mildew and dry rot." She took another hit of her drink. "One hat box had disgusting little snails living in the tissue paper."

Mary Alice matched her mother's snail grimace. "New dresses will be so nice," she said, eyeing the buffet. Things were getting cold.

"But I got a promise of pink for all the Linnley dresses. The Periman twins will be in the master bedroom. I'm personally paying extra for ruffled pantaloons for them. Ready to eat?"

Mary Alice had never figured out why her mother, with all her money, made the pilgrimage organization pay Linnley's pilgrimage expenses. Every year Elizabeth wrested her share of the funds to spiff up and decorate the antebellum home and gardens. However, at other times, such as when Hurricane Katrina had leveled the Mississippi coast, she could be extremely charitable.

Elizabeth frowned but said nothing as Mary Alice crowded some of everything onto her Limoge plate—Eggs Benedict, bacon, biscuits, crab in puff pastry and fresh fruit salad. As she added a second crab puff, she tried to calculate what the waistband on her Liz Claiborne slacks would permit.

"Poor Vallie is stuck with the Carter girl," Elizabeth said, selecting a single biscuit and a small mound of fruit. "Child must weigh 200 pounds. I suggested elephant gray moiré, but Vallie thinks—"

Mary Alice concentrated on her food. Occasional nods and "hums" fueled her mother's detailed monologue about fat. She believed that obese people were undisciplined louts who, if they didn't quit shoveling food down their throats, would get what they certainly deserved—diabetes, heart problems and early death.

"Oh," Elizabeth said, talking around a bite of pineapple, "Vallie asked me to ask you if you might could get together a play for next year like the Natchez Pilgrimage has."

Mary Alice swallowed the last of her biscuit. She wanted another one but knew her over-filled plate had already set her up for a discussion of her recent weight gain, which would lead to a lecture from her mother on eating junk food. That sermon might segue into a harangue about any number of Mary Alice's shortcomings.

"It's a satire on the pilgrimage itself," Elizabeth said. "Natchez grosses over $3,000 per performance."

Mary Alice knew about *Southern Exposure* although she'd never seen it. The last thing she wanted was to organize Cana's version of the same. She could imagine the egos that would emerge in full battle gear.

"Minerva Weeds is the writer, ask her," Mary Alice said. "Who knows if there'll be a Cana Theatre by this time next year?"

Elizabeth dropped her head and raised her gaze. "It's just too awful. I didn't go to Jamie's funeral, but I sent a nice spray. Flashy birds of paradise. The Irish like that sort of show."

Mary Alice felt a now-or-never sensation and put down her fork. "Mama, I'm worried about Chase, and I think I should help him." She braced for a maternal explosion, but Elizabeth merely refilled her coffee cup. "Anything I find out, I'll tell Bill Burgess. I won't do anything dangerous."

"A man has been murdered," Elizabeth said. "By definition, doing is dangerous."

"Mama, Chase didn't kill Jamie. Bill's only looking for some technical reason to get him off or get the case thrown out. The cops are doing nothing; they have Chase."

"That Detective Potts is doing something," Elizabeth said. "She called on me."

"What'd she say?"

"Wanted me to tell her about Jamie," Elizabeth said. "That and where I was the night of the murder. Can you imagine?"

"You weren't here?" Mary Alice asked.

"Of course I was, and thank God Maria was too, or I'd be a suspect. Vallie is so upset with that Potts woman. She acted like Vallie was lying."

"That would be like her," Mary Alice said. "Potts not Vallie."

"Vallie pulled every string in Cotashona County to get Ms. Potts sent back to the pit from which she emerged, but she's FBI."

"MBI. The Mississippi FBI."

"Whatever," Elizabeth said. "She's a carpetbagger. But don't get me off on Potts. We were talking about your involvement in a murder investigation."

"Mama—"

"Does Bill approve of your helping him?" Elizabeth asked. She held her eyebrows up until her daughter answered.

"If I tell him something pertinent, he'll check it out," Mary Alice said, wanting to return to Claire Potts.

"That's not what I asked."

"Chase won't survive in prison," Mary Alice said. "He's my friend, and he's innocent." She chose not to add that Elizabeth's rancorous relationship with Mary Alice's father was the main reason for Mary Alice's close tie to Chase Minor. He had been there for her when her mother wasn't.

"What in heaven's name can you do?" Elizabeth asked. Her mouth drew up like a draw string bag.

Mary Alice pushed down the irritation that rose and blushed her cheeks. "I've come up with a list of suspects."

"My God. Who's on it?"

"First things first. What'd you tell Potts?" she asked her mother.

"Same as everybody else. I hardly remember Jamie. It's been two decades. No family here anymore, bla, bla, bla." She pulled her chair closer to the table.

"But you do remember him, don't you?"

"Who could forget Jamie?" Elizabeth said, drawing out the name and shifting into a conspiratorial tone. "All charm and malarkey. Everybody liked him. Had a power over women. The girls," she laughed, "even a few matrons threw themselves at him, and he was never good at keeping it in his pants." Her eyes glinted.

Mary Alice had been right about locals closing ranks against the outsider detective. She wondered if that might hurt Chase's case.

"Jamie was promiscuous?"

"Please."

"I was still a kid when he was in high school," Mary Alice said.

"I thought everybody in Cana knew his reputation." Elizabeth seemed to grow larger the more she gossiped. "Joyce Tufts had an abortion in New York, and everyone said Jamie was the father."

Mary Alice noticed a game of squirrel-chase outside the window. She needed information from her mother, and her mother was in a talkative mood. Mary Alice didn't want to blow it.

"What about after he'd left Cana, but came back to visit his Mama," Mary Alice said. "Did he fool around with any of the local girls?"

"A primal drive like his doesn't just dry up." Elizabeth plainly enjoyed being a font of knowledge.

"You ever hear his name linked with Melissa Corbin?"

"Amos Corbin's daughter?"

"Yes. Maybe around 1991, the summer Jamie's mother died."

Elizabeth turned toward her daughter. She looked like she'd just discovered her three carat diamond was missing. "Good lord, I don't know. Mary Alice you're scaring me. Do you know something?"

"I hope so Mama. That's the whole idea if I'm gonna help Chase."

"What about Melissa?" Elizabeth abandoned her fruit.

"She never left Cana. She knew Jamie. She has a son." Mary Alice took the last sip of her Bloody Mary which was now sloppy with melted ice.

"So?"

"This is just a theory. If I tell you, you have to promise not to tell anybody."

"My lips are sealed," Elizabeth said.

"I mean it, Mama. This is serious."

"I might gossip some, but I wouldn't betray your confidence."

Mary Alice looked at her mother and weighed the pros and cons of disclosure. Common sense and her Private-I book both said not to reveal any information she didn't have to reveal. However, there was a good chance that her mother might know something useful. Elizabeth Tate knew all the dirt and had a mind for detail.

"Jamie wrote a play that seems autobiographical. In it a man comes back to the small town he grew up in to claim his illegitimate son."

"Jamie had a bastard?" Elizabeth said.

"Possibly. If so, the mother or maybe her husband had a motive to kill Jamie to keep him quiet."

"Oh my God, they could do one of those tests."

"DNA." Mary Alice sucked a sliver of ice.

"Melissa married Larry Don Leach," Elizabeth said as if she were giving Mary Alice a vital clue.

"That's it?"

"There's nothing very interesting about Melissa Leach," Elizabeth said.

Mary Alice shrugged. "Bill Burgess can check her alibi."

"What if the Leaches find out you're digging up dirt?" Elizabeth asked.

"I won't tell her. Neither will Bill and you won't, will you?"

"Promise me you won't do anything without Bill." Elizabeth frowned, creasing her surgically enhanced face.

"I'll promise if you tell me if you're the one who told Potts about Jamie plagiarizing Chase's play."

"No. I didn't even know about that until—"

"Until?"

"Vallie told me." Elizabeth said it as a confession.

"And Vallie told Potts?" Mary Alice asked.

"She didn't mean to," Elizabeth said. "That woman acted like she already knew things and Vallie—well, that woman tricked her."

Mary Alice wondered how Vallie Leonard had found out about Chase's stolen play. Chase swore he'd only told Mary Alice. But of course, Jamie could have told Vallie. But why would he?

"Vallie didn't think it was important, and she was trying to seem cooperative with that awful detective woman. Anyway, everybody knew there was no love lost between Chase and Jamie."

Mary Alice nudged the last bite of watermelon. All alone, it looked forlorn. She speared and ate it.

"Jamie was a damn fool to put his private business in his plays," Elizabeth said.

"I bet he'd agree."

"Promise you won't do anything without Bill Burgess?"

"Promise."

"Who else besides Melissa is on your list?" Elizabeth asked.

"Promise you won't tell anybody." Mary Alice knew she needed help. Eliminating even one name from the list cut the work by an eighth.

"Yes, yes." Elizabeth held up her right hand as if she were swearing in court to tell the whole truth.

"And you'll tell me anything you know?"

"Everything."

"Swear it."

"I swear I won't blab about your list. Okay?" She pushed her plate aside.

"Fine."

"Lord knows I don't want my friends to know you're involved in this sordid mess."

Mary Alice took the paper from her purse. "My theory could be wrong, Mama. You can't talk about this."

"I swore. Now give me the damn list." Elizabeth's long tapered fingernails clattered on the glass topped table.

Mary Alice handed it over and watched her mother's eyes jump from name to name.

"Sarah Clooney," Elizabeth said. "Well, how can I say this charitably? She got around, so I doubt she skipped Jamie."

Mary Alice knew that Sarah Clooney, now Sarah Clooney Brown, had three children. Mama Sarah had effused at length about her brood in the Cana Reunion Booklet. The boy, his mother had bragged, earned an A average and played JV football. Mattie Catherine had told Mary Alice that the Browns had built a huge house in the new Tara subdivision, but Mattie Catherine was ignorant of the source of the Brown's wealth.

Her mother looked at the list again. "Why is Paige Leonard on the list but crossed off?"

"She fits the profile." It was hard to imagine Paige blowing a hole in Jamie's chest. "She has a sixteen year old son."

"But she was home with her family," Elizabeth said. "I mean the night Jamie was murdered."

"Which is why I crossed her off."

"Oh," she sounded disappointed. "Vallie would have a coronary if she knew Paige was ever on your list." Elizabeth smiled. Her tongue flicked.

"But she'll never know. Right?"

"Absolutely." Elizabeth again raised her right hand.

"I'm trusting you," Mary Alice said.

"It's ironic. Vallie did everything she could to keep her precious son from marrying Paige Thompson. Bobby can do better than that little piece of trash, she used to say."

Elizabeth was caught in the throes of gossip fever, and Mary Alice was glad to let it rage.

"Paige wasn't trash. Was she?" Mary Alice asked.

"Her family was pretty far down from the Leonards. And don't forget, Vallie is old South, one of the Brittains, DAR, UDC, and FFV with fortunes from everything from cotton to real estate. And Paige didn't kowtow to Vallie. Of course after Jim was born, Vallie was so delighted to have a grandchild period, she forgave Paige her rude heritage."

"Paige shadows her now."

"That's now."

"No other names on the list ring bells?"

"Nothing to say they'd bear Jamie O'Malley's son and kill him to hush up the fact." Elizabeth handed back the paper. "Wait. Rosemary Olsen's boy, I think he's called Jonathan. I know him."

"It's his parents I'm interested in."

"He's the spitting image of his papa," Elizabeth said. "They're Swedes or Finns or something Nordic. Any blonder and they'd be albino. Does that help?"

"Yes, maybe so," Mary Alice said. But the way it helped was to make her see what had been right in front of her all the time. She needed to get a look at the children themselves. One might look exactly like Jamie O'Malley. "Mama, I have to go. Thanks for breakfast. It was good."

"Stay a minute. I want you to see the invitations for the party."

Mary Alice looked at her watch. It was nearly two o'clock.

"Did I tell you that Vallie got Mrs. Dickens to agree to cook for the party?" Elizabeth asked remaining rooted in her chair.

"Paige said Mrs. Dickens isn't all there anymore," Mary Alice said. She pushed away from the table.

"Paige says," Elizabeth snorted. "The doctor said Mrs. Dickens only has short term memory loss. Besides-of-which, Mrs. Dickens was thrilled. And Clotil will help. Clotil could run the White House." She rose and posed beside her chair. "Now don't be difficult and come see my pretty invitations."

"Mama, Boon's in the house, and he's going to need to go out. Soon." She saw no need to tell her mother where she really was headed.

"Dogs are such a lot of trouble." She tossed her napkin on the table but didn't argue.

Mary Alice suspected her mother didn't like Boon because he'd been her father's dog.

Her mother followed her into the foyer and deadheaded a bloom on the massive arrangement that topped a green marble table.

"I saw Cham's big brother, Rollins, yesterday," Elizabeth said.

"Oh, joy." Mention of the Mauldin boys made Mary Alice's breakfast sour in her stomach.

"He said to tell you hello. I think he liked you, but his brother got you first."

"He sure did. Get me, that is." She considered that perhaps Elizabeth was preparing the way for Rollins Mauldin to marry Mary Alice.

"Don't be so touchy. Rollins is a nice man." Elizabeth pulverized the dead blossom between her fingers.

"He's all yours, Mama."

"Are you seeing anybody?" Elizabeth asked. Her frustration with a thirty-five year old divorced and not remarried daughter was apparent. Further, that daughter was almost thirty-six and didn't have many childbearing years left.

Mary Alice played with the idea of telling her Mother about the night she'd just spent on the floor in front of a fire with Tom Jaworski.

"No one yet. I'll let you know."

"I just worry about you, sugar."

Mary Alice held up her hand. "I know. I'm fine. I'm digging out the wet-suit tomorrow and am going to start swimming again. When Georgia gets back in May, she has a project for me. Trust me. I'm fine."

Elizabeth Tate looked at the floor trying to say something. Mary Alice knew her mother didn't believe her daughter would ever get her life together and live as a lady at the top of Cana society should. Mary Alice should have had two children by now. In addition to being Elizabeth's daughter, Mary Alice should have been an active Daughter of the American Revolution and of the Confederacy. And she should not be eking by on the small trust fund her father left her. At minimum, she should accept large infusions of cash from her mother and be properly obligated.

"Honey, life isn't a rehearsal. And it flies by faster than you can imagine."

"Actually, I think life is a rehearsal," Mary Alice said. "But I'm just not sure what it's a rehearsal for."

"That's your father talking. You'll be old and alone, and you won't like it."

Just like you?

Letting her mother have the last word, Mary Alice turned and walked out the door. Tiny leaves, barely visible, glowed on the sun-drenched trees. A sweet breeze teased her hair as she walked to her car. Inside, she struggled not to let her mother depress her. Had she ever spent time with Elizabeth Tate and come away feeling good? But at least her mother had been generous with information.

Mary Alice had promised Chase she'd visit, but she was itching to research Melissa Corbin Leach and Sarah Clooney Brown. Mary Alice tried to think of who would know if either woman ever dated or hung out with Jamie. Maybe Mattie Catherine. Elizabeth hadn't known anything specific, but she'd confirmed Jamie's promiscuous behavior which confirmed Mary Alice's belief that Jamie's play was about him. She was also interested in the other six women on her list and the three unknown people who didn't have alibis. If Potts wouldn't tell Jaworski who they were, maybe Bill Burgess would know. She wondered what Chase would make of the fact that Vallie had spilled the beans to Potts about Jamie stealing Chase's play. Had it really been a slip?

In the rear-view mirror, she saw Elizabeth Tate standing on her grand front porch taking in the view of her magnificent rolling lawn. Mary Alice fought to maintain her private investigator persona but felt her mood slipping. By the time she left Linnley's driveway, she was Elizabeth's odd-and-not-in-a-good-way daughter.

She'd sacrifice me to Rollins Mauldin.

Her ex-husband, Cham Mauldin, now an obscenely wealthy Dallas physician, had been narcissistic and emotionally cruel. But from what Mary Alice knew, Rollins was capable of topping his brother. Would Mary Alice's unhappiness be worth it to Elizabeth Tate if she got a grandchild and heir?

The Do-Mama-In picture showed Elizabeth Tate up to her neck in a vat of Bloody Marys, being force fed hundreds of biscuits sopped in red-eye gravy, hams, buckets of grits and an entire pineapple upside-down cake.

Mary Alice pulled up and parked beside her house, liberated Boon and in five minutes was hiking the trail that led to the Weeds' cabin. Boon ran ahead and returned with a brown snake writhing in his mouth.

"Let it go. Right now."

The crestfallen dog dropped the snake, which retreated into the woods.

As they approached the cabin, Mary Alice noticed another car parked beside Chase's. It was Kate Bishop's.

CHAPTER 12

March 11, Sunday

As MARY ALICE REACHED FOR the brass fox-head knocker, the door burst open. Kate Bishop stepped out, knocking Mary Alice backward onto the porch floor.

"Jesus H. Christ," Kate said. "Are you okay?" Kate crouched over her friend.

Mary Alice examined a fan of splinters in her left palm.

"I had no idea anybody was out here." Quietly, Kate closed the cabin front door. "I'm so sorry."

"I'm okay." Mary Alice rose and brushed the seat of her pants. She wondered if her butt would be bruised.

Kate continued to hover. "Sure?"

"No permanent damage," Mary Alice said, forcing a smile to show she was fine. "Where's Chase?"

"Asleep," Kate said. "I gave him magnesium chloride. Mary Alice, he's a wreck." Kate shifted into a whisper. "He watched that *Shawshank*-something movie on HBO, and it flipped him out."

Mary Alice remembered *Shawshank Redemption* with Mississippi's own Morgan Freeman. Tim Robbins played a man doing life for a murder he didn't commit. However, as violent as the movie was, it was set back in the fifties. Prison life was considerably worse now.

"There's TV here?"

"Satellite. A channel for each star in the galaxy."

Mary Alice knew Kate didn't approve of television.

"He was shaking, Mary Alice."

Mary Alice wanted to wake Chase and tell him what she'd found out. Her experience with Sheree Delio taught her that victims knew things that would help, but often they didn't know the importance of what they knew.

"I don't want to wake him up," Kate said, anticipating her. "Let's walk down to the shore."

"I really need to talk to him," Mary Alice said.

"He just dozed off," Kate said. She sounded like a mother talking about a fussy baby.

"It's not like he doesn't have lots of time to rest," Mary Alice said. A battle of wills over Chase seemed ridiculous, but she didn't want to give in to Kate.

"He feels betrayed," Kate said. "Even people who don't think he's guilty are keeping their distance."

Mary Alice reached for the door knob and felt Kate's hand cover hers.

"Half an hour," Kate whispered.

Thirty minutes wasn't long. Mary Alice relented, but she didn't like how it felt. It meant that Kate was right, and Mary Alice was wrong. Her mother often told her she was wrong.

It was an old battle for Mary Alice on a new battlefield. Her father had told her that, "Being right isn't any fun. Being right won't make you happy." Years after his advice, she still struggled to let go of the need to know, to be right. Now she felt irritated at Kate and at herself.

"Okay."

"Come on. The shore."

Kate headed down the path that looked like the National Park Service had built it. Mary Alice followed. Boon leapt and danced beside Kate, who baby-talked him. Mary Alice felt her irritation shift to jealousy.

The Weeds' cabin was situated on a knoll tucked into a paisley-shaped inlet. Mary Alice remembered parties here, but the narrow sand beach had eroded in the last flood and now looked forlorn. She walked to the water's edge and attempted to sort out her feelings which she knew had nothing to do with Kate or Boon. She felt frustrated and helpless and needed a toehold on the investigation's slippery slope.

Kate threw a stick to Boon.

Mary Alice wormed the list of women's names from her pants pocket and held it out to Kate.

Kate glanced over it. "What's this?"

Boon chewed the stick spitting out small chunks of wood.

Mary Alice explained her theory based on the content of Jamie's play, *Redemption*. "I need to talk to Chase. I need his help."

They perched on bare pine logs beside a charred fire pit. A heron alternately dipped and soared over the blue gray water.

"You know all these women?" She scanned the names again.

"Yes, or I did." Mary said.

"Lynn Jacobson couldn't have done it," Kate said. If she sensed Mary Alice's exasperation, she didn't show it.

Squeezing down her feelings, Mary Alice said, "Everyone is equally innocent and guilty right now."

"Not Lynn."

"Kate, at this point it's important to—"

"Lynn's dead."

"Dead?" Mary Alice vaguely remembered Lynn from girl's tennis.

"She died in Katrina. Was in the paper," Kate said.

When Hurricane Katrina laid waste to Waveland, Bay St. Louis, Gulfport, Biloxi, and Pascagoula, Mary Alice had been in Dallas failing at being Mrs. Doctor Cham Mauldin. She'd missed the storm, but Kate had joined the rescue efforts, first with the Red Cross and then on her own, saving abandoned animals.

"Oh. Then that leaves seven with sons about the right age," Mary Alice said. She didn't explain that Rosemary Olsen wasn't a likely candidate. Nor did she thank Kate for shrinking the list by one.

"Why's there a line through Paige Leonard's name?" Kate asked, handing the list back to Mary Alice.

"Verifiable alibi," Mary Alice said.

"You ought to add Brenda Lee Chinault." Kate collected a handful of short branches and snapped them into even smaller pieces.

Mary Alice knew where Kate was heading. "She talked to you?"

"She's missed two periods," Kate said. "She asked me for something to cause an abortion."

"Shit. What'd you say?"

"I told her to get a test kit and make sure," Kate said. "She thought I could mix up some herbs and take care of her problem." Kate switched from twig snapping to tapping between her eyebrows. It was her Emotional Freedom Technique, EFT, that supposedly unblocked chi. Kate did it as easily as Mary Alice scratched a mosquito bite.

"If she tests positive, you're going to help her?" Mary Alice asked. She remembered her own recent experience with a pregnancy test kit and her dilemma: she wanted the result to be simultaneously positive, baby-yes and negative, baby-no.

"I don't have the potion she wants, but I can help her other ways," Kate said.

Although Kate's folk medicine wisdom had helped Mary Alice in the past, she now found Kate's wise woman persona grating. It wasn't so different from the power medical doctors wielded. "I overheard her in the school bathroom. I think she was sleeping with Jamie," Mary Alice said, glad to know something Kate probably didn't.

Kate ceased tapping. "If you saw how she looked at Jamie at rehearsals, well—"

"Jamie apparently promised her that a reviewer friend from Atlanta would take a look at her performance," Mary Alice said.

"And Brenda Lee saw the lights of Broadway," Kate said. "I thought he had more class than that."

Mary Alice wondered what else Kate thought about Brenda Lee and Jamie. It was never pleasant to find your lover was doing it with another woman, especially one half your age. But then Kate had unusual ideas about relationships. Kate insisted on honesty and freedom in all her relationships. She said she didn't want anyone sticking with her out of duty or obligation.

Mary Alice imagined that most of the marriages in Cana would dissolve without those twin glues.

Mary Alice took a deep breath, again trying to adjust her mood. Kate had her own point of view, but she wasn't an enemy.

"She's just a kid," Kate said. She shook her head slowly and scattered the pile of sticks.

Mary Alice wondered. Brenda Lee hadn't sounded that naive in the high school rest room. Maybe the girl had her own agenda. "Mama says Jamie always had quite a reputation. She called him a Lothario." Mary Alice picked at the splinters in her hand. "You think Brenda Lee could have done it?" she asked. "Marry me or I'll shoot?"

Kate shrugged. "Maybe."

"She's kin to a pack of mean ole Chinault boys who'd see it as a matter of honor," Mary Alice said. "I know Dale Chinault. Huge, hairy and hateful."

But putting Brenda Lee Chinault into the mix troubled Mary Alice, who had begun to count on the killer being on her list, which she was whittling down. Her theory made sense. But if Brenda Lee Chinault's relatives could be guilty, so could half of Cana.

"Kate?" Chase's voice floated down from the cabin porch.

Kate and Mary Alice rose and waved.

"We'll come up there," Kate called. "Damn, he needs sleep," she whispered.

They headed up the path. Boon skirted the water's edge, looking back at them as if they were crazy to leave the beach.

"I didn't know you were here," Chase said, hugging Mary Alice.

To Mary Alice, Chase looked ten years older and a couple of inches shorter. He'd given up on fashionable country attire and was missing a belt and a shave.

"Your nurse here said you were napping," Mary Alice said.

He waved a hand dismissively. "It'll take more than minerals to put me out." He tucked his shirt in his pants. "So what's new, Nancy Drew?"

Mary Alice took a deep breath. "Vallie Leonard was the one who told Potts about your falling out with Jamie."

"What?" He frowned as if he'd just tried an unpleasant mouthwash.

"She told Potts that Jamie plagiarized your work," Mary Alice said.

"I never told Vallie that—" Chase shook his head in disbelief.

"Somebody did. Mama says Vallie didn't mean to tell."

"And she told Elizabeth?" He shook his head again. All of Cana knew if those two knew.

Mary Alice handed him the list of suspects.

"And these would be?" he asked.

"I found Jamie's plays in the theatre like you said. One seems autobiographical."

Chase looked simultaneously alarmed and glad.

"She thinks Jaime is the main character who has an illegitimate son he's come back to claim," Kate said.

Mary Alice explained her idea, how she had created the list and why Paige Leonard and Lynn Johnson had been eliminated. She hoped the news would encourage Chase. If he gave up, it was all over. At the same time she felt as if she were the one who needed encouragement or at least empathy.

"Y'all come in," he said. "I need a drink."

A chilly trickster of a breeze blew up off the lake and followed them inside.

They sat at the round oak table and caught Chase up on the news about Brenda Lee Chinault. Chase didn't say much except that from what he knew, Chinault girls were almost expected to get knocked up.

Chase poured glasses of wine to the rims. "But none of the women on your list seem like—"

"Everyone's capable of murder under the right circumstances." Mary Alice thought of her own recent brush with death.

"Any of the other plays interesting?" Chase asked. He took a deep draw on the glass.

"They're all pretty melodramatic, filled with dirty family secrets," Mary Alice said. "Catholic titles like Penance and Contrition."

"He copied Lillian Hellmann once," Chase said. "A colonel who hid in a well when the Yankee soldiers came." His color rose with the memory.

"If he copied Hellmann, you're in pretty good company," Kate said.

"There's a play about incest," Mary Alice continued. "A brother can't save his pregnant, incested sister, and she dies."

"How original," Chase said.

"But *Redemption* stood out," Mary Alice said. "Jeb is Jamie. I'm sure."

"I don't think we should ignore Brenda Lee and her clan," Kate said.

Mary Alice noticed Kate's use of "we." Was she committed to helping or only to easy opinions? "Can you find out if she's really pregnant?" Mary Alice asked.

"Yes."

"This is preposterous," Chase said. He drained his glass and refilled it.

"What is?" Kate asked. She looked at Chase's glass as though her gaze could neutralize the alcohol which wasn't going to help Chase sleep well.

"What we're talking about," Chase said. "It's ludicrous."

"Chase—" they said together.

"If you were out on bail, accused of murder, would you want me as your only hope for exoneration?" he asked.

Mary Alice sipped her wine. No, she admitted, she'd want a crack private investigator and a barracuda lawyer. "Chase, we're—"

"Yes," Kate interrupted. "Yes, I'd want you. You'd care, and you'd be tenacious."

Chase stared at the blue and maroon wool braided rug beneath the table. Mary Alice was afraid he was going to cry. She wished she'd said what Kate had.

"But Chase, we're not the entire team," Mary Alice said. "The police are doing what the police do. And Bill Burgess is on it, believe me. I just dig in the local dirt." She calmed her voice. "I believe somebody in Cana knows who shot Jamie. Hell, we probably know the killer. It's like a puzzle we need to put together. Maybe the play I found is a vital clue. Bill's reading it, by the way. Maybe Vallie telling Potts about you and Jamie will add up. Wait a minute."

"What?" Kate said.

"Something Mama said this morning. Vallie was mad that Potts didn't believe her story. Three of the people so far interviewed don't have verifiable alibis. I bet Vallie Leonard's one of them."

"She's not on your list," Kate said.

"My list is of women who have—"

"Has no son but she's got a grandson," Chase said. "Jim Leonard."

Mary Alice remembered her meeting last week at Thorpe House where Vallie and the others had been eager to convict Chase. Vallie had seemed glad to fuel the fire of suspicion. Mary Alice remembered her words: "But anybody can get angry and lose it. A loaded gun presented itself." And Vallie had been at World Oasis the morning after the murder all aflutter with the news. Mary Alice knew she needed more information and wondered who, besides her mother, she could pump for Leonard family history.

Kate stood. "I gotta get back to the store. Workshop on homeopathic remedies."

Kate hugged Chase multiple times and promised to bring him a different herbal sleep-aid the next day. All three walked outside into the fading light.

"Is a Lothario the same as a libertine?" Kate asked.

"Lothario is a libertine in Rowe's play, *The Fair Penitent*," Chase said. "Why?"

"That's how Mary Alice's mama described Jamie," Kate said.

"Machiavelli suits better," Chase said.

Mary Alice hugged Kate, attempting with the embrace to say she was sorry for being jealous and divisive when she really valued Kate's help and friendship.

Mary Alice and Chase watched the dust plume behind Kate's car. She stuck her hand out the window and waved.

"I better go, too," she said. "We're on foot. Boon, come."

"I actually feel like I could go to sleep." He faked a yawn.

She knew he was trying to reassure her that he'd get rest, grow strong and fight to the end. She wished she believed him.

"I want to call Bill Burgess," she said. "Is he staying in touch with you?"

"You know lawyers," he shrugged. "When he has something to say."

Boon sprang from the woods and rubbed his damp fur against them. He'd had a dip in the lake.

Mary Alice wondered if Chase realized Burgess was putting all his effort into getting the case thrown out.

"I'm swimming tomorrow," she said. "I'll stop by."

"Ye gods. In those frigid waters?" he said, turning to look at the darkening lake.

"Wet-suit."

"It's March."

"It's spring."

"Ladies do not swim in ice water."

"*Au contraire.* Diane de Poitiers swam every day in the River Cher. Credited the practice for her beautiful complexion."

"Bully for her; the only clean female in France."

"Tomorrow."

Chase gave Mary Alice a hug. "Thanks for your help. I know I'm useless. I'm a disaster."

"Day by day," she said holding on to his hand and squeezing. She hoped to press some confidence into him. Boon led the way to the path. She resisted looking over her shoulder at her sad, frightened friend alone on the porch.

Back at her house, Mary Alice went directly to the office which was taking on the look of a war room. The index cards fanned across the desk.

Boon whined for his dinner

"You gotta wait baby. I have to get this down before I forget something." She wrote: *Vallie Leonard told Potts about Jamie plagiarizing Chase's play. Why? How did she know? Not from Chase.*

On a fresh card she wrote: *What's Vallie's alibi?*

Then she made a series of cards each with only the full name of the six women: *Melissa Corbin Leach, Sarah Clooney Brown, Stacy McMillan Davis, Paula Wilson Stein, Amy Louise Pickens Rice and Rosemary Peel Olsen.* She included the maiden names the women had when they were involved with Jamie. If they had been. She also noted Rosemary's Scandinavian husband whose children probably wouldn't look like Jamie. Reluctantly, she created a card for Brenda Lee Chinault.

Boon banged his bowl around the kitchen floor.

"Hold on."

She sorted through the cards again and then wrote out a final card: *Vallie Leonard, What else?*

Everyone had to be interviewed, alibis verified, but more important was the background information on each woman. Mary Alice didn't want to ask her mother for more gossip. She made another note: *see if Burgess read Jamie's play.* He'd had four days—probably not enough time.

Mary Alice mixed Boon's dinner of special dry food with cooked veggies and two vitamins. As he inhaled it, the phone rang.

The caller ID said it was her mother. She picked up.

"Hi Mama."

"That always gets me. You're not supposed to know it's me."

Mary Alice had read how private investigators usually had two cell phones—one for incoming calls which provided the caller's name and another for outgoing calls that used a phony name for the PI. That way, the person called didn't know an investigator was on the line. But she didn't share this tidbit with Elizabeth Tate.

"Sorry. I'll start over. Hello? Who's this?" Mary Alice asked politely.

"You don't ask the caller's name," Elizabeth said. "Well-mannered people will tell you in the next sentence."

Mary Alice's jaw tightened. The grammar SWAT team had kicked its way in and rappelled down five miles of phone line. She thought of a scenario she'd used before in which the phone cord turned into a boa constrictor, and as Elizabeth talked and talked, it coiled its sinewy body around hers and slowly took up the slack each time Elizabeth exhaled.

Mary Alice marveled at how her mother could annoy her and then expect her to do a favor. But then her mother didn't know she'd been annoying. "What is it, Mama?"

"I need you to go over to Pontotoc tomorrow and carry Mrs. Dickens back over to Vallie's. She's agreed to help cook for us, but she hasn't seen Vallie's kitchen for a long time, and anyway, Vallie wants to make sure she's okay."

"Okay as in not out of her mind?"

"In her right mind," Elizabeth said. "Paige swears she's dotty and refuses to be a party to employing her. Prophesizes disaster. Can you pick her up?"

Mary Alice hesitated. "What time?" she asked. She didn't want to seem eager.

"Ten. Do you know where the home is?"

"Off Highway 6 just short of Pontotoc?"

"Vallie can take her back," Elizabeth said. "So you won't need to wait. Vallie has to go to the mall in Tupelo anyway."

Mary Alice hadn't considered waiting. "Very considerate," she said speaking carefully, sounding, she hoped, helpful but not overly so. A car trip with Mrs. Dickens presented an incredible opportunity. Here was the person who knew the Leonards the best and for that matter, knew a lot about a lot of Cana people. Maids and cooks always knew the dirt and shared it with each other.

After she hung up and gave Boon a short run, she flopped on one of the worn sofas in the living room and took out her note pad. Mrs. Dickens had worked for Vallie and Spence Leonard for years; even if she had Alzheimer's, her long-term memory might still be accurate. But Mary Alice would have to be careful with her questions. She knew the former cook, but not well, and she hadn't seen her in over ten years.

She wrote: *Lead with food/cooking. What Mrs. Dickens cooked for other pilgrimage parties? What about Paige and Bobby Leonard's wedding at Thorpe House? Did Vallie help plan the wedding? (The Leonard's not Paige's family paid for the whole shebang.) Who else on the list had a cook? The Alexanders?* Then Mary Alice thought about a journalism class she'd taken.

The professor reminded reporters that interviews required intimacy. The source had to trust. And it was important not to lead. Interviewers don't know what the real story is going to be. They must be ready to follow and remember talkers are getting something out of the experience too even if it's catharsis. Interviews could be manipulative, but they didn't have to be.

Mary Alice crumpled her sheet of note paper and sailed it into the brass waste paper can her father had bought in a Turkish souk. All she wanted the old woman to do was give her a lead that would make somebody besides Chase a suspect.

CHAPTER 13

March 12, Monday

MARY ALICE PAUSED IN THE glass foyer of Golden Meadows Manor and surveyed the large room ahead. Damask Victorian wallpaper and burgundy print carpet contrasted with the practical railings and ramps. Next to the reception desk stood an elderly woman in a navy J. C. Penny-type suit. Her beauty parlor hairdo looked like an armored animal, maybe an armadillo.

Mary Alice stepped inside. She supposed the floral air freshener was an improvement over whatever it was covering up.

"Make sure Lavar tapes my programs," the woman in blue said. "I can't say when I'll be back." Her accent twanged, maybe Mississippi backed by Smokey Mountains.

"Mrs. Dickens, we aren't supposed to do personal things like that," the plump woman behind the desk said.

"Corky always does it just fine."

"She's off today."

"And I need my trash emptied."

"Wednesday is your garbage day."

"It's piling up and stinking up."

"Mrs. Dickens, you're not supposed to cook in your apartment. Just snacks. We provide meals."

From the look on the old woman's face, the meals weren't much.

Mary Alice noticed that the bingo players in the far corner had paused to watch the drama.

Mrs. Dickens tossed her head and made a plosive scoffing noise. "I'm just saying—" She pointed at a huge clock behind the desk. "She's late."

Mary Alice sprang forward. "Mrs. Dickens?"

"Where's Paige?"

"Do you remember me? Mary Alice Tate? I'm your chauffeur this morning."

"Where's Paige?" Mrs. Dickens squinted.

Mary Alice glanced at the woman behind the desk whose name tag said *Chandra*. A wandering right eye animated her otherwise dull demeanor.

"I'm so sorry." Mary Alice forced her volume down and kicked up her compliant southern girl tone. "My mama said I was to pick you up. You think that'd be okay?"

"Who'd you say? Mary Alice?"

"Yes, ma'am. Tate." She offered her brightest Mouseketeer smile.

Mrs. Dickens surveyed Mary Alice as though she were hiring her to edit her memoir. "Well, come on then. You're late." She started toward the glass doors. "Chandra, you tell Lavar." She turned and glared at the bingo women. Their heads snapped back to their cards; a wavering voice said, "G-4."

"Yes, 'um," Chandra said, the irritation in her voice distorted by the caramel in her mouth.

Mary Alice looked back at Chandra whose good eye said, *you ain't the boss of me.* She ran ahead to hold the door for Mrs. Dickens.

"That your car?" the old lady asked, blinking through the sunlight. She sounded incredulous as if the vintage BMW were a Russian Volga.

"Yes, ma'am."

As they headed toward Cana, Mary Alice felt helpless to steer Mrs. Dickens toward any productive conversation. For the first ten minutes, the woman quizzed her about what was going on in Cana. If Mrs. Dickens knew about Jamie O'Malley's murder, she wasn't interested in discussing it.

"What's this?" Mrs. Dickens asked, tugging a copy of *The Cane* from between the seats.

"The Cana High Yearbook." She hoped she wouldn't have to explain that the yellow sticky notes marked potential murderesses. But Mrs. Dickens was already through the faculty section and on to the Who's Who.

"I never thought she should have won most beautiful," Mrs. Dickens said. "Too much gum shows and her eyes are squinty." She tapped the smile of Babs Fisher, most beautiful in 1984.

They passed the Chevron station that sold hand-made ice cream sandwiches from a freezer set beside the night crawler ice box. Halfway to Cana.

The annual fell open to the senior photos and a picture Mary Alice had marked. It was Sarah Clooney, now Sarah Clooney Brown.

"I remember her," Mrs. Dickens said stroking Sarah's moon face.

Heading off questions about why Sarah's photo was marked, Mary Alice said, "She's an interior decorator now."

"She any good?"

"I don't know." Mary Alice slowed for man walking inches from the blacktop. "It's a competitive business."

"She ran with those wild girls," Mrs. Dickens said. "Drove her mama crazy. But then her mama—well, the apple never falls far from the tree."

Mary Alice made a guttural noise she hoped would encourage more.

Listen to the story the interviewee wants to tell not the one you think you want to hear.

"But I always said you can't have bad girls without bad boys, now can you?" She looked at Mary Alice, her eyes fever-bright.

"Exactly," Mary Alice said. Mrs. Dickens egalitarian view surprised her. In Cana, even now, if a girl got pregnant, it was her fault. Period. But what about the boys? She pictured guys who had smoked dope, ridden motorcycles and totally enchanted her. "Sarah ran with bad boys?"

"You were there, weren't you?"

They stopped at the four-way. There wasn't much more time. "Yes but I was only—"

"Sarah Clooney married Eli Brown," Mrs. Dickens said. "My brother-in-law was his boss at the casket company in Batesville one summer." Mrs. Dickens took off down the rabbit trail about her brother-in-law who had been wonderful to her but died of liver cancer. But not from drink.

Something didn't seem right. The woman clearly loved the power and attention knowing gossip provided. Yet she didn't want to talk about bad boys. What was juicier than that? Mary Alice made noises of concern about liver cancer. She slowed to a crawl. Maybe Mrs. Dickens knew something about Melissa Corbin whose photo was on the next page.

"She left him once. Sarah did," Mrs. Dickens said. Her voice was comically conspiratorial. "Her boy wasn't yet a year old."

"Sarah left Eli?"

"That's who we're taking about, ain't it?"

"Why?" Mary Alice asked struggling to negotiate the twists and turns of Mrs. Dickens' memory.

"He abused her."

"Hit her?"

"Mental." Mrs. Dickens smiled the smile of a wise woman familiar with the wicked world.

"Goodness sakes." Mary Alice nodded and relaxed. She knew she had a big fish she needed to play. With enough time, Mary Alice suspected Mrs. Dickens could air everybody's dirty laundry.

As they entered the city limits, the old woman put down the annual and began a commentary on every structure they passed. "That used to be a bowling alley; that's the colored's mortuary; that's the parking lot where they shot that deputy." She read aloud billboards, signs and marquees. *Are you ready? Jesus is coming. Now hiring all shifts. Lab puppies $100.* At the huge State Farm billboard, which encouraged faith in insurance sold by Billy Coggins, Mrs. Dickens asked, "Ain't they the ones that wouldn't pay after Katrina?

Mary Alice nodded. "It's so nice of you to help with the pilgrimage this year."

"It's hard for me," Mrs. Dickens said. "I'm not well."

"You're a legend, Mrs. Dickens." Mary Alice knew that in spite of the woman's put-upon tone, she was thrilled to be called upon.

"I cooked for the Leonards and for Judge and Mrs. Weeds I don't know how many years. Babysat Bobby. Wasn't anything I didn't turn my hand to."

"You must have done Bobby and Paige's wedding." Mary Alice said, fishing.

"I told Mrs. Leonard and her husband it'd work out fine."

"What would?" Mary Alice said.

"Bobby and Paige." She paused. "Mrs. Leonard got so depressed she had to take tranquilizers. I told her Bobby was gonna marry Paige no matter what, and she better make peace with it or she'd lose him too. That turned her thinking because she'd lost a baby. Bobby was her only chick."

"Mrs. Leonard had a miscarriage?"

"Yes, two as I recall, but her little girl died of a respiratory ailment. About 1962."

"I was only ten." She slowed to twenty miles per hour. Thorpe House was just ahead. She vaguely remembered a Leonard baby dying.

"But like I told her, it all worked out fine. After Jim was born. Well, Mrs. Leonard was hard on Paige before that. I tell you. But Paige took it. Never said one word against her mother-in-law. Bided her time. Mrs. Leonard took one look at grandbaby-Jim, and it all changed in the blink of an eye. We going in the back way?"

"Unless you want the front," Mary Alice said. Navigating Mrs. Dickens' stream- of-consciousness dialogue was a challenge, but Mary Alice felt heartened by the woman's solid memory.

"Back suits me."

Mary Alice was about to ask more about grandson-Jim, when Vallie Leonard appeared on the upper veranda waving energetically. She sallied down the stairs and across the lawn, her high heels sinking in the cushy turf.

Mary Alice had to hand it to Vallie; she knew how to coddle her former cook. She complimented Mrs. Dickens' appearance and commiserated that she wasn't allowed to cook in her room at the home. Before Vallie ushered Mrs. Dickens inside, Mary Alice volunteered to drive whenever Mrs. Dickens needed a ride.

From Thorpe House, Mary Alice headed toward the square to Dotty's Café and the Monday meatloaf special. Mrs. Dickens was a mother lode of fractured information, but it wasn't clear that she could be mined. Did it matter that Eli and Sarah had separated for a time? Had he caught her with Jamie? And the stuff about the Leonards. If a mother would kill to keep her dirty secret, might a grandmother do the same? Young Jim Leonard was Vallie and Spense Leonard's only heir. What good was a million acres in timber and another in cotton if you had no heir, no future through your offspring? She stuffed her thoughts about her own lack of offspring.

For the time spent, Mary Alice hadn't gotten much, but Mrs. Dickens was able to remember specific dates of events that happened over forty years ago.

She parked in Dotty's Café lot and tried Kate on the cell phone but got no answer. The same happened with Tom Jaworski. "I'm a big girl. I can eat alone," she said aloud. Inside Dotty's she headed for the pearly-green plastic counter with the squeaky swivel seats. She spotted one open at the end. She wouldn't be eating alone at all.

Distracted by greeting a dozen diners in the café, Mary Alice didn't notice that the rotund body next to the vacant seat was occupied by Detective Claire Potts. Once in the seat, it was too late to escape.

"Ms. Tate, I was going to call you today," Potts said. She worked her tongue to free something green stuck to a molar.

Mary Alice looked around for an excuse to bolt. Dotty filled the ice water glass in front of her, paused and moved on.

"Afternoon, Ms. Potts." Surely Potts wasn't going to question her in a public place over lunch.

"After I saw you at the theatre last Saturday night, I started thinking. Wondering why you were at the theatre so late," Potts slurped the bottom of her coke glass. "I mean, given that you found the body there, it can't be a place you'd want to return to unless—"

Mary Alice watched a weary fly light on the top of the glass cake dome. She couldn't believe how crass Potts was.

"Unless you were looking for something you didn't want anybody to see you looking for," Potts ploughed ahead. She shifted on the seat; it squealed, begging for help.

"The whole cast, including me, had been at the theatre all day building the set," Mary Alice said. She turned the menu over and read.

"Still, going back at midnight alone."

"I had my dog," she said, knowing she should shut up. "And I've been working in that theatre since I was child. It's a very familiar space."

Shut up, Mary Alice, shut up.

"And you went to get a list you'd left there?" Potts dug in her purse for her little notebook.

"Kate and I are doing props for the play," Mary Alice said.

"Props."

"Short for properties. All the stuff: ashtrays to zebras." She turned her head to look at the detective, showing she had nothing to hide. But Potts was deep in her tiny notebook.

Potts tabbed through several pages and read, "A grocery list that included potatoes for ice cream. That correct?"

"I'd have to check," Mary Alice said. She knew being evasive indicated guilt. Her PI book said so.

"Okay, but you theatre folk do sometimes use mashed potatoes instead of ice cream because ice cream melts. Right?"

"Yes, we theatre folk do just that." She wondered if Potts would mention the fuchsia feather.

"What I can't figure is that while there is a meal in the play, in the script I read that Mr. Pike gave me, they don't eat the meal. A family fight interrupts the dinner."

"Empty dishes would be noticeable," Mary Alice said. She knew she could get up and walk away. She hadn't been charged with a crime. But she realized Potts would just come at her again. She hoped no one in the café could overhear.

"True, but no dessert is served. I asked Mr. Pike. The director would know about dessert." Potts put on her baffled look.

"When I made the list, dessert hadn't been decided. Norton—Mr. Pike trusts his prop people to provide an array of choices," Mary Alice said. "And potatoes are cheap."

"Wouldn't you use instant mashed potatoes?"

"That would work too."

Potts looked at her little book. "But your list just said potatoes."

"And I wouldn't write out Trappey's Black Eyed Peas with snaps and fat back. I'd just write black eyed peas."

"You're not telling me the truth, Ms. Tate." Potts looked directly at her, and Mary Alice could see an underlayment of minuscule bumps across her face. "What were you doing Saturday night at the theatre?"

Mary Alice examined the scratches on countertop. Potts seemed to believe Mary Alice had been removing evidence that would incriminate her or further incriminate Chase. Or maybe the detective thought she'd been there to plant evidence. Why had she let this uncouth creature lure her into an inappropriate interrogation? How was she going to get out?

"Here you go, hon," Dotty said placing before Mary Alice a large Styrofoam to-go-box. "One meatloaf special, mashed taters with gravy, beans instead of slaw."

Mary Alice looked up, but Dotty did nothing to betray the fact that Mary Alice had not made a to-go order.

"Tell your mama hello."

"Thanks Dotty," she rose, seizing the moment. "Excuse me, Ms. Potts; don't want Dotty's meatloaf to get cold."

Potts swiveled toward Mary Alice as far as the stool would take her. "We know we have the right guy, but I don't like loose ends."

"Have a nice day," Mary Alice said. She forced herself to stroll through the café to the cashier by the door. As she paid, she glanced around. Potts looked like a giant mushroom topping the café stool. Across the way, she saw Bill Burgess lunching with three other lawyers. He didn't look at her. She wondered if Bill had sent over the lunch or if it had been Dotty's idea to rescue her. Cana closed ranks against outsiders for its own. She depended on her status as a local. It was the one power she had that Potts didn't.

She drove to the parking lot behind Kate's World Oasis and ate Dotty's famous meatloaf made with Pickapeppa Sauce and undisclosed quantities of top secret ingredients.

Great, she thought, Potts knew she was lying and would be watching her. Wait until she found out Mary Alice had a list of suspects. But why was Potts still interested in her? Did it mean the detective wasn't completely sure about Chase's guilt? She wished she could share her theory with Potts about Jamie, the father claiming his son. Potts had resources and the ability to interrogate suspects. Squeezing information from the honeysuckle vine of gossip was slow. She finished the mashed potatoes and wished Dotty had put in a slice of black bottom pie.

A haze covered the sun. She'd promised herself she'd swim today and drop by Chase's. And she needed to track down the women on her list and scrutinize their sons. For a pretext, she'd ask the women to volunteer to help with the pilgrimage. Even if they refused, she'd get to talk to them and possibly to eliminate one or two. It would be easy to segue from talking about the pilgrimage to talking about Jamie's murder.

She started to go into World Oasis, but she knew what she longed for wasn't inside. Instead she stopped at the Quick Mart and bought a box of Little Debbie Brownies, three of which she ate on the drive home.

Avoiding the full length mirror, she struggled into the wetsuit. She knew she weighed at least ten pounds more than she had six months ago. But it was March 12, warm enough to start swimming every day. Would the extra pounds melt? She'd never before had to melt pounds and wasn't sure about the process or the rate.

She dove in.

Stroking hard through the chill water brought calm. Certainly Potts was one of the ones her Daddy had warned her about. Be careful who you talk to, she'd heard him say.

She swam past the cliff with the z-slash in the rock and headed for the tiny cove and the Weeds' cabin. She had nothing new, and Chase would see that immediately. It was important to involve him. Maybe he could help devise better ways—a ruse he'd call it—to check out the women on the list.

There was no answer when she knocked on the cabin's door. Chase's car was gone, but she called his name and pounded again. Nothing. Maybe he'd driven up to Memphis. Was he allowed to leave the state?

Halfway back across the lake, she rolled on her back just as clouds obliterated the sun. She turned and kicked hard. If a storm came up, she didn't want to be in the middle of the lake or slogging barefoot around its rocky perimeter. Answers to questions about Chase's whereabouts, why Eli had left Sarah, if he really had, and if Brenda Lee Chinault were pregnant had to wait.

Thunderless lightning flashed.

CHAPTER 14

March 12, Monday

M ARY ALICE ARRIVED EARLY FOR rehearsal. She hoped to corner Brenda Lee Chinault—maybe push some buttons. Girls Brenda Lee's age liked to talk about themselves.

The theater auditorium was empty, but she heard Garth Buchanan holding court in the dressing room and followed the sound. Garth, who played the patriarch in Jamie's play, was about sixty with military bearing and a Barrymore voice.

"I've never been treated with such disrespect," Garth said. He snapped his script against his thigh.

Most of the cast stood in the crowded room looking at Garth. Mary Alice could see him catch his reflection in the make-up mirrors.

"Everybody connected to the play got questioned," one of the lighting guys said.

"Not at the police station," Garth said. He shook himself as if to fling off the memory.

Mary Alice couldn't tell if he was claiming abuse or superiority. She stood in the doorway, listening.

"Who does that woman think she is?" Garth sat on a bench in front of the mirror; the naked bulbs framed him. "You're lying," he imitated Potts. "She said that right to my face in that nasal, Yankee sneer." He puffed his cheeks and twisted his mouth creating a startling likeness to the detective.

"Where'd you say you'd been?" Fran Zimmer asked. Her mouth formed a tense line as though it still held straight pins.

"Home alone, which is where I was," he said. "They're checking my phone records, but I didn't make any calls."

Anger swelled his voice, but Mary Alice didn't believe he was really worried. No doubt he disliked being hauled in for questioning, but Garth liked the lime light and every face in the room was trained on him.

One mystery solved, Mary Alice thought. Vallie and now Garth. Who was the third person without a verifiable alibi?

"It's impossible to always have an alibi," Garth said. He gestured broadly, sending a shelf full of rehearsal shoes to the floor.

The group crowded around him seemed to be feeding on his pain. Sounds of agreement rippled like barnyard animals at the trough. Not one even glanced at the shoes tumbled around them.

Mary Alice wanted to shake them and shout that Chase was no different than Garth. But she knew it wasn't true. Garth's prints weren't on the murder weapon. She retreated to the auditorium and spotted Brenda Lee alone down front, hemming a costume. Fran Zimmer was always assigning sewing jobs to the younger women.

Mary Alice took a seat behind her. Brenda Lee didn't look pregnant, but what did Mary Alice know about that?

"Hey Brenda," Mary Alice said. Brenda Lee was the same age Mary Alice had been when she'd run away from home. It broke her heart to look at Brenda Lee's youth, beauty and innocence tangled with ambition, naiveté and ignorance.

"You got a cigarette?" Brenda Lee spoke with the same country twang that Mrs. Dickens had. However, onstage, there was no trace of her trailer-up-the-holler background. It occurred to Mary Alice that Brenda Lee used this vocal skill to seem older or more interesting to men like Jamie. Mary Alice had effectively used the same ability. Only now did she realize she need not have bothered.

"No, I quit." She didn't explain that she'd quit years ago, a week after she'd started. "And we'd have to go outside anyway."

"Damn. Don't nobody smoke no more." Brenda returned to jabbing the needle in and out as though she were repairing pirate boots.

Mary Alice leaned forward. "I heard Norton say how good he thinks you are in the play." The director had actually said everyone was doing marvelously.

Brenda Lee dropped the skirt and turned toward Mary Alice. "He did?"

Brenda Lee Chinault was way too easy. "Yes. He thinks we ought to get a big newspaper to review us. Jamie was pretty well-known." Mary Alice hoped playing the reviewer card would gain Brenda Lee's confidence. Actresses could bond over reviews.

Confusion flushed Brenda Lee's face. Maybe she thought Mary Alice could read minds. How else could she have known Jamie promised the girl a professional review? "That'd be good," Brenda Lee said. "Do they make a difference?" Everyone knew Mary Alice had majored in theatre in college. To Brenda Lee, Mary Alice was a snail's breath away from an Actor's Equity union card.

"To what?"

"Your career." She returned to her crude slip stitches.

Mary Alice didn't like manipulating the girl. Even if Brenda Lee hadn't shot Jamie, she'd been involved with him and might know something useful. Too much was at stake to worry about Brenda Lee's feelings.

"Good ones do," Mary Alice said. "But with the director arrested for murder—"

"You think he did it?" Brenda Lee asked a straight question without a hint of what she wanted to hear.

"Do you?"

Brenda Lee looked around the auditorium. "I know for a fact," she whispered, "he didn't respect Mr. Minor."

Mary Alice almost laughed at the understatement. "What did he say?"

"Called him a silly fag, a faggot. Said Chase Minor couldn't write cereal box copy. Fuck!" She jerked her hand to her mouth and sucked the blood from the finger she'd stabbed. "Sorry."

Mary Alice affected a bored, cuss-all-you-want look. Rough language indicated trust.

"I was with him," Brenda whispered. She resumed sewing, leaving tiny blots of blood on the skirt.

"Jamie?"

"That night."

"You saw?"

Hadn't Kate said she was the last to leave? How many women did Jamie have hanging around after rehearsal?

"I waited in the restroom 'til everyone left."

Mary Alice waited for more.

"Sometimes, you know, Jamie and me, we'd talk. He didn't treat me like a kid."

Mary Alice could easily imagine how Jamie had treated Brenda Lee. As a teenager Mary Alice's appetite for cheap thrills had led her to more than one older man. But didn't Brenda Lee realize Jamie had manipulated her? Maybe he'd manipulated all of them. Maybe that's why he was dead.

"So you talked that night?" Quit leading the witness she told herself.

"No. He was too pissed off at Chase. Said he wanted to rewrite a scene. Told me to leave."

"And you did?"

"I went on out to my Uncle Earl's. Will they arrest me if they find out I was the last one to see him alive?"

Brenda Lee shrank into a big-eyed third grader scared of a spanking.

"You didn't tell them?"

"They'll think I did it."

"I think you'd better tell them."

"But I didn't see nothing. I left fifteen minutes after you did." Brenda Lee rubbed away tears along with most of her mascara.

Mary Alice thought that the girl was in love, had been in love with the playwright. She found a Kleenex in her coat pocket and handed it over. "I'm not going to repeat anything you just said," Mary Alice said, "but if someone later remembers you hiding in the bathroom, maybe your girlfriend, what's her name, Annette, and they talk, it'll look a lot worse."

"She'd never—" Her realization stopped her. "I am so fucked."

Mary Alice moved a seat closer. She figured there wasn't anything Brenda Lee wouldn't tell her now. "Not necessarily. Unless you killed him you weren't the last one to see him alive. There was—"

"Places everyone," Norton Pike barked from the rear of the theater. "Fran, get those people out of the dressing room, please."

"Anybody seen Kate Bishop?" the stage manager asked.

Nobody had.

The moment with Brenda Lee was lost. Mary Alice gave her a pat on the shoulder that she hoped said, we'll continue later. But Brenda Lee looked away.

"I want to run the second half of act one to check the blocking," Pike said as the actors drifted on stage. "No acting please."

Everyone chuckled.

They ran the scene twice, and the director fine-tuned who moved where and when. Mary Alice, having little to do in the scene, replayed the conversation with Brenda Lee. What had the girl told the cops? Had her uncle corroborated her story? Mary Alice had the distinct feeling she didn't have all the facts on Brenda Lee.

The assistant director called a ten minute break.

Mary Alice stepped outside the theatre into the cool darkness. A hand gripped her arm.

Before a scream could gather, she heard Kate say, "It's me. Chase is in the hospital."

"What?"

"I'll tell you in the car."

On the way to the hospital, Kate told Mary Alice how she'd found Chase collapsed in the cabin late that afternoon. "I called 911. They took forever to get out there. All I know about healing came to zip-zero. He was sprawled on that stupid sofa, barely breathing."

"What? How?" Mary Alice could barely talk.

"Overdose, I'm pretty sure."

Mary Alice took a deep breath and tried to accept what Kate was telling her. Chase might die. Had he been lying on the floor when she'd knocked on the door? Her Daddy had explained that resistance to what *is* only brought pain. His logic, gleaned from an assortment of Eastern religions, made sense to her but getting to that place of acceptance eluded her. Her mind could only pump out no, no, no.

In the hospital waiting room the two women sat together on the only sofa. The sallow fluorescent light made both look ill. Cotashona County Hospital hadn't spent much on space for healthy people. Mary Alice prayed it had spent well on whatever it would take to save Chase.

Kate went to the desk and using her healer persona, asked about Chase. The nurse on duty wasn't impressed. Alive was all she could find out. She returned to the sofa.

"I should have told them I'd played a doctor on television," Kate said.

Mary Alice smiled remembering Chase's story about once having dinner with a famous heart surgeon and quoting an old TV ad. Chase had said, "I'm not a doctor, but I played one on TV." Overheard by the waiter and diners who took him seriously, Chase became an instant celebrity. No one cared a fig about the famous heart surgeon, and they all claimed to remember Chase on early episodes of *ER*.

"I talked to Brenda Lee tonight," Mary Alice said. "I'm pretty sure she was in love with Jamie. And he told her he hated Chase—made fun of him, called him a fag."

"She's pregnant," Kate said.

"Oh my God." Mary Alice turned to face Kate. "That gives her a motive."

"Can't be sure it's Jamie's."

"That might not matter to Brenda Lee," Mary Alice said.

"I just can't see it." Kate rested her head in her hands. "She wasn't sure she was pregnant until after Jamie was dead."

"Maybe. Maybe not."

Kate shrugged and threw up her hands.

"Kate, tonight at rehearsal, she told me that the night Jamie was murdered, she hid in the bathroom until everybody, including you, left. Apparently she often hung out with Jamie. But this time he told her to leave, and she went to her uncle's."

Mary Alice could see Kate putting it together, coming to the same conclusion she'd reached.

"Suppose she told him she was pregnant, and he rejected her or made fun of her the way he did Chase?" Mary Alice could imagine a cornered Jamie changing from lover to libertine. "A pregnant teenager wouldn't fit his plans for the future."

"You think she waits for him, tells him and when he doesn't go for it, she grabs the gun in a fit of passion and shoots him?" Kate asked. "Kind of cliché."

"Clichés exist for a reason," Mary Alice said. "And remember, she didn't know the gun was loaded."

"Threatening him?"

"Possible."

"She still wants an abortion." Kate poked at the stack of ancient *Reader's Digests* on the table.

"I might too if I'd murdered the baby's father." Mary Alice didn't approve of abortion, nor did she approve of mostly old white men telling mostly young poor women they couldn't have one. She hoped she'd never have to make such a choice.

"Just a thought but it's possible Jamie might have wanted the baby. He didn't have any children except maybe Jim who wasn't exactly his," Kate said.

"Possible." Mary Alice remembered that the Jeb character in Jamie's play worried about sexual potency and dwindling chances to produce children. She wondered what Kate might say about Jamie's ability in bed, but she wasn't going to ask her.

They sat in silence, feeling time creep by. Mary Alice remembered a time she'd been in trouble, and Chase had stood by her.

A dark wraith of a man pushed a dust mop down the hall. He sang and rolled gently with his music. "God's not finished with me yet."

"What are you thinking?" Kate asked.

"About Chase."

"Attempted suicide's bad. They might lock him up," Kate said.

"When I was about Brenda Lee's age, Mama and Daddy were practically having public brawls. I ran away to New Orleans. Took money out of Mama's purse and caught a Greyhound south."

"How'd that work out for you?"

"Some dude spotted me ten steps out of the bus station."

"Bought lunch?"

Mary Alice nodded. "Walked me around the Quarter, smoked a joint. Very cool."

"Think he knew he had a Miss Cotashona County on his arm?"

"I expect he thought he had some US prime on the hoof 'cause he wouldn't let me out of his sight. I told the dude I needed to pee, and I called Chase from a pay phone. I had no idea what I wanted, but unconsciously I must have known I was in trouble. I told him I was starting a new life in New Orleans." She shook her head at her naiveté.

The janitor, still singing, ambled through the hall in the opposite direction.

"Chase said, terrific. He loved New Orleans. He spoke like he was saying lines in a play. He got me to give him the number of the pay phone in case we got cut off. All the time he was saying that splitting might be a good idea, he was making me see how it was a bad one."

"What about the pimp?" Kate asked.

"Chase said if I wanted, he'd come for me, or he could send his friend, Marvin, who lived in the French Quarter." Mary Alice paused, again overwhelmed by the caring Chase had offered.

"What happened?" Kate, caught up in the story, urged her on.

"So me and my new boyfriend are finishing our coffee and beignets. He's making plans for us to visit his wonderful friends at the proverbial house of joy when up comes a black guy who looked like a Saints linebacker. He said, 'I believe you have my baby sister. I'm Marvin'."

"How did Marvin know what you looked like?"

"I must have told Chase what I was wearing," Mary Alice said. "I know I told him where we were. I wanted to impress him."

"What'd your parents do?"

"They never knew," Mary Alice said. "Chase took care of everything and everybody."

"You didn't run away again?" Kate asked.

"I thought about it. Daddy moved to the lake house. Mama and Daddy switched from fights that would clean the house to psychological warfare which was lots worse. But Chase cast me as Babe in *Crimes of the Heart*. I couldn't run out on that." Mary Alice pushed down the tears the memory had stirred. She couldn't lose Chase. For years he had popped in and out of her life, magically sensing when a surrogate parent was needed.

Kate looked at her watch. "No one's ever going to tell us anything."

"Maybe I can find out something." Doing something, anything, distracted her from free falling into the abyss of poor little hard-done-by Mary Alice. "I must know somebody here." She heard her mother joke, what was the good of being a Tate if you couldn't pull rank?

Mary Alice took the elevator to the third floor, bypassing a nurse's station. She walked to the other side of the hospital and went down the stairs ending up in the triage unit. She saw Raymond Shore, a physician's assistant, scribbling on a clipboard. Raymond smiled and took her through a full course southern greeting before asking why she was in triage on a Monday night.

"Chase Minor," she said.

"I haven't seen the lab report," Raymond said, "but they pumped him out in time. I think it will come out that he took pills and chased them with alcohol. Unofficial, of course." He pointed a cautionary finger at her.

"He's an old friend. I'm worried." Mary Alice couldn't bring herself to say the word, suicide.

"They're probably still checking his insurance," he said, trying to lighten the mood. "Don't worry."

All Mary Alice could think about was that it looked like Chase had tried to kill himself. When she got back to the waiting room, she found Kate asleep on the hideous sofa. "Let's go home."

Kate half-rose. "You saw him?"

"I'll tell you in the car."

CHAPTER 15

March 13, Tuesday

MARY ALICE'S BEDSIDE CLOCK READ 12:13 PM Tuesday was half gone. Synonyms for *paralyzed* inched across a tiny screen behind her eyes: leaden, frozen, gelatinous, stuck. She pulled her knees to her chest and felt sure that was the only movement possible for the rest of the day. Chase hadn't managed to kill himself, but now what? Jamie had been murdered two weeks ago. The cops had Chase, and what did she have? A pile of index cards and an insupportable theory. Nancy Drew would have had more by now. What Mary Alice also didn't have was a life as in a husband, a child, a career.

She heard scraping noises from the kitchen as Boon inched his bowl across the tiles. She got up and trundled down stairs.

"I know. You're hungry. It's coming."

However, even after coffee and a loaded bagel, she felt depression settling in like old relatives with hard eyes and inflexible opinions. She called the hospital, but no one answered in Chase's room.

The wet-suit, still damp from yesterday, chafed and grabbed her flesh. She forced herself into it and into the lake. The spring sun warmed her back, but after only two miles, she came in and toweled off.

She usually crossed the lake and didn't like to admit that nearly being murdered had made her more cautious, even fearful. Peeling off the wet-suit, she ignored the extra pounds she'd gained. She dressed and padded back downstairs. The phone system told her she had messages from Tom Jaworski and her mother. She didn't want to talk to her mother at all, and she wanted to be more prepared—in the right mood—to talk to Tom. She called the hospital again but hung up after a maddening series of automated voices led her in circles. Chase probably wasn't going to go AWOL.

Dressed in her comfortable pants and her father's denim shirt, she made a nest on a chaise lounge on the deck. The table beside the chaise was piled with Cana High yearbooks, Mattie Catherine's alumni booklets, the index cards and Jamie's plays. Boon sprawled beside her. On a new legal pad she wrote: *Of concern: Chase's physical and mental health. Alibis: ask Burgess to check. Make up a story for Potts, avoid Potts, contact Mrs. Dickens, call Jaworski, call Mama, check on the band for the party, buy dog food.*

She thought of adding Brenda Lee Chinault, but asking the girl if she'd shot Jamie was all she could think of to write. Instead she tried to prioritize the items but ended up gazing at the water and wiggling her toes into Boon's thick fur. Dog food seemed as important as anything else. But as she woolgathered, her subconscious nudged her to pick up the high school annuals. She flipped the pages of 1984 ending with a section of candid snapshots. George Orwell had been wrong. These kids were having fun, and Big Brother wasn't watching anybody.

She pulled out a few of the Cana reunion booklets and opened the thickest. In 1990, several classes had joined to host a big party. She'd been a sophomore at Ole Miss and not yet interested in reunions. Even when CHS didn't schedule official reunions, the locals had an unofficial one, and Mattie Catherine and her committee put together a booklet of photos and updated bios. Classmates were advised to check the Cana High website.

Although nothing clicked with either collection of pictures from the past, her intuition about old photographs persisted. She closed her eyes. Perhaps a shot fraught with meaning of one of her suspects laid waiting for her to discover. Instead, youthful images of nearly two decades ago sent her tumbling backward in time. The unlined faces and constant smiles brought up a well of emotion that mixed raw innocence and sentimentality. How many terrible things had happened to how many of them?

She dozed.

The tinny song of the cell phone snapped her out of a dream about flying a vintage biplane that was chiefly powered by her abdominal muscles.

"Hello." She caught a breath.

"It's me. Tom."

"Hey. Where are you?" She sat up and checked to find Boon still asleep beside the chaise.

"On my way home."

"You heard anything about Chase?"

"Released him from the hospital an hour ago."

"He's okay?" She held her breath.

"He says he is. Says it was an accident."

"You believe him?" She looked up at the blue sky. Mississippi skies, usually heavy with humidity, rarely were so bright a blue.

"The D.A. wants him back in jail. Burgess is negotiating."

She bit her lip. "Exactly where are you?"

"Just passed Lonnie Cooper's cotton field."

"I'm out on the deck. Want to stop by?" She made it sound like it's a beautiful day, drop by, no big deal.

"Yes, but I'm late." He sounded evasive. "Have to leave town for a couple of days."

Later when she remembered the conversation, she would wonder why she didn't immediately guess his destination.

"Where you going?" she asked as if she expected the answer to be the NASCAR-Daytona.

"California."

California meant his wife. What was her name, Alicia? The wife he couldn't let go or maybe she wouldn't let go. Mary Alice hated the jealous feeling that raked her insides like tentacle hooks of a malignant tumor. She changed the subject and hoped her voice didn't betray her. "Brenda Lee Chinault is pregnant. She told Kate. And Brenda Lee as much as told me she was having sex with Jamie." Mary Alice knew Jaworski would see the implications. "She also admitted she hid in the bathroom after rehearsal, waiting to see Jamie."

"She can't prove her alibi," he said.

"Potts told you?"

"Yeah."

"Brenda Lee told me she was at her Uncle Earl's." Even as she discussed the case, Mary Alice couldn't let go of California. She wanted him to explain why he was going—something like Alicia was dying of cholera, or Alicia wanted to marry somebody else.

"Maybe she was but the uncle wasn't," he said.

Again Mary Alice wondered how much of what Brenda Lee Chinault said was true. The girl had incriminated herself. She'd been there, knew about the gun and had a motive.

"Who else is on Potts' list?" she asked.

"Vallie Leonard and Garth Buchanan."

It had taken days, but now she knew who couldn't corroborate their alibis. She tried not to eliminate anyone. The detective-how-to book said to use factual evidence, not emotional response. "Tom, are the police even looking for another suspect?"

"There's nothing new."

She could tell by his voice—the formality and brevity—that he needed to get off the phone, needed to pack, needed to visit his wife.

"Potts is still asking questions though," he said. "She doesn't want any surprises."

"She thinks I lied about why I was at the theatre."

"You did," he said.

"I had a good story, and I haven't done anything wrong," she said.

"I haven't talked to her about you, but if she thinks you know something, she's not going to leave you alone."

"Like what do you mean?" A cold tightness, not unlike a too small wet-suit, zipped up around her brain.

"Withholding evidence. Obstruction of justice," he said. "Your detective book mention any of that?"

"Could she arrest me?"

"Depends on what she has," he said.

Mary Alice felt a watery-sick feeling creep in and take hold of her core. She couldn't help Chase if she were in jail. But handing over the plays wrecked her chance to check her theory. She needed time. She was the only one who really believed Chase was innocent. Potts wasn't going to look for Jamie O'Malley's bastard son. In fact, Potts might suppress the evidence or the plays might disappear. Potts needed a slam dunk guilty verdict to make her reputation in Mississippi.

"What if Potts found out about Brenda Lee?" she asked.

"She's already a suspect, but she's a kid," he answered. "Chase looks guiltier."

And more easily convicted. She wished Jaworski wasn't leaving town. She wondered if he had sex with his wife and hated that she speculated.

"Did you check out the kids—the sons of your suspects?" Jaworski asked.

"Not yet."

"Who's topping your list?"

Nobody was. That was the problem and here she was wasting time with jealousy.

"All equal contenders at the moment," she said, feeling like she hadn't done her job. She knew she should have checked out the sons a week ago.

"I'll call you when I get back."

When would that be? Ending the call this way felt awful. She remembered that he had called her, twice, and that she was wildly projecting his reasons for the trip. He wasn't shutting her out. He'd given her privileged information about the case.

Get a grip.

"Thanks, Tom. Be careful." She purged her voice of clingy-whiny and hung up. Acting training came in handy. But then the wounded feeling rushed back. It hurt to be intimate with a man and find out he— She admitted she didn't know what he'd do with Alicia. But why couldn't he just call the wife? He'd made it clear how manipulative she was. What he hadn't made clear was how strong he was. Perhaps he'd never be free of her. Alicia Jaworski.

She knew her irritation was really irritation at herself. She had no hold on Tom Jaworski, wasn't sure she wanted one. She realized what she liked as much as the sexual chemistry, which she liked a lot, was that he treated her like a partner. And now she'd all but shown him a pissy-possessive female persona, one sure to drive him away permanently.

"Damnit to hell." She wanted to hurl the phone into the lake. Her anger broke her depression. In an hour she was dressed and driving into the subdivision called Tara Estates, not to be confused with just plain Tara, another subdivision that was never built because a number of sink holes swallowed the project.

The homes, all large and the same age, possessed stereotypical southern mansion elements: porches, columns, mullioned windows, gabled roofs, uniform landscaping and white paint. It wasn't hard to imagine Scarlet O'Hara sashaying across any one of the cropped lawns. But in the differences lay the sameness. It'd be easy to get lost in Tara.

She found the Brown's faux mansion, a white wedding cake of a house, and rang the bell. Gracing the wide porch were six identical white rocking chairs that sat like movie set props. She heard footsteps.

"Yes?" the woman Mary Alice recognized as Sarah Clooney Brown said. She smiled and raised her eyebrows.

"Sarah, I'm so sorry to just drop by without calling first, but—"

Sarah Brown was huge. In spite of expensive, draped clothing, she looked to weigh in excess of 250 pounds, a significant portion of which rested on her chest. Mary Alice locked eyes to keep her gaze from flitting to the biggest breasts she'd ever seen.

"Mary Alice? I didn't recognize you. Come in." Sarah pushed open the ten foot high door. "I just got home from Catholic Daughters. I thought I heard the bell, but Steve said I was crazy. I hope you weren't out here waiting long. Come in, come in." Sarah effused at length without taking a breath.

Good. Son Steven was in residence. "I won't keep you long. It's about the Garden Club's Pilgrimage." She looked past the foyer into the Olympic-size living room. Elizabeth Tate would have loved to dive in.

Sarah, moving like a Zamboni, guided them into a sitting room that could have come straight out of the June pages of *Better Homes and Gardens*. The furnishings, drapes and wallpaper looked as if a magazine photo crew had just left. Everything was coordinated, clean and slightly bland.

Mary Alice chattered mechanically to hide her amazement. Sarah, who Mary Alice knew was forty, would have been beautiful minus half her body weight. Skin, hair, eyes, teeth, nose, and fingernails looked like they were out of an air-brushed advertisement for high-end perfume. She tried to imagine Sarah standing on the stage holding a gun on Jamie. Hell, Sarah could have just sat on him.

"We need a couple more volunteers," Mary Alice said cranking up the charm. "I know it's late, but mama and I thought of you. Do you have any time next week?"

Sarah explained her busy schedule that revolved around her three children and her decorating business, but Mary Alice could tell she'd say yes.

"And of course you and Eli have to come to the infamous wrap party." She strained to hear evidence of a teenage boy in the house.

Sarah beamed.

"It's at Thorpe House this year," Mary Alice said. "The Leonards refuse to be outdone."

Sarah smiled again, her pearly teeth showing between plump pink lips.

"I love your home," Mary Alice said. "You've done such a—"

Sarah Brown took her cue and asked if Mary Alice would like a tour. After twenty minutes, Mary Alice felt like she'd been through the Biltmore Estate, but she soldiered on, hoping they'd stumble upon the teenaged boy. From the granite counter-tops and stainless steel appliances to the hard wood floors and twelve foot ceilings, the house was a realtor's dream home. Every feature was what buyers thought they wanted; there were no surprising color choices—or any surprises at all. Sarah unnecessarily explained each feature. It occurred to Mary Alice that Sarah was auditioning for membership in the exclusive pilgrimage garden club of which Mary Alice herself was not a member.

"Steven, honey, come meet Ms. Tate," Sarah called to a closed door.

A heavy-set teen emerged. His eyes were nearly hidden by a prominent forehead and a curtain droop of dark hair. "How do you do?" he said, a perfect southern gentleman hidden inside the Neanderthal.

Steven Brown could not have looked less like Jamie O'Malley. Where this boy was thick and awkward, Jamie had been lean and light. As she watched him amble back to his room, Mary Alice felt certain he was none of Jamie O'Malley.

She promised to call Sarah with details of what the pilgrimage would require. Driving out of Tara Estates, she wondered at the source of the Brown's wealth. Mattie Catherine hadn't known much. And more interestingly, had Eli Brown once left his wife as Mrs. Dickens said? Mary Alice reminded herself that caches of booty often housed a venomous snake and a trap door or two.

The progress made with Sarah and her son lightened Mary Alice's mood, and she pulled into Sonic Drive In and ordered a large root beer float. Taking Sarah Clooney Brown off the list based on her son's appearance was huge. Now she needed to check Melissa Corbin and the others.

The girl brought the float. Mary Alice paid, adding a fat tip. She lifted the cup and with roller coaster anticipation, waited for the ice cream to slide into her mouth. Eyes closed, she moved her tongue through the cold sweetness giving each taste bud a chance. It was bliss until she flashed on a picture of Sarah Brown poised on the bow of a ship—a formidable figurehead. Mary Alice left a quarter of the drink, also called a brown cow, and cranked the engine.

Motivated by a skyrocketing sugar level, she drove to Bill Burgess' office. Tom Jaworski could fly to California and be damned. She had work to do.

Burgess sat behind his desk. Even at the end of the day, he looked suave as if he were going to have his photograph taken with the Ole Miss Chancellor. But Burgess always looked cool. His office reflected him: neat and classy with a studied casualness.

"Don't you ever work? Have clients?" she asked, sinking into the leather chair opposite his desk.

"Have a drink?" he asked, heading to the liquor cabinet.

"No, just had one, but thanks." A sticky sweetness still coated her mouth.

He refilled his glass. "I was going to call you tonight."

"Is Chase okay?"

"He's back in his own house," he said. "Our deal to keep him out of jail."

"The cops going to check on him every hour?" she asked.

"That's the idea," he said. "His neighbors aren't too happy about having him back."

Mary Alice guessed which homophobic neighbors they were. They'd disliked Chase before they thought he was a killer.

"At least he doesn't have to wear the anklet," Burgess said.

"God almighty." How much worse could it get? She stopped herself. Negative thoughts wouldn't help. "Bill, did you read the play I gave you?"

"I did. Very interesting."

"It's not just the plot that makes me think Jamie had a child here in Cana," she said. "It's the way the Jeb character suffers over it. The little details from Cana and Jamie's life."

"I agree."

"You do?"

"It creates an interesting scenario," he said. He rose, crossed the room with purpose, but then sat in the chair beside her. "Is there any proof Jamie actually wrote the play? It's not published, is it?"

"I don't know," she said. She could feel heat from his body.

"May not matter. Pans out or it doesn't."

"You'll check it out?"

He gave her a vague nod.

She took out her list.

"This is?"

"My list of suspects." She handed him the sheet. "Lynn Jacobson's dead, Paige has an alibi, Rosemary Peel married a Swede and all her kids look like him, ditto for Paula Wilson except her husband is Lebanese and their sons could be Boys of Beirut poster children. Oh, is that racist?"

"Probably, but I'm not offended."

"I haven't checked on Melissa Corbin, Stacy McMahan or Amy Louise Pickens. But I saw Sarah Clooney's boy, and he's no son of Jamie."

Burgess looked impressed. "How'd you get the names?"

She explained about her cousin's resources. "If we checked alibis—"

"I see," he said. He held her in his gaze as though he was setting up a portrait.

"I'm going to check out the sons of these women," she said. "Genetics can be tricky. I'd feel more secure if—" She wished he wouldn't stare.

"What's the V by Paige's name?" He held up the list.

"Her mother-in-law, Vallie. As you know, she can't corroborate her alibi, and she's the grandmother. Jim's her only grandchild and heir. Heirs matter to Vallie Leonard."

"So Vallie Leonard's on your list? With Paige—or instead of her?"

"Yes and with."

"Anybody else in your sights?" He didn't seem to be making fun of her.

"In confidence?"

"Yes," he said.

"Jamie was fooling around with Brenda Lee Chinault. She was the last person to see him alive, she doesn't have an alibi and she's pregnant." She counted off the four items on the fingers of her right hand, knowing that it wasn't certain who last saw Jamie alive. She also recognized that Burgess probably knew some of this either from Chase or from small town gossip. But she wanted him to know she had the facts too and had gotten Brenda Lee Chinault to talk. She wanted Burgess to see her as important to Chase's acquittal not for her own ego gratification, but because she believed she was important, perhaps essential.

Burgess raised his eyebrows. "Betrayed pregnant teen shoots lover," he said. "Ironic that all your motives involve Jamie O'Malley's illegitimate children."

"She could have done it," Mary Alice said. "Maybe accidentally."

"You don't want to just turn over all this to the police and let them investigate?"

"Yes, hell yes," she said. "But I have some experience with Cana's finest. The cops don't want a new suspect." She thought about Jaworski. It drove her crazy that she had to keep people and information separate. It was like the CIA. She wondered what pieces of the puzzle might emerge if everybody got together and had a fat sodium pentothal cocktail.

"I'll get these ladies checked out." He rose. "May take a few days."

"Thanks, Bill. I—"

"The reason for my call was to see how you feel about St. Patrick's Day."

"In a religious sense?"

"Think green beer, Hal and Mal's parade, and Jackie O'Shaunesey's annual party," he said.

"In Jackson?" Here it was. Another date with Bill and this one out of-town which meant a hotel room.

"Jill Conner and all the Sweet Potato Queens will be there," he said. "It's next Saturday."

Somehow, through a series of books, Jill Conner Browne had established a Sweet Potato Queen organization. Worldwide, over five thousand chapters of sisters existed, many of whom descended on Jackson for Hal and Mal's annual St. Paddy's Parade. The wild women espoused their founder's philosophy, part of which stated that well-behaved women rarely made history.

Mary Alice had an uneasy feeling that if she wanted Burgess to let her help Chase, she needed to accept his invitation. The basketball game had gone all right. Maybe spending more time with Burgess would actually help Chase. Bill Burgess wasn't going to give her a roofie. He might use her, but he wouldn't hurt her. And wasn't she trying to use him in a way?

"Sounds terrific. I love Saint Paddy," she said. "Anybody who can get rid of snakes is okay in my book."

She left Burgess' office and drove the short distance to Kate's store. The square was choked with afternoon rush hour traffic and out-of-town drivers who didn't understand how roundabouts worked. She maneuvered into the inside circle, avoiding a collision.

She still held an icky feeling—like being a hostage. What was Burgess' intension? If she'd said no to the St. Patrick's party, would Burgess distance himself or cut her out of the investigation altogether? She compared how Jaworski treated her. Everything but the recent stuff with his wife. Even considering the sexual attraction between them, Jaworski never had a hidden agenda. She could still feel Burgess' even, cool gaze that captured her every exhalation.

She pulled in behind World Oasis. Kate was standing by the back door.

"Want to drive to Oxford for supper? Maybe Newk's?" Kate asked.

"Why not?"

"Park. I'll drive."

CHAPTER 16

March 13, Tuesday

A T NEWK'S COUNTER, KATE ORDERED a Greek salad, dressing on the side and a water. Mary Alice chose Newk's Favorite—greens, chicken, gorgonzola, cranberries, grapes, artichokes, pecans, croutons with Newk's vinaigrette—and ice tea presweetened with Splenda. Kate frowned at the tea but said nothing. Mary Alice had heard Kate's lecture on Splenda. She predicted that aspartame would be proven to be more deadly than saccharine. Drinks in hand, they wove through tables and chairs to a booth by the window.

"You sleep?" Kate asked. "You look tired."

"Some," Mary Alice said and shrugged. Everybody had problems. But then she whined to Kate about how Jaworski was 2000 miles away, Burgess was nowhere, Potts was relentless, and Chase was suicidal. She sipped her drink, but the gulp outmatched her and tea splashed down the front of her jacket into her crotch. She blotted, the napkins turning to lint on her clothes.

Kate handed her a wad of napkins.

"Thanks," she blotted again. "How about you?"

"Mr. Bennett isn't responding, and I'm pretty sure he has liver cancer. The lease on the store is about up. The health department is hassling me about tinctures. Pebble wants to quit, and I'm so, so sad that Jamie's dead."

Mary Alice reached across the table and placed her hand over Kate's. They broke apart when a beefy waiter arrived.

"Who had the Greek?" he boomed.

Mary Alice ripped open a packet of Barbero Breadsticks. She felt depressed. She sensed the personifications of all her neuroses joining them at the table, lips tight, scribbling furiously in thick spiral bound notebooks. One wore a badly pilled cardigan and licked the tip of her pencil. She was Ms. Paranoia. Next to her sat Doubt and Confusion wearing a good suit but a bad comb-over. They were all hungry.

"At least I can take Sarah Brown off my list of suspects." Mary Alice said, determined to say something positive.

"How come?" Kate asked around a mouthful of spinach and feta.

"I saw her son," Mary Alice said.

Kate nodded. "Who else is still on the list?"

"Stacy McMahan, Melissa Corbin and Amy Louise Pickens," Mary Alice said. "And I added Brenda Lee Chinault."

"You don't think that girl shot him, do you?" Kate said.

"She lied about where she was that night. That makes her as much a suspect as any of the others even if it's for a different reason." Mary Alice dug through the greens searching for cranberries. "You're the one who pushed to put Brenda Lee on the list."

Kate put her fork down disappointment written on her face. "I know, but now…she's a scared pregnant teenager."

Before Mary Alice could respond, a group of teenaged boys jostled past their table.

"Hello Ms. Bishop," a boy wearing a Cana High sweatshirt said. His friends filled in around him.

"Hey Leo. What are y'all doing in Oxford?" Kate asked.

Before they answered, Mary Alice knew it was sports related.

The boys chattered, talking over one another about the track team win.

"Y'all know Mary Alice Tate?" Kate asked.

In a blur, the boys delivered a collective "how do you do" and exchanged pleasantries that would have made their mothers proud of their good manners.

"Nice to see you Ms. Bishop," the one called Leo said. They headed for the large corner booth.

Mary Alice watched their youthful exuberance charge the air. These were nice boys from good families who probably drank beer and looked at porn on the Internet and tried to get laid whenever possible, but they'd stayed out of trouble. "Who's that? The one in the middle?" There was something familiar about this boy. The subtle body language, easy slaps, position in the pack, said that he was the leader.

"You know him," Kate said. "Jim Leonard."

Mary Alice had thought she knew what Paige and Bobby Leonard's son looked like. Obviously Jim Leonard had grown up since she last saw him. But it wasn't his looks exactly that caught her attention. It was the way he moved, held his head, pushed another boy, laughed.

The recognition and what it meant stunned Mary Alice. She felt as she had when oxygen masks had dropped on a flight to Miami and the crew prepared for a water landing.

"What's the matter?" Kate said.

Mary Alice grabbed Kate's arm. "Look at him, Jim Leonard," she whispered.

Kate turned. They both watched the teenager elbow his buddies and then stand to wave at two girls across the restaurant. Another boy jerked his shirt tail, and he fell back. His laughter bubbled; the other boys joined in. Kate turned back to Mary Alice.

"He remind you of anybody?" Mary Alice asked.

Kate casually turned again, looking without looking. "Jeez Louise."

"You see it too?"

"Jamie O'Malley," Kate mouthed the name.

They finished their salads stealing looks at the boy who looked mostly like his mother, Paige Leonard, but whose nonverbal language was all Jamie O'Malley. The kid was easy in his body, confident. The girls in the next booth vying for his attention leaned toward his brightness like sun starved plants. And if genetics determined the sound of laughter, this boy had Jamie O'Malley's laugh chromosome.

As Mary Alice stood, collected her purse and pushed in her chair, she caught the boy's eye for an instant. His smile at her had a secretive, cocky even sexy quality.

Christ Almighty. He's almost twenty years younger than I am. But then significant age differences wouldn't have mattered much to Jamie O'Malley either. Jamie had been forty-nine; Brenda Lee Chinault, just eighteen.

On the ride back to Cana, they strategized to prove the boy's parentage.

"Only a DNA test would prove it," Mary Alice said. "If Paige admitted that Jim was or could be Jaime's, that would make my theory credible."

"When pigs fly," Kate said.

"I didn't mean she'd confess to murder."

"Like you'd trick her into admitting her indiscretion, and she never see that it implicated her until it was too late?" Kate asked.

Mary Alice smiled. "That happened in a movie I saw."

"What was Paige's alibi," Kate asked.

"Burgess said Paige, Bobby and Jim were at home together all night," Mary Alice said. "Pretty tight."

"Why'd they even check on Paige?" Kate asked. "I understand why they'd ask Vallie, but Paige?"

"She's on the theatre board of directors," Mary Alice said. "Vallie got Paige on when she rotated off." Everyone knew that Paige voted as Vallie would have. Mary Alice wondered if Paige made any of her own decisions.

Kate slowed as they entered the Cana city limits. "If little Jim Leonard isn't a Leonard at all, but is an O'Malley—well think of it. Bobby would divorce Paige, and Vallie would kill her. Jim's all they've got to keep the precious Leonard line going."

"I think that even if Vallie knew the truth about Jim's real father—"

"Assuming we're right," Kate said. She paused at a stop sign.

Mary Alice nodded. "I think that as long as nobody else knew, Vallie would just go right on pretending. And Jim wouldn't ever know."

"So Grandma Vallie's still on the list," Kate said.

"Yes," Mary Alice said. "Maybe she had even more motive than Paige."

"You think Jamie told one of them he was going public?" Kate asked. "Force a DNA test?"

"You knew him better. Would he be arrogant enough to think he could have his way?" Mary Alice asked.

"Yes. It was part of his charm," Kate said. "He thought he was special and most of the time everybody else did too."

"That's it. That's what I saw in the kid. Jim."

"What?"

"Conceit. Nice, friendly conceit, but a certain self-satisfaction. It's in his bones."

Kate pulled into the parking lot behind her store and let Mary Alice out beside her car. "What are you going to do?" Kate asked.

"Think about it," Mary Alice said. "Damn, Jaworski told me to look at the boys."

"You thought you knew this kid."

"I should have looked at all of them a week ago." She shut the car door.

"Go give yourself a C in sleuthing and then kick yourself a few times," Kate said.

"I should lighten up? Have some fun?" Mary Alice mocked.

Kate rolled down her window. "Mary Alice, be careful who you talk to. There's a real murderer out there, and pretty soon they're going to catch on that you're getting close. If they killed Jamie, they'll think they have to kill you too."

"I know. I'll be careful." There it was again, *Be careful who you talk to.*

CHAPTER 17

March 13, Tuesday

ON THE DRIVE HOME, MARY Alice tried to imagine Vallie Leonard shooting Jamie. Guns were part of the Leonard's way of life. Spense Leonard had cases full of rifles, pistols and antique weapons. Vallie would know how to use a gun. She had a key to the theatre. Somehow she could have loaded Chase's gun.

She drove through the navy darkness. Only the brightest stars shone like pinpricks in a felt sky. Spring was trying to hold back, but very soon she'd fling off her winter coat and reveal her effulgence.

Mary Alice shook her head. She didn't want to think about effulgence.

Maybe Vallie had tried to pay Jamie off if he'd leave the Leonard dynasty in tact. Mary Alice could almost hear Jamie's earnest, slightly Irish lilt explaining how the boy had a right to know his real father, and how with or without the Leonard's help, he intended to lay claim to his son. How could he not?

Maybe Jamie first tried to persuade Paige to reveal the truth. Maybe she refused to listen, and he then went to the grandparents. Too many maybes.

Mary Alice pulled the car into the garage and let Boon out of the house to run. The evening's cool had turned chill. As she watched Boon make his rounds, Mary Alice remembered when Paige and Bobby had married. Jim had been born soon after, which meant that, if Jim wasn't really a Leonard, Paige was fooling around with Jamie at the same time she was becoming Mrs. Bobby Leonard. Had Paige married Bobby only for his wealth and position? Well duh-uh. But Cana was small, and affairs were difficult to hide for long. Why had she risked it?

Boon returned and demanded supper. As she mixed the vitamin powder into the dog food, she ran a scenario.

Maybe Vallie had gone to the theater that night to make a deal. Everyone has his price. But Jamie had refused her offer. Perhaps later he would have relented, but initially his vanity would have been insulted. After all, it was his son she was trying to steal. They argued. Things got out of hand. Then Vallie, in a rage or panic, grabbed the gun and shot him. But again, how did it get loaded? And why was Jamie in the bed and not twisted on the floor center stage?

She needed to talk to somebody. Tom Jaworski was with his wife, and Mary Alice couldn't bring herself to call him. She didn't want to call Bill Burgess because she didn't feel comfortable about the St. Pat's party, only five days away.

Chase, just out of the hospital and likely hysterical or sedated, was of little use.

"Want to go to rehearsal?" she asked the dog who with great huffing slurps scoured his emptied food bowl. She knew what Boon really wanted was a long walk.

Mary Alice wasn't called to rehearse, but she knew Brenda Lee would be there. And there was something about the the-atre-as-crime-scene that helped her think things through. And they'd all be buzzing about Chase, calling the episode a suicide attempt. And other details might surface, information that was greater than the sum of its parts.

Halfway down the driveway, she remembered the gourmet food she'd put in the cabin's freezer. Chase, now back in town, wouldn't have had a chance to clear out of the Weeds' place. She backed up, and parked next to the house.

Waste not, want not, for you may live to say, O how I wish I had the coq au vin and that very good '69 Chateneuf de Pape that then I threw away.

"Come on, boy," she called. "Let's take a walk."

She grabbed a tote bag from the utility room and took off into the dark with Boon alternately trailing and leading her on the well-known path around the lake to the cabin.

She located the cabin's key under the third rock, opened the door and switched on the lights. If Chase had been back, he hadn't taken much of his stuff. She loaded Latrice Latcherie's frozen to-go gourmet entrées and Chase's fancy mustard, almond stuffed olives, tapenade, and some imported things in jars and tins that she couldn't identify.

Chase's leather briefcase sat upright on the table he'd used as a desk. Mary Alice swept the loose papers into it. She noticed a paper stuck to the back of a manila folder and when she separated it, she saw it was a letter. The signature made her read it.

Dated February 23, it read:

Dear Chase,

The enmity between us must cease. What else can I do to persuade you of my deepest regret for using your work all those years ago? I was young and greedy then, and it all came to naught anyway. I made no name or money from your script.

Your sarcasm and disdain upset me, but your recent threat to kill me, frankly has me worried about your mental health. I know you'd never really kill me, but how can we work together for the next few weeks?

Life is too short. Can we not please talk and work something out? Perhaps after a rehearsal. I am and have always been your friend,

The note had been written on a word processor and signed in black ink, *Jamie.*

Mary Alice felt a meat locker chill rise in her. Had Chase threatened Jamie? Then the heavier question weighed in. Had Chase murdered him? She noticed her hand was shaking.

She remembered Kate's view that Mary Alice protected Chase too much and that her very protection prevented him from helping himself. Maybe Kate was right. Mary Alice's protection prevented her considering that Chase might be guilty. She felt like she was onstage in a play, but when she looked around, she saw that the scenery was slowly fading until the stage was empty. Nothing felt familiar. She had the idea that if

Chase were guilty, it would be a long time before anything felt right again.

Carefully she put the letter in the briefcase and turned out the light.

But as she touched the door knob, she saw car headlights bouncing among the trees. Her gut told her it wasn't Chase. He was still recovering. Ducking below the window sill, she scooted toward the back door, calling Boon as she went. The briefcase and the loaded canvas bag slowed her, but she had no time to put the food back, and she couldn't leave it out. She wasn't about to let anyone else read Jamie's letter to Chase. The vehicle's engine quieted.

She eased open the back door and held Boon's collar so he wouldn't race around to the front and investigate. There were footsteps on the porch, but there was no knock.

Boon seemed to sense danger and let Mary Alice lead him.

Pulling the bags and the dog, she crept to the edge of the lake. She expected light to flood the cabin, but it remained dark. Just as she made it to the cover of the trees, she saw a flashlight's beam swing across a window. Probably the police taking advantage of Chase's absence to see what he might have left behind.

Struggling down the path in the dark, she made her way around the lake and back to her house. She imagined that the gloomy characters that judged her and took notes on her short comings followed her like the furies of Greek tragedy screaming what ifs. What if the police knew about the letter? What if they knew that frozen food was supposed to be in the freezer? What if they knew that stupid Mary Alice had been in the cabin and had stolen evidence in a murder investigation?

What if Chase Minor had shot Jamie O'Malley and was letting Mary Alice drive herself crazy trying to help? What if Chase was even amused in a cool Cole-Porter-sort-of-way at her ineffectual gyrations?

She made it home and crouched in the darkened living room afraid to turn on a lamp. She clutched Chase's briefcase containing the letter. It was only when she realized that Latrice Latcherie's gourmet food was thawing that she moved. And it was when she loaded the freezer she wondered why the police hadn't knocked. Didn't they usually bang on the door and shout, "police." She was sure the door had been locked. How'd they get in? Cops would have turned on the lights. Who was inside the cabin, and what were they after?

She raced back to the car and blasted down the drive to the main road that circled back to the entrance of the Weeds' place. She figured she had only a couple of minutes. Fifty yards short of the driveway, she slowed to find an old hunter's road and turned in. With the car parked in a copse of elms, she killed the lights and eased out of the car. Crouched behind a bank of scrub oak and azaleas, she waited for the mystery car to emerge from the Weeds' place. There was only one road in and out. From her position on the hill, she'd be able to see the car clearly and maybe who was inside. If she hadn't missed them.

She waited, glad it was too early in the season for ticks.

She saw lights. The car appeared and turned toward town. The driver looked to be alone. As the car approached, the driver lit a cigarette and in the flash of sulfur, Mary Alice clearly saw Claire Potts of the MBI.

Back home minutes later, she'd called Bill Burgess and reported everything but the letter. Potts' visit had to mean something important.

"If she had a warrant, why would she have acted like that?" she asked him. "I know the front door was locked." She tried to sound calm. Hysterical women were not believable witnesses.

"Interesting," he said. "I can't say how useful it'll be, but it's good to know the activities of the enemy."

She had expected more praise. Who else would have had the presence of mind to hide in the dark and make a clear identification? Hadn't Burgess told her that Potts would make a mistake like breaking and entering, searching without a warrant and probably ten other crimes?

But Burgess was more interested in telling her what he'd done. "Melissa Corbin and Amy Louise Pickens have solid alibis for the night of the murder. That leaves only Stacy McMahan." He said it like he was dismissing her theory as implausible. He didn't mention Brenda Lee Chinault, and she didn't tell him that Jim Leonard resembled Jamie O'Malley.

They said good night. She hung up.

She felt conflicted. Shouldn't she and Burgess and even the police be working together to solve the crime? If she was holding back, no doubt they were too. But there was no way she was going to tell him about the letter. Even if Chase had threatened Jamie, it didn't mean he'd killed him. And how did Chase's overdose fit in? That question begged the question of was it an overdose? She didn't want to think about suicide.

But the letter, like the Ancient Mariner's albatross grew heavier with each hour. Would it be possible for Chase to have killed Jamie and for Jim Leonard to be Jaime's son? How could those two pieces both be true? Coincidence?

She wanted to call Jaworski. Even if she didn't tell him about the letter, he could help her sort things out. He was an experienced detective. He'd know what to do. But she couldn't. No matter what she said, it'd look like a pretext. And anyway, what was there to sort out? Jaworski had said he'd call her when he got back. But why wait? His cell phone worked in California.

She went to bed lugging the figurative albatross.

No wonder Coleridge's mariner carried on so about the bird.

Chapter 18

March 15, Thursday

On Thursday Mary Alice met with the band Vallie hired for the pilgrimage wrap party. She liked hanging out with The Confederate Survivors—Dwayne, Larry, Hog, Earl and Skeeter Ray—who flirted with her and took her out of the world of lawyers, court and jail. With them she felt like a risk taker, a bad girl, a hell-raiser. After two beers, she sang back up with Skeeter Ray.

They invited her back any time.

She knew she needed to call Bill Burgess to cancel the St. Paddy's weekend ASAP. It was a matter of giving him enough time to get another date. No big deal.

He answered on the first ring.

"Bill, I'm sorry, and I should have called sooner, but I have to cancel on the St. Pat's party."

"Oh?"

He wasn't making it easy.

She knew lying to him would be a bad idea. She burbled on, "I'm just not feeling comfortable. The overnight part." She knew she sounded like a tight-assed, prudish imbecile.

"Mary Alice, I'm sorry I made you feel like that."

"Well, it's not—" Why hadn't she told him last night on the phone? Why had she ever accepted?

He cut her off. "I was going to call you in a minute. Seems Jackie O'Shaunesey's in the ICU at St. Dominick's. Heart attack, probably a bad one. Obviously the party's cancelled."

"Oh." She apologized again wishing she'd known before she acted so prissy

Can you kick yourself with the same foot you put in your mouth?

Burgess, ever suave, said no big deal, but she thought that later on his male ego would sit him down for a chat after which Mary Alice wouldn't look so good. It wasn't fair. Not at all.

But the problem of the letter quickly overshadowed that of alienating Burgess. If he cut her out because she wouldn't date him, no, sleep with him, so be it.

By two o'clock she was at Chase's door, letter in briefcase, heart in mouth.

"Precious, enter," Chase said in his Vincent Price voice. He wore his vintage olive dressing gown over casual slacks, shirt and ascot. The green accentuated his pallor, but the costume looked more like the old Chase.

"Where's your pipe?" she asked following him into the living room and setting her purse and briefcase on the sofa.

"With whom are you confusing me, Miss Smarty Pants?" he asked.

"Sherlock Holmes?"

"I like the irony of that," he said. "A detective who can't save his own neck. Tea? Juice? It's all I'm allowed."

"Nothing for me," she said.

"Oh, dear, refusing refreshment." He sat on the edge of a gold club chair watching the briefcase as though it might explode. "What's in there, Miss Muffet?" He pointed to the briefcase. "It must be totally-awesomely-atrocious. You're being so jolly."

She opened the case, extracted the letter and held it out to him.

"Don't tell me. You're putting me in Whitfield," he said.

"You've got to be lots crazier," she said, finding the banter increasingly painful.

"For the record, that was no suicide attempt," he said. "If Chase Minor decided to exit, there'd be no resurrection." He slipped gold wire reading glasses from a breast pocket, put them on and read the letter.

Mary Alice gathered her resolve to make him see that she had to know the truth. She couldn't let him explain away damning evidence with smoke and mirrors. As he read, she searched for some flick of expression that would give him away.

Chase looked up. The cliché "wind out of his sails" came to her.

"Where'd this come from?" he asked.

She described the scene from two nights ago ending with her identifying Potts by the light of a match. "I told Burgess about Potts in the cabin, but I didn't tell him about this."

"You waited until now to tell me?"

"I thought you were indisposed." She didn't add that she was scared that the letter made him guilty and had been in no hurry to prove it so.

"And you want to know, what?" He held the letter as though it might burn his fingers.

"Have you seen this? Did you meet with him?"

"Unequivocally no." He took a deep breath and let it escape through pursed lips. "However, if you think that I did, I suggest you immediately withdraw your support." His effort to sound firm wavered.

"I believe you, Chase," she said. She still felt uneasy as though something remained unexplained.

He looked up at the ceiling, not letting the tears crest. "It's a fake."

"Don't you dare get emotional," she said. "It won't help. Sit. Let's figure this out."

They sat side by side on the stiff sofa that had belonged to his great-great grandparents. Chase placed the letter on the antique cherry coffee table.

With her arm around his shoulders, Mary Alice could feel how despair had hollowed him out. She doubted he had the energy for many tears.

"This is actually the most hopeful thing that's happened," she said.

"Someone's trying to frame me and you think—"

"If Jamie didn't write this, whoever did is getting antsy." But why they were getting antsy confounded her. Was it something she'd done?

"But the D.A. would use it," he said. "Proof of premeditated murder. It's all they need to put me away for a very long time."

She could imagine the D.A. saying just that. She could also imagine a jury buying it.

He stuck his fists into his robe's pockets. "It's by sheerest chance that you and not the police found it."

"But we do have it," she said. "Let's stay with that." But as she spoke, she wondered if the writer perhaps had forged a reply from Chase that would be discovered.

"Then they'll try again. Something else." Panic rimmed his voice.

"Maybe, but let's look at the letter," she said. His terror exhausted her. She needed all her energy to figure out what was going on. "How do you know Jamie didn't write this?"

"You found it on my desk?" he asked.

"On the back of a folder. Something sticky held it."

"The folders held audition forms I intended to send to Norton."

"Someone must have put it there after you left for the hospital," she said.

Chase looked hopeless, his color matching his robe. "Which means they had over twenty-four hours."

"They wanted the police to find it," she said.

"Hence the timely arrival of the portly Miss Potts," he said. "Tipped off, we presume."

She could tell Chase was having trouble considering the letter as a tool to help them discover the killer. While she was thankful that he was trying to participate in his defense, she had the feeling they were in a British-drawing-room murder mystery and another body was about to be discovered. Maybe Chase's.

She picked up the letter and handed it to Chase. "Read it out loud."

He read aloud line by line. "It's Jamie O'Malley doing James Joyce." He attempted a wry smile. "But the D.A. won't understand about Jamie and his Irish pretensions."

"And he ain't gonna see it," she said. "But what do you see?"

He looked at the letter again. "There is the matter of word processing," Chase said.

"How do you mean?"

"Jamie despised computers. I grant the signature's a fair copy, but Jamie never used a PC. Had an old Underwood or paid a typist."

Mary Alice examined the font. It wasn't a common one. Maybe it was chosen because it looked arty or literary.

"It's an educated person."

"Why?" he asked.

"Proper letter format, for one thing," she said.

"Format is easy on a word processor."

"Okay. Word choice."

"Ha!" he said. He rose and led her into his study where cherry bookcases lined the walls. Elegant and homey at once, it looked like a place where Gilbert and Sullivan could have written *Pirates of Penzance*. Behind cupboard doors a PC hibernated. He rubbed the mouse, clicked Word, typed *hostility* and clicked Synonym. *Enmity* was one of the four choices. "See? Instant appearance of education."

He was right.

"I know about the Thesaurus," she said. "But it's more than words."

"Exactly. Look, *'it all came to naught'* and *'I made no name'*, he said. "Jamie made fun of phrases like that. Never spoke or wrote such drivel." He paused and opened a smaller cupboard door and the drawer behind it. "But that's not the reason I know it's a fake." He removed a heavy mahogany box, simple in design but obviously expensive.

Mary Alice thought it resembled a tiny coffin.

He opened and spread a packet of letters on the desk. All began, *Dear Cody* and closed, *Happy trails, Jaime.*

"He called you Cody?" she asked.

"When I was a kid I watched *Roy Rogers* reruns, *Bonanza*, anything cowboy. Cody was my cowboy name and the name I planned to use when I became an actual cowboy. Only Jamie knew that."

All doubt vanished; the metaphorical albatross was cut from Mary Alice's neck. The salutation clinched it for her. Jamie wouldn't have written Dear Chase. The letter she'd found was a forgery planted to convict Chase of murder. Chase was innocent.

"What do we do with it?" he asked.

"Burn it," she said.

In mystery novels, incriminating evidence that didn't get incinerated came back to haunt the owner. And she'd been the one who found the letter and who stole it. Every action had a consequence, but it was impossible to guess what consequences might arise from Chase hiding a letter meant to further frame him for murder.

"You think Bill Burgess should see it?" he asked.

"I don't know." Burgess didn't seem interested in finding the real killer.

"What next?" he asked. He tucked the letter into the inside pocket of his dressing gown.

She thought about her theory of Vallie Leonard as killer. "You think Vallie could have written it?"

"Christ only knows, but somehow I think she'd have done a better job" he said. "This is quite amateurish when you examine it."

"I saw Paige's boy, Jim."

"You lost me. We were on Vallie-as-author."

"Kate and I saw him with his pals at Newk's over in Oxford," she said. "Tuesday."

Chase repacked his letters in their box. He performed the action as though the letters were valuable anthropologic artifacts. "And?"

"It's not his looks exactly," she said. "Chase, if you could have seen him. Full of himself. He flirted with me. He's a young Jamie."

"You believe Jim Leonard is the bastard of Jamie and Paige?" He shook his head, no.

"Kate agreed with me."

"We see what we want to see," he said.

"But it fits. It gives Vallie motive." She wanted to shake him. Blanket negativity wasn't going to help.

"What about opportunity and means?" he asked.

"Vallie has no reliable alibi: she knows the theatre, knows guns," Mary Alice said. "And she was the one who told Potts about your falling out with Jamie. Why else would she volunteer that bit?"

"What about the other mothers on your list?"

"All well-alibied except Stacy McMahan," she said. "Burgess is still checking on her."

"And the talented Miss Chinault?" he asked. He picked up a netsuke box and ran his fingers over the delicate carving. "Norton says she's missing."

"Since when?" she asked. She'd talked to the girl Monday.

"She missed rehearsals on Tuesday, her big scene," he said. "Norton's thinking of replacing her."

"A pregnant teenager might want to disappear," she said.

"Didn't she tell Kate she wanted an abortion?" he asked.

"Then she'd be in Jackson or out of state." In spite of Roe v. Wade, there was only one place in the entire state of Mississippi where legal abortions were performed.

"Brenda Lee isn't a silly child," he said. "She's obsessively driven. She intends to be a professional actress." He repeatedly opened and closed the box.

"You think she planned to use Jamie?"

"I can't think." He shook his head. "But if I could, I'd think he wouldn't give her money, and they fought about it." He set down the miniature box.

"I can't see Brenda Lee pulling the trigger at close range," Mary Alice said. But a new thought fledged. What if Brenda Lee or any of the other suspects had help? Someone who could easily pull a trigger.

"Did you know she and her friend Annette used to strip in Memphis?"

"Strip? Like strip tease?" Mary Alice said.

"Strip as in bump and grind in a titty bar."

"She's just a kid." She imagined leering faces watching Brenda Lee pole dancing in a blue haze.

"Apparently those establishments don't check such facts very carefully."

"How'd you know?" Mary Alice was agog. Less than a week ago she'd been sitting in the theatre watching Brenda Lee hem a costume.

"She told me when I interviewed her for the role. With nary a blush she couched it in terms of having recent stage experience."

"And why back in Cana?"

"One of several burly uncles happened by the gentleman's club employing her."

"Did he snatch her off the stage?" Mary Alice imagined the thick necked uncle wrapping his hairy arms about Brenda Lee's naked torso and hauling her away in a fireman's carry.

According to her, Uncle Brute explained to the management she was underage. I believe they gave him some compensation to keep quiet."

"She told me she was last to leave the theatre that night," Mary Alice said. "Planned to hang out with Jamie, but he was mad at you and he sent her home. She said she left right after I did."

"Maybe she thought you'd seen her," he said. "Felt she had to explain."

"Incidentally, Kate was home waiting for him."

"Brenda Lee is talented and knows it," Chase said. "If Jamie threatened her perceived chances to become an actress and consequently to get out of Cana, she might— Hell, any soap opera writer could spin a dozen possible scenarios."

"I've got to find her," she said

"Can't Burgess do that?"

"Maybe, but she knows me," Mary Alice said. "Opened up with me. She's still a kid. She can't be that tough."

Chase made them a snack, which they ate in the kitchen. She did most of the eating. He'd lost over ten pounds. She remembered how flattened her friend Sheree Delio had looked when twenty years in the women's prison stared her in the face. Fear was corrosive. The Fear diet worked.

From Chase's she returned to her home and her computer. With Boon under the chair chewing what had once been a toy duck and with her PI book and Cana High annuals by her side, she searched cyberspace for leads to Brenda Lee. In less than an hour and for less than thirty dollars in database fees, she had names, addresses, tax records and criminal backgrounds for twenty-three Chinaults in the area.

She chose Brenda Lee's oldest sister, Wilma, but marked her county map with four other possibilities. None of the Chinaults on her list lived in town, and most had addresses on dirt roads the county supervisors neither graded nor graveled. She didn't have a firm story as to why she wanted to find Brenda Lee. She'd start with missing-from-rehearsal and see how receptive sister Wilma was.

She collected her purse and car keys. Boon emerged from under the chair and shifted his weight, clicking his dog-toenails on the floor.

"Stay," she commanded.

Boon looked at her as if she were nuts.

If he got out in the boonies, she'd never find him. He wasn't named Boon for nothing.

As she headed for the door, the phone rang.

"Oh. I can't believe you actually answered," Elizabeth Tate said.

"Hello Mama." Why did her mother always start with a barb?

211

"Could you pick up Mrs. Dickens tomorrow afternoon? Vallie thinks she needs to talk to her again. Maybe Paige was right about the old biddy."

"I'd be glad to," Mary Alice said. She'd been thinking about inveigling another invitation to talk to Mrs. Dickens. Didn't the PI book repeatedly state that the job of a good PI was to ask, ask and ask. No stone unturned. Since last Monday, there were lots of new stones to flip over.

She headed west on an empty county road toward a tangle of smaller roads where she hoped to find Wilma Chinault Cumbest, who would tell her where little sister Brenda Lee had skedaddled off to. Watching the western sun through a dusty windshield, she thought of Cody Cowboy and his pal. *Happy trails to you, until we meet again.*

CHAPTER 19

March 16, Friday

MARY ALICE ROSE WITH FRIDAY'S dawn. Before the dew dried, she'd swum the lake shore to shore, hoping the cold would fire a few synapses. The brief Thursday foray into the deeper recesses of Cotashona County had produced one relative of Brenda Lee's who offered nothing but vague notions as to the whereabouts of more Chinaults. She'd given up at dark. But spurred by her discovery of the forged letter and Chase's evidence that Jamie didn't write it, she felt a foggy clairvoyance struggling to break clear. Something was going to happen.

Fanned on the floor in front of the sofa lay the index cards. She sat with Boon on the smooth leather and composed a list of items to investigate. *Where is Brenda Lee Chinault? Who wrote the letter? Who tipped Potts to search the cabin? Who had access to the cabin?*

Mary Alice looked at one of the cards written several days ago. *Did Chase kill Jamie?* She started to toss it, but didn't. The cards were tools to stimulate her thought processes. They didn't mean anything except what she decided they meant.

The last item on her list was to follow the Jim Leonard trail. *Interview Minerva Weeds, Mrs. Dickens, Mama. What do they know about him?* She added Stacy McMahan. Good detective work insisted no clue be left unexamined. Suppose Stacy's son also resembled Jamie? Hells bells, suppose he had bastards all over Cotashona County? She circled Minerva's name.

She had rehearsal at seven o'clock. Minerva wouldn't be hard to pull into a discussion. A romance writer, Minerva was always trolling for material. And wasn't Minerva the Roman goddess of wisdom? And of war too.

She looked at Boon, who cocked his head to the right in his charming-quizzical expression.

"Okay, the letter was a plant by the killer to cement suspicion about Chase. Did the killer do this because of my digging? How'd the killer know what I was doing? Do I know him or her?"

Boon cocked his head to the left and smiled.

"Where was the leak? Brenda Lee Chinault? Sarah Clooney?" Boon studied his front paws.

"No? Did Kate tell someone I was looking for Jamie's illegitimate son? Burgess, Chase and Mama know about my Jim Leonard theory. Maybe one of them said something not even thinking it would matter."

Boon twisted to bite at the fur on his flank.

"Hey, pay attention." She nudged the dog. "All killers make mistakes, but some never get caught, which means that their mistakes went undetected. In detective fiction, often the killer confides in someone. Or maybe Jamie's killer didn't act alone."

Boon rolled onto his back on top of the cards.

"You're not helping much," she said, scratching his belly and pulling cards from beneath him.

She scrawled the questions on yet more cards. She wondered what Kinsey Millhone, who used the card system, did with all the cards when a case closed. Mary Alice still had the crisp index cards she created to help Sheree Delio last year. However, she had to admit that in the end, the cards hadn't helped Sheree's case much.

After lunch Mary Alice gassed up the BMW and headed out in search of Chinaults. She found Bessie Chinault's mobile home. Immobile for at least thirty years, the aqua aluminum structure featured a vaulted ceiling and multiple ornamental shutters. A woman who said she was Brenda Lee's aunt told Mary Alice it was none of her damn business where Brenda Lee was. The woman, barely five feet tall, her face aflame with broken veins, further informed Mary Alice that if Brenda Lee was gone missing, and the aunt insisted she wasn't, but if she was, she'd turn up. Brenda Lee was a growed woman. Mary Alice was sure the aunt was lying. The aunt banged the door in her face. As she walked to the car, Mary Alice felt multiple eyes peeking through ragged curtains at every tiny window.

She figured the aunt would alert other Chinaults, but that if Brenda Lee actually was missing, even the Chinaults would eventually worry and might talk to Mary Alice. By four she was ready to give up the search for the day.

Dressing for rehearsal in her Ralph Lauren gray slacks and oversized gray sweater, choices that wouldn't upstage Minerva Weeds' couture, Mary Alice looked at herself in the mirror. *Elephants wear gray*. She heard her mother's axiom. Compared to many women her age, she was still trim, but her addiction to junk food kept her weight yo-yoing. Just thinking about it made her want a Moon Pie. She grabbed her keys and headed for the theatre.

At rehearsal, Mary Alice found that Minerva was only too glad to talk. She suggested coffee after rehearsal at Cana's only coffee bar, Caffeine Up! which bragged *We never sleep* and stayed open all the way to midnight to prove it.

The rehearsal dragged. An actress couldn't remember stage right from left, even though Norton Pike explained twice that right and left were the actor's right and left when facing the audience, not his. Garth Buchanan took the opportunity provided by the basic acting course to question Norton's constant demand that the actors at all times know what their characters wanted.

"I can't remember my lines, I'm so busy probing for some want," Garth said.

Others, the lazy ones, hummed in agreement. Jaws drooped, eyes glazed.

Norton Pike swiped his slick head with both hands and explained how action on stage came from unseen motives. Motivation wasn't a joke. It was fundamental to convincing acting just as it was to human behavior.

Mary Alice thought that the killer's motivation now was to not be caught and to remain undetected and free. To that end, the killer could wait it out. But if someone found new evidence, the killer's motivation would change to *I want to silence the busybody who's trying to expose me.* Stirring things up might force the killer to act and show himself. That usually worked in mystery novels. But she wasn't sure she wanted to make herself a target. She might end up dead, with Chase in jail and the killer free. Still, wasn't the letter a sign that Jamie's killer was anxious, if not panicky? Doubt about Chase's guilt would jumpstart the investigation.

She could imagine a nervous Vallie Leonard writing the letter and forging Jamie's signature. The Leonards and Weeds were close friends. Vallie probably had a key to the cabin. She would have known that Chase was ordered to return to his home in town. Nothing easier. Mary Alice returned her attention to the stage where Norton was grilling Garth.

"Why does the general react to the old man's threat?" Norton asked.

"I want to, I want to—" Garth floundered.

"Garth," Norton said, "try this. We'll cut it if it doesn't work for you but just try. I, the general, want to in ensnare my sister so that I may possess her. I want to make her love me. I want to kill the idea that she could marry Jack Gilbert because—"

"Possess?" Garth asked. He said the word as if he were about to spit out a medicinal cough drop.

"Have her totally." Norton leveled his dark gaze at Garth.

"Sexually? Incestuously?" Garth sputtered. Likely he envisioned his sister's naked limbs wrapped around his thrusting loins.

"Just try it, Garth. Don't worry, he fails in his intent." The director looked heavenward for an inspiration that would make Garth Buchanan, who mostly acted in plays for ego gratification, motivate the general's lines. "No one but us will know this, Garth. It will buzz in the deepest recesses of the general's mind. Can't you see how such a motive juices things up?"

Garth Buchanan could. He could see the severe pastor of First Baptist personally kicking him off the deacon's bench for even thinking of having sex with a make-believe sister.

"Chase never made us do things like that," Garth said, his mouth pulling out, making him look like a post Civil War Ulysses S. Grant.

Mary Alice knew Garth was wrong. Chase was relentless in pursuit of motive, of want, of human desire. *Desire under the Elms, Art, The Real Inspector Hound, The Little Foxes* and dozens more plays that Chase had directed demonstrated irreversible human desire of such force that entire families crumbled and lives were lost.

Again Mary Alice pictured Vallie Leonard. Would she be ferocious enough to defend her family at any cost? What motive buzzed in the remote recesses of the killer's mind?

And what about Vallie's daughter-in-law, Paige? Could she have been having sex with Jamie just as she was about to marry into the Leonard clan? Was it passionate, irresistible longing for whatever Jamie gave her that Bobby Leonard didn't? Or would Paige's motivation have been *I want to annihilate the*

Leonards who look down on white trash me. I want to get a little of my own back. Years of watching the Leonards unsuspectingly dote on a boy who shared none of their royal blood might have been satisfying to Paige. She could take pleasure in the buzz of revenge against a family and all its ancestors for snubbing, belittling, mocking. Her husband, Bobby, would have been an unfortunate but necessary victim in her plan.

She was about to consider Brenda Lee Chinault's motivation when the director called for places at the top of the scene. Mary Alice took her place a foot from where Jamie O'Malley died. A heavy sadness flowed around her, causing her to miss the single line she had in the scene.

The rehearsal moved on and just before ten concluded with the director's notes. He had nothing specific for Mary Alice. Her role was so small. He stated that he was generally pleased and expected everyone off book by next Monday. As the cast disbursed, he reminded the stage manager to call Brenda Lee Chinault again.

MINERVA AND MARY ALICE SANK into the nubby, beige sofa in the back corner of Caffeine Up! Both had decaf lattes with caramel over whipped cream. The place had successfully copied cool coffee joints, but its cliental looked too well-behaved and starchy. Few slouched, no feet were up and only one laptop was in evidence. It was more a fifties soda shop than a Starbuck's knockoff.

Mary Alice asked Minerva what she thought of Norton Pike's direction of the play.

"Fine. Norton knows his stuff." She waved her arms dramatically erasing all doubt about Norton Pike's abilities. "That's not why we're her though, is it?" Minerva's green eyes flashed over the dome of frothy cream.

"I need information," Mary Alice said. She still had no idea how to find out what she really wanted to know.

"About?"

"Jamie and Chase to start."

"Together or separate?"

"Both."

Minerva set down her coffee and assumed a diva pose in spite of the spongy sofa. "Chase Minor was a good writer. I write romance, but I read literature. He had chops."

Mary Alice remembered her PI Book and resisted leading. She nodded.

"Few writers garner a living writing, but Chase could have or at least had a lucrative avocation." Minerva paused for effect.

"But?"

"That devil Jamie O'Malley belittled Chase—stole his self-confidence at a critical juncture," Minerva said. "I remember once at a party, Jamie goaded Chase to tell us about the short story he was working on. As Chase told his story, Jamie completely undermined him. Made the story sound trite and stupid. Then, at the end, Jamie assured Chase it'd be wonderful when he finished. 'Don't pay any attention to my bullshit,' Jamie said. But of course the damage was done."

"Why would Jamie do that?"

"Jealousy? Or maybe just because he could."

"You think Chase hated Jamie enough to kill him?"

Minerva lifted her coffee cup and gazed at the whipped cream. "I'm pretty sure Chase has always been in love with Jamie."

Mary Alice struggled not to choke. "They were lovers?"

"Sugar, in north Mississippi we don't acknowledge carnal activities between two men. But I imagine Jamie could have been bisexual. He required large infusions of attention and wasn't picky about who doled it out."

Mary Alice's head spun. She'd not considered such a liaison.

"We writers have to be good observers," Minerva said. "Chase used to look at Jamie with so much admiration his mouth hung open. And whenever Jamie agreed with him or praised him, Chase would practically levitate."

They drank their coffees and watched Caffeine Up! fill with the late crowd. Mary Alice hated to think about Jamie humiliating a vulnerable Chase.

Mary Alice didn't want to tell Minerva her father-son theory about Jamie and Jim, and mention of the boy might arouse suspicion. Minerva Weeds, both a successful author and wife of a judge, would spot subterfuge faster than a goldfinch finds suet.

"Have you eaten at that new place on Barnett?" Mary Alice asked. She knew she sounded stupid—a stall and not a clever one. The whole meeting seemed contrived. She supposed she'd hoped Minerva would open up with juicy details providing dramatic insights. But that wasn't happening.

"Dreadful fare, worse service," Minerva said. "The waiter wanted to tell us all about his life and how he managed to eat dessert and stay slim. Christ."

"You sound like my mama."

"Why do Americans settle for such mediocre food?" Minerva swirled the liquid in her cup.

"I'm not sure."

"Flannery O'Connor said ours is an age that has domesticated despair and learned to live with it happily," Minerva said. "I think it relates to the restaurant debacle."

As Mary Alice's gaze tracked Caffeine Up's perimeter, she tried to think of how to pump Minerva. She'd decided to just tell Minerva her theory when Paige Leonard walked in. If she saw the two women in the back corner, she didn't show it. She ordered and fixated on a menu while waiting.

"You know she saw us." Minerva bristled, but then shrugged. "Bless her heart, she didn't come up easy." In the south, poverty usually was not an excuse for bad manners.

Mary Alice gave Minerva a questioning look. Investigators needed to listen, not talk. Elizabeth George's character, Detective Barbara Havers, was excellent at getting more by saying less.

"Vallie worried that girl was going to give Bobby a social disease," Minerva said.

"I heard she got around," Mary Alice said, hoping to spur Minerva to tell a story that would link Paige and Jamie.

"To say the least," Minerva said. She flared her eyes wide.

"Who'd she go with?" Mary Alice asked. "Before Bobby Leonard."

At the counter, Paige mined her studded designer bag for money to pay for the coffee.

"I don't remember names," Minerva said. "Uncharitable souls said she had what we used to call intercourse with every male in the wedding party. Mostly I remember how upset Vallie was. But then baby Jim came along and Vallie forgave Paige for her carnal excesses."

"Must have been quite a change for her, becoming a Leonard," Mary Alice said. Mrs. Dickens had given her version of the same information. Mary Alice sipped her coffee and thought about the scones in the lighted glass case.

"Andy somebody," Minerva said and clapped her hands.

"Andy?"

"Yes, him and that terrible Billy Overton. God, but all the mothers were glad when the Overtons moved to Hattiesburg."

Mary Alice leaned in and attempted to appear interested but not too interested.

"Vallie worried that when the minister asked, 'Does anyone know why this couple' *et cetera*, one or more of Paige's former beaus would pipe up." Minerva laughed.

"I thought Vallie wanted to stop the wedding." She wanted to ask if Jamie might have been such a beau.

"But not after she'd paid for it."

Mary Alice smiled. "I must have been in Dallas then." Divorce memories always accompanied the name, Dallas. A familiar tinny taste leaked into the back of her mouth. She took a drink of coffee that didn't completely wash the taste away.

"I'm sorry things didn't work out for you and Cham," Minerva said. Everyone knew about the divorce. Bitter and contested, friends had taken sides driving the animosity deep into Cana.

"Me too." She wanted to tell her that her ex was a mean son of a bitch who'd treated her miserably for years. He'd been so successful at driving her crazy that she still felt guilty about the collapse of the marriage.

Paige was leaving with her coffee.

Minerva waved broadly, but Paige scurried out into the dark without turning. "Why would she avoid us?" Minerva asked.

"Maybe she didn't see us," Mary Alice said. She was pretty sure Paige had noticed them because it'd be hard not to see Minerva posed in her draped and fringed outfit, a cross between an Indian sari and a Mexican hammock.

"Perhaps." Minerva tossed her glance to an oversized picture of a coffee cup and then zoomed back looking thoroughly put out. "Damnation, I wish I could smoke."

"You can," Mary Alice said. "Just not in here."

"That's why I like you, Mary Alice," Minerva said, gathering up the swathes of fabric and her bag. "Let's go."

They retreated to the patio where smoking was permitted, even encouraged. Minerva, likely bored with Mary Alice's sleuthing, explained the plot of her in-progress book. "They're going to have sex on the sailboat, I think. I used a boat once before but it was a trawler and that was thirteen books ago. Shouldn't be hard to imagine."

"On deck or below?" Mary Alice asked.

When Mary Alice got home a phone message from Bill Burgess waited. He asked her to call. Eleven o'clock was too late. Good news? The inscrutable lawyer was impossible to read.

Minerva's gossip had been interesting, but nothing had connected Jamie with Paige. And Minerva's speculation that Jamie and Chase had been lovers could be twisted to further heighten the perception of hostility between them. A scorned lover. She could imagine the trial as the D.A. laminated one thin damning layer of evidence on top of another. No one bit significant; all together meant ruin.

Boon waited for her on the stairs, thumping his tail impatiently.

"What? You figure out who done it?" she asked him.

Boon tossed his head and raced ahead.

Later, lying in the dark with Boon hogging the middle of the bed, she caught the dog up on what Minerva had said. Then she felt her father's presence. He seemed alternately to sit and hover on the foot of the bed. She'd agreed with her therapist that he was likely a product of her subconscious—a method to talk to herself and to recapture her Daddy's love. But at times he felt quite real.

"Don't overlook the obvious," he said.

"At the cemetery you said be careful who I talk to."

"That's important too."

She remembered years ago her father telling her that most of what she needed to know, she already knew if she'd just turn off her monkey-mind and listen. She took a breath.

Had the killer realized the letter hadn't been found by the police? What would he or she do next? Whatever Mary Alice had done, she needed to do more of it. How could she go public with her theory without hurting Jim Leonard? And how could she take Brenda Lee off the list or put her at its top?

If she scootched down in the bed, she could see the moon, a wispy cloud overtaking it. Earlier, she'd felt something was going to happen, but now she felt stuck. She remembered Norton lecturing the cast on motives. Somewhere under the same moon a murderer was acting on new motives. She'd thought the killer's motivation would be to not be discovered, but now she realized that was a negative—a not wanting. What did the killer want? Maybe something more than getting away with murder. What if she or he felt justified in killing Jamie? *I, the killer, want to revel and glory in the murder of Jamie O'Malley because he deserved to die for what he did to me.* That idea produced a different kind of killer than one skulking in the shadows avoiding detection.

Mary Alice pulled the covers over her head. I want to— She stopped. She wanted to get Chase out of trouble. Was she ready to blame someone else for the murder? What if that person were innocent? She didn't like thinking she was no different from Detective Claire Potts.

CHAPTER 20

March 17, Saturday

A THIRD HUNT FOR BRENDA LEE'S kin sent Mary Alice into areas of north Mississippi that made her feel as if she were in another country. After the second wrong turn, she vowed to buy a GPS as soon as she could save enough. Her mother's fat Christmas check had been exhausted by utilities, taxes and vet bills. She dodged another pothole and vowed to follow her New Year's resolution to live within her means. Why couldn't the small trust inherited from her father meet her needs? When her mother, who would likely live a very long time, passed away, Mary Alice would be wealthy, unless Elizabeth managed to spend it all. Elizabeth would love to give her daughter a generous allowance, but the strings Elizabeth would attach were many and coated with itchy obligation. Mary Alice imagined herself a gray, mad octogenarian roaming the halls of Linnley spending all her inherited money on QVC and a herd of dogs whose names she couldn't keep straight.

The sun through trees created a strobe effect as the car rolled over bars of shadows on the pavement. It was St. Patrick's Day, a Saturday in the sticks, and she had it all to herself. No developer would likely slash and doze this part of the county.

She skidded to a stop and backed up. A mailbox with some of the required numbers leaned precariously over the shoulder next to a steep driveway. It curved up a low hill which gave the residents ample warning of visitors. Much of deep rural Mississippi hadn't fully entered the twenty-first century. They had cell phones and jumbo TVs, but they also had poverty, little education, poor health and deep mistrust of outsiders. She counted on her Mississippi roots for entree. The country accent, quaint idioms and tortured grammar were easier for her to duplicate than to defy.

Halfway up the drive, she rolled to a stop on the edge of a mucky puddle bigger than her car. Entering it would be like playing Russian roulette. She got out, locked the car and tottered around the abyss and up the drive whose ruts and craters reminded her of history class films of the Battle of the Bulge. Through the trees, thickly protective even in March, she spotted the unmistakable metal box on wheels. She wondered why they still called them mobile homes. The ancient trailer sat on a flat patch of sandy hardscrabble that had been bulldozed into the hill. Truck tire tracks laced the dirt. She had thought trailers were sheathed in aluminum, a metal that didn't rust. But it wasn't true. Rusty lines stripped the exterior and rimmed the camper sized windows. Rust had consumed the skirting and the whole structure seemed about to exhale and collapse.

No one appeared, not even a hound. She climbed the rickety wood steps and knocked. She hoped she wouldn't have to go inside. It would smell like cabbage and despair. Her mission seemed to be to tell little lies to get a little truth that would free one person and convict another. She pulled back her shoulders in an effort to look less manipulative.

No one answered. The windows, covered on the inside with tin foil, looked like mirrors no longer capable of even distorted reflection. She walked around the back where a small clearing ended in dense hardwoods and pines. There was a back door such as all old trailers had, but it didn't look like it'd been opened in a couple of decades. She could see one window whose foil had been ripped. What would a peek hurt? She had her accent and her story ready.

She got no closer than ten feet before feeling something hard hit below her shoulder blade.

"Right there, Missy," the man's voice said.

She opened her mouth to explain she was not a trespasser, but a visitor, a friend of Brenda Lee's who wanted to talk to her sister, Wilma. He could relax and take the shotgun out of her ribs. They could joke about it; no harm done. She thought she'd pee her pants.

He poked her spine hard. "G'wine 'round front."

She stumbled toward the front door stoop, trying to recall a self-defense class of ten years ago. If someone held you at gunpoint in your car and told you to drive, you were to floor it and take your chances with the air bag. Probably the perp would run. People noticed a crashed car. But here, there were no airbags or people to hear her scream.

Outside the front door, the man called, "Open up. Spider caught a fly."

The trailer door opened releasing a pulse of fetid air. She gagged as he pushed her inside. In the middle of what had once been a living room stood a wiry man who moved like a cockroach on a shit pile. Another in the corner, smoking, turned his back as she entered. He'd looked like Elvis Presley, the young Elvis.

Mary Alice struggled to speak, knowing her silly excuses wouldn't matter. She'd run up on a drug lab, crack or meth or both. She was a liability no matter how valid her reason. "I-I-I didn't—"

"Shut up," the cockroach man said. He spoke quietly with dammed up hatred. She nearly fell to her knees and vomited.

"Put her in the back room 'til I can figure."

Her captor set his hand on her shoulder and with the gun still gouging a rib, he marched her down a narrow hall. The heat and smell made her dizzy. Mold competing with a burning chemical odor dominated the hall and stung her eyes. Terrified, she moved forward as though in a Kurosawa film, noting the quaint details of the old trailer. The paneling was real maple; the miniature light fixtures were made of copper and brass. It reminded her of a yacht.

The captor-man opened the door at the end of the hall and shoved her inside.

"Don't turn around." He handed her a worn, blue-striped pillow case. "Put it over your head," he said. Head sounded like *haid*.

She did as she was told, gulping in a final glance at the room: one tiny window covered with foil, a twin bed, a closet with a sliding door.

In one smooth move, he wrenched her arms behind her and wound tape over her wrists. She offered no resistance. He laid a strap of tape around her neck to hold the pillow case in place. She knew ankles were next. She had an image of herself sprawled helpless on the bed.

"Let me sit. I'm sick. If I vomit I'll choke," she said.

He paused. Had to think about that. Killing her was an option, but nobody had told him to.

When he turned her a half turn, she sat down fast, avoiding the shove that might put her on her back. He yanked off her running shoes and taped her ankles. He left, and she heard a lock slide in place. She wasn't going anywhere.

She couldn't stop the tears that soaked the pillow case. They'd break into her car and go through her purse finding out she was Mary Alice Tate, the one who'd been in the newspaper who'd brought down a drug trafficking operation just a few months ago. These rednecks weren't murderers, but they couldn't afford to have her report their laboratory in the woods. Didn't victims in thrillers always promise their captors they wouldn't tell? No one ever listened to them. She tried not to think what they might do to her, but fear clutched like a vise.

They're just thoughts. They're not true. Not yet at least. Think other thoughts.

She knew she had to stop her mind from spiraling down to a dungeon of insanity. She had to do something. Some action, even simple physical movement.

With effort, she scissor kicked and loosened the tape on her ankles enough to permit her to stand. Slowly, she leaned forward off the bed, stood and found she could walk like a Chinese lady with bound feet. She felt her panic lessen. She took three deep breaths. On the last one, she pulled the tear-stained pillow case into her mouth and chewed, biting the threads that tasted like dead skin. The worn out fibers finally gave way, creating a small hole through which she could see the floor. She could hear talk, some shouting in the living room.

She inched to the closet. Maybe guns were stored in it. Maybe sharp things that could cut duct tape. Turning her back to the sliding door, she worked it open and began a slow search, seeing only what the half-inch opening in the pillow case afforded.

"How much longer 'til it's cooked?" the cockroach-man asked.

"'Bout three hours."

The wooden closet conducted sound from the trailer like a speaker. She froze.

"She don't look like DEA," the captor–man said.

"Shit-for-brains, that's the whole idea. They don't look like DEA."

She thought the Elvis-man who'd been smoking said that. He had been the only other person in the room.

"Maybe she's that cop Kenny told me about," Cockroach-Man said. "Bitch from Jackson."

"Plates are Cotashona," Captor-Man said.

"It don't matter. She seen. She knows," Elvis-Man said.

Mary Alice wanted to crawl out and promise that she'd never tell. They could hold her until whatever was cooked. She'd be no trouble. She really hadn't seen much. She was starting to shake.

"I'll call Harlan," Cockroach-Man said. "He'll take care of it."

"That'll cost," Captor-Man said.

"You're the dumb fuck what drug her in here," Elvis-Man said. "Mr. Viet-fucking-Nam Special Forces. She might'a just gone on."

Mary Alice thought it was good that they weren't in agreement although all her knowledge of similar circumstances came from movies. But then she thought of Capote's *In Cold Blood*. Disagreement between the two convicts had sparked the murder of the whole family.

"I'm calling Harlan," Cockroach-Man said.

She knew she had to think fast if she didn't want to be delivered into the hands of Harlan, the man who took care of things. It was clear that to them the situation was serious. Getting busted for cooking drugs meant years and years in the pen. There was no way they'd just let her go even if they wanted to. They couldn't risk it. And if they were going to kill her, wouldn't it occur to at least one of them to rape her first? Why waste the opportunity?

She slid down the wall of the closet to the floor. Minutes passed. There were no more voices. She chewed the pillow slip as if she could escape through a large enough hole. Her only hope was that killing her was more trouble than it was worth. Murder brought on risks too.

She remembered someone else coolly telling her why she had to die. She knew secrets. She had to die, and she'd brought it on herself. Her relentless snooping on behalf of that crack-head whore, Sheree Delio.

She heard a door open and voices. A new voice. Harlan's?

"You kidnapped a girl?" it said.

"Rayburn done it. Mother-fuck."

That was Cockroach's voice.

"Where is she?"

"In yonder," Elvis-Man said.

"She the Avon Lady?" the new voice said.

"Funny," Elvis-Man said.

"Don't matter now," Captor-Man said.

"That her car out there?"

"Harlan'll take it too. He said so," Cockroach-Man said.

Mary Alice's fog of terror shifted. The new voice didn't belong to Harlan. She heard steps in the hall and felt the rush of air as the door opened.

"What's she doin' in the closet?" the new voice asked.

She felt the pillow case being jerked from her head. The tape caught and tore her hair, but she didn't scream. Her hands were almost numb. She concentrated on the pins and needles sensation to keep from losing it completely.

"Shit," the new man said. "Mary Lyle? 'at you?"

She worked her mouth to say *Marshall*, but nothing came out.

The man looking down at her was Marshall-the-meth-man, whom Sheree Delio had dug up as a street contact for Mary Alice. He'd met her at a Laundromat and taught her all he knew about cooking meth and the nuances of illegal drug sales and purchases in north Mississippi. He'd been charming in a speedy sort of way. She'd helped him with his wash. Later, he'd called and asked her if she'd like to drive over to the Delta with him to Morgan Freeman's joint. He'd gotten her name wrong.

"Mary Lyle?" he repeated.

The other three had crowded in behind him filling the elevator-sized room.

"Y'all done got Mary Lyle," Marshall announced as if they had captured his grandmother. "Get her up outta there," he said taking the lead to lift her without breaking her arms. "You dumb asses."

"You know her?" the captor-man said. He sounded simultaneously skeptical and relieved.

"Hell yes. What y'all gone and done?" Marshall asked, pulling the tape from her hands. No one stopped him. "You remember Sheree? Friend of hers. I sold her couple of rocks. She's okay."

The Elvis-man slipped out of the room. She wondered if they'd force her to do meth. She'd heard once was all it took to become addicted. First divorce and then Betty Ford. She'd have to leave town.

"Hi Marshall," she managed to say. Something in his look told her to say as little as possible and to play along. She wasn't out of the woods until she was out of the woods.

"Were you looking for me?" he asked.

She nodded.

"Well, you done found me, girl." He led her to the bed where she sat as he stripped the tape from her ankles. "Sorry," he said. Red marks ringed her legs.

"You vouch for her?" the captor-man asked Marshall.

"Goddamn yes. Mary Lyle's a friend. I know her," Marshall said.

The captor-man touched Marshall's shoulder. "If they's trouble, we'll get you before they get us. You know that."

"Mary Lyle ain't going to say nothing," he pulled her to her feet and handed her her shoes which she clutched to her chest.

She could tell she'd wet her pants and was glad for the black jeans to hide the spot and for the stench of the place that would cover a rotting hog.

"Better call Harlan back," Cockroach-Man said and left.

Mary Alice's body sagged against Marshall. She wasn't going to be raped, strangled and dumped in the river by someone named Harlan.

"Better move," Marshall whispered in her ear.

As he pushed her down the narrow hall and out the front door, she sensed the men's nervousness at letting her go. But keeping her was more of a problem.

She didn't remember stumbling barefoot down the drive to her car or how she got around the huge puddle. She didn't recall fastening her seatbelt or turning the key. Maybe Marshall had helped her. But she did remember the look on Marshall's face when he told her not to say anything. He'd saved her life; she had to do the same for him.

She drove fast down the middle of the road. Everything hurt from adrenaline burn. The last time she'd hurt so much, she'd awoken in the Cana hospital aided by a fleet of nurses and doctors. She could barely drive.

She found a half bottle of water and sipped it.

I'm alive.

It was over. No one followed her, and Cana was only a few more miles. She let herself cry. She didn't think she'd ever feel quite the same about St. Patrick's Day again.

CHAPTER 21

March 17, Saturday PM and March 18, Sunday

HOURS AFTER SHE WAS SAFELY home, Mary Alice still felt like her skin was pulled too tight. She spilled Boon's food on the floor, knocked over a lamp and had trouble turning on the water in the shower. Sobs pulsed from deep inside. The palsy of fear controlled her even after the hot water ran tepid, and she emerged from the shower minus at least one layer of epidermis. She believed she'd washed away the captor-man's touch, but the duct tape burns reminded her that some marks were slower to heal.

Dressed in jeans and one of her Daddy's flannel shirts, she placed everything she'd worn in a black plastic bag, tied off the top and put it in the garbage can. She didn't want Goodwill to have to deal with the bad juju.

At eight she started cleaning the house and by eleven that night had the entire contents of the kitchen cabinets spread on every available horizontal surface. She wiped each item as though removing fingerprints and then Windexed the shelves. At two in the morning, with all lights ablaze and her dog by her side, she fell asleep on one of the living room sofas. Over and over again, she dreamed of the men in the trailer. Twice she awoke in a panic; the second time the sofa cushion was damp with her tears. How did women survive worse violation?

Bright sun woke her at nine. She felt hung over but glad to see a new day. It easily could have been otherwise. As she wandered into the kitchen to feed Boon and make coffee, she noticed the message light on the phone blinking. Tom Jaworski was the only one she wanted to talk to. But what could she say? *Leave your conniving wife and come back and comfort me.* No. She'd survived. She'd be more careful. However, she fully understood that any trouble at ye-olde-dope-trailer would come back not only to Marshall but also to her. They'd find her easily enough. Telling Jaworski about her ordeal was out. He was a cop with cop responsibilities. But what if the crystal meth crew got busted without any help from her? How could they know she hadn't tipped off the law? They couldn't.

What have I gotten myself into?

Goldilocks came to mind, and Mary Alice understood a little about what had made the naive girl take a nap in baby bear's bed. But Goldie had escaped.

She moved to the living room with coffee and a thousand-calorie, buttered Honey Bun. The phone rang.

She'd almost stopped shaking, but the ring set her off again. The boogie man calleth. "Hello."

"What's the matter with you?" her mother asked.

"Nothing Mama." She cleared her throat and laid on a perky Disney tone.

"You haven't forgotten Mrs. Dickens, have you?" Elizabeth Tate asked.

She had.

"No, Mama, you said two, right?" Mary Alice said. "I'm fixing to go in a few minutes." She started up the stairs, unbuttoning as she went.

"You didn't call me back last night. Where were you?"

"Stuff for the play—props," she said.

"You are aware the pilgrimage opens in twelve days?" She sounded as if the opening compared with the Second Coming.

"March 31st, right?" March had faded so quickly. She'd had the sense that the pilgrimage opened some time in the distant future and that the play opened some time well after that. Chase's trial date was the only anchor in time she had paid attention to, and because it hadn't been set, she felt trapped in a limbo, a race without destination.

"Is that dreadful band all set to appear?" Elizabeth asked.

"All set."

"Vallie called at seven this morning fit to be tied," Elizabeth said. "It seems the Carter girl is pregnant."

"Who?"

"The fat one," Elizabeth said. "Hell's bells, the costume won't fit anyone else, and there's no time now—"

"She can't be that pregnant," Mary Alice said.

"You are or you aren't pregnant, my dear. There are no degrees."

Mary Alice couldn't tell if her mother was being witty or bitchy. Mary Alice knew all about being and not being pregnant. "She's showing?"

"No, but we can't have a knocked up teenager describing the art work in the Madonna bedroom at Thorpe House."

"Put her in the dining room." Mary Alice pictured the overweight Carter girl who had likely been used by some boy who now wouldn't speak to her. "I take it nuptials are not in the picture?"

"Who knows," Elizabeth said. "The dummy told her girlfriend who blabbed it all over school so now everyone knows. But that's not what's important."

"What is?" It felt reassuring, even comforting to gab about others' misfortunes and short comings. So much better than a dark ride in the trunk of a car.

"Vallie, the girl's replacement and upholding the standards of the Cana Pilgrimage."

"Ah," she hummed in agreement. The pregnant Carter girl was now only *the girl,* and she was soon to be cast into oblivion.

"And Paige," Elizabeth said. "Did I tell you Paige has gone and made a mess of the party favors?"

"How so?" Mention of Paige put her on alpha alert.

"The idiot penny pinched to impress Vallie with her business acumen. The crap UPS delivered wouldn't be acceptable at a VFW barbeque."

"With all her money—" Mary Alice wondered what it was with rich women who wanted to go cheap. Elizabeth, who could certainly afford it, refused to absorb Linnley's pilgrimage expenses.

"Vallie's furious. They're not even speaking."

"Who's getting the favors? The replacements?" Mary Alice asked.

"Nobody. Paige spent most of the money on the junk and can't get a refund."

"You want me to help?" She tried to imagine what Paige had selected. Thai elephant incense burners, coupons for carpet cleaning?

"You want to?" Elizabeth switched from irritated to incredulous to delighted in less than two seconds.

"I have a couple of ideas," Mary Alice said.

"Darlin', that would be wonderful," Elizabeth said, sounding jubilant as if her daughter had just been named Junior Auxiliary volunteer of the year. "How much will you need?"

"Let me make some calls first," Mary Alice said. "I'll let you know."

Elizabeth oozed gratitude. This girl was the daughter she'd always wanted.

"I better get going, Mama."

"I pray to the Lord that Vallie hasn't made a mistake using Mrs. Dickens," Elizabeth said. "Vallie said she acted a little funny last time."

Mary Alice remembered the former cook in her navy blue suit ordering the staff around at Golden Meadows Manor. "She seemed okay the last time I saw her." In truth, Mary Alice had thought there was something a little off with the old lady. In fact, Mary Alice counted on Mrs. Dickens to be a little off.

"You let me know," Elizabeth said.

After the phone conversation ended, Mary Alice quickly changed into gray slacks and a light, white fleece jacket. There was no time to launch the party favor plan which she hoped would give her a direct way to check the alibi and children of Stacy McMahan. She knew where she'd get absolutely free some cool stuff to give away. Favors were easy if you knew who to ask, and Mary Alice knew everybody. Her generations-deep network of friends and relatives was her chief asset as a sleuth. She forgot that sometimes.

As she drove just over the speed limit to pick up Mrs. Dickens, it occurred to Mary Alice that Paige Leonard wasn't going to like being shown up in the party favor department. She suspected that somehow Paige's failure and her own success would hearken back to family roots. Cana's upper crust liked to believe that it instinctively and naturally knew how to maneuver in tricky social situations. It was an inborn skill not shared with lowborn climbers, who, try as they might, usually would fail. But what if Mary Alice managed to get the favors and let Paige take the credit? A friendly Paige might be useful with an unfriendly Vallie.

She drove the back roads, meandering through breathtaking green. In the south, spring trumped the other seasons. She let her thoughts drift among the hills, but one thought kept returning. The pregnant Carter girl had blabbed her secret to a friend. Teenaged girls did that sort of thing. Had Brenda Lee confided her secret to her friend, Annette? Chase or Norton would know Annette's last name. The girl came to all the rehearsals.

As she approached Golden Meadows, Mary Alice formulated a subterfuge to question Annette. She didn't like manipulating the girl. It felt creepy to flatter the callow teen, but it felt worse to imagine Chase in jail. Much worse.

Mary Alice parked and went inside to get Mrs. Dickens, who wasn't waiting in the lobby this time. The same staff member as before, Chandra, sat at the desk. This time she was sucking hard on a Tootsie Roll Pop. She looked up, her good left eye recognizing Mary Alice.

"Mrs. Dickens is in her apartment, hon, but I don't think she's gonna be able to go out today," she said. Her tongue was candy purple.

"Is she okay?" Mary Alice asked.

Chandra slipped her hand inside the neck of her blouse and tugged over her bra strap. "She had her a spell early this morning—" She stopped, possibly remembering rules about patient confidentiality. The way she said, spell, conveyed fit or tantrum, not seizure.

Mary Alice vocalized reassuring sounds. She understood cranky old folks.

Chandra looked relieved to find a sympathetic ear. "Something set her off and—She's got her a potty mouth." Chandra's eyebrows arched.

But spell or not, Mary Alice needed to see Mrs. Dickens. Chase was still about to go to jail for murder, and there were suspects the police weren't even looking at. The letter she'd found indicated to her that the real killer was anxious. Mary Alice bet the old lady knew something useful. She'd been around the Leonard home for years, and Paige had more in common with Mrs. Dickens than she did with any of the Leonards. It was a matter of asking the right questions.

"She's in one-eleven," Chandra said. "Through the double doors and to the left.

"Thanks."

"You gotta sign in," Chandra said, pointing to a book on the desk.

Mary Alice wrote her name and March 18, 2:10 PM

The faux Victorian luxury of the lobby vanished two steps beyond the double doors. Here the carpet was plain and stained. The hand rails affixed to the walls were slightly askew. The predictable nursing home odor sneaked between layers of cheap lavender deodorizer and pine disinfectant.

Outside number one eleven Mary Alice heard a woman's voice.

"You son of a bitch."

Mary Alice knocked. She imagined beefy orderlies forcing Mrs. Dickens into a wheelchair. Elder-abuse was commonplace. Some studies showed that scrappy oldsters with some fight in them were twice as likely to suffer attacks.

"Help," the old woman's voice screamed.

Shoulders square, Mary Alice pushed open the door and strode into the room to find Mrs. Dickens confronting TV ASPCA agents, who appeared to be rounding up a passel of yapping beagles.

"Jesus Christ. Look at that. They're starving," Mrs. Dickens shouted and jerked loose a snap. The pink print house dress, worn inside out, had nearly succumbed to the heavy duty washers of Golden Meadows Manor.

The rescued beagles were being loaded into vans. Mary Alice wasn't sure whose side Mrs. Dickens was on. Muttering, Mrs.

Dickens leaned forward toward the television. When the vans drove away she turned to Mary Alice.

"Paige? Paige. Honey, why didn't you tell me you was coming?" she asked.

Mary Alice smiled in reply. Later, she'd remember this moment when she'd chosen to impersonate Paige Leonard. The two didn't look much alike, but as Chase had said, you see what you want to see.

Mrs. Dickens fingered glasses that hung on a metal chain around her neck.

"Let's set on the couch," she said. Mrs. Dickens rose and padded to the sofa. Her slippers looked like mummy wrappings.

"That'd be nice," Mary Alice said. She felt she was having a version of the actor's nightmare. The curtain had gone up, but she didn't know her lines and worse, she wasn't even sure what play she was in.

"Turn down the TV. Not off, just down. Set over here by me." She slapped the sofa.

Mary Alice punched the volume button on the TV. A commercial for an erectile dysfunction drug was barely audible. A twinkle-eyed actor-doctor described its effectiveness as a glowing almost middle-aged couple beamed in agreement.

"What'd you bring me?" Mrs. Dickens squawked a laugh.

Mary Alice laughed too, but she wasn't sure what was funny.

Mrs. Dickens' eyes tracked the circling fan blades overhead. "I put the Estee Lauder bath gel you brought yesterday in yonder." Using the hem of her housecoat, she swiped the lenses of her glasses. "They'll steal it if they can."

Mary Alice realized her opportunity to find out about Paige while playing Paige could be cut short at any second. Mrs. Dickens' brain might reshuffle itself or someone could come in and identify Mary Alice. "They stole other things," she said.

"Them cleaning gals got the chocolate you brought," Mrs. Dickens said. "Said they thought I didn't want it. With it setting right out." She pointed.

Mary Alice looked at the bureau topped with what appeared to be gifts: a basket of fancy jams, a teddy bear, a fuzzy throw and some chocolate swathed in thick cellophane that hadn't been opened. She wondered if this were the stolen chocolate.

Mrs. Dickens rambled on about her ill treatment at the facility.

At the pilgrimage lunch meeting Paige Leonard hadn't wanted to hire the old woman to cook for the wrap party. Paige said she hadn't seen the former cook but understood she had dementia or some such. Clearly Mrs. Dickens regarded Paige as a frequent visitor who usually brought goodies. Why would the Paige lie about seeing the old lady?

"I'll bring you some more chocolate next time," Mary Alice said. "Need anything else?"

Mrs. Dickens said no, but then said she needed a can of anti-static cling spray and a card of brown bobby pins. She patted her armadillo gray hair-do.

"Now don't you worry," Mrs. Dickens said. "I ain't forgot what we talked about yesterday." She clapped the glasses back on and peered at Mary Alice through the smears.

"Good," Mary Alice said, feeling her way through the forest of manipulation and deceit. She felt like Dorothy miles short of Oz. She was lost and had no idea of how to ask Mrs. Dickens if Jamie O'Malley had fathered Paige Leonard's son. To Mrs. Dickens, Mary Alice was Paige.

Mrs. Dickens upped the volume on the TV which now advertised yogurt. "Ain't nobody's business what you two done. Let sleeping dogs lie, I say."

"Not everybody feels like that," Mary Alice said. Apparently, Paige had told Mrs. Dickens something and sworn her to secrecy. Were Paige and Jamie the two of "you two?"

"Too bad about that fella getting shot," Mrs. Dickens said. "Stirred everything up."

"That's for sure," Mary Alice said. No, it didn't seem like Jaime was one of the two. Calling Jamie, "that fella" distinguished him from the person alluded to in "nobody's business what you two done." She had no idea how to find out what she wanted to know.

It was even possible that Mrs. Dickens was aware of Mary Alice Tate's sleuthing—stirring things up. And then there was the niggling thought that maybe Mrs. Dickens wasn't all there and nothing she said was true.

Mary Alice knew from checking on Jim's birthday that Paige had been pregnant with him in 1990. That year Mary Alice had been getting ready to go to Ole Miss. Could Paige Thompson have gotten herself married to a rich man and pregnant by someone else? If it wasn't Jamie O'Malley, who was it and why was Paige telling Mrs. Dickens to keep it secret?

"I'll never tell nothing about any of this. I swear," Mrs. Dickens said. "Skin me like a catfish, boil me in the crab pot, but I won't tell. He's suffered enough."

He? Mary Alice couldn't recall Jamie suffering. Chase had suffered, but Jamie had enjoyed remarkable luck and good fortune. But Mrs. Dickens seemed to have regressed into the past when the man in question was still young. Weren't parents chiefly responsible for suffering in the young? She took a leap.

"His pa." Mary Alice shook her head and looked at the floor.

"May that evil son of a bitch rot in hell." Mrs. Dickens backed down the TV volume. Her face darkened and contracted until her nose nearly met her chin.

With two words, *his pa*, Mary Alice had opened a floodgate.

"He was just too young to save his sister from that bastard," Mrs. Dickens said. "He tried once and the old man beat the living tar out of him and still got onto the girl."

"He was way too little," Mary Alice said venturing closer to the quicksand.

"When she died, part of him died," Mrs. Dickens said.

Mary Alice nodded. But simultaneously another part of her brain lit up in recognition. She'd heard this story before. Where?

"He's the one got her the money for the abortion," Mrs. Dickens whispered.

Mary Alice must have looked shocked because Mrs. Dickens jumped in to explain.

"It's what she wanted—didn't want to have her own daddy's baby."

"No girl would," Mary Alice said. She felt like Alice in Wonderland. Incest and abortion could have lurked in Jamie O'Malley's past, but from what she knew Jamie didn't seem like the tortured soul Mrs. Dickens was describing. But Jamie did have a sister. She couldn't remember how she knew that. Nor could she remember why the incest-abortion-dead-sister scenario sounded so familiar.

"He told you everything?" Mary Alice couldn't figure out how to get Mrs. Dickens to say his name.

"I knowed him since before his momma died," she said as if the fact explained everything. "I got to get the Ford in for a valve job. You tell your Papa to call me. I need them to pick it up."

Mary Alice remembered that Paige Thompson's father had run the garage at the Ford dealership. She also remembered he drank a lot and climbed on and off the wagon like a seasonal picker.

"I will." Mary Alice promised. Mrs. Dickens seemed to have reverted to an even earlier time.

Mrs. Dickens advanced the channels on the remote without looking at the set. "My program's coming on in a minute. Want to watch?"

"No, ma'am, but thanks. I better get back." It was certain that Mrs. Dickens wouldn't be coming along and that any minute she might ask "who the hell are you?"

But the program didn't come on. Instead a local news report topped the hour. Someone had escaped from Parchman Prison Farm and was armed and dangerous. Mary Alice glanced at the set to see Elvis-Man from yesterday frozen on the screen. Even in the photo he seemed to be looking right at her with his Elvis sneer and scary-sexy look. She cried out.

"Parchman's a horrible place," Mrs. Dickens said, patting her shoulder. "Cousin Maynard went there for a time. Made him work the farm in the sun without a hat. That's how he got the skin cancer, you know."

Mary Alice felt too rattled to talk. Everybody knew about Parchman. Mississippi's John Grisham had described it well in *The Partner*. Chase could end up in Parchman.

Mrs. Dickens' program began. They stood and hugged, the music on the television obscuring most of their good-byes.

"You come again soon, you hear?" She squeezed Mary Alice's arm. "That a different perfume?"

"I'll come soon," Mary Alice said without answering about the perfume. She'd tell everyone that Mrs. Dickens had a spell and would come another day. It was true.

The old woman winked and mimed zipping her lips, locking and throwing away the key. Then she turned to the television as if she were alone.

Mary Alice let herself out. In the hallway she recognized Miss Vivian Harris who had taught her piano. Miss Harris didn't recognize her or probably anyone. Again in the well-appointed lobby, Mary Alice paused at the desk. No one was around. She heard a woman giggle.

In the glass foyer Chandra flirted with a UPS delivery guy whose gaze never veered from Chandra's bosom.

Mary Alice looked at the sign-in book and flipped back a page. Paige Leonard had visited yesterday afternoon. While Mary Alice had been duct taped in a meth-lab trailer scared out of her wits, Paige Leonard was making sure her tracks were covered. But where did those tracks lead?

On the drive back to Cana, she tried to imagine if anything Mrs. Dickens had said made Jim Leonard the child of Paige and Jamie. She heard, "what you two done." The possibility existed that Mrs. Dickens was deluded or was lying. She liked attention just as she liked to try to run Golden Meadows. By the time Mary Alice passed the larger Jesus Saves sign, a first class headache pulsed.

But if Mrs. Dickens wasn't dissembling, the woman believed she had been asked to keep quiet about Paige and someone, who Mary Alice considered was Paige's lover. "Nobody's business what you two done." And who was the he that had "suffered enough?" She wanted to pull over and write down everything the woman had said.

There was a lot of new information, but would it help Chase? Paige protecting a past indiscretion didn't mean she had anything to do with Jamie's murder. And if Jamie wasn't Jim's father, didn't that shift the search back to Brenda Lee Chinault? Mary Alice shivered at the thought of tracking her through Cotashona County. She could still see Elvis-Man leering at her from Mrs. Dickens' TV.

New-born springtime didn't look so tender and sweet on the drive home.

In the office she sat at her desk covered by index cards. They looked like rows of clean rectangular windows. They also resembled grave stones.

"Maybe Bill Burgess could hire a PI to find Brenda Lee," she said to Boon who rested under the desk. She looked at the cards again.

It was possible that the meth trailer had belonged to Brenda Lee's older sister or at least to some Chinault. Even excluding the escaped felon, Elvis-Man, the men there were a rough bunch who had been ready to turn her over to a man who likely would have killed her. They were murderers if you looked at it that way. What if, on Brenda Lee's behalf, one or more decided to scare Jamie into doing right by their cousin? But what if Jamie didn't scare easily and things got out of hand?

Her head pounded. She phoned Vallie Leonard to report that Mrs. Dickens didn't feel well enough to come to Cana. She strained to hear anything in the woman's voice that could indicate—what? Nervousness, guilt? Paige was shielded by her alibi, but not Vallie. But if Vallie Leonard had shot Jamie O'Malley to protect the secret of her only grandson's birth, she wasn't telling.

Mary Alice lay down on the worn leather sofa and visualized her headache as a furious handball game that slowed as the players tired. *Bop, bop, bop.*

CHAPTER 22

March 19, Monday

ABOUT FOUR THE NEXT MORNING, Mary Alice snapped awake. She'd been dreaming she was in line at a Quick Mart. The man in front of her was telling the cashier about how he wouldn't miss a Neil Young concert anywhere in the U.S. When she tried to interrupt to pay for a case of caramel corn, he started reciting Neil Young lyrics: *Old man take a look at my life, Cinnamon girl, Are you ready for the country?*

But when Mary Alice sat up on the sofa, she only had one thing in mind. She knew where she'd heard Mrs. Dickens' incest-abortion-death story. Snapping on lights, she went in the office and yanked open drawers until she found the file containing Jamie's plays.

She reread *Absolution.* Just as the old woman had said, a boy named Drew had been unable to stop his father's sexual advances on the boy's little sister. The girl got pregnant and asked her brother for money for an abortion. He stole to get the money, but the abortion killed the girl. The boy tried to kill his father but failed. He lied about his age, joined the army and ran away from his past. However, just as Tennessee Williams never let his character Tom Wingfield off the hook for his sister, Laura, Jamie had crafted a tortured future for his character, Drew.

The play harkened to Eugene O'Neill's style, as if the writer had just finished reading *Mourning Becomes Electra*. However, it lacked the tragic proportions of the domestic dramas of O'Neill, Williams or even Arthur Miller. Sentimental, predictable and maudlin described it well. Unpolished as it was, Mary Alice doubted if the play had ever been produced. But it smacked of truth. Jamie had co-opted a local Cana story. If Jamie knew it and Mrs. Dickens knew it, others would too. Mary Alice thought of her mother, Mattie Catherine, and Chase. Dozens more might remember if the right questions were posed.

But how was Paige Leonard connected, and of course, who was the Drew character? The answer to the second question might answer the first. While it was clear to Mary Alice that Jamie was Jeb, the main character of *Redemption*, it didn't appear that he was Drew.

All she had were bits of information, but they had a congruency. The key seemed to lie in *Absolution's* plot. Mrs. Dickens, who wouldn't know about Jamie's play, knew the real story on which Jamie's play was based. Thinking Mary Alice was Paige, the old woman had talked about the shameful family drama that apparently Paige was part of. Jamie, Paige and the Drew-person were linked somehow.

Mary Alice stripped off yesterday's clothes she'd slept in, showered, brushed her teeth and fed Boon. The whole time she ran the questions. Paige and whoever Drew was had done something that had to be kept secret. But when? Two days ago Paige evidently had reminded Mrs. Dickens to keep her mouth shut, but the deed seemed to have occurred long ago. Maybe when Mrs. Dickens worked for the Leonard family.

Mary Alice needed someone to play *what if* with. Elizabeth Tate knew decades of old dirt, but Mary Alice would have to tell her mother more than she wanted. In any case, Elizabeth wouldn't be in gossip mode until at least ten. It was barely eight. She called Chase, who was awake because he hadn't been asleep.

"Come over," he said. "My phone's probably tapped."

"I'll be there in fifteen minutes."

On the drive over, Mary Alice tumbled the parts of the story again. It didn't smell like a red herring, nor did it link with Jamie's murder.

At Chase's sunlit breakfast table, they read *Absolution* aloud.

"It's the worst soap opera crap I ever read." Chase whacked the pages on the table beside his uneaten breakfast.

Mary Alice told him what had happened with Mrs. Dickens. "She told me the story. Incest, abortion, sister's death, all of it. She's never read Jamie's play. It's the same."

"More than that, it's true," Chase said

"You know this story?"

"Not personally, but—" He squinched his eyes tight. "What were their names? The old man. Heavens, it has to be in the newspaper. The girl died." He ran his fingers over the deep crease in his napkin.

Mary Alice felt a tiny flutter of hope. Through blind luck Mrs. Dickens had confused her with Paige. Her gut told her this clue mattered.

Chase sighed. "Jamie never made up a story if he could borrow one."

He picked up a triangle of buttered toast and chomped it down in two bites.

Mary Alice took this action as a good sign.

"If they'd been somebodies, instead of nobodies, there would have been a big scandal, but only the dead girl knew the abortionist, and the boy couldn't prove squat. It was just ugly and sad. The boy left town, and the gossip faded. Damn, what was their name?" Chase dramatically pressed his fingertips to his temples and closed his eyes.

"I can find the newspaper story on the computer," Mary Alice said.

"I'll think of it in a minute," he said. "Let's call him Drew for now." He licked butter from his thumb.

While she hoped the story would help Chase, Mary Alice felt slightly sick at the facts of the story—incest, abortion, attempted patricide—and that Jamie copied it so closely with no thought of the pain the play could cause the family. If the boy who'd tried to save his sister was still around, what would he feel? She imagined seeing a play in which her parents' tragic soap opera and her own divorce were featured. While her story paled in comparison, if she were this boy, she thought she'd want to run away to one of the small towns in Paraguay where international criminals hid out.

Chase, talking around a second piece of toast said, "We have to get into the heads of the characters." He became a director, employing the tools of his craft. "We have Drew and Paige." He wiped his mouth and flourished the napkin.

"And Jamie," Mary Alice added. She watched Chase stab a bite of cantaloupe. He'd lost over ten pounds since his arrest.

"And Mrs. Dickens. She may be a player too," he said.

Mary Alice paused, letting Chase set up the scene.

"So back in the day," he said, "Paige and this Drew did some secret something or other that now, because Jamie's murder stirred things up, must be kept secret."

"Or, or whatever they did caused Jamie's murder," she said.

"There will be a big price to pay if the secret is exposed?" he said.

"Yes. But what did they do?"

"Or see?" He forked another bite of melon.

"See somebody else do," she said.

"Hold on," Chase said. "Drew, Paige and Mrs. Dickens are from the same, shall we say, social class."

"Wrong side of the tracks," Mary Alice said. "And she said she knew Drew since before his mama died."

"Could any of the three be blood kin?" he asked.

"That's the kind of stuff I can find out."

"Mrs. D. works for the Leonards and Paige marries into their dynasty. There's bond between the two women."

"Both feel inferior," she said.

"Put down," he said. "Believe me, Vallie Leonard knows how to put underlings in their places." Chase's phone rang, but he waved at it, ignoring it.

"And both women use the Leonards to move up in the world. They help each other," Mary Alice said.

"Yes, likely so," he said.

"Ever been any gossip about Paige and Bobby?" she asked.

"He hunts. She travels. Not close but no scandal. The Leonards don't do scandal." Chase rose from the table. "I'm going to whip up a little herb cheese omelet. Want some?" He approached his six-burner Viking.

She didn't, but she wanted him to eat. "Yes." She watched Chase don his white chef's apron with the New Orleans-Central Grocery logo.

"Back to Drew." He cracked half a dozen eggs with one hand. "He's a teenager, mother dead or gone and his father gets his beloved little sister pregnant. The boy is powerless. He can't talk to anybody. It's too shameful—"

"He has no money—"

"So his motivation is to rescue the sister." He whisked the eggs in a stainless steel bowl.

"Because?"

"It's obvious. He loves the sister and hates the father."

"And he wants to cover up the family mess. Doesn't want people to know, especially about the incest."

"He gets the money for an abortion. They're still illegal. In Jamie's play he stole the money and got in trouble." Chase poured the eggs into the waiting pan and adjusted the flame.

"But the abortion kills the sister. End of rescue, beginning of guilt."

"So the motivation shifts. He wants revenge." Chase skillfully lifted the edges of the omelet, allowing the runny egg mixture to slide under.

"He wants to kill the father to avenge his baby sister's death."

"He's still a powerless, penniless boy. How can he get revenge?"

"In the play, he fights with the old man, loses and runs away to the army to forever carry the guilt for his failure."

"And in life," Mary Alice asked. "What's he do?"

"Joined the army and came home after his stint."

"How do you know?"

"I'm guessing, but you can find out once you know his name." Chase added the cream cheese and herbs. "Grab us some plates. Not the Haviland."

"How you think Paige figures in?" Mary Alice set two red Fiesta Ware plates on the warming shelf above the stove.

"They were childhood friends. Maybe. She tried to help him either with the money for the sister or to kill the old man."

"And Mrs. Dickens, like all maids and cooks, knew everything. Maybe Paige confided in her," Mary Alice said. "She knows a lot more. I can tell."

She wasn't an old woman then. Maybe she helped." He turned off the flame and covered the omelet.

"Maybe Mrs. Dickens knew the name of an abortionist." Mary Alice winced at the idea of a young girl, pregnant with her own father's baby, subjecting herself to an amateur abortion.

"Or was the abortionist."

"Lord."

"How did she act with you yesterday when she thought you were Paige?" Chase asked. "Her attitude. What was the feel?"

"Chummy, loyal, supportive. She didn't think whatever I'd done was wrong."

"Think of her tone. Not what she said, but how she said it."

"Conspiratorial. She winked at me. The secret's dirty." She felt again the sensation she'd had when Mrs. Dickens promised to keep quiet. "The secret holds forgiveness and says, 'I know what you did, but women like us have to survive.'"

"And stick together."

"Yes."

"Sex not murder."

She shrugged. "Drew and Paige?"

"The only other character is Jamie."

"Jim Leonard resembles Jamie."

"Let's say Jamie and Paige had a love child, Jim."

"How does Drew fit in?"

"Patience, *mon aimee*. At the same time she's married Bobby Leonard. That's one secret Mrs. D. could know."

"But Drew—"

"We don't know his part yet. But the play's called *Absolution* which means forgiveness or even release. To get forgiveness Drew helps Paige whereas he failed to help his sister." He halved the omelet and slid it onto the plates.

"So no abortion this time. A marriage and cover-up," she said. "Well, it's a stretch."

"It's all a stretch. We're improvising. But if my little sister's death lay on my conscience, my motivation, after failing at revenge, would be to find forgiveness, absolution."

She carried the omelets to the table.

"Wells." Chase smacked the spatula in the pan.

"What?

"Wells. The name. Randy Wells. You said well and—"

"I know him." She could clearly picture Randy Wells from high school. Several grades ahead, he'd been one of the bad boys whose sexy good looks made up for his trailer trash pedigree.

"You know him?" Chase tucked into the omelet.

"Sure. I saw him a couple of weeks ago. He was with Stony Colley at the BP."

"Then Randy Wells must be our Drew, *n'est pas?*"

Chase's phone rang again and with a pained expression, he rose to answer it. "Excuse me. Could be my esteemed attorney."

Mary Alice picked up the heavy sterling fork and took a bite of the omelet whose texture, temperature and taste were perfect. She heard Chase on the phone in the next room. He mostly listened. It had to be Burgess. Who else had Chase's number? When he returned all the vigor brought by the breakfast and their sleuthing had washed out.

"That was Bill Burgess on the phone."

"What'd he say?"

"The judge set a trial date this morning." He reached for the back of a chair to steady himself. "Discovery, motions, stuff. Has a schedule. Trial in six months."

Mary Alice dropped a cup on the slate floor.

"He'll argue for more time." He gripped the chair. "He said."

They both stared at the porcelain shards as if they could read them and divine the future.

"What else?" She tried not to sound frantic. A trial date made it real. By Thanksgiving Chase could be in Parchman.

"He doesn't think it looks good for me. He didn't say so directly but—nothing has popped up, dead-ends, you know. Mentioned changing my plea. Wants me to stop by his office later."

The headache that had retreated twelve hours ago now returned as if a toggle switch had been flipped. Her temples pulsed hot. She held her breath waiting for the splitting throb. Chase guilty. Chase incarcerated. Little time and less hope.

Without another word, together they picked up the pieces of the shattered cup.

CHAPTER 23

March 21, Wednesday

YEARS AGO, A DOCTOR HAD told Mary Alice that her headaches weren't technically migraines and that the best thing to do was to lie down in a dark room until the pain eased. Her physician ex-husband had at first loaded her up with drugs and later in the marriage, suggested the headaches were psychosomatic. At the end, he accused her of faking. She took to her bed Monday evening and with few exceptions, didn't get up until Wednesday morning.

After breakfast and a long walk with Boon, Mary Alice called Bill Burgess. He was in Greenville for the day so she made an appointment for Friday, March 23. She felt relieved at not having to coax Burgess into telling her what was going on with Chase's case, although the absurd suggestion that he change his plea worried her. And a little more time might be useful. She wanted to mull over Randy Wells' possible involvement in the murder.

Part of her brain constantly shuffled the clues that led nowhere. The private investigation book had great faith in the Internet. Mary Alice struggled to have any faith at all.

Before signing up with the pay data banks she'd used to locate Brenda Lee, she tried the weekly, *Cana Herald* and Tupelo's *Daily Journal*. First, she found a brief notice in both papers that Randall Wells had completed basic training in the Army. He was listed as the son of Margery and Tyrone Wells of Cana. It was 1985, and he'd been eighteen years old.

Next she found an obituary for Margery Wade Wells in the Cana paper from September, 1982. Typical of small southern newspapers, no cause of death was named, but she'd died when she was only thirty-five. Her husband, children and dozens of relatives were listed as survivors. Mary Alice knew the surnames but none of the individuals, except for Randy.

She walked out onto the deck into the spring morning air hoping a composite of the Wells' family would emerge. Randy would have been fifteen when he lost his mother. It didn't take much to imagine that without the mother, the girl was especially vulnerable to her predatory father. Mary Alice pictured a young, loving brother powerless to help his sister against a strong, hateful daddy. Maybe the father kicked the boy out. She almost didn't want to search for the little sister's obituary.

The phone rang.

"Hello."

"Mary Alice Tate, please," he said.

"Speaking."

"Mary Alice, it's Walker Bates down at the Hallmark Shoppe."

She could see him. Wide as he was tall with suspenders over a starched shirt. Bad breath and a smarmy habit of touching ladies on the arm or shoulder.

"Hey Walker. What can I do for you?"

"Your mama said I might be able to do something for you."
He smacked.

"She did?"

"Party favors sound familiar?" He drew out the words.

Mary Alice couldn't believe her mother had meddled and
pre-empted her efforts by calling Walker at Hallmark. Mary
Alice knew exactly what she wanted and where to get it. Free.
Why couldn't Elizabeth have an attack of shingles? Who else
had she called? "Well, Walker, I am getting together some
things for favors for the wrap party, but—"

"There not all matched up," he interrupted, "but I have lots
of cards that would be nice." He sounded very pleased with
himself. "I have some Ole Miss and State paraphernalia too but
maybe that wouldn't work. Oh, and packs of paper fingertip
towels in assorted patterns and colors."

Mary Alice could imagine the top dollar donors of the
pilgrimage pulling from their goodie bags dusty cards with
winsome bunnies or paper towels in stiff yellowed cellophane.
She could kill her mother.

"Walker, I'm working on a theme, and I'd have to see what
you have to know if it'll work," she lied. "It is so nice of you to
think about donating to us. Would it be okay if I stopped by?"

"Absoluta-tiva. I don't suppose I could wrangle an invitation to
the party," he snorted a laugh. "You know I am a party animal."

"Let me ask, Walker. I'm favors, not invitations. Mama
will know." There were no extra invitations to the party. Well,
Elizabeth could take care of her buddy, Walker Bates.

After she hung up she called her mother. No one answered;
she left a message. "Mama, do not call anyone about the favors
without checking with me first." She didn't say please or try
to sound polite. And she knew her mother would ignore the
message.

Rather than return to the computer to search for the dead Wells girl, she made another call. She'd lost nearly two days to a headache and the party wasn't far off. Wanda Fuller at the Cana Chocolate Company answered and in five minutes had promised a mountain of free chocolate candy.

"We can't sell it because it's not perfect; 'specially the mini-turtles," Wanda explained. "But it tastes exactly the same and most looks fine, but—"

"Thanks Wanda. We'll bag it up real cute and give you credit for the donation."

"I got bags too."

Mary Alice checked chocolate off her party favor list and went back to the PC. Continuing in the obits, she easily found Tyrone J. Wells who'd died in Cana in July, 1987 and was buried in the Veteran's Cemetery. He'd been forty-six, eleven years older than his wife. Both seemed awfully young to be dead.

The obit for Lilly Ruth Wells who'd died at age fourteen in 1985, the same year Randy joined the Army, was only three sentences, but there was a story a week later that said the coroner would hold an inquest in her death. She hadn't died of natural causes. Her body had been found by her brother in her bedroom. The Cotashona County sheriff was investigating. Nothing else followed about Lilly Ruth Wells, but in another issue Mary Alice did find a notice that US Army PFC Randall Wells had received a medal in marksmanship.

Mary Alice turned off the computer. Bam, Lilly dies in 1985. Bam, bam, Randy joins the army, same year, and bam, bam, bam, the father dies in 1987. Randy was back in Cana now. Had he come back after the army and taken out his father? There wasn't a report that Tyrone Wells had been murdered, but that didn't mean he hadn't been. No matter, the dead sister and the army tour were facts that echoed Jamie's play, *Absolution*.

Clearing away the breakfast remains—two Jimmy Dean Sausage, Egg and Cheese Biscuits—she shuffled through the stack of index cards, selecting a half dozen. On a sheet of newsprint, she made a bubble diagram of the most important clues.

At the top right she wrote:

Secret: What does Mrs. Dickens know that Paige and Randy did?

A. *Help with illegal abortion? Lilly died in 1985; Paige was 16 & Randy 18.*

B. *Attempt to kill Tyrone Wells in 1985?*

C. *Murder of Tyrone Wells in 1987?*

D. *Paige's pregnancy 1990-91? Hide it, esp. from Leonards?*

E. *What else?*

F. *How does Jamie's death stir up this secret???*

In a second bubble she wrote: *Jamie's play, Absolution, reveals Randy's family's shameful past. Is Randy Drew? Does Randy know about the play? If so, would that knowledge give him motive to kill Jamie?*

The bubble beneath read: *Paige's son, Jim, resembles Jamie O'Malley. Paige and Jamie could be Jim's real parents. No proof whatever that Jim Leonard is Jamie O'Malley's son.*

Another said: *Paige and Randy childhood acquaintances. How close? Same background. How does Paige fit into the Randy Wells story?*

And then in a rectangle, Mary Alice wrote: *Brenda Lee Chinault pregnant. Father is Jamie? Or? She is now missing. Why?*

After reading the diagram over and over, Mary Alice reached three conclusions which she jotted on a fresh legal pad. First, she needed to quiz her cousin Mattie Catherine about Randy and Paige. He was only two years older than Paige. Were they related in any way? What was their bond? She dialed Mattie Catherine but got no answer.

Next, she toyed with the idea of again impersonating Paige to Mrs. Dickens. With what she now guessed about the secret, she could risk going over it with the woman, probing for particulars. Mrs. Dickens might confirm or deny details of Mary Alice's suppositions. Maybe, in a foggy state, Mrs. Dickens would dump the secret. The plan had few risks. If, in the middle of the interview, Mrs. Dickens realized Mary Alice's real identity, so what? No one would take Mrs. Dickens' accusations seriously. The bigger danger was that the old woman was unreliable. She wrote, *Pump Mrs. D.*

Her third conclusion was that she had to talk to Randy Wells about Jamie's play. He'd be easy to find. All the old Cana High guys hung out at Mickey's reliving the glory days. Maybe she'd hand him a copy of the play and tell him how she realized it was about his sister. Jamie was dead, she'd found the play, had Jamie ever talked to him, bla, bla. It was fishing, but maybe he'd react. It was also cruel, but a court date had been set. *Tempus fugit.*

And if Randy knew about the play, did that mean he had a motive for killing Jamie? Nobody had checked Randy Wells' alibi. Why would they? She reminded herself that Randy Wells had a medal in marksmanship. She wrote, *Weekend, find R. at Mickey's.*

What if her theory that Vallie Leonard had killed Jamie to protect her grandson's true identity and Randy, with his own reasons for hating Jaime, had pulled the trigger for her? The story made more sense if Paige had arranged the murder and used Randy, but Paige had witnesses as to her whereabouts on February 26. Mary Alice studied the diagram sure she was missing some link.

She took a break and called Latrice Latcherie at Laissez Le Bon Temps. She was only too glad to donate all manner of sample sizes of gourmet food items.

"Baby, I got a bunch of little tinned and jarred thingies," she said in her deep Cajun accent. "They're gonna expire before they sell. I'll write 'em off."

Latrice promised to comb the storage room for more stuff. Anything from Laissez was going to be good. She thought of greasy Walker Bates at the card shop. She'd have to stop by and be nice. She called cousin, Mattie Catherine again. When she got no answer, she pulled out her Cana High yearbooks and for an hour searched the group photographs. Paige and Randy hadn't been in the same grade, but Cana was small and by junior high, girls were going to high school parties. She hoped for a shot of the two, but there wasn't anything. On the bottom of her diagram she made a note to check the childhood addresses of Paige Thompson Leonard and Randy Wells.

Flipping back to the party favor list, she called Doug Lenhoff of Lenhoff and Lambert Jewelry on the square. A gushy young female asked her to hold please.

"Doug Lenhoff. May I help you?" He had a red velvet cake southern accent, rich and moist, that made clear there were stark class and regional differences among southern ways of talking. It wasn't unreasonable that southerners got testy when outsiders lumped together all southeastern states as though the Ozark accent equaled that of the Gulf Coast and both were about the same as East Texas.

After minutes of chatting about family and dogs and weather, Mary Alice made her pitch.

"I think we can help," he said. "How about silver-plated pens that look like sugar cane stalks?" He explained how a supplier thought the town's name, Cana referred to cane as in sugar cane and had given the store as a bonus for a big order dozens of the pens. "They don't write as well as the free pens at SouthBank, but they're better than the ones at First National."

Mary Alice could see the pens packaged with high end note paper. The goodie bags were filling up. At least something was working.

She remembered when some speculated that Doug Lenhoff might marry the widow, Elizabeth Tate. They'd dated, but then Elizabeth had spent a month in Europe and somehow when she got back, the relationship didn't take up where it left off. Or maybe it did. Mary Alice, at the time mired in a dissolving marriage, believed that her mother loved the attention of men, but that she wasn't about to risk what money she had by marrying. At least not for a jewelry merchant worth not much more than a million.

At five she fed Boon and brought in the mail which she sorted as she squirted pimento cheese from a can on Ritz crackers. Rehearsal was at seven. If Brenda Lee didn't show up, Mary Alice vowed to track down the girl's friend, Annette. She ate the crackers and fixed six more.

Boon gave her a soulful-mournful look.

"Okay, but just one," she said.

The mail consisted of bills, Ole Miss Alumni requests for money, and a Coldwater Creek Catalog. Then she found a thick envelope with a return address from her ex-husband, Dr. Cham Mauldin. Whatever was inside, it wasn't good news.

When the phone rang, she let the answering machine take it.

"Mary Alice. Walker here. You won't believe what I found in the back store room. I think they'll suit your party favor requirements just fine. Come on by soon, ya hear?"

CHAPTER 24

March 23, Friday

F RIDAY MORNING, MATTIE CATHERINE McBRIDE returned
Mary Alice's call.

"I'm so sorry, Mary Alice. I ran Big Mama down to the sale
at Hurwitz-Mintz."

Big Mama, Mattie Catherine's hundred pound grandmother,
was called big because of her age. Ironically, Big Mama's daughter, Little Mama to her family, weighed two hundred pounds.

"I didn't mean to worry you with all those messages." Mary
Alice recognized the clicks of cigarette lighter.

"What's up?" Mattie Catherine asked on a deep inhale.

"I have a question I just know you'll be able to answer."

Mattie Catherine adored her role as the unofficial keeper of
Cana's stories. "Is this about Chase Minor?"

"Yes, but it's mostly to help Bill Burgess take suspects off his list. I'm seeing him this afternoon. We don't want him to spend time on stuff that's not going to pan out."

It wasn't all true, but it wasn't all lies either.

"Okay, shoot."

"What do you know about Randy Wells and Paige Thompson? Leonard now; she was a Thompson then."

"I know." She blew smoke. "How do you mean?"

"From school. Did they date? Any connection to each other."

"Let's see. Randy's older than Paige. I'd have to check the yearbooks, but I think two years."

Mary Alice knew their ages but didn't comment. The good stuff would come, if there was any good stuff.

"And of course they lived real close. Until his little sister died."

"Where's that?" Mary Alice asked trying not to lead the conversation.

"Out in the county. You know the road to the Indian Mound?"

Mary Alice walked to the map tacked up on the office wall. The county road meandered west and then curved sharply north ending in a spaghetti bowl of turns.

"I know where that is."

"Are they suspects?" Mattie Catherine asked. She sounded like she hoped they were.

"No, no." She placed a sticky arrow on the Indian Mound road. "Bill says it's confidential so he doesn't even tell me why he wants to know things. Maybe it's because Paige is on the theatre board." She knew she couldn't tell her cousin the truth.

Mattie Catherine blew smoke into the phone. "Randy was like a big brother to Paige way, way back. I think he even called her Cissy."

Mary Alice made an encouraging humming sound.

"One time Paige got sent home from school for head lice—maybe third grade—and some boys made fun of her."

"Uh-huh."

"Randy tore those boys up. Got suspended from school."

"What about Randy's little sister," Mary Alice asked.

"She was the first young person I ever knew who died."

"You knew her?"

"Barely. You don't remember her?"

"No."

"I'll think of her name in a second. She was retarded. Not Downs but just simple-minded. Real sweet girl. Poor little thing."

Mary Alice vaguely remembered a girl in a grade behind her who had died. "The paper said there was an investigation into her death."

"It was hall hush-hush. Lots of gossip but no proof."

"I heard she died after an illegal abortion."

"That's what the gossip was about."

"The sheriff ever do anything?"

"They had to do an autopsy, you know. I guess the result must have made the sheriff suspicious," Mattie Catherine said.

"But she was pregnant?"

"Mary Alice if you tell Bill Burgess this stuff you have to promise not to say who told you."

"Word of honor."

"My Aunt Myrna's maid, Adine, was kin to Randy's mother. I don't know how Adine found out, but she said Lilly, that was her name, Lilly Wells. She said Lilly bled to death in her own bed. Hemorrhaged."

"That sounds like a botched abortion."

"Everybody thought that. Abortion was legal, but there were illegal ones too. And just like now, the only legal clinic was in Jackson. Lilly Wells could hardly get herself to school much less to a clinic two hundred miles away."

"Must have been hard on the family."

"Randy took it hard. Quit school."

Maybe Randy had dug up the abortionist's name. Maybe he'd driven Lilly there. Roe v. Wade came in 1969. Safe abortions had been legal for years. Again, Mary Alice imagined what the experience must have been like for the girl. And legal or illegal, what did it matter now?

"What about her father?" Mary Alice asked.

"Oh, him. I think people suspected she was taken advantage of. You know, her weak mind and having no mama."

"Rape?"

"I guess it would be, but maybe she consented. She had the mind of a child, but by fifteen, she looked like young woman."

Mary Alice easily pictured girls who developed fully and early. Now girls flaunted bouncy breasts and bared their navels. Back in 1985 some modesty ruled in Mississippi, but nubile female bodies occupied the minds of most boys and lots of men.

"Any rumor about incest?"

"Aren't there always when white trash comes up pregnant?"

"What do you think about that?"

"It wasn't Randy. He loved her. But the daddy was a mean old cuss. They're all dead but Randy. We'll never know."

Mary Alice thought, unless Randy knows and tells.

"If Chase weren't in so much trouble, I'd never bring it up," Mary Alice said. "They set a court date. It doesn't look good."

"You think Randy Wells is involved?"

"He might know who is," Mary Alice said. "It's like unraveling a sweater. You have to keep pulling threads."

"What else can I tell you?" Mattie Catherine, the font of secret information so far unstaunched.

"When Randy got out of the army, did he come back here?" Mary Alice asked.

"I don't know the dates, but he wasn't gone more than a couple of years."

"And Paige married Bobby Leonard."

"Randy was probably at the wedding. He and Paige were always close."

"I don't suppose they're close anymore." Mary Alice floated the supposition, hoping for comment.

"We're all still close, Mary Alice." She sounded miffed as though the bonds forged in the Cana culture could never be weakened.

Mary Alice imagined her cousin thought that if Mary Alice attended more of the alumni picnics and reunions, she too could be wrapped closer in the Cana fold. Living in Dallas for ten years until recently was no excuse.

"I mean close, like before."

275

"They're in different worlds now." The lighter flicked again. "But at our reunions, we pick up like we never left off."

"Randy comes to reunions?"

"He comes by but then goes on down to Mickey's. A quarter of his senior class practically lives there."

"Mama used to call Randy and his buddies hoods." Hoodlums, boys with motorcycles, tattoos, and attitudes who smoked and skipped school. Fast boys who carried knives and the intoxicating scent of trouble.

"Mary Alice I can't imagine how you could forget all of this. You were there."

"Partly, but my head must have been somewhere else." *Up my ass most of the time*, she thought. Preparing to become a vacuous beauty, a deb, a sorority belle and ultimately the lucky wife of a soon-to-be prosperous lawyer or doctor. Dr. Jekyll.

She thanked her cousin and hung up. If there'd been any doubt about a link between Randy and Paige, Mattie Catherine had erased it. And clearly, Jamie O'Malley had used the Wells' story in his play. Mary Alice carefully made notes and then put everything away in a locked desk drawer. She had just enough time to swim across the lake and back, dress and make her two o'clock with Chase's lawyer.

"Pilgrimage opens next week, doesn't it?" Burgess asked. He remained behind his desk and didn't offer even a cup of coffee.

She chatted briefly about the fact, bent on not getting distracted. He took the hint.

"What can I do for you, Mary Alice?" He sounded professionally cordial, but then Bill Burgess was a master at masking his thoughts and emotions. District attorneys and judges statewide knew it.

Mary Alice spoke softly. "Are you going to be able to get Chase's trial date put off?" She didn't want to challenge him.

"As I told him and no doubt he told you, I'm trying," he said. "Six months is short for a murder trial, but it's manslaughter, and Judge Williams likes to finish big cases before Christmas."

She shook her head. Locked up for the holidays.

"Nasty cases depress Judge Williams, and he wants to be happy during the yuletide season." He twisted a button on his vest as though he were opening and closing a tiny valve.

"Chase said you mentioned changing the plea."

"That's one possibility. Right up 'til the eleventh hour."

"He's innocent."

"I think so too, but the D.A. doesn't agree. Nothing new has come up. Potts is being circumspect. Nobody knows anything." He sat back in his leather chair and fingered his cuff links.

"I do."

"You do?"

"Yes. I do."

"Tell me."

"First, there's Brenda Lee Chinault," she said.

"The pregnant runaway actress. What's up?"

Burgess sounded genuinely interested. Could he be that desperate? Maybe Chase should have told him about the phony letter from Jamie.

"We need to find her. Mary Alice skipped describing her ordeal in the meth lab trailer. "Can you hire a PI?"

"Sure. But they don't work for free."

"I talked to her best friend, Annette Severs." At the last rehearsal Mary Alice had sought her out. Annette, however had practically run away from Mary Alice and her questions.

"She tell you anything?" Burgess asked.

"It's more what she didn't say. Bill, she knows where Brenda Lee is and probably the name of the baby's father. In spite of her cool bluff, Brenda Lee's a scared girl. Now she's got a baby and a dead man mucking up her plans to be a movie star."

"You think she shot Jamie?" He ran his fingers under his collar, loosening it.

"She's involved somehow." Mary Alice stood to stretch as she recalled why she felt so strongly about the girl. "She told me she hid in the theatre bathroom until everyone, including me, had left for the night. She wanted to talk to Jamie, who she said liked to talk to her and didn't treat her like a child. She's pregnant. What do you think she wanted to talk about? And she was the last known person to see Jamie alive. If they didn't have Chase to blame, wouldn't this be enough to at least make her a suspect?"

"Sure. Without Chase you'd still be a suspect," he said. "Ms. Chinault is interesting; what else you got?"

She'd rehearsed in the car what she'd say and not say about Paige and Randy. Burgess knew that Vallie Leonard was on Mary Alice's list of suspects. But the discovery of Jamie's play brought involvement by the Leonard women into sharper focus.

"Jamie wrote a play called *Absolution*."

"Not another play. Please."

"Hear me out." Mary Alice told him about the play, about Randy Wells' life and his connection to Paige. She ran the scenarios she and Chase had created. Burgess stopped fussing with his clothes, sat up and scribbled a few notes.

"So you think Jim Leonard is Jamie's son, and Jamie tried to claim paternity."

"It's possible."

"And to keep this secret Paige's old friend, Randy shoots Jamie?" Burgess went back to twirling his vest button.

"Maybe."

Burgess, leaping ahead, said, "And if Randy Wells knows about the play, he has his own reason to hate Jamie O'Malley. Dragging his family's name in the dirt, as my mama used to say."

"Exactly."

Burgess shook his head. "I don't think I'd murder somebody for airing my family's sordid past in a play that nobody even knows about."

Mary Alice sat on the edge of her chair facing him. She thought about all the hours in theatre class and rehearsal during which directors had driven her to see the psychological reality of a character.

"What if you're a poor kid, your mama was dead by the time she was thirty-five and your daddy's having his way with your little sister. You love your little sister. She's mentally challenged and vulnerable. Maybe she looks like your dead mama. You're all the girl has. Then she tells you she's pregnant and both of you know why. She begs you for help. You pay for an abortion. She hemorrhages to death. You find her lying dead in her own blood-soaked sheets. And you're too weak to avenge her death—can't even tell anybody about the shame of it. You've failed as a brother and as a man. Basic training in the army can't begin to distract you from the guilt and pain." Mary Alice saw Burgess' eyes harden. He'd become Randy for a minute.

"Then later on some playwright has the gall to write your private, painful story to put on the stage for all to gawk at. Your family will likely be recognized. Shame and hatred overwhelm you. Worst of all, everyone will know that you didn't protect your sister. You helped kill her, and the father got off." She sat back in the chair, exhausted.

Burgess sank back too. "That your closing argument?"

She shrugged.

"Can't prove much, but it's worth a look," he said. "Having a name helps a lot. I'll check on Annett Severs. Check Wells' alibi." He leaned forward on his desk. "You're not suggesting a link between your dual scenarios, are you?"

"There can't be two killers, of course, but somehow they're all characters in the drama." She twisted a strand of hair.

Burgess smiled. "Would you like a coke?"

She declined.

He offered dinner—Dutch if she insisted, but Mary Alice had plans for Friday night. He saw her out.

What else he might do with the information was unclear, but Bill Burgess was smart, crafty and wanted to win. The repetition of the story, however, charted a course for Mary Alice. She knew she had to talk to Randy Wells. And soon.

She stepped away and then turned back. "Will you tell me again about Paige's alibi?" Mary Alice asked.

"Sure. The whole family was home."

The whole family was just three people.

"Watching a movie together?" she asked. "What?"

"As I recall they were in the house aware of one another but engaged in different activities."

Mary Alice imagined Jim in his room plugged into an electronic device and deaf to everything else. Everyone knew Bobby drank a lot. He likely ended his evening with his friend Jack Daniels in front of the TV. What would Paige have been doing? Painting her nails; checking her stock portfolio?

Mary Alice said goodbye and headed for her car. On the walk she realized that she gave everything to Burgess and except for the alibi info, he gave her nothing. She remembered her PI book talked about this problem.

There was no way to tell if Paige were lying about her alibi. And anyway, the police didn't suspect Paige. The Leonards would stick by their story. But Paige could have slipped out for an hour that February night, without her husband or son knowing.

As she left Cana and crested a rise, a vista of chartreuse hills appeared. Mirroring this fresh view, Mary Alice realized that if Paige Leonard's alibi were shaky, an entirely new perspective opened.

As she fed Boon, Mary Alice eyed the unopened envelope from her ex. However, her evening's mission took precedence over bad news from Dallas. She sensed an energy that she could only describe as something was going to happen. Good or bad, something was going to crack open.

She chose her clothes carefully. Nothing fashionable, too casual or too sexy. She tossed tops and bottoms on the bed trying to remember which colors made people look friendlier. Yellow? On the bed scratching Boon's ears, she decided a girl-next-door look was her best shot. She pulled her brown hair into a ponytail, added only lipstick and mascara and practiced wholesome smiles in the mirror.

At ten she pulled into Mickey's crowded parking lot, pretty sure Randy Wells would be inside.

CHAPTER 25

March 23, Friday night

Inside Mickey's Bar, country music and heat pulsed. The doctors and lawyers drank downtown; Mickey's was mostly good ole boys and girls, and on a Friday night it was packed. Mary Alice imagined that the hard, often boring work these people did to get by made an end-of-week gathering at Mickey's essential.

She caught her reflection in the bar mirror. The red-gold hues of light flattered everybody. Even beer-gutted rednecks looked ruggedly picturesque. She smiled at her wholesome image and hoped it would have the right subliminal message for Randy Wells.

She remembered her outfit for her first meeting with Tom Jaworski. The miniskirt had worked, but manipulating men with costumes made her uneasy. When did minor dishonesties cross the line? She didn't want to think about the fact that her entire mission this night was duplicitous.

Scanning for Randy, she took the long way to the bar, greeting acquaintances as she wove among the crowded tables. A group of school teachers about her age dominated a large table in the corner. Half a dozen regulars in gray work clothes with name patches over breast pockets took up one leg of the bar.

"Mary Alice Tate."

She heard her name barked from near the bar and recognized Olivia Gillespie, who waved as though requesting Mardi Gras parade beads.

Over six feet tall and well-upholstered if not fat, Olivia pulled focus in any room. She grabbed Mary Alice and hugged the air out of her.

"I haven't seen you," she paused, "in years," Olivia said.

Mary Alice supposed it had been at her daddy's funeral.

"Ditto. How are you?" Mary Alice struggled to talk above the noise.

"If my dancing partner doesn't show up before the band does, I'm gonna be pissed. That's how." Olivia took a slug of beer from the bottle and without looking at the bartender, signaled him for another. "What you drinking?"

"Whatever's on tap," Mary Alice said. She climbed onto the vacant stool next to Olivia.

"Lonny, make it two," Olivia bellowed over the din, two fingers shooting into the air.

Mary Alice was about to quiz her high school classmate about her dancing partner when she caught sight of Randy Wells at the back of the room. In tight faded jeans and a black tee shirt, he leaned against a brick wall watching two men shoot pool. The cock of his head, tilt of his pelvis and squint of his eyes made him look like a model for men's cologne. He had the five o'clock shadow and the rippled abs too. Maybe an ad for men's underwear.

As Olivia updated Mary Alice on the local gossip which mostly consisted of who was sleeping with whom, Mary Alice kept an eye on Randy. Two different women approached him. He smiled, but his body language said he wasn't interested. They left him alone.

"That Randy Wells over there?" Mary Alice asked.

"That's him."

Mary Alice hoped Olivia would elaborate, but she got off on how she and Johnny Wylder had won a country and western dance contest in Shreveport. "See, folks don't expect a big woman like me to be able to move like I do."

Randy disappeared into the dark hall that led to the restrooms. It was her chance.

As if she were reading her mind, Olivia said, "Randy's a loner. Don't waste your time."

"No girlfriends at all?"

The band dragged up onto the stage and started its sound check.

"He got married years ago, some gal he hardly knew. Was when he got back from the army. Didn't last a year."

"You think that's why he's a loner?"

"He always was a loner, if you ask me." Olivia craned her neck to look for Johnny.

"His baby sister died," Mary Alice said. "That had to be hard on him."

Olivia gave Mary Alice a look that said she knew about the rumors. "Maybe that's it."

Mary Alice could see that the band was about to slam into some overly-amplified tune about good love gone bad. Randy was still in the men's room. She needed to get back there.

"You know how some people can't get an even break?" Olivia asked, still checking for her dance partner. "That's Randy. Trouble always finds him."

Mary Alice wanted to be in place by the pool table when Randy emerged, but Olivia was now talking about Randy. Maybe she knew if Randy and Paige were still close.

"He doesn't even have to look for it," Olivia said.

She was about to ask Olivia for an example of trouble that found Randy when Johnny Wylder sidled up.

"I believe I'll go say hello," Mary Alice said.

But Olivia hardly heard her. "Johnny, goddamn it; we said nine-thirty."

Johnny Wylder laughed, signaled the bartender and gave Olivia a hug all at once.

Mary Alice slid off the barstool and arrived at the pool tables just as Randy came out. She only knew him in the way everybody in a small town knew everybody else. He'd know her too, but if he wanted, could pretend ignorance. She counted on the beer and the bar atmosphere to help.

"Randy Wells," she said. "I was hoping I might run into you." She thought she had just the right amount of down home familiarity

She saw a blip of wariness flare in his eyes, but he recovered quickly.

"Howdy, Mary Alice," he said. His southern accent held a hint of Mississippi country.

She smiled her best cheerleader smile.

"Well, you found me," he said. He opened his arms in a here-I-am gesture.

Her stomach tightened. What if he got crazy-upset by what she was going to tell him? Terse introductions of musicians burst over the mike followed by "two, three, four." The band blasted, matching the energy of the dancers who swarmed onto the floor. Couples barely missed one another, stepping and spinning through the chaos.

"Can we sit down?" she shouted.

He nodded and moved stiffly toward an empty booth away from the stage. She could tell he didn't want to go. Again trouble had found him.

Settled with fresh beers, he waited for her to speak. She felt him watch her, but there was nothing flirtatious about him. She asked where he was working, and he told her about his job with a furniture manufacturer. He asked about what she did now. He seemed aware of her divorce.

She told him about working with Georgia Horn at the Women's Center and how that job had dried up when Georgia went to finish her master's degree. Telling Randy Wells how she really hadn't ever earned a living wasn't the way she wanted to start the conversation. She couldn't ask about his family.

"I guess you know about Jamie O'Malley getting murdered," she said plunging in. She watched for his reaction. Even seasoned poker players had tells that showed their intentions and feelings.

"Just what folks said." He examined the table's wood grain beneath the thick layer of varnish.

So far he was cool or at least unreadable.

She explained her connection to Jamie through the theatre and the production of his play. Then she pulled from her purse a photocopy of *Absolution*.

He sipped his beer, tipping his head way back.

"What's that?" He eyed the papers seeming to intuitively sense danger.

"Jamie wrote this. It's a play." She pushed it to the center of the table. "He wrote several plays using personal stories—people from here. He's even in one of them."

Randy didn't react. She hoped she'd remember later on to write down that he hadn't moved when she brought up Jamie using personal stories. "I found a box of his plays. Now that he's dead, they might get more attention." She worked hard to not say too much and not repeat anything. Babbling sounded guilty.

His thumb flicked the Budweiser label.

"I think he used your family's story in this one."

"Oh?"

She could feel the energy shift with the words, *your family* as he slid from curious to surprise. She expected horrified to follow quickly.

"Why you think that?" he asked.

She couldn't read him. Was he really dumbfounded or ready to grab her throat and choke her?

"I might be wrong," she said. "You read it. I thought you ought to know."

She didn't want to describe the play to him and certainly wasn't going to mention incest or abortion. She didn't have a good feeling. It was like lying to a favorite teacher about breaking in line or stealing the milk money.

After a long pause between two sips of beer, Randy said, "He's dead now."

"But his plays might get more production than when he was alive. It works like that."

"I know that."

"There're libel laws that could protect your privacy whether the stuff in the play is true or not." He might know that too. Did she sound that patronizing?

He looked at her like he was trying to comprehend the real reason for her visit.

"I thought you ought to know," she repeated. She didn't like the look on his face, but the whole point was to push his buttons and get a reaction. Hitting hard on every clue might keep Chase out of jail. A muscle in his jaw jumped and griped. It was impossible to tell if he'd known about the play's existence. But he sure knew now.

"Did Jamie ever ask you if he could write about your life?" she asked.

He closed his eyes. "I never talked to him a'tall." When he opened his eyes anger had leached in.

"Did you know about the play?" she whispered.

"No and I can't see it matters much. I ain't read it, but there's no story in my family."

"Okay, but—"

"There's no family." He leaned back, glaring at her, daring her to try to shame him.

She finished her beer and gathered her purse. "I'm sorry Randy. I just thought you—"

"You said." He leaned across the table, his beer breath frosting the air. "Who else knows about this?" He poked the script.

"I don't know. Maybe there're other copies. I don't know. Getting a lawyer would be better protection than trying to get all of the copies."

"Fuck. My mama, papa and sister are all dead. There's no story, and I don't need protection."

The band finished its first number to hoots and applause.

"I'm so sorry. I just—" What could she say? She'd heard nasty rumors and believed them? She slipped from the booth and stood.

He swept the script toward her. "Take this shit with you. It's not about me."

Ignoring the script, she turned and walked away half expecting to be tackled or feel the Budweiser bottle smack her head. She could claim she was just the messenger, but she knew even that wasn't true. She left him glowering at the polished table. She'd dropped a bomb and about all she knew so far was that he was in denial about much of his youth. That, or he just didn't want to claim his unhappy past with her as witness. She'd have to wait and see if the bait attracted a hit.

She sat in the dark parking lot sucking her least favorite color Life Saver, green, and hating that she'd just made Randy Wells a victim. There had to be a better way.

A man came out Mickey's front door, and she knew by the way he moved that it was Randy Wells. He held the script in his fist. He looked around the parking lot, walked past a row of cars and searched again. Was he looking for her? She scooted down in the front seat below the level of the dash.

Maybe he wanted to yell at her for stirring up old memories and turning them into new problems. She sank lower like the coward she felt she was.

Randy found his white pickup, tore out of the lot and sped away. She wondered if the PI book would have advised her to follow. If she'd wanted to push buttons, she'd succeeded. Seen one way, she'd as much as told him that she believed he had a motive to kill Jamie O'Malley. She couldn't guess how he'd see it all or what he'd do.

A light mist began as she started home. She looked through the streaked windshield that the worn wipers tracked but didn't clear and tried to imagine Olivia and Johnny Texas-two-stepping to a country beat. To her they seemed honest and pure. They didn't put on or try to be other than they were. She couldn't imagine Olivia manipulating Randy as she had just done. She felt dirty.

At home the fat envelope waited. She held it to the kitchen light and then flipped it between her fingers trying to guess what was inside. Maybe something to do with the recently finalized divorce? Perhaps Cham had found a way to take half of her meager trust fund.

He'd cheated, lied, betrayed and then acted as if he were the injured party. She hadn't turned out to be the wife he'd been led to expect. He demeaned and bullied her almost to insanity, and after her father died and she was bereft of real support, he'd taken full advantage of her vulnerability. It had taken everything she had to pack a single bag and run.

The last time she'd seen him, he appeared at her home demanding she return with him to Dallas. No wife, however inferior, left Dr. Cham Mauldin. She'd shot at him with her Daddy's gun, obliterating the deck railing. She'd missed on purpose.

She slit the envelope. A bundle of papers fell out with a one page letter that informed her that she and the doctor were being audited for the previous tax year. The US Treasury letter pointed out that she was equally responsible for additional taxes and possible fines. They'd filed jointly; she'd signed the form. Cham's note said he'd found a tax attorney with a good reputation and wanted to hire him. The retainer was ten thousand. Cham wanted her half by April first.

The other papers were various photocopied IRS documents and letters that made no sense, but brought home the seriousness of the matter.

Face hot and stomach queasy, she stuffed the pages back in the envelope. She didn't have five grand. Of course, Cham knew that, and he knew that her mother did have it. He also knew how Mary Alice felt about taking money from her mother.

She laid her face against the cool surface of the breakfast bar. Boon, standing by the door, watched. Even if they won, a fight with the United States government would be expensive. What if she lost the house? Boon, sensing trouble, didn't whine to go out.

"I have to get a job, a real job," she told the dog. "I must know somebody who will hire me." She took a pen with her father's name embossed on the shaft and on the back of a phone bill made a list of everyone who owned businesses, had government or university jobs or worked at the hospital. It didn't take much to imagine herself exhausted by mind-numbing work that paid barely enough to cover bills. She could see herself on a Friday night in Mickey's Bar, distracting herself from her dreadful life.

Climbing the stairs to her bedroom she wondered how things had skidded so fast. Chase's case didn't look good, Tom Jaworski hadn't called, and now the Feds and her ex wanted what little she had left.

Fully clothed, she fell on the bed. Boon sprang and landed with a bounce beside her. The phone rang. She made up her mind to ignore it but after five rings grabbed it. Maybe it was Chase or Tom.

Someone named Connie told her that her mother had fallen and been taken to the hospital.

CHAPTER 26

March 30, Friday

"MAMA, I REALLY HAVE TO go now," Mary Alice said. "Paige is waiting."

Paige smiled over her glass of chardonnay.

"Are you sure that Connie-creature knows what to do?" Elizabeth Tate asked from her over-priced bed in the Memphis convalescent center. "I wasn't going to keep her—"

"Connie will do fine. Mama you need to rest and let your bones heal." Actually the creature was doing very well.

"I still can't believe Maria isn't coming back," Elizabeth said. "After all I did for her."

"So ungrateful," Mary Alice said.

Maria, the only housekeeper who had lasted with Elizabeth Tate for more than a few months, had the audacity to quit her job when her aunt in California died. Actually, Mary Alice was enjoying, Connie, the eccentric housekeeper who had arrived from a temp agency hours before Elizabeth Tate tumbled down her grand staircase breaking an ankle and cracking three ribs. Connie freely admitted her housekeeping experience was limited to on-job-training for three different husbands.

"Call me in the morning before the doors open," Elizabeth commanded. "I haven't missed a Cana Pilgrimage in over twenty years."

"Paige and I are right here at home, and we have things under control. Don't worry about Linnley."

"You call me."

"Yes, ma'am." Mary Alice replaced the phone on the desk and went to the tiny bar her father had built into an office bookcase.

"Is she still in a lot of pain?" Paige held out her glass.

Mary Alice topped it off and refilled her own. "Depends on when you ask her. Thank God she isn't here ordering everybody around." Mary Alice sank onto the sofa next to Paige. She loved the cozy office nook. She'd spent years on the same sofa doing homework and watching her daddy work at the desk.

"What timing." Paige looked heavenward and shook her head.

"Without your help Linnely wouldn't be on the tour this year. Thanks Paige."

"You're more than welcome. I've enjoyed working with you. Getting to know you better."

"Mama thinks Connie is a gypsy who's going to steal the silver."

"She's unusual, Connie," Paige whispered looking over her shoulder at the door. "Why'd she cover the foyer floor with old pool towels?"

"So the gardeners wouldn't track up the fresh wax."

"And gardeners are coming inside because?"

"Lunch. Connie feeds them."

Paige laughed. "Your Mama would die."

"Connie says a hungry man is a useless man." Mary Alice sipped the cold wine. "Now they're more loyal than dogs. When the window washers didn't show up, Connie had them do it."

"Sakes."

"They fixed her car too."

"Which I do hope she'll pull around the back. It looks like an oil tanker." Paige slipped off her shoes.

"Didn't Earl Ritchey have a car like that in high school?" Mary Alice remembered stories of the infamous Earl and his seduction-mobile.

"A green Chevy Caprice," Paige laughed. "Is that a Caprice out there?"

Mary Alice shook her head. She hadn't known when her chance to talk to Paige about Randy Wells would come. She'd rehearsed dozens of opening gambits, waiting for the right level of trust. The week of organizing a fleet of maids, florists, decorators, caterers, landscapers, docents, hostesses and Connie had bred something close to trust. To seal the deal, Mary Alice had turned over to Paige the cache of wrap-party favors and the credit for obtaining them. Paige Leonard was her new best friend.

But how do you ask a friend if her oldest friend, Randy Wells, could have killed Jamie O'Malley either because of the play Jamie wrote or because Paige or her mother-in-law asked for his help to protect the secret of Jim's father?

Mary Alice poured the remainder of the wine into their glasses. Outside dusk settled and before the light completely faded Mary Alice told Paige about the IRS investigation and the trouble she expected from her ex.

"I don't know how you bear up," Paige said. "Especially this mess with Chase."

"At one time Jamie was Chase's best friend."

"People change."

"It's weird how even in death Jamie haunts us through his plays," Mary Alice said.

"I heard he plagiarized a play Chase wrote. Is that true?"

Mary Alice suspected Paige had heard from her mother-in-law. "That's one reason why the cops think Chase killed him." She also wondered what Paige would think about Jamie's play, *Redemption*. As far as Mary Alice was concerned, that play was about Paige and her son. "He wrote a play about the Wells' family tragedy too."

"Huh?" Paige whirled around to face Mary Alice

"Seems tasteless to use a real story like that." Mary Alice took her time. She couldn't ask direct questions. All she could do was plant ideas and hope for a telling response. "You and Randy were friends in school, weren't you?"

"We were neighbors out on Indian Mound."

"Then you know what happened to his sister." She swirled the wine in her glass.

"Yes." Paige chewed her lip. "How do you know Jamie wrote a play about all that?"

"I found it. With a bunch of others."

"Well the son of a bitch never produced it, and now he never will." Paige pulled herself out of the cushy sofa and circled the coffee table. It went unsaid that perhaps someone else could produce it.

"I can't imagine Jamie writing it," Mary Alice said. "It'd be so painful to the family."

"Randy told him way back that if he used anything about his family, he'd be real sorry."

If Paige knew about the play so did Randy Wells. He'd lied.

"Jamie asked if he could write about his family?" Mary Alice asked.

"He wanted the gory details," Paige said. "Can you imagine? Said he didn't want to get anything wrong. He thought Randy would like the idea of putting out the truth." She perched on the edge of the desk.

"Jamie had no conscience." And few morals either. It seemed ironic to Mary Alice that the chronicled Cana melodramas in his plays were now his only public legacy.

"He was a piece of work all right. I can see how he could have provoked Chase to shoot him."

Mary Alice wanted to ask more but couldn't risk that Paige might connect the dots and realize she'd just confirmed Randy Wells' hatred of Jamie O'Malley and therefore possibly a motive for murdering him. She also wanted to defend Chase, but instead she steered the conversation back to bad husbands and worse luck.

Fifteen minutes later Paige left.

Mary Alice took a long walk with Boon around the grounds of Linnley sorting through the meaning of what Paige had said. Randy had disavowed knowledge of the play about his family. Why? Was he shamed by Mary Alice knowing about his past or nervous about appearing to have a motive to kill Jamie? Paige said Randy had threatened Jamie. Told him he'd be real sorry.

Judging from Paige's reaction, she hadn't known about Mary Alice's and Randy's meeting a week ago at Mickey's. What did it mean that Randy hadn't told Paige that people knew about the play and his history with Jamie? If Randy Wells had shot

Jamie because Paige wanted him to, surely he'd let her know the play had surfaced with all its implications. Or maybe he was still protecting Paige.

She debated if she should tell Bill Burgess what she'd found out, but it was after eight on a Friday night. He'd said he'd find out where Randy Wells had been the night of the murder. It'd be interesting if Randy couldn't verify his alibi. She thought about calling Chase but decided against it. If Chase had drowned his fears in eighty year old scotch, she didn't want to know. What about Kate?

Except for rehearsals, Mary Alice hadn't seen Kate Bishop since their lunch in Oxford when they'd spotted Jim Leonard. Kate had said she was busy with the store.

"Boon, come. Car."

The dog met her at the garage door and in minutes they were speeding through the cool spring air. "We're going to visit Kate," she told the dog who couldn't have cared less where they were going as long as he was going too. Kate loved the spontaneity of unplanned visits. But even as she justified her sudden action, Mary Alice realized something she couldn't name was urging her to go see Kate. Not to call first, but to drop in unannounced.

She parked. The front of the house was dark, but lights were on in the back. Boon, sensing familiar territory, leapt from the car and circled the yard and tiny porch. She rang the bell and heard it echo. No one answered. She rang again. There was movement within.

"Mary Alice?"

"Me and Boon." She waited for Kate to move aside and let them in.

"I was asleep."

It was too early for bed, and Kate was in jeans and a tie-dyed tee shirt. "I wanted to run some things by you."

Kate didn't move. "About Chase?"

"About Randy Wells."

"Could we do it in the morning?" Kate asked. "I have such a headache. I can't think straight." She rubbed the back of her neck.

Kate Bishop, the queen of homeopathic remedies, never had headaches or was sick at all. Mary Alice didn't say anything.

"I wouldn't be any good to you," Kate said. "Come by the store in the morning, and we'll go for coffee."

Someone's here, and she wants me to leave. "I'm sorry we woke you up. Boon." The dog came to her side. She didn't remind Kate that the pilgrimage started tomorrow.

"I'm sorry." Kate backed away and slowly closed the door. "See you tomorrow." Outside security lights popped on.

Mary Alice returned to the car. She saw the outside lights go off. Kate seemed to have someone visiting she didn't want Mary Alice to know about. Kate had never cared before who knew about her men. She slowly drove down the street.

A block away she turned around in a driveway and drove back past Kate's house. Lights came on through a basement window. If Kate were going back to bed with a headache, what was she doing in her basement? It occurred to Mary Alice that Kate was in danger. In movies killers always told the main character to answer the door but to get rid of the visitor. But Mary Alice didn't think Kate was being held hostage. She thought her friend was lying to her.

Mary Alice was up and dressed by six the next morning. Paige, Connie and an army of helpers arrived at seven. For two hours, the dozens of flower arrangement were refreshed, antebellum costumes were donned, and Connie removed the towels from the shining foyer floors. Just before the doors opened, Mary Alice dutifully telephoned her mother, who reminded her about making sure a hostess was in each room at all times. The *hoi polloi* might steal an heirloom.

"Time to open the doors, Mama. Gotta go."

But the first visitors, a tour busload from Corinth, wouldn't arrive for another twenty minutes. Mary Alice and Paige walked through Linnley's twenty plus rooms to make sure every antimacassar and poesy was in place. In the dining room, guarding a fortune in silver, china and cut glass, stood Annie Carter.

Paige didn't seem to remember the plump teenager, who having become pregnant had been dismissed from Paige's mother-in-law's mansion. Mary Alice had persuaded the girl she'd be doing Mary Alice and the pilgrimage a huge favor to serve at Linnley.

The perfect late March weather brought out the crowds. Groups waited on the verandas until rooms cleared. Over and over Mary Alice heard docents explain how the Cana Pilgrimage had been started by the Cana Garden Club after the Natchez Garden Club had begun theirs in an act of desperation.

"The ladies of Natchez were hosting the annual meeting of the Mississippi Federation of Garden Clubs when just days before a late freeze killed off all the camellias and azaleas. It was a disaster as you can imagine." Emily Jane Pelan, in dark green moiré skirts, bodice and a picture hat, touched her hand to her breast. She wasn't kidding. "Plans couldn't be changed so fast. This was 1931. But the garden club rallied, and members opened their homes to the visitors for tours of antebellum Natchez homes instead of gardens."

Emily Jane moved to the table under a crystal laden chandelier. "Now remember the youngest of these homes was seventy years and none had enjoyed any significant restoration. The south was broken by the civil war, the boll weevils and the Great Depression. The ladies weren't sure anybody would want to peek inside the old homes.

But lo, the visitors found riches galore. The paint might have been peeling and the wallpaper dull, but priceless silver, antiques, carved woodwork and chandeliers like this one above us eclipsed the dilapidated conditions. And the visitors adored the stories about the homes which the owners found they were delighted to tell.

The event was such a success that the next year the Garden Club repeated the tour of historic homes adding period costumes pulled from dusty attics. Over 1,500 people came. The Natchez Pilgrimage has continued every year since except for three years during World War II."

Emily Jane herded her group through the twelve feet high sliding doors into the second parlor. "The Cana Pilgrimage, started in 1952, is younger by nearly two decades, however..." Emily Jane, having set the stage, proceeded to describe how special the homes in Cana were.

Docents demonstrated the dumb waiter, theorized about the button collection of the original owner and kept sharp eyes on the Meissen, Limoges and Severs. They knew details of how and when the panes of glass were made, the history of the mint julep and the Tate's restoration of the home. They answered hundreds of questions, many about slavery, a topic they knew a lot about but never brought up.

If queried about slavery as a cause of the War Between the States, docents demurred, relenting only to say it was one of several causes. Only occasionally did a visitor argue. When that happened, the hostess smiled, admitted it was a complicated matter and ushered her group to the next room. Mary Alice suspected her response would have been different and that was why, since junior high, she'd not been asked to hostess.

In the dining room Annie Carter held forth admirably about the complete set of Haviland china and how the famous French dishes were actually the product of an American, David Haviland, who fascinated by a near-transparent tea cup searched for the maker and ended up moving to France where he and his decedents created some of the world's most beautiful and treasured hand-painted porcelain.

By six PM, Mary Alice was too tired to hobnob on the back veranda with all the volunteers, but Paige insisted she had to. It was tradition. How would it look?

She drank two rum punches and by ten was in bed. As she fell asleep she considered that being sucked into the south of 1860 might be beneficial. Worrying about the details of the Battle of Shiloh or if southern belles wore any sort of makeup provided a complete break with reality. Perhaps real detectives should take breaks. She vowed to think only about the pilgrimage and allow her brain to marinate the facts and clues of the case. She remembered Scarlet O'Hara's line, "I'll think about that tomorrow. After all, tomorrow is another day."

CHAPTER 27

April 7, Saturday

THE TOMORROWS ROLLED FASTER AND faster toward the last syllable of the last hour of the pilgrimage. After each day's final horde passed through, Mary Alice, often with her mother on the phone dictating, oversaw cleaning, flower arrangement refurbishing, costume mending and a thousand other details. They were all exhausted by Wednesday, snappish by Thursday and near-dead on the final Friday. And it wasn't over yet.

Mary Alice prayed for a second wind to get her through the wrap party. Vallie had decided that even if Mrs. Dickens was wacko she had to cook for the party. People expected it. Mary Alice had secured the job of picking up the eccentric old lady who, apron in bag, waited in the lobby of Golden Meadows.

"Let's go," Mrs. Dickens said. "I need all afternoon. Them girls they got helping me don't know nothing." The woman seemed consumed by her role and barely noticed Mary Alice.

Mary Alice helped the woman fasten her seatbelt. She pulled out of the parking lot and headed towards Cana. Hoping to find out more about Randy and Paige, she was alert to any indication that Mrs. Dickens might be receptive to further confidences. Mary Alice had only done one thing to prepare.

For fifteen miles Mrs. Dickens recited recipes and cooking secrets long buried in her head. Mary Alice reported on the success of the pilgrimage and drove as slowly as possible.

"How many are coming tonight?" Mrs. Dickens seemed to be calculating servings of peach cobble.

"Over a hundred accepted," Mary Alice said. She was careful not to identify herself. As they got closer to Cana, her anxiety escalated. She might not have another opportunity to question this woman who obviously knew secrets. Those secrets might identify the killer.

"I pray she ordered the brand of flour I favor," Mrs. Dickens said. "I don't mean to judge, but sometimes she goes too cheap." She adjusted her black wraparound sun glasses.

Mary Alice missed her chance to follow a school bus. They'd be at Thorpe House in less than five minutes. It was now or never. "My mother-in-law doesn't understand cooking the way we do." There, she'd identified herself as Paige. She held her breath.

The woman threw back her head and guffawed. "She don't understand a lot."

Mary Alice took a deep breath. "As long as she never understands who Jim's daddy is. I'm just saying—"

Mary Alice felt a hand on her arm.

"Them Leonards won't never hear nothing out of me," she turned to Mary Alice and rasped. "Sometimes thinking about it all was what got me through. Of course, she always paid good, but you know—" The hand squeezed then retreated.

They were in front of Thorpe House and out of time. Mary Alice's job now was to hustle Mrs. Dickens into the kitchen. But Mrs. Dickens had mistaken her for Paige again. Probably the perfume. After Mary Alice had asked Paige about the scent, Paige brought her a small spray bottle of Celine. Mrs. Dickens didn't see well, but her nose worked fine. Mary Alice couldn't wait to sponge off the scent.

Once inside, Mary Alice had time only to deposit Mrs. Dickens and to slip into one of the bedrooms and change her dress. The old lady had all but confirmed that Jim Leonard wasn't Bobby Leonard's son. She knew she had to be careful, but if it was true, who was Jim's father? Mrs. Dickens had indicated on the last visit that Paige and Randy had a secret. Could Randy be Jim's father? The boy didn't look a bit like Randy Wells. But then Jim's resemblance to Jamie O'Malley was not literal. The boy moved and laughed like Jamie, a man Jim hardly knew.

Someone knocked on the door. "Mary Alice, Paige needs you downstairs to help her with her party favors as soon as you can."

She fluffed her hair and wished she borrowed one of her mother's girdles. The raw silk sheath pulled across the hips and cupped under her butt. Too late now. She scampered down the curved, suspended staircase to help Paige with *her* favors.

The band started at eight and by nine the Thorpe House was packed. Attendance at the pilgrimage had beaten all records, and Cana's upper crust was ready to celebrate. As the music poured through the open doors and across the lawns, liquor poured into glasses and down throats. Mary Alice saw Minerva

Weeds dancing with a congressman. A group in a corner erupted with laughter. She felt the absence of Chase Minor. Folks congratulated her on stepping in for her mother and hosting Linnley on the tour, but by ten she found herself gravitating to the veranda, alone. She wondered if Tom Jaworski had been in town, would she have invited him.

The night was cool with only a sweet hint of humidity. She walked the length of the front veranda and turned to do another leg when she saw a new cherry red pickup truck in the small gravel parking lot. The radio played. Behind the wheel sat Jim Leonard tapping the beat on the steering wheel.

"Hey," she said, yanking open the cab door and sliding in.

The boy jumped and reached to turn down the volume.

"No, leave it," she said. "I like it. You're Paige's son, Jim aren't you?"

"Yes Ma'am." He sounded like he'd been caught doing something inappropriate but didn't quite know what it was.

"I'm Mary Alice Tate. Your mama and I've been working on this crazy pilgrimage for the last week. I appreciate your family letting her spend so much time at Linnley." She smiled, leaned toward him and saw that he barely had to shave. He'd be a man in a few short years, but he wasn't one yet.

"Oh, yes, ma'am." He relaxed.

"I think we're both glad it's almost over and life can get back to normal." In the soft light from the house, he looked more like his mother than anyone else. "Lord, I need a cigarette."

He looked puzzled for only a second. Then he smiled. Reaching across her to the glove box, he pulled out a pack of Marlboro's and held it out to her. She recognized the sexy flirty look from the restaurant in Oxford. And she hadn't missed that he'd brushed her bare knees getting the cigarettes. She imagined the boy thought he had a slightly drunk older woman sniffing around. Anything might happen. If he was Jamie's boy, it probably did.

He lit the cigarette.

She hoped she wouldn't choke on the smoke. "What are you doing out here alone in the dark?" She let the suggestiveness of the question ferment.

"I could ask you the same thing," he smiled.

"Well, neither one of us is alone now, are we?" She blew cloud of hot smoke out the truck window.

"Mama called and told me to bring over some more ice. Somebody's supposed to come out and get it." He turned a quarter toward her and looked straight into her eyes.

She felt he was practicing, like *this is how you talk to real women*. His body language in no way resembled that of a high school boy talking to his mother's friend. He made her smile and wonder if in different circumstances she could have a fling with a boy so much younger. The possibility held an attractive risk factor. She wasn't sure of the creepiness rating. She refocused on the boy as a source of information.

The band, back from a break, started again. He switched off the radio.

She wanted to ask him if he knew who his father was. She wanted to ask him if he'd really been home the night Jamie was killed and if his parents were home too. But of course she could ask neither question. However, she knew her age, experience and the strangeness of the moment gave her a certain power. Jim Leonard had no idea she was looking for a murderer.

"You hear about that playwright that got shot at the theatre?" she asked.

"I guess everybody has."

She started to ask if he knew Jamie but instead said, "You ever talk to him?

"No. Never did."

"He was kind of famous," she said.

"I didn't."

"It's terrible. Your grandma was worried the murder was going to ruin the pilgrimage. You know bad publicity." She blew a stream of smoke and watched it burst against the dash and spread like a hydrogen bomb cloud.

"Grandma would."

"Doesn't seem to have hurt us."

"They caught the guy, didn't they?"

"But I heard they're not sure he did it. Still looking."

"But there's gonna be a trial."

"Is there?"

"I heard there was," he said.

"But the one they arrested hasn't said he's guilty, so I think they still have to look until the jury's in."

He shrugged and looked out the side window. "I heard he's gay."

"That doesn't make him guilty." The cigarette made her light-headed.

"No, but—"

"Oh, like a motive. I see," she said. "Or maybe somebody's counting on that. Maybe the real killer's framing him."

If Jim Leonard knew anything about the murder, he wasn't showing it. He'd stopped flirting, but he didn't seem to be trying to protect any family secrets such as phony alibis.

From around the back of the house, she saw a man approaching.

"Your Mama told me the police talked to everybody at your house. Your grandmother's too," she said.

"I bet that's the ice man." He opened the truck door and jumped out, walking back to the bed to help unload the bags. "Excuse me."

She got out of the truck and called to him. "Nice to have seen you, Jim." She waved and headed back inside.

He hefted four bags of ice and flashed a smile—Jamie O'Malley's smile.

She didn't like playing him as she had. He was only seventeen. And having been sheltered all his life, he was about as tough as one of Mrs. Dickens' buttermilk biscuits.

In the back hall she passed Mrs. Dickens. A man was guiding her down the hall to the back of the house. Mary Alice felt the woman turn to watch her as they passed, shoulders almost brushing. Mary Alice, eyes straight, kept going.

The party had entered its final phase. The light-weights were gone, and the remaining patrons were drunk or getting there fast. Vallie Leonard was dancing with a man who hardly moved. The grand dame, however, gyrated wildly. Everyone looked older. Mary Alice found her belongings. As she quietly left, she passed a table with the remaining goodie bags looking like a pile of silken pies. They'd been a big hit. No one seemed surprised that Paige had done such a good job.

Driving home, she let the spring air wash over her. Maybe because winter in Mississippi usually was lousy, spring tried to make up for its predecessor. Her head ached from the cigarette. As she drove she recalled her chat with the boy. Had Jim wanted the killer to be caught and the matter done with or was she projecting? He cut the playful behavior as soon as she mentioned the murder. Was he thinking about protecting his mother's alibi? At least in her own mind she was one step surer that young Jim Leonard was really an O'Malley.

It was nearly eleven when she turned into her driveway. After the week at Linnley, it felt wonderful to be back at her house. She could see the lake reflecting the moon. She also saw a car in the parking space by the garage. It belonged to Tom Jaworski.

CHAPTER 28

April 7 Saturday night and April 8 Sunday

SHE PULLED UP BESIDE HIM and cut the engine. "I do something wrong, officer?"

"You're way past curfew, Miss."

"It's not a school night."

"It's not?"

"No sir."

"You kept a peace officer waiting for an hour."

"Is that against the law?"

"It ought to be." He opened her car door.

Tom Jaworski looked better than a man had a right to. She half-stumbled getting out of the car. He caught her, and an hour later she was still holding on to him. Thighs touching, they sat on the soft leather sofa.

"Miss me?" he asked.

"Private investigators don't have time for foolishness like that." His lengthy disappearance, likely with his wife had made her crazy, but he was with her now, and being in the now made more sense that anguishing about the past or for that matter, the future.

"How's it going?" He shifted, cradling her.

She told him the story, finishing with her suspicion that the killer was Paige Leonard with or without Randy Wells or alternately, it was Brenda Lee Chinault.

"Not the grandmother?"

"Her motive seems weaker."

"Everyone else off your list?" he asked.

"Gone. Burgess is checking on Randy Wells."

"And the letter you found. Nothing else like that turn up?"

"Not that I know about."

"And nobody's reported the girl missing?"

"I don't think so."

"Then she's not missing."

"But—"

"She has too much family. Somebody would've filed a report."

"I tried to find her." Mary Alice described the afternoon in the meth trailer and her rescue by Marshall. She left out the part about Harlan and the Elvis-man-escaped-convict, making the experience sound more stressful than life-threatening.

Jaworski jerked away and faced her. "They could have killed you. Do you know that?"

"But they didn't." Of course she knew. She braced for the lecture.

For the next ten minutes Mary Alice heard how stupid she'd been and how lucky. He told cop stories about innocents caught in the middle of drug deals. "You may still be in danger."

"Hold on. I've knocked on doors out in the county before and never been abducted. I'm not going to stop living because something bad might happen. Could you live like that?"

Jaworski admitted he couldn't and curtailed the harangue. "I remember the first time I met you. You looked so, so—"

"Hot?" She joked trying to take them back to the mood when he was kissing her as if he wanted to consume her.

"Beautiful. I acted rude because I was overwhelmed." He sank back into the sofa pulling her with him.

"I thought it was because you thought I was trying to get a cop killer off."

"No. He paused. "The second time was at the police station after you were almost run off the road." He took her hand in both of his and kissed the palm. "I don't like to think about you in danger—being that scared."

"What about you? You were almost killed because of what I told you. And don't tell me you're a trained police officer. It's only luck the rollover didn't kill you."

"I'm a trained police officer."

"And how is your back, officer?"

"Better. I did physical therapy in California. Some fancy sports medicine place. That's why I stayed so long."

So he hadn't been cozying up with his wife. She'd squandered hours worrying. She wanted to ask about the wife and the divorce but knew it would contaminate the rest of the evening. "So, are you staying?"

"I'm invited?"

"If it's not illegal."

Boon made his final run outside; they turned off the lights and holding hands climbed the stairs.

"You said Burgess was getting a PI on the girl? What's her name, Brenda?

"Brenda Lee Chinault. Why?"

"He needs to find her. If she's not a suspect, it'd be good to know soon. And if she knows something, you need to know now."

He amazed her. He clearly wanted to take her to bed and at the same time understood her concern for the investigation. No wonder there had been so many TV male-female detective teams.

"She's still a kid," he said. "She'll crack easy if she knows anything. She probably wants to talk."

"When I find her, what do I do?" They paused at the top of the stairs as if they had to finish their detective work before entering the bedroom.

"Start with the obvious. Who's the baby's daddy?"

"Think she'll tell me?"

"Eventually. And once she tells you that, she'll tell you anything."

"I can't force her to talk to me."

"Tell her that if she doesn't talk to you, she's going to talk to the police. Give her my name."

"But—"

"You can't always get what you need to know by being straight forward. You must know that. You fooled the old lady."

"Mrs. Dickens is half blind and completely dotty."

"The girl's scared, pregnant and maybe involved in a murder. Her vulnerability quotient is ten."

She had a hard time imagining grilling Brenda Lee. What if the girl said "fuck you" and walked out? "I don't know."

"It'll be a piece of cake. But let the lawyer find her," he said.

Mary Alice started to respond, but he put a finger over her lips.

"Forget about them." He pulled her into the bedroom. "As I recall, you still have some 'splaining to do about being out so late."

In spite of the dark she could tell he was unbuttoning his shirt.

Jaworski left at dawn. Woozy with the sex, Mary Alice rolled into the space he'd occupied. The man-smell radiated from the sheets. Was he her boyfriend now? She didn't want to think about it. They'd avoided topics of his wife and if either of them was ready for a relationship. The L-word wasn't even on the radar.

That he hadn't stayed for breakfast was fine with her. She looked forward to a day alone to think. The pilgrimage was over, the party done and her mother was still captive convalescing in Memphis. She'd just had sex for the first time in many months—great sex. The day outside looked glorious. What could possibly go wrong?

A tiny misgiving niggled as she ate the huge slice of Connie's banana bread. It raised its spiky head during her shower, and by the time she was walking Boon around the lake, the feeling had morphed into a problem.

Back in the kitchen Boon pushed his bowl around the floor while she punched in Kate's phone number. She answered on the first ring.

"Kate, it's me, Mary Alice."

"Hey. How'd the pilgrimage go?"

"Exceeded all records."

"I bet you're exhausted."

"Somewhat."

"Your mama home yet?"

"No. They're spoiling her rotten up there, and the fun's over here so she's in no rush."

"The store was packed all week."

"Good."

"Did I tell you I got the lease on the building extended another year?"

"Good. I guess. Is that good?"

"Very. Same deal for one more year. Gives me time."

"I want to apologize for dropping in on you last week. Waking you up."

"No big deal."

"I wouldn't have even rung the bell, but I could tell someone was home. The TV was on."

Everyone knew Kate hated television. She frequently held forth on the destructive violent programming that celebrated everything low. She believed the fast, flashing edits harmed the brain and were why so many children were crazy, ADD or worse.

"How come you got a TV?"

During the long pause Mary Alice imagined Kate's expression. She'd been busted.

"I have a house guest."

"You're importing the spawn of Satan via cable for a guest? Who?"

This pause was longer, and Mary Alice knew her friend was struggling. Kate never lied. She hated lying more than she hated TV.

"Brenda Lee. Brenda Lee's staying with me for a little while."

"Brenda Lee Chinault?"

"How many Brenda Lee's do we know?"

"Were you going to tell me?" She sounded pissed off. "I almost got killed looking for her, and all the time she was here?"

"Killed?"

"I stumbled on a meth lab." She knew she didn't have to say more.

"But I didn't know that you'd—"

"Kate, this running around I'm doing?" She sounded more than pissed off now. "It's not a silly game, a diversion. Chase could start serving time at Parchman by this Christmas. He'd be lucky to be alive by next."

"She asked me not to tell. I'm sorry. Mary Alice, she started bleeding; because of the baby. She came to me for help. She's so confused. I thought I'd give her some time to rest, to think."

"She's okay? Her and the baby?"

"Yes."

Mary Alice felt a second tirade about to boil over. Didn't Kate want to help Chase? What was Brenda Lee's confusion compared to a prison sentence? But she said, "I'm coming over there. Leaving right now."

She figured Kate would understand that alerting Brenda Lee would be stupid. Brenda Lee was safe with Kate.

Boon accompanied Mary Alice. She thought animals, especially dogs, were reassuring to most people. She reasoned that a detective who had a dog couldn't be bad. She hoped Brenda Lee would see it that way.

When she arrived Kate and Brenda Lee were on Kate's tiny back patio. Both held steaming cups. The box on the table read Common Sense Herbal. A box of organic flax cereal stood at the ready beside a bowl of bananas and apples. Mary Alice regretted she hadn't brought the rest of Connie's banana bread.

Although she couldn't have been more than two months pregnant, Brenda Lee looked different. The cliché that she was no longer in control of her body fit. There was no bulge yet, but she moved like a swollen sleep walker. All her sass and sexiness had vanished into a body preparing for only one thing—motherhood.

It wasn't fair. Here sat a girl who had eons left to reproduce. A girl without a husband or even any support. She was pregnant while Mary Alice, even under the most accelerated plan, was years away from becoming a mother. Her anger-laced sadness made her harder than she meant to be.

"How could you just disappear? There's a lot at stake here for people other than just you."

Brenda Lee burst into tears.

Boon moved in close absorbing tears and permitting the crying girl to tug his fur.

Kate patted Brenda Lee and frowned at Mary Alice.

"Brenda Lee, I need to talk to you. I think you're in some trouble, and I don't just mean baby-trouble," Mary Alice said. She sat close and made the girl look at her.

Brenda Lee erupted in a fresh frenzy of sobs.

"Calm down," Mary Alice ordered. "We can help you." She didn't want to talk about the baby's father yet. "Tell me about the night Jamie O'Malley was killed."

"I already told you—"

"Tell me again." Mary Alice recognized Claire Potts in her tone and manner.

Brenda Lee, through snuffling, repeated what she had said before, that she had waited in the ladies rest room until everyone had left the theatre because Jamie had asked her to stay behind. But when she appeared, he'd told her to go home. He'd said he had to rewrite a scene and that it was late. He'd apologized for making her wait. He'd asked her to meet him the next night.

"I wasn't with him five minutes," Brenda Lee said.

"Where did you go when you left?"

The dog set his muzzle on Brenda Lee's lap and gave her a soulful look.

"I went to Uncle Earl's." She stroked Boon's ears.

"Was your uncle home?"

"No."

"And you stayed there all night alone?"

"He—" Brenda Lee hesitated. "I—"

Mary Alice guessed that a boy, maybe the father of the baby, dropped by. Probably she'd called him. "Brenda Lee, you can't protect anybody. It's all going to come out one way or another." Mary Alice had no idea where her questions were headed, but she had the girl talking. "Nobody's going to hurt you." She depended on Brenda Lee's familiarity with a certain kind of southern religion that taught confession and valued testimony. She invited the hurt, sobbing girl to unburden herself.

"He came over," Brenda Lee said. Involuntarily she touched her belly. "And we had a fight. We never had a fight before." Her face, red and wet, contorted as ugly sounds like giants breaking loose rose in her chest. "Don't tell. I swore to him I wouldn't tell he came over."

"Who came over?" Mary Alice asked.

Brenda Lee forced the answer out of her mouth like the last bit of toothpaste in a spent tube. "Jimmy. Jim. Jim Leonard."

Mary Alice sat back hard in her flimsy metal chair. She hadn't seen this coming. Her brain zinged. Jim Leonard hadn't been at home with his parents the night Jamie was murdered. Paige had lied. Why had she made the point to the police that Jim had been home?

Brenda Lee resumed sobbing.

"Mary Alice, take it easy," Kate said.

"Brenda Lee, look at me. Is Jim Leonard your baby's father?" Mary Alice spoke softly. She thought she knew the answer, but that there was value in getting the girl to tell her. Jaworski had thought the revelation might open a flood gate.

Brenda Lee covered her face and wept.

Mary Alice let her cry for a minute. All this time she'd got it wrong. She'd conjectured that Brenda Lee had shot Jamie. She'd envisioned the scene where the girl had demanded help or money, and that Jamie had dismissed her, laughing. In a fury, she'd picked up the gun and shot him. But now it seemed clear Brenda Lee had hooked up with Jim Leonard. Not Jamie but Jamie's estranged son.

"Who's the father, Brenda Lee?"

"I don't—I'm not sure." She laced her bitten fingernails into Boon's neck fur.

Mouth agape, Mary Alice looked up at Kate whose expression said she'd been told. "You don't know the father?"

"I think I do, but there was the one time—" More tears flowed.

Mary Alice remembered from childhood being unfairly slapped by her mother. She felt the same stunned amazement now. This plot just got thicker and thicker.

"Who?" Mary Alice could tell Jaworski had been right. The girl was dying to talk. "Who else?"

"Mr. O'Malley."

The absurdity of calling the man who might have impregnated her *Mister* made Mary Alice laugh. She was back to the first scenario of the pregnant teenaged Brenda Lee demanding Jamie's help. Except now Brenda Lee appeared to be innocent.

"But it was just the one time," Brenda Lee blathered. "It was way more with Jim. He thinks it's his. Please don't tell him. Mr. O'Malley's dead. I think it is Jim's. I really do."

Slow motion took over. Mary Alice couldn't speak. What difference did this revelation make to the question of who murdered Jamie? She shook her head hard. The thought that Brenda Lee's baby could have been fathered by either Jim Leonard or by Jamie O'Malley was stunning enough, but if Jamie turned out to be Jim's father—it was a southern melodrama of gargantuan proportions. She became aware of Brenda Lee talking.

"We can't get married on account of his family. He's a Leonard." She said the name as if she were saying the pope's name. "You know. But when he's eighteen and goes to college he can do what he wants."

Mary Alice couldn't imagine Jim Leonard giving up pledging Sigma Chi at Ole Miss to marry and support Brenda Lee and child. But what did she know?

"So you plan to keep the baby?" Mary Alice asked. She envisioned Jim handing over his allowance to buy diapers and formula.

"I don't know what to do."

Even though the girl was nearly hysterical, Mary Alice knew Brenda Lee was practical and manipulative. Chase had thought so, and she'd planned to use Jamie to further her theatre career. She was the classic "Fancy" of the Reba McEntire ballad whose mother gave her everything they had to go to town, find a benefactor and never come back. To survive one rung up. Perhaps once Brenda Lee had found out she was attractive to men and that she didn't want to marry Joe Bob Nobody and get fat watching TV, she formed a plan. Maybe Jim Leonard had been part of it. In any case, as the girl had just said, 'Mr. O'Malley is dead." There was no margin in attaching to him.

"You don't have to decide anything right now," Kate said massaging Brenda Lee's shoulders.

"But soon," Brenda Lee wailed. Her growing body was evidence enough of that.

"But not today," Kate said. "That's enough, Mary Alice. For now."

"Okay. Just let me get this straight." Mary Alice rose from the rickety bistro chair. Boon pulled in behind her. "Jim Leonard was with you the night of the murder?"

"He came out to Uncle Earl's trailer. I didn't expect him. He just came."

"Stayed all night?"

She nodded.

Mary Alice had more questions, but Kate was adamant. The girl was done for the day.

At the door Mary Alice hissed, "Don't let her leave."

"She didn't do anything but get herself knocked up," Kate whispered.

"Probably so but she's connected. I can't see it yet, but the play Jamie wrote—hell, I don't know but it's looking certain to me that Jim is Jamie's son just like in the play—"

"Brenda Lee doesn't know anything about that part," Kate whispered.

Mary Alice rolled over her. "—and now I find out that his parent's airtight alibis are full of holes. They lied."

"Slow down, Mary Alice. She's got no where else to go."

On the drive home Mary Alice felt schizophrenic flipping between stories. The sheer shock of finding out that Brenda Lee's baby could be Jim Leonard's or Jamie O'Malley's made her reel. Would a DNA test be conclusive between father and son? But the paternity of Brenda Lee's baby had no implications for the murder case. The melodrama was just a barnacle on the skin of the important story. Paige Leonard had gone to some trouble to establish an alibi. But Jim Leonard hadn't been home as the police had been told. Jim had been out most of the night, half of it with Brenda Lee Chinault.

Again she played the scene in her head where Paige and Randy shot Jamie. There was no shortage of motives. Maybe Jim found out or suspected what had happened and was now trying to protect his mother. He'd told Brenda Lee not to tell anyone he'd come out to her uncle's. Was that why he acted funny when Mary Alice brought up Jamie's murder? It wouldn't be in his best interests to have his mother convicted of murder. Who cared about a visiting playwright?

Once home, she put on her oldest bathing suit and dove in the chilly waters of the lake. Swimming hard, she cleared her head and slowed the useless repetitive thoughts that churned in her head. After a mile, she felt a calmness born of the rhythm. She imagined her daddy rowing his little boat beside her, encouraging her. She rolled on her back and looked up. He smiled at her. She smiled back and thought about how the snobby Vallie Leonard was going to look when somebody told her that her first great-grandchild was on the way and that its mother was none other than Brenda Lee Chinault of *the* Chinaults of Gravel Hollow.

But she didn't smile when she thought of Vallie Leonard finding out that her daughter-in-law, Paige, the mother of Vallie's beloved grandson, Jim, had killed Jamie O'Malley in order to preserve the secret that Vallie's grandson wasn't hers at all.

CHAPTER 29

April 9, Monday

MARY ALICE SAT ACROSS FROM Bill Burgess at Dotty's Café. The Monday lunch crowd had thinned. Burgess started in on his hamburger steak lunch special with creamed potatoes, gravy, snap beans, carrot-raisin salad and cornbread muffins. In a supreme act of will power, Mary Alice had ordered the chef salad with low fat dressing.

"You talk to Chase this morning?" she asked the lawyer. She poked the hard boiled egg half that looked like a large disapproving eye.

"No. You?" He raised his iced tea glass, the signal at Dotty's for a refill.

"Yes. He could barely talk."

A waitress filled both tea glasses and vanished.

"Doc has him on some heavy anti-depressants."

"They're not working. He's out of control." She flipped the egg over.

Burgess cut two neat bites and popped one into his mouth. "The fear builds up over time. Constant stress zaps the body's resources."

Mary Alice separated the slivers of purple cabbage, corralling them at the edge of the bowl. She wished she were eating Burgess' lunch.

"Are we here just for lunch or you know something I don't?" He continued eating rapidly but smoothly, swapping cutlery, effortlessly chewing and talking at the same time. Burgess working his blue plate special reminded Mary Alice of a modern dance performance.

"I don't think Brenda Lee Chinault killed Jamie." She'd never been sure how seriously Burgess took her dual theories about the murder, but she was sure she'd have his attention for the next few minutes.

He wiped his lips. "Why's that?"

"Because she had company at her uncle's trailer that night. Stayed all night."

"Thus supplying an alibi at least for most of the night?"

"Probably, but the alibi isn't the important part."

"Who?" Burgess speared a snap bean.

"Jim Leonard." She could see in his face that he understood that if Jim Leonard had been with Brenda Lee, he wasn't at home. The Leonards had lied. They'd said they'd Jim that night at home, all night, no doubt.

"Paige's boy, Jim," he repeated.

"He's the one."

"He the father of the baby?" He drank deeply. Sweet tea at Dotty's was legendary.

"She's not completely sure. But he thinks he is."

"Mary Alice I cannot imagine how you got this girl to tell you all this stuff. Well go on. Finish."

"Paternity is in question because Brenda Lee had one assignation with the now dead playwright, Jamie O'Malley." She moved aside a cherry tomato that behaved like the rubber ball used in Jacks.

Burgess choked on the tea, sending out a spray. "Oh, man." He mopped furiously. "Please excuse me."

She enjoyed watching him recover. "So while it seems I was right about her having a motive, pregnant by the playwright, she now has an alibi."

"Bringing the focus back to the Paige Leonard," he said.

"Exacta-mundo. Jamie's autobiographical play, what old Mrs. Dickens told me and now that Paige lied about her alibi. It adds up."

"This might be a good time to tell you that your boy, Randy Wells didn't do well on his alibi test." He finished blotting the spilled tea. "I hired Bruce Harkey to check him out. Bruce said Wells claimed to be home alone that night, and it was none of Bruce's goddamned business anyway. Bruce asked him some other routine stuff, and the guy went crazy. Nearly threw him down the steps."

"So he essentially has no verifiable alibi."

"He may, but he is disinclined to share it," Burgess said. He tidied up his silverware.

"Randy doesn't want anyone probing his past." She could still see him standing outside Mickey's clutching the script she'd left with him, fury in his every fiber. And she could still feel crummy for having given it to him.

The waitress came and asked if they'd like dessert. Mary Alice declined.

"How about we share a piece of Dotty's sour cream apple pie?"

Apples were fruit. How bad could a few bites be? She smiled.

"Make it a la mode," he said. "And two coffees."

The waitress took Burgess' plate and handed him a fresh napkin from her apron pocket. Mary Alice gazed at the river of dressing that bisected her mostly uneaten salad.

"You told me that Paige told the police that all the Leonards were home the night Jamie was killed," Mary Alice said. She wanted to move Burgess to some conclusion, some action before he dashed away to his office to work on somebody else's case. "She said Bobby was watching ESPN and Jim— What was Jim doing?"

"The report said Paige checked on her son, who was in his room playing a video game. About ten o'clock."

"She didn't, and he wasn't."

"So you think, just like in the play, Jamie wanted a stake in his son's life. He was getting older, had no other children and felt the primordial need to claim his only son?" Burgess leaned back in his chair.

Mary Alice took up the scenario. "Jamie must have begged Paige to let him into their lives. Maybe he just wanted to meet the boy."

"But Mama Paige, who is no dummy, saw what an authentic connection would ultimately bring."

"Jamie would want a public acceptance of his paternity," Mary Alice said. "He was used to getting his way. He betrayed friends to get what he wanted."

"And that would unhinge the Leonard dynasty in more than one way."

"So Paige had to get rid of Jamie."

"Maybe she tried to buy him off first."

"But when that didn't work, she knew she had to kill him." Mary Alice wondered if it were hard for Paige to come to such a decision.

"She knew about the play rehearsals, the gun."

"And she knew how to shoot a gun."

"Maybe she was just thinking about saving her boy, saving their relationship, hell the whole family," he said.

"Or about Bobby kicking her out and sending her back to a dirt-road trailer."

"She confided in her old friend, Randy Wells," Burgess said. "Her protector, whose little sister had died because of his inability to save her."

"Now Randy has a chance to make things right for Paige even if he failed for Lilly."

"And he knows Jamie wrote a play using the Wells' sordid past," Burgess said.

"Jamie told him about it. Tried to fact-check with him."

"Two reasons to kill Jamie O'Malley." Burgess smiled at her. "Who's the shooter?"

"Randy's the strong protector. He'd insist. Maybe she drove the car. Helped."

Mary Alice felt carried by the excitement of the story. If they could say it, it could be true.

"If she picked him up, he wouldn't have to park a car—"

"—that could be noticed and reported by someone."

"What about the gun?" Burgess asked. "It's premeditated; they wouldn't take a chance on a weapon being there."

"I'm guessing they didn't," she said. "Brought a gun, but things worked in their favor. Maybe Jamie grabbed it, but Randy got it away from him and fired. He might have been surprised it was loaded."

"There wasn't a scuffle," he said.

"Forget the gun for now. They faked it; it worked. They leave undetected and set Chase up."

"Maybe they had no idea they were setting up Chase."

"But when it turned out that way—well, you don't look a gift horse in the mouth," she said.

The waitress brought a huge slice of sour cream apple pie with two balls of vanilla. "I'll get your check ready, Bill. Y'all enjoy." She left them, heading for the sound of her name being called.

They ate in silence. Having just solved a crime and convicted the killers, they needed carbohydrates.

"There's one more little thing," Mary Alice said half-way through the dessert. "I saw Jim Leonard at the pilgrimage wrap party. He brought over some ice."

Burgess looked up but didn't stop eating.

"I went out to his truck to talk to him. Just digging, trying to see if he was Jamie's son or if he knew anything. I'd never talked to him before. At the time I had no idea he was hooked up with Brenda Lee."

"And?" He draped the soft ice cream onto a wedge of crust and lifted it into his mouth.

"He flirted with me at first. Gave me a cigarette, practically put his hand on my thigh."

"Little young for you isn't he?"

She ignored the jest. "But when I asked him if he knew about the murder at the theatre, he stopped flirting and acted nervous. Wanted to get rid of me."

"What'd you say?" He edged the plate an inch toward Mary Alice. "About the murder?"

"I lied. I told him the case was still open."

"And that made him nervous?"

"I think he found out something. Overheard something, read an email, whatever. And of course he knew he was lying about his alibi and that his parents were too. He might have wondered why." She took a big bite of ice cream and felt the fat race straight to her thighs.

"Wait. You think he thought his mama killed a man?"

"He's just a boy," she said. "When I talked to him I could see that. He's a kid and a sheltered one. He doesn't expect to explain why adults do things, but he might have an instinct for survival. If mama's in trouble, he's in trouble."

"I take it you've dismissed the grandmother as the killer?"

"She's the backup scenario. No alibi she can prove, but she has a weaker motive, less opportunity and means.

"Very interesting," Burgess said. He nodded to a couple leaving the café.

"What can we do?" she asked. Burgess was winding down, and Mary Alice wanted an action plan. Something to tell Chase.

"I'll have to think about it." He aligned the dessert dish and folded his napkin. "Questioning Miss Paige about lying about her alibi might flush something."

"Everybody's been lying." Mary Alice fought the sensation to stand up and shout at the lackadaisical lawyer. Couldn't he see they had a break? Couldn't he tell that Chase needed some good news?

"People do. You can count on it."

Mary Alice felt like she was drowning. They'd just been over the whole murder. Sure, some details were flaky or missing, but the story hung together. What did Burgess mean 'he'd think about it'? Had the last half hour just been a murder mystery fantasy lunch for him? "Bill, you've got to do something and do it now." She felt her cheeks flush.

"Hang on now," he said. "If I take this story to the D.A. with no proof of much except that Paige Leonard fudged the truth about her whereabouts the night of the murder, I'll lose any advantage I have by knowing all this."

"But—"

"She'll say she was only trying to protect her family, and she didn't know Jim had slipped out. She and Bobby will still validate each other's alibis."

"I know but—"

"However," he interrupted, "Randy Wells isn't a Leonard with all their insulation. He's a hothead. I think he can be manipulated."

"Like how?"

"Mary Alice, this isn't a crime thriller. I don't know. But if he's lying about anything—"

She could see that Burgess had an idea.

"Suppose somebody tells him they know he's involved and that he ought to save himself," he said. "Paige's alibi has fallen apart, they know she had motive, and she's trying to pin the murder on him."

"Would he fall for that?"

"Nobody knows, but it's worked before. Many times it's worked."

"But she's not trying to pin the murder on him," Mary Alice said.

Burgess smiled. "Just brainstorming, Mary Alice. Conjecture. Speculation." He looked at his watch. "Sorry, I really have to get back."

The waitress placed the check beside his plate, patted him on the shoulder and sailed away.

"Let me handle this, Mary Alice. "I have an idea." He fished a huge tip from a wad of cash.

In two bites, she finished off the pie, every scrap.

Outside, Burgess promised to keep in touch. He also warned her to stay away from Randy Wells.

She walked south; he headed north. She'd wanted to ask about Claire Potts. Wasn't she supposed to screw up by now and by doing so help Chase's case? Wasn't there any good news?

She needed a nap before the rehearsal at seven. The play opened in a week. She walked to the parking lot wondering how Brenda Lee could have had sex with a son and with his father. Of course the girl hadn't known the relationship, which admittedly remained unverified, but she was certainly aware she was having sex in the same period of time with two very different males. Something didn't seem right.

In the car she went over Burgess's idea to get Randy Wells to talk.

But what about Paige? What if someone in authority told her that her son's identity was about to be exposed. Show her how easy it would be to prove that Jim wasn't Bobby Leonard's son, and that quite likely the boy was the dead playwright's son. Paige knew about Jamie's play based on Randy's family history, but Paige didn't know about the one in which she was a main character. Maybe it was time she did.

CHAPTER 30

April 8, Monday night

MARY ALICE SAT IN THE back of the theatre auditorium beside Kate. Norton Pike stood on stage in front of the newly finished scenery. He'd thanked them for their hard work especially under the circumstances and for fully accepting him as replacement director. Then he got to the heart of his talk.

"Ladies and gentlemen, we have four rehearsals remaining. We open perhaps Jamie O'Malley's best play on Friday evening, and we are sold out. I think the great director William Ball said that openings usually are about as good as an average of the final rehearsals. And that's why these next four are critical."

"You think Garth learned all his lines?" Kate whispered to Mary Alice.

"I heard him asking Norton about a prompter. Said he knew the lines but sometimes didn't know who was supposed to say them."

"We'll run tonight without stopping," the director contin-ued. "Be at places on time. Don't turn the stage manager into your personal assistant. If you screw up, keep going just as you will do on Friday in front of several hundred people."

Mary Alice could see Garth Buchanan. At the mention of audience he'd turned the color of oatmeal.

"Remember," Norton said. "Always focus on what you, as the character, want in each scene, beat by beat. Really listen to the other characters' lines, but get into the head of your character. See things through his or her eyes." Head high, he walked away and then stopped. "And have fun. Don't forget to enjoy this."

The stage manager took over ordering everyone to check props and the notes from the last rehearsal. "If you haven't checked in with Miss Frannie, do it now. Places in ten."

Mary Alice and Kate stayed put. Their scenes didn't come up for over a half hour.

"How's Brenda Lee?" Mary Alice asked.

"Up and down. Says she's going to keep the baby."

"Has she seen the Baby-Daddy?"

"He came over yesterday. He calls a lot."

"Hard to imagine them getting married," Mary Alice said.

"You mean 'Patches' and the rich boy?"

"And that they're both children."

"Look at his mother," Kate said, "as an example, I mean."

Mary Alice thought about Paige Leonard, who it seemed had shot the father of her son because the father had wanted to be the boy's father. Why Paige married the innocuous and wealthy Bobby was a no-brainer, but then risking it all by fool-ing around with Jamie didn't make much sense. Had Jamie known she was pregnant? Or a better question, when had he found out Jim Leonard was his son?

Mary Alice heard the stage manager call, "House fade to black; go cue one."

The buzz in the theatre quieted as the house lights faded and the stage lights came up on a five count. The play began.

But Mary Alice didn't pay too much attention. Instead she imagined the entire murder investigation as a drama with characters each of whom wanted something, each of whom had a perspective. "See things through his or her eyes," the director had just said.

At lunch she and Burgess had conceptualized Paige and Randy's motivations and actions. Mary Alice closed her eyes and tried to get inside Paige's skin to feel her panic when Jamie came demanding paternity rights. She couldn't give him what he wanted. She was trashy Paige Thompson from a trailer out by Indian Mound who'd come so far. Admitting Jamie was her son's father meant admitting that she was a con, a charlatan, a gold digger in designer dresses who had accepted the Leonard's largess all the while lying about what mattered most to them. For Paige, Jamie had to be eliminated. If he wouldn't accept a pay off, somebody would have to kill him. Of course she'd ask Randy to help her. She knew he'd want to.

Little effort was required to see through Randy's eyes. Randy's dead sister and the play Jamie had written about her were time bombs. Paige's plight provided the fuse. Mary Alice doubted Randy Wells had hesitated even a second to sign on.

Mary Alice wondered if either Paige or Randy had understood Chase's vulnerability. Likely so. Lots of people knew the two men had been arguing since Jamie's arrival. Others knew about the plagiarized play and the gun being used in the current production. What an opportunity. All they had to do was keep quiet.

But they hadn't counted on Jim, the boy for whom the murder was committed, hooking up with Brenda Lee Chinault. The boy had busted Paige's alibi.

Mary Alice and Kate scurried backstage to wait for their entrances. Garth Buchanan said his lines perfectly, and when the scene was over, Mary Alice told him what a good job he was doing. He hugged her. She returned to her seat in the auditorium and resumed her imaginings, this time trying to see things through the eyes of Brenda Lee.

Pretty, smart, but dirt poor with zero opportunities, Brenda Lee instinctively had learned to do whatever had to be done not just to survive, but to get ahead. She'd stripped in a seedy Memphis club to get the money she needed. Brenda Lee must have seen Jamie O'Malley's arrival in Cana as an opportunity. She wanted to be an actress, knew she had talent and believed the playwright could get her some critical attention. Sex with Jamie wouldn't have been a tough decision. Mary Alice doubted it had just been the one time.

And how had she come to be entangled with Jim Leonard? Had she gone after him or vice versa? There were always slutty girls who were used by rich boys. But Kate had just told Mary Alice that Jim called and visited Brenda Lee. Was it possible he was in love with her? Maybe Mary Alice's cynical view of wealthy seventeen year old males didn't apply to Jim Leonard. Maybe he was an innocent.

She tried to see things as he would, want what he wanted.

Intermission came and went. Act two struggled a bit after the seamless performances of act one. The director paced and took notes furiously. The light cues cross-faded smoothly, but the telephone ring came a second late. The set looked wonderful with period furniture, crown molding and a curved staircase; however, Mary Alice couldn't help seeing the space as a crime scene. Just over a month ago she'd discovered Jamie O'Malley's body down stage on the same bed that sat there now. In her mind she repeated the journey remembering her panic and how she'd sat on the edge of the stage clutching her dog. She could still see Jamie's dull eyes looking at her from his blood-soaked bed. What a stupid waste. She tried to see the murder taking place on the stage. Jamie sitting on the edge of the bed. Not expecting a bullet. An argument. The gun. Then she stopped and saw something else.

"Oh my God."

After her final scene, she told the stage manager that she felt sick, had cramps, and had to leave before notes. "I'll call you tomorrow," she promised and ran to her car. Pulling out of the lot, she punched in numbers on her phone.

She drove toward the square. It was a Monday and not quite nine. The warm spring evening had brought people out. The square was packed. She circled twice before she found a place to park.

The French doors of Caffeine Up! lay open to the street, and patrons spilled out onto the sidewalk and into the paved alley alongside. Mary Alice ordered a decaf latte at the counter. The frivolity in the air contrasted with her mood. She waited at the counter until she saw him come in and take a table near the open door.

"Mind if I sit here?" she asked, pulling out a chair.

"It was just waiting for you."

She didn't know how to begin and was still surprised she'd reached him. There'd been no time to rehearse. She looked at him. He was certainly good looking in that sexy, bad-boy way. Not movie star handsome, but there was that something in his eyes.

"I didn't know it'd be so crowded," she said, edging closer so he could hear her.

"It's okay," he said, settling in his chair, relaxed and confident.

"I just got out of rehearsal," she said gulping her latte and burning her lip. "Yikes."

"You all right?

"I hate these plastic tops. The coffee either leaks or scalds you," she said.

"I got cold beer in the truck. Want one?"

It was up to her. Maybe alone was better. Unless he was dangerous.

"Absolutely." She rose.

Leaving her coffee on the table, they walked away from Caffeine Up! to the parking lot at the end of the block. From a cooler in the back of the truck, he removed two Budweisers, opened both and handed one to her. Spill from a single street light warmed the darkness.

"Want to get in?" He was already opening her door.

"We better. I think it's against the law to drink beer on the sidewalk."

They got in, rolled down the windows and sipped the beer. The sounds from the coffee shop wafted down to them. Happy sounds.

"What's up?" He kept looking at her.

"I was going to ask you the same question."

"I asked first." He took a long draw on the beer.

"Well, I wanted to talk to you."

"Yeah?" He rotated the beer between both hands.

"The last time we talked, I didn't like the way it ended," she said. "It didn't really end."

He smiled a cocky grin and leaned his head back against the headrest. "I agree."

"Of course, I don't know you very well, but—"

"What'd you have in mind?" He looked like he expected her to reach over and unzip his jeans.

"First, I have a question."

He said nothing, but turned to look at her. His expression implied he thought her question would be sexual in nature. After all, she'd invited him to meet her. After all he was male.

"Can you tell me where you were February 26?"

He looked at her blankly, all innuendo gone from his face.

"That was the night Jamie O'Malley was murdered."

The energy changed as if a vacuum cleaner had sucked out the cab.

"I told the police. Home."

"But that's not true, is it?"

He rested the beer on the seat and looked away.

"Sure, you were probably home for awhile, but then you went out," she said. "You went to the theatre."

"I don't know what you're talking about."

"The rehearsal was over, everybody gone but one person. Jamie O'Malley."

"You were there? You saw me?" He laughed unconvincingly.

"I'd just left. Brenda Lee Chinault had just left too."

"You're full of shit," he said. "Look, get out. I have to go."

The keys were wedged in his tight jeans; she knew she didn't have long.

"You wanted to have a little talk with Mr. O'Malley," she said. "You believed the charming writer seduced your girlfriend.

Had sex with Brenda Lee. And you went to stake your claim. She was your woman, right?"

"Fuck you. Fuck you, you bitch. You don't know anything."

"And the charming playwright told you all about the girl whose honor you were defending. How she was a slut and how sluts had their uses in the world, but that you certainly, especially you, shouldn't be getting serious about her. There were lots of girls worthy of you. This one spread her legs for any guy. She didn't even care about you."

The boy sat frozen.

"But you love Brenda Lee, don't you, Jim? She's having your baby." Mary Alice spoke slowly, watching everything. "You couldn't let him talk like that. He used her. Had power over her. Had charisma. Girls fall for men like that. You had to do something. A gun was sitting right there. How could you not pick it up? The bastard."

The next image reminded Mary Alice of the way Oz's wicked witch of the west had melted. Jim Leonard let go of his beer. It poured over the seat and onto floor like a foamy waterfall. He sank inches behind the wheel.

"Did you know it was loaded?" she asked.

"He didn't think it was. He laughed at me."

"Surprised you both, huh?"

He took a deep breath.

She had the sense it was the first deep breath he'd taken in a long time. "Did you tell Brenda Lee what happened? You went out to her uncle's right after."

"I didn't tell anyone."

"You care about Brenda Lee and the baby?" she asked. She wasn't about to tell him Brenda Lee was unsure if he really was the father.

He nodded.

"Then let's not make this any worse." She put her hand in her purse to get her phone, but stopped. Here it came. What he'd held inside for so long.

"He acted so weird. I came in the back way. He was on the stage. When I went over to him he tried to put his arm around my shoulder."

She nodded. She'd guessed right.

"Said he was glad to see me. Said son, good to see you. Acted like he knew me. But he didn't know me. I told him to go to hell. Told him to leave Brenda Lee alone. She talked about him all the time. How he was going to help her; how she was going to New York. It was shit. He just wanted to fuck her."

"You're probably right."

"He said she was—he called her a piece of ass. Said he'd had her right there on the stage." His voice sounded ragged, one tick from tears. "Goddamned liar."

She tried to sound like a therapist. "I guess he made you angry talking about her like that. He insulted both of you." She could well imagine the scene: Jamie, delighted to encounter his son and offer advice about his choice of girlfriend—a girl not good enough for Jamie O'Malley's son. And Jim Leonard coming from an opposite reality trying to save Brenda Lee from a dirty old man, trying to protect his love.

"It was an accident," he whispered. "He said it wasn't loaded. I never—" but he didn't finish. Emotion overcame him, and he dropped his head and sobbed.

"I believe you, Jim. I really do." She let him vent the pent up anxiety. How he'd managed for so long not to explode she couldn't imagine. She pulled her cell phone from her purse and punched Jaworski's number. He answered.

"Tom, I'm at parking lot down from Caffeine Up! I need help."

JAMIE'S PLAY WAS HAILED A huge success. A reviewer from an Atlanta newspaper did come and commented that the community theatre's work was easily as good as any LORT B theatre in the south. Brenda Lee Chinault received a special mention. Chase Minor had stood in the back at each performance. In the dressing room sat a huge but tasteful bouquet of flowers he'd sent Mary Alice.

Mary Alice hosted the final cast party at her home on the lake. As the party heated up, Chase joined Mary Alice on the broad deck looking over the dark water.

"How can I thank you?" he asked.

"You'd do it for me. Did do it for me," she said hugging him.

"I'm free because of you. I have my life back."

She heard his voice catch. "Burgess was getting close," she said. "I was never worried."

They laughed.

"What will happen to the boy?" he asked.

"He's a juvenile. Bill says he'll get a few years. They're calling it accidental." They both understood that the Leonard name had been helpful to his case.

"How could a kid like that go to classes, practice ball, carry on? Even if he hadn't meant to, he'd shot a man dead."

"It's called disassociation," she said. "The event is so horrible the mind can't handle it. So it compartmentalizes it, closes it off. It's almost like it didn't happen."

"All of this over some foolish jealousy," he said. "A man's dead because a boy thought the man was seducing the boy's girlfriend. Incomprehensible."

Chase didn't know that there were two possible fathers of Brenda Lee's baby. Only Kate, Burgess, Mary Alice and of course Brenda Lee knew, and the first three agreed no good would be served by letting the world in on the secret. Brenda Lee certainly wasn't talking. The official view was that Jim was the daddy.

And Mary Alice had also chosen to say nothing more about the other paternity secret—that Jamie O'Malley was likely Jim Leonard's father. A few including Chase knew her theory, but there was no proof. However, their close physical resemblance and the way Jamie had behaved toward Jim, acting paternal and warning him about girls like Brenda Lee, cinched it in Mary Alice's opinion. The boy would suffer enough for his crime without believing he'd killed his own father.

"If the gun hadn't been there, Jim would probably have taken a swing at Jamie."

"I suppose the shooting really was an accident," Chase said. "But I don't understand how the gun got loaded. I know it was empty when I brought it back to the theatre."

"We've been over that a ga-zillion times," she said.

"I'm partly responsible if—"

"You may have accidentally provided a means, but also remember the gun was left alone for what, four hours before Jim fired it? Someone could have loaded it."

"Jamie, Jamie, Jamie," he said.

"Jamie loved to play with fire. No pun intended. He was partly to blame."

"We all are, in a way." Chase rubbed his hand over his forehead.

"I cringe to think how I had Paige all but convicted. Randy Wells too," she said. "I owe Randy Wells."

"It was good detective work," he said. "About the only good detective work. When I think of that viper Potts woman—"

"Burgess won't tell me, but I think he had something to do with her being pulled off the case," she said.

A burst of laughter rolled across the deck. Through the wide glass windows, she could see Tom Jaworski talking to Garth Buchanan.

"She did break into the cabin, after all," Chase said.

"I hear she's been assigned to the coast. Mosquito Point, I believe."

"What about the forged letter?" Chase asked. "How could the boy have written and planted it?"

"I don't know. She shook her head. "I wished I'd asked when I had him all guilty in the truck. Once I called the cops, he got lawyered-up pretty quick. And of course nobody but us knows about the letter."

"It's one thing in anger to accidentally shoot someone, but another to frame someone else for murder," Chase said.

"I don't think Jim wrote that letter," she said.

"Who? Vallie?"

"Brenda Lee?"

"Maybe Potts wrote it, planted it and then came back to find it."

They looked out over the lake, each imagining who could forge a note intended to place blame on Chase. There were things they'd never know.

Boon wandered out onto the deck and sniffed the perimeter.

"Is Brenda Lee still with Kate?" he asked.

"No. Now that is a story," she said.

"Tell." He led her to a bench by the railing. They sat and were joined by the dog, who nestled at their feet.

"You may recall one of my earlier theories that Vallie Leonard did it?"

"She had no verifiable alibi," he said.

"Yes. I thought maybe Vallie would do anything to secure immortality through her blood line. She wasn't about to let her grandson Jim turn into Jamie O'Malley's bastard. That would mean Jim was no blood kin to her. And there weren't going to be any more grandchildren."

"The Leonard dynasty would end. Ka-put." Chase loosened his salmon silk tie. "That would be too, too sad."

"I hypothesized Vallie would cover up the facts if she found out. She'd go right on and who would be the wiser?"

"And she'd have little choice if she wanted an heir, in name at least."

"Usually people invent ancestors, but in her case—"

"No," he said. "Don't tell me—"

"So in a way I was right. Brenda Lee has moved into Thorpe House with Vallie and Spence, her soon to be in-laws where she enjoys every luxury. Vallie is ecstatic to be having a great-grand-child and is said to dote on the girl. No one dares comment on the circumstances." Mary Alice couldn't help but wonder if Vallie Leonard suspected Brenda Lee's baby had been fathered by Jamie O'Malley.

"And in five years most won't even remember them," he said. "Not all, but most."

"You always say 'you see what you want to see.' The Leonards see a victimized young girl. Two young people in love but inexperienced and therefore manipulated." "The Leonards see their future," he said.

"Bingo."

"What do you think Paige sees?" he asked.

"She and Brenda Lee will understand one another. Cut from the same cloth."

"I suppose next year Brenda Lee Chinault Leonard will be a pilgrimage hostess at Thorpe House."

"She always wanted an acting career," she said.

They smiled at the irony. Pregnant and unwed Annie Carter had been banished from hostessing at Thorpe House, and she was from a good family.

"Mama's coming home tomorrow. I'll let her know."

They watched a breeze shift the branches of the Loblolly pines along the shore.

Chase crossed his arms and turned his head away. "What a waste."

She felt him shudder and struggle for control. "Yes," she whispered.

He shook his head. "A man is dead. Jamie's dead." Chase sounded incredulous as if he'd always imagined there would be a time to patch things up.

Mary Alice wrapped an arm around his shoulders and felt him lean on her. Chase had always loved Jamie O'Malley. And now finally, Cowboy Cody could grieve for his lost friend.

Happy trails, 'til we meet again.

The End

ABOUT THE
AUTHOR

DINAH LEAVITT SWAN, A NATIVE of the Gulf Coast of Mississippi, is the author of *Cana Rising* and *Now Playing in Cana*, the first two books in the Mary Alice Tate Southern Mystery Series.

She's also written eighteen plays—all produced, five national award winners—and the women's lit novels, *Romantic Fever* and *Hacienda Blues*. She lives in Colorado with her husband and dog.

You can write Dinah at <u>dswanstory@yahoo.com</u> .

An excerpt from the first book in the series,

CANA RISING:
A MARY ALICE TATE SOUTHERN MYSTERY
by Dinah Swan

Prologue

"SHEREE, YOU'RE A STOOGE AND a druggie," Scott Bridges said. "You can't just boogie. You want to go to jail?" He eased his gun belt onto the dresser where it coiled next to her pink hairbrush.

"I done my part," Sheree said. "You got two arrests. I'm scared." She looked at her bare feet and the nail polish in bad need of a touchup. She knew he'd be hard to convince, but she also knew her days as a drug informant were dwindling. Pretty soon some dealer was going to put it together, and she'd get nailed. She felt her breath coming fast and fought to stay calm.

"I'm protecting you, baby." He pulled her down onto her bed.

"Scott, this part ain't working either." She avoided his eyes by staring at the Cana Police Department badge on his chest.

"It's working for me," he said in his playful bad-boy voice. He leaned back, relaxed and in control.

"I appreciate what you done for me but—"

He sat up. "You appreciate what I done? Do you remember where I found you?"

"Yes, but I don't do that no more and—" She was drowning. She felt like a child arguing with a sadistic stepfather who enjoyed setting her up and trapping her in her own words.

"Lap dances at The Pink Pony?" His voice heated up. "Selling meth in the bathroom to support your own habit? What else?"

"Scott, Georgia Horn says I got a right to an attorney—"

"That bitch runs a women's shelter, not the police department. You talk to a lawyer, our deal is off and you go to jail. You listening?" He grasped her jaw and twisted her face toward him.

"Scott, this ain't TV. It's scaring the shit out of me." She started to cry, and the squiggly mewings she heard herself make frightened her even more.

"I can take care of you." He released her and shifted into his good cop voice. "Sheree, look at me. Tell you what, a month more, or just until the deal I'm working on is done, and I'll get the D.A. to cancel the informant contract. You can go away. I'll help you." He relaxed back on the bed.

"You swear?" She got control of the tears. She didn't trust him.

"Swear." He ran a finger down her bare arm.

"Scott—"

"Cross my heart, hope to die." He drew an x over his heart and raised his right hand.

She sat on the edge of her bed and finished off the fifth of Southern Comfort she'd been sharing with him. The blackout drapes made the room dark, but the clock said four PM It was going to be a long night.

"What do you want to do?" she asked. She looked at him sprawled on her bed and tried to remember why she had ever thought he was fascinating. Somehow Scott's games made her feel more used than any of the things she'd done to get drugs.

He sat up close to her and tapped each button on her blouse.

"Well, Miss Delio, ma'am, looks like I'm going to have to strip search you."

She acted her part without enthusiasm; he didn't seem to notice. Afterward, she listened again to his secret drug bust plan. It was coming to a head quick and big fat heads were going to roll, he said.

Later in the blackness of her bedroom, Sheree couldn't see Scott lying beside her, but she could feel his heat. She hoped he'd leave the apartment before she sobered up. As she sank into the hazy layers of drunken sleep, she sensed a shadow slide through the dark like hawk wings over the night desert. The compressor of the AC window unit cut in, grinding up the sultry air. Before she passed out, she felt Scott kick her lightly and jostle the bed as he turned.

Chapter 1

MARY ALICE TATE KNEW HOW to put on a party. She'd been in training most of her life. But it had taken courage to throw this one. She realized she was the target of gossip: Why had she divorced her successful doctor husband and come back home to Mississippi? Why did she live alone at her late father's lake retreat? Why was she spending all her time with Georgia Horn at Cana's Women's Center?

In fact, the party was a fund raiser for the center. No doubt it seemed odd to some that her reintroduction to Cana society should coincide with the event. But, she reassured herself, at the party everybody would see she was fine. It would be as though she never left Cana. Thirty-five wasn't too old to start over. She was a lot wiser now.

I'm not some loser divorcee skulking back home to live with my mama.

She inspected the softly lighted living room one last time. Heavy wood paneling colored the room like honey. A gigantic stacked stone fireplace dominated one wall. Antique Turkish carpets, some nearly threadbare, covered the oak floors. Leather and muted fabrics upholstered a hodgepodge of sofas and chairs. A wall of glass exposed the panorama of lake and woods outside. She wiped off a wet dog nose mark from a glass door.

"Come on, Boon. Help me check the food." The yellow lab followed her into the kitchen.

She peeked in the refrigerator at the trays of hors d'oeuvres: baby artichoke hearts with proscciuto, miniature crab cakes, crudités, shrimp kebabs, and mini spring rolls. The counters were laden with cheese straws, rumaki, antipasto, brie with cranberry marmalade and a spiral cut smoked ham. A copper chafing dish held spicy Italian sausage bites; a silver one warmed Swedish meatballs. Sneaking a taste of pâté, she danced to a Kenny Chesney tune on the radio. She hoisted a tall service bucket of punch from the kitchen counter, turned toward her Grandmother's sterling punch bowl and collided with Boon.

The bucket popped into the air while her feet scrambled but found no purchase. Boon shied away as the bucket hit the floor and spilled its load.

From her position sprawled on the kitchen floor, Mary Alice watched eight gallons of the famous Tate family champagne punch sluice across the tile floor like a wave over Panama City Beach. Boon watched intently, perhaps waiting to see if the liquid that covered half of the kitchen floor was palatable.

The punch tide leveled out and washed back toward Mary Alice, surrounding and then soaking her. "Boon, don't move." The canine padded through the foamy punch making doggy tracks on the dry half of the kitchen floor. "Oh, shit."

Fifty guests were due in half an hour. As she poked her finger in the rip in the knee of her new DKNY slacks, the door between the garage and kitchen opened and in stepped a statuesque, attractive woman wearing a garnet silk summer dress. Behind her stood another woman holding a large, white box.

"Mary Alice." Elizabeth Tate stepped gingerly through the flood toward her daughter. "What have you done?" She snapped off the radio.

"Mama."

"Maria, get my cell phone from the car," Elizabeth said. "Call Mr. Treadwell at Star Liquor and tell him to send out six cases of champagne. Put it on my bill."

Maria set down the box, turned, and without a word went back out the way she entered. Boon followed her.

Mary Alice worked her mouth like a goldfish. How had her mother known it was champagne punch?

"Tell him I said to shake it," Elizabeth called. She scowled at the departing dog.

"Mama," Mary Alice protested, her voice sounded whiney. Thirty seconds with her mother, and Mary Alice was a ten year old.

"I'll get Maria going cleaning up this mess," Elizabeth said. "You go change. Put on a dress."

"Mama, I have more champagne." She got up from the floor and felt liquid running down her legs and into her shoes. The opening bars of "You Make Me Feel So Young" tinkled from the living room. She wanted to tell her mother to butt out. She wanted to quote Tennessee Williams and tell her mother to get on her broom and ride up, up over Blue Mountain the way Tom had finally told his mother, Amanda to do. She felt her hand clutch a heavy silver cold meat serving fork.

"Who's banging on that piano?" Elizabeth turned an ear toward the music, striking a dramatic pose like Norma Desmond in *Sunset Boulevard*.

"I hired Parker Fisher."

"He still does parties?"

Maria entered with a sponge mop and bucket. She gave Mary Alice a blank stare and looked to her boss for orders.

"Thanks, Maria," Elizabeth said. "Nobody will come in the kitchen for awhile. We should have enough time."

Mary Alice stood gaping as her mother, the most southern of all southern belles, grand dame of Cana, Mississippi society, swooshed off her fringed, chartreuse silk stole and launched into action.

"Go on, Mary Alice, before anybody gets here." She fluttered her right hand in a four-fingered point toward the door.

Mary Alice slunk out. As the swinging kitchen door fanned back and forth, she heard her mother's voice rhythmically loud-soft, loud-soft. "Maria, put those awful shrimp-thingies in the fridge. All we need is to poison everybody in Cana who matters."

Zombie-walking up the stairs to her room, Mary Alice remembered that less than an hour ago she'd been putting the finishing touches on her party after nearly ten years in Dallas with ex-husband, Dr. Cham Mauldin III. She had stood on the deck that overhung the lake, looking back at the retreat her Daddy had built and left to her. She had smiled, thinking how pretty the Tikis and twinkle lights around the deck would look after dark. That was an hour ago...

CANA RISING is available wherever fine books are sold.

Made in the USA
Charleston, SC
14 April 2013